Dissolution

J.L. Campbell

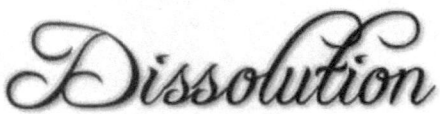

Copyright 2016 © J.L. Campbell
Published by The Writers' Suite

ISBN-13: 978-976-95586-2-5

Acknowledgments

Diana Hockley and Alan Sugano, my beta readers, offered invaluable advice and guidance that helped mold Dissolution into a story I'm proud to have written.

Tawanda Gregory-Johnson and Kamika Williams-McKellop, my friends, sisters, and guinea pigs, read not only as wives and mothers, but with an eye to keeping things real from a Jamaican perspective.

As always, my writing pals make the journey a little less lonely and a lot more interesting. Thanks to Michael Amrein, Nathan B. Childs, Donna (DCP62), Susan Etheridge, Caroline Kellems, Sybil Nelson, Chris Stralyn, and Patti-Anne Yaeger.

Detective Constable Carlos Ellington and Officer Michael Lawrence put up with my questions to do with police procedures, and the Jamaican justice system.

Desrene Miller, enrolled nurse, guidance counselor, and social worker, offered insight into the challenges our youths face every day, as well as their coping mechanisms.

Despite being missing-in-action so many times while writing and editing, I still have a supportive family. Thanks for putting up with my frequent absenteeism, even when we share the same space.

I am all too aware that on my own I can do nothing, but that all things are possible through Christ, who strengthens me.

One

Sherryn wanted to close the door on the proof of her husband's infidelity, but there was no going back.

She avoided looking at the child in front of her, whose cupid's bow of a mouth and tawny eyes confirmed that he shared the same genes as her children. But the similarity ended there—his ashy skin, underweight body, and wash-worn clothes pointed to a lack of concern for his well-being and appearance. The woman with him smiled—a smug grimace that deepened Sherryn's suspicion.

She didn't hide her distaste at the sight of the snug tank top holding in a belly about to surge out of control, or the denim skirt that did little to cover a pair of lumpy thighs. A lustrous, blonde weave complemented the woman's caramel complexion, and false eyelashes emphasized the spite in her gaze.

A quick scan tagged her as the stereotypical product of one of Kingston's ghettos. For timeless seconds, Sherryn felt as though she was stuck in an early 1900s silent film. The wind stirred the flowers and shrubs in the front yard, dried leaves blew over the lawn, and a car drove by, but she heard nothing.

Then the dancehall queen look-alike pushed the little boy forward, dragging Sherryn back to the unthinkable scene unfolding on her doorstep. "Tell Maurice him can have him pickney."

Sherryn suppressed a shiver by pulling her shoulders back. She stood tall, squeezing the doorknob as a shipwreck victim might cling to a life-saving piece of flotsam. After a glance at the boy, she whispered, "Oh no, you're not leaving him here."

"You ca'an decide dat. Since Maurice won' take care of him, him can keep him."

The woman dropped a knapsack, and spun away with an exaggerated wiggle of the hips and the jangling of gold-plated jewelry, to saunter down the driveway to the gate, where a marked taxi waited.

Ghetto rat! Why leave her child on my doorstep like unwanted baggage?

The boy's bottom lip trembled and he blinked hard several times. Sherryn's chest heaved, and she struggled to slow her breathing. It wouldn't help either of them if she fell apart. Pressing her lips together to keep her focus, she picked up the threadbare knapsack and touched his shoulder. "Come with me."

She left him sitting on the sofa inside Reece's office.

Over the years, Maurice had been shortened to Reece. The inane thought reminded her that she had spent half her life with a man she doubted she would ever really know, and here again, was proof.

The purpose for leaving the boy in Reece's study was twofold. First, he was hidden from her, as if he didn't exist and second, Reece's world would spin off its axis—just as hers had—to find his secret tucked away in his private space. She hoped the experience turned out to be as gut wrenching and devastating as hers.

In the living room, she perched on the edge of the settee and hugged herself. She tilted her head back and stared at the high ceiling. Then she skimmed the familiar paintings, family portraits and oddments, absorbing all that meant home and family.

Everything she'd invested in her relationship with Reece lay in invisible pieces around her like shattered glass.

Cold and sterile on the inside, she sighed, forced herself to get up and climb the stairs to their bedroom. Once there, she lay down and allowed the tears to fall, searing her sinuses and then her eyes. Other than anxiety over her children when they were ill, and tears shed while watching sad movies, no drama had touched her life.

And now this.

She wasn't sure how much time passed before she heard Reece's Land Cruiser throttling in the yard. He was home on one of his afternoon stopovers. Her heart thumped painfully at the confrontation to come.

She hurried into the bathroom to wash her face, staring into her dull eyes before returning to sit on the bed, facing the doorway. She ran an unsteady hand over her close-cropped hair and glanced at her watch, surprised to find that two hours had slipped away since she answered that fateful knock at the door. Briefly, she spared a thought for the boy. He had to be hungry.

Concern fled as Reece bounded up the stairs, calling her name. The door opened, and the energetic man at the center of her world entered the room. He crossed the patterned tiles in a few steps. "Sher, you never hear me calling you?"

She met his eyes, sure her expression would tell him something had gone wrong.

"Sherryn, what happen'?"

She stood up, willing herself not to scream or lash out at him for destroying her near-perfect life. Instead, she said, "It's not what, but who."

He attempted to touch her, but she edged away, ignoring the hurt and bewilderment in his darkening eyes.

"Come downstairs," she said, not waiting to see if he followed.

His footsteps fell heavy on the wooden treads behind her.

Sherryn blinked hard to prevent fresh tears from forming as she turned left at the bottom of the stairs. She paused outside his study and sucked in her belly to pull herself upright. Then she turned the knob on the door and it swung inward to reveal the boy curled up on the settee. He was asleep with a thumb in his mouth.

She pushed sympathy aside and composed herself. Reece's breath bathed the back of her neck, and he grunted in what she supposed could only be surprise.

She faced him and spoke to his pinstripe shirt through the obstruction in her throat. "Don't bother to say anything. I don't want to know."

She brushed past him, and on the way out of the house, picked up her keys from the table in the hallway.

Two

Reece had sensed that whatever lay inside his study meant the end of eighteen years of happiness. When Sherryn opened the door, shockwaves pulsed across his brain.

The result of one regrettable encounter lay asleep on his couch.

Now he understood her coldness. Panic forced sweat out through his pores and he wiped a sleeve across his forehead, but kept his mouth shut. Anything he said would make little sense and serve to tee Sherryn off, but he swore in his mind to kill that piece of trash, Gloria. She'd done this deliberately, because he refused to play along with her latest bit of blackmail.

Hoping he was trapped in a bad dream, he passed one hand over his mouth while his stomach churned.

Sherryn mumbled indistinct words and glared at him with glittering eyes before hurrying out of the house.

That was no dream.

Certain he would go mad, Reece stalked around the massive desk, along the edges of the carpet, past the bookshelves and the sofa. He refused to think about the implications of the child's presence, thereby avoiding thoughts of losing Sherryn.

He couldn't face that possibility. Death was better than forfeiting his home and family.

He sank into the executive chair, his heart beating a heavy tattoo in his chest. The discomfort was such, he wondered if he was having a heart attack.

Moving at the speed of an old man, he dragged himself out of the seat to pace aimlessly, his mind a blank space. The enormity of the situation left him numb and he couldn't think. What was he going to do? The boy stirred, rubbed small hands over his eyes and pulled himself upright.

Unable to contain his resentment, Reece glowered at him. The child shrank into the settee, his knees drawn up to his chest. Reece wanted to tell him to get his sneakers off the sofa, but instead shut his eyes to calm himself and get rid of the frown he wore. None of this was the boy's fault. He, Reece

Allbright, was the stupid adult who had created the current mess in a moment of drunken weakness.

Intuition had warned him a hundred times since the boy's birth that this day would come—for all his wishing it wouldn't. The day had arrived, taking him by storm and leaving him with a sense of powerlessness he hadn't felt in more years than he cared to remember. He tried to root himself in the present by running a hand over his prickly chin. His voice was loud in the silence.

"You hungry?"

The boy shied away, looking ready to dart out the room and hide, but instead he nodded.

"Come."

They walked down the passage and through the dining room, which adjoined the kitchen. There, further dread settled over Reece at the sight of a fire engine on one of the tiled counters. He stared at his son—he had no doubt the boy was his—and tried to work out what he was going to tell his other children. His stomach clenched again because he had no solution.

"Sit down."

Reece made a tuna sandwich and placed it in front of the child he wished had never been born.

The boy crammed the food into his mouth, apparently too hungry to remember his fear.

On the way back from the refrigerator with a glass of apple juice, an idea hit Reece. He'd take the child back to the tenement yard where Gloria lived before his kids got home and started asking questions. Justin, his eldest, would take one look at the boy and know he was a relative.

Disappointment and hurt were sure to come, if he did nothing to derail Gloria's plan.

Disgusted with himself for his cowardly approach, Reece flung a napkin at the boy.

"Wipe yuh hand and mouth and come."

He grabbed the knapsack from his office and rushed out the door with his sixth offspring.

Three

Sherryn adjusted the mirror to get a better view of the kids in the back of the van. She had just completed her rounds and picked them up from their schools.

Sixteen-year-old Justin had Melaine, his thirteen-year-old sister, in a headlock. Their younger sibling, eleven-year-old Celia, had her face hidden in a book, while Kyle—the baby at three-years-old—chattered non-stop to himself in the booster seat. Brandon, who was super-mature for his six years, played a video game in the passenger seat beside her.

Her insides ached as if a debilitating disease had ravaged her. What had possessed her to give in to Reece's wish to have so many children? And if she didn't stand strong, he wanted to round out the family with a sixth Allbright. Her lips curled in disgust. He had obviously made time to complete his family elsewhere.

Reece had no relatives worth staying in touch with, so together they had fulfilled his desire to have a complete family unit. One corner of her mouth twitched at his single-mindedness, but what was there to be amused about? The joke was clearly on her.

What am I going to do?

Kyle, catching her eye in the mirror, giggled and hid behind his fingers. In return, she made a funny face. He laughed—a joyous sound that pushed away the unpleasant thoughts.

She didn't regret giving any of them life. They were good kids. Their father was the one who had wrecked everything. Images of Reece naked with that woman flooded her mind, filling her vision. How many times had he been in her bed over the years? Did he love her?

She forced herself to focus on the road when Brandon, along with his brothers and sisters, shouted, "Mom!"

She'd missed hitting another passenger van by inches.

"Oh, God," she whispered and then apologized to the children over her shoulder, while ignoring the string of swear words the wronged motorist hurled at her.

She whispered a prayer of thanks, only to see two police officers riding up behind them.

One pulled alongside the Toyota Noah and pointed toward the sidewalk. Sherryn parked and reached for her license and registration, hoping to avoid a ticket. The heat of the afternoon sun intensified with the van at a standstill. She swiped her forehead as sweat covered her skin.

One officer got off his bike and crowded the window, peering inside the vehicle. "Good afternoon, Ma'am. You aware you just run the red light?"

Sherryn settled her thoughts and hoped the children wouldn't take her to task for the humdinger of a lie she was about to tell. "Yes, officer. I wasn't paying attention because I thought something was wrong with the baby."

She pointed to Kyle and put on her best penitent expression. "That's how I ran through the light. Officer, please, don't ticket me. You understand how it is when you have so many children in one vehicle ... "

The policeman removed his dark glasses and slipped one of the arms into his mouth, eyeing her from her hair to the jeans covering her legs. In a low voice, he said, "We can sort this out easy, easy. Leave a t'ing wid me and mi partner, nuh?"

Reece would have a fit at what she was about to do, if he knew, but who cared what he thought? She reached into the space between the two seats and rifled through the handbag for her purse. She pulled out a crisp, blue thousand-dollar note bearing a picture of one of the island's past Prime Ministers and deftly folded it into the policeman's hand that rested on the window.

"Respec', Ma'am." He stepped away from the van, smiling. "And remember to keep yuh eyes on the road."

She eased into the traffic and mere seconds passed before Justin exploded. "You shouldn't give him nutten! Damn thiefin' police!"

She looked at him in the mirror. He knew how much she disliked when he spoke badly, but he often did it to irritate her. "Excuse me?"

He sat back, grumbling. "Daddy woulda handle him differently, fi real!"

"That's how they're teaching you to talk in school these days?"

Refusing to give up, he continued, "Mommy, you know that's why they harass people on di road. You shouldn't give him a dollar."

She sighed. Why did this have to happen today of all days? "Justin, you're right, and I'm wrong. I shouldn't have done it, okay? Now, relax."

Their eyes met in the mirror. "Just don't say anything to your father."

He avoided her by squinting at his watch, and she smiled, knowing he was unwilling to be in cahoots with her when he could score points with his father.

Justin sprawled on the seat in his khakis, arms folded, defying her in silence.

She stopped watching him, disturbed by how much he resembled Reece, but then all their children did. Somehow, they all inherited his amber eyes and the distinctive shape of his mouth. Justin and Brandon also shared the deep bronze undertone of his skin. The others had her dark-honey complexion.

Sherryn gripped the wheel tight to keep her mind on the road, but something occurred to her. If their home was destined to go topsy-turvy, she had some groundwork to do.

"Um, guys." She glanced behind her. "Your father may have a visitor."

Brandon raised his head, frowning. "So?"

"Well, he's a-a relative."

Justin leaned forward. "You mean like a cousin or something?"

She nodded and chanced a peek in the mirror.

Justin frowned at her. "But, Mommy, where this cousin come from all of a sudden?"

"Your dad will explain," she said, hoping to stem his questions.

Justin resumed his position, but the taut way he held his body said he wasn't satisfied.

Sherryn cursed on the inside, wishing she knew how to brace them for the coming upheaval.

Four

Reece was gone when she returned.

The children spilled out of the van with their belongings, oblivious to her turmoil. She reached in to release Kyle from his seat, grateful for the reprieve. What could she say to Reece?

The stuff and nonsense he'd filled her ears with over the years now worked out to be just that. So much for his promises of never cheating because theirs was a special kind of love.

She used to insist he was a man and couldn't keep his word to himself, much less her, but he swore he had never touched another woman since their marriage. That turned out to be a devastating lie. How many others had he told her?

After eighteen years, their passion for each other was alive as ever—or so she'd thought. With their vibrant love life and hectic family schedule, where had he found time to maintain another relationship?

Obviously, he carved some out of his busy days.

Kyle's hands caught her in the face.

She'd zoned out and hadn't lifted him from the seat.

He struggled to get out. "Mommy?"

"Yes, hon?"

"Want sleep."

He crawled into her arms and rested his head on her shoulder.

Holding him close, she abandoned her mental wandering and took him to the bathroom.

In the water, Kyle came to life, darting behind the shower curtain to hide. She teased him, directing the shower spray at his tummy. He squealed, as he did every time they played this game.

After a quick soap and rinse, she wrapped him in a towel and carried him to the room he shared with Brandon. She listened with one ear while he nattered about his day in pre-school and sang the nursery rhyme he'd learned, the desire for sleep forgotten.

Hand-in-hand, they walked to the kitchen, where all the kids congregated as soon as they changed out of uniform. Celia was the exception. She usually grabbed a snack and locked herself in the bedroom she shared with Melaine. She'd read for most of the afternoon and then have to be reminded to do her homework.

Having settled Kyle with a tuna sandwich—for he currently refused to eat anything else—Sherryn restored order to the kitchen.

Miss Emelyn, their household helper, had not come in that day. Her son was in trouble with the law again for beating up his girlfriend.

When Sherryn finished wiping the counter, she reminded Justin, Melaine and Brandon to clean up after themselves and Kyle.

In her bedroom, she faced the mirror trying to unclog the pipeline to her brain. She needed some sort of game plan. But what? She didn't have a clue where to start. She felt like all the other women who had invested their time raising a family, only to find their spouse had moved on to discover new and exciting relationships elsewhere.

She supposed she could be dramatic and throw Reece's things out on the doorstep. But to what end? Did she really want him to leave? Did she want to start over on her own? No. But how could she live with him, knowing he had been in another woman's bed, spilled his sperm inside her and worst of all, started another family outside of the one he'd promised to love and cherish?

Her eyes smarted and she sniffed, feeling sorry for herself. How long had he been sleeping with that ghetto woman, and without a condom too? What did she give him that he wasn't getting at home?

A chill ran over her skin and anger twisted her face. Though she hadn't noticed anything out of the ordinary, she needed to make a doctor's appointment. What if he'd brought home something more serious than an STD? Something she wouldn't know about until it was too late?

Reece had pulled himself out of the ghetto, but hadn't lost his taste for the women.

Her breath puffed out in a slow stream and she blinked hard, wishing her thoughts would stop churning. She felt like a fool. Humiliated. Didn't want to see him or talk to him. She couldn't avoid him forever, but what was there to say?

Five

Reece battled traffic on Molynes Road, trying to ignore the silent tears the boy cried.

As they traveled down Seaward Drive toward Waterhouse, the area started to drag on his spirit. Many a time he wondered how people who lived in the ghetto avoided constant depression.

The evidence of poverty was all around—the shacks, the abandoned buildings, the ever-present streams of mucky water, the men hanging about on the street corners.

He glanced at the child huddled against the window. He had no choice but to return him to his mother. However, guilt ate at him, as it had in the five-and-a-half years since the boy's birth. Reece had little contact with him by choice, but provided money for food and clothing. He suspected the boy wasn't even in school and that Gloria used his money to support her other two children. She also had a liking for shoes, clothes and synthetic hair. Just like his mother, Cynthia.

Thoughts of her made his mood worse and his thoughts returned to the problem at hand. Truth be told, he hated himself for what he had done to the child strapped in beside him.

Gloria lacked the capacity to love. She was hard from the inside out and had always been that way. Ghetto life had toughened her at an early age, stripping away any compassion she might have been born with.

He approached the neighborhood through the nearby complex of factories, driving with caution as the road condition deteriorated the closer he got to Waterhouse.

The lanes were populated with a combination of weather-beaten wooden houses and unpainted concrete structures, clustered together behind broken fences.

While navigating the pothole-riddled roads, he wondered why he continued to visit. Those who escaped hadn't looked back, but he kept returning even after realizing that the so-called friendships he nurtured were mostly one-sided. He dropped money here and there and the men respected him, but Reece knew they were loyal only to themselves. Their gratefulness to him lasted as long as it took to spend his money on a ganja spliff or whatever else they needed in the moment.

The van entered the lane, battened on both sides by zinc fences. He pulled up outside Gloria's gate, un-strapped his son and lifted him out. The little boy clutched the knapsack and stuck a thumb in his mouth.

Reece banged the gate, setting off bedlam from the band of mongrels inside.

The boy shrank behind him when he shoved the gate and it slammed back on its hinges. A half-hearted kick sent the black-and-white pack leader scrambling away, yelping. The others scampered behind him, barking over their shoulders.

It never ceased to puzzle Reece that these people could barely feed themselves, but always had a gang of half-starving dogs.

Reece tramped up to Gloria's ramshackle house and pounded the door. Nothing moved behind the glass louvers. A sound from the house next to hers stopped his abuse of the plywood door.

"She not dere."

He stepped back and turned toward the frail woman he knew as Miss Ivy. "Weh she deh?"

She squinted at him, her face a network of wrinkles. "She move out today."

He had to have heard wrong. "Move out?"

"Yeah. She neva say weh she a go, but before she leave, she pack up di two other pickney dem and carry dem go to dem fadda."

Reece closed his eyes and rubbed his jaw. He was as good as dead.

The easiest solution was to ask Miss Ivy to keep the boy. She could use the money he'd pay for his son to stay with her, but she was raising two grandsons who were already members of a gang. Leaving the child there would condemn him to following in their footsteps.

The condition of the yard suddenly registered in his mind. Rivulets of water ran over concrete, green with morass. Bits of rubbish blew over the otherwise dusty ground, which was an incubator for germs and hookworms because of the dog feces littering the yard. The smell rose then as if to cement his disgust with the way Gloria chose to live.

Shame clogged his throat; he'd thrown money at Gloria and allowed her to keep his son under conditions which none of his other children could imagine.

Resigned to taking the boy back home with him, Reece waved at the woman. "All right. Thanks, Miss Ivy."

"All right, mi son."

On impulse, he took out his wallet and gave her a thousand dollar bill. She thanked him, slipped the money into her bosom, and showed him a toothless grin.

He touched the boy's shoulder, nudging him forward.

Not daring to think further than the road in front of him, Reece drove home with his newly-acquired problem.

Reece got out of the vehicle in front of their home in Queensborough—leaving the child inside—tilting his head toward the upper floor of the house. The burgundy awnings shaded the bay windows, behind which the drapes were drawn. The verandah between the two bedrooms held the usual crush of African violets, philodendron, and spider plants.

From the driveway, he called Sherryn's cell phone, hoping she'd talk to him. After an interminable wait she answered, sounding shell-shocked. "Yes. What is it?"

"Sher, I'm outside, and I have him with me." He swallowed and then sighed before continuing. "I can't find his mother."

She said nothing.

"Can I bring him inside? I don't have anywhere else to take him."

"It's your house. Do what you want."

She hung up, leaving him nowhere.

He opened the passenger door, gestured for the boy to climb down, and held him by the shoulder. As they approached the house, Reece prepared himself for the first of many difficult days to come.

Justin lounged on the couch in the living room watching television. "Hey, Dad. Hello, little man. Is this the relative Mommy told us about?"

Reece breathed out through his mouth on a sigh. "Yeah."

Justin cocked his head and inspected the boy. The wrinkles in his forehead flattened, but suspicion lurked in his eyes.

Reece warned himself not to fight imaginary battles brought on by guilt. "I, uh, where are the others?"

Justin avoided him by fixing his attention on the television. "Doin' homework."

"Okay. I'm going to get him something to eat."

Justin's gaze flicked over them and skimmed away. "Cool."

Reece guided his son into the kitchen, dragging a hand over his damp face.

"You hungry?" he asked for the second time in an hour and a half.

The boy nodded, and Reece fixed another sandwich from the bowl of tuna they kept ready for Kyle in the refrigerator. Clearly, this child didn't get much to eat.

After he devoured the sandwich, Reece gave him fruit juice and tried to figure out what to do next. A bath maybe?

"When last you bathe?"

"Yesterday."

"Come."

In the bathroom, Reece tossed an order at him. "Tek off yuh clothes."

After a hunt through the drawers below the counter, Reece found a new rag and soap. He handed them over and sat on the toilet seat. The boy stood in the shower, waiting.

"You ca'an bathe yuhself?"

He shook his head.

Sighing, Reece got up and pointed with his chin. "Gimme dat."

The child lifted the snake-like showerhead, holding it as if it would bite him.

Reece bathed him, told him to dry off, and went to find the knapsack. When he returned, the boy was sitting on the lid of the toilet with beads of water coating his body.

Irritated, Reece barked. "You madda don' teach yuh to do anythin' fi yuhself?"

Tears glittered in his son's eyes before he lowered them to stare at the floor.

Reece pawed through the bag, ashamed, because he doubted any child of five was as self-sufficient as he expected this boy to be. Annoyed, he upended the bag on the ceramic tiles for easier access.

"What Gloria do wid mi money?" he muttered.

Judging from the meager selection of clothing, the boy owned next to nothing. Apart from the jeans and polo shirt he had worn, there were two other pairs of jeans and tee-shirts, two pairs of shorts, two briefs, and a merino filled with holes. The only footwear was the sneakers and worn out socks Reece had taken off him.

Exasperated, he asked, "You don't have no more t'ings?"

A small jerk of the head signified no.

Shaking out a pair of shorts, briefs, and a tee-shirt, Reece muttered every expletive that came to his lips and then some. He rammed the items he didn't need back into the knapsack and hurled it in a corner. Only then did he notice the boy cowering between the toilet and the shower, like a dog used to human abuse. Reece held out the clothes and in a gentler tone than he'd used before, said, "Here, put these on."

After the child did as instructed, Reece left him in the office and went to find Sherryn. He didn't know what to say to her, and on the way to their bedroom, nothing came to mind. But as much as he dreaded facing her, he had to voice his outrageous request.

Six

Sherryn sat in the rocking chair next to the window, her attention fixed on the pale blue and white plumbago blooms in the front garden. Yesterday, she contemplated their beauty; today their splendor paled beside her problem. The blossoms remained vibrant, but so much had changed. Her life had turned into ploughed soil from which Reece had uprooted everything good.

The door opened, and she sensed his presence. She didn't turn her head, because the sight of him might throw her off-kilter, and she wanted to stay mad at him.

Oh, she was upset, no doubt about that, but she was in no mood to listen to any apologies or the reasons why he'd found himself in another woman's bed. If she had no mental image of her competitor, things would have been a hundred times different, but she had a vivid picture of the woman who shared Reece's body and perhaps his heart.

At his approach, she took labored breaths.

He stayed beside her for some time, before moving to stand in front of her.

She ignored him and finally, he stooped so he was below her eye level.

Sherryn pretended he wasn't there.

Long moments slipped by before he sighed and went to sit on the bed. His explanation was raw as the words spilled out. "Sherryn, I have no excuse. The only thing I can say is that it happened a long time ago."

Slowly, she said, "It ... might be the end."

Gathering her thoughts she continued, too dazed to question the lethargy that held her in its grip. "It's one thing for a man to cheat on his wife." She swung her head to stare at him. "And quite another to have the evidence—a real, live human being—thrown at her."

Her words emerged in a low and languid fashion. "She could eventually forget, if there was nothing tangible to tie a man to his adultery, but you, you had to take things to a different level. You had to breed that slut. You led me to believe we had something exceptional, but it clearly wasn't enough, for you had to start another family. I just hope you can give your other children a good explanation why you couldn't keep what God gave you in your pants."

She turned away, unable to bear the sight of him as he examined his hands folded between his legs.

"'Course it never occurred to you that if you caught anything from that ghetto gyal, you'd give it to me too."

She sucked her bottom lip into her mouth, savoring the blow she was about to land. "You can take a man out of the ghetto, but you can't take the ghetto out of him."

If she didn't expect it, she might not have caught his whole-body twitch—but it was unavoidable, because at forty-three, Reece was still sensitive about his origins.

He opened his mouth, and Sherryn lifted a hand to stop him from speaking. "Like I said, I don't want to know. Not tonight. You've had your secret for how many years? Four? Five? Another night of not hearing all the details of your nastiness won't kill me."

Puckering her lips, she gave him a 'so there' expression.

His hunched shoulders and gloominess spiked her temper. She flung restraint aside and scourged him with native Patois she forbade her children from using. "You can tek off di hangdog expression, 'cause dat don' faze me."

Rocking gently back and forth, she hung on to her composure. When he called her name, she eyed him with all the hatred burning her insides.

"What you want?"

"Uh, the boy, he's downstairs."

"What, your little hood rat don't want him no more?"

He muttered something she was too incensed to hear. When he repeated himself, she launched out of the chair to stand, arms akimbo. "What di hell you just say, Maurice Antonio Allbright?"

He rubbed his chin and kept his gaze on the floor. "I took him back to her yard, but she gone. She move out."

Sherryn's hands turned into fists, which pressed into her sides. "Mek mi understand dis."

She walked over to stand in front of him. "You," she said, jabbing him in the forehead with her index finger, "cause dis woman to bring her pickney and leave him on my doorstep and then vanish into thin air. You and she must be mad to hell! I don' know where him goin' sleep, but is not in here wid my pickney dem!"

Shaking like a leaf tossed by a vigorous wind, Sherryn hugged herself and moved away from Reece. The blood pounded in her head, making it impossible to hear, or form a coherent thought. She stopped, having the sensation of standing frozen in the middle of a highway watching an eighteen-wheel trailer about to run her over. When communication resumed between her brain and feet, she marched to the chair and fell into it with tears scorching her eyes.

This boy was not her child; therefore, he was not supposed to be her problem. Her anger turned to fury. Instead of giving her space to grieve for what she'd lost, her jackass of a husband expected her to find a solution for his indiscretion. She threw her head back. "Jesus in heaven, why me?"

Turning toward Reece, she said, "God know why your last name is Allbright, 'cause I can't believe you so damn bright as to want me to do somethin' 'bout dat unwanted pickney you have downstairs."

Silence claimed the room, and when she couldn't take it anymore, Sherryn gave in. "You know what? I'm not heartless, and it's not the boy's fault that him have a loose, irresponsible mother and an oversexed donkey for a father."

She stomped away, hoping that by some miracle, Reece would jump out the window and kill himself by the time she returned.

She found him in Reece's office. He leaned in the corner of the settee, sucking his thumb. Fresh scabs and faded spots covered the stick-like legs stretched out before him. His dark knees were evidence of too much time spent kneeling on the floor. The crinkled blue shorts and washed out tee-shirt typified what old people called 'less-care'. The boy was in desperate need of attention.

A youthful version of Reece's face searched hers—wary and frightened. Based on Reece's account of his early life, it couldn't be far different from this child's—an absent father and a mother who couldn't have cared less whether he lived or died.

She closed the door and approached him.

His sober eyes were huge as he watched her. Salt lines from the tears he'd cried left crooked lines on his face. He pulled the finger out and propped it on his thigh, as though he didn't want to get it dirty.

A smile tried to break through her anguish, but Sherryn held it at bay. "What's your name?"

"Likkle."

His voice was low and husky as if he didn't speak often.

"Your given name," she said, "the one your teacher calls you by at school."

He frowned as if thinking hard. "Maurice."

"Oh."

What she wanted to say was, 'How dare your careless mother name you after my husband'.

"My name is Sherryn. Your fa—Reece's wife."

She could have been speaking another language for all the reaction he gave.

"D'you know where your mother is?"

Maurice shook his head.

"Has she left you before?"

A small age went by before he answered. "Sometimes she go 'way and leave me wid Miss Ivy."

"For how long?"

He shrugged, then said, "Whole day sometimes."

"You go to school?"

"No. Mi madda say mi don' have to go 'til mi six."

Sherryn couldn't help thinking that her children lived in a totally different world from the one this child inhabited. Her children had all been in pre-school by the time they were three.

"You got something to eat?"

"Him did give mi two sandwich."

"Your father?"

Maurice's wrinkled brows said he believed that was a trick question. Either that, or he didn't know Reece was his father, and that wasn't possible.

He didn't answer.

She sat beside him. "Since we don't know where your mother is, you'll have to stay here for tonight."

His eyes grew wide again. "That mean I will get more sandwich to eat?"

She held back another pained smile and nodded. "Where's your knapsack?"

"In di bathroom. Him did t'row it in di corna."

A search of one of the bathrooms yielded the discarded backpack. Sherryn cringed at the condition of the clothes inside. His mother was worthless. She refused to believe Reece was not providing for the child. She knew him that well. She also understood that the priority of the flighty ghetto woman was different from hers. Bling was all that mattered, as Maurice's mother had proven by the heavy necklace, big earrings, and assorted jewelry she wore.

Sherryn shook her head and went back to Reece's office. With Maurice in tow, her steps slowed as she approached the living room where Justin, Melaine, and Kyle were watching television.

Brandon was engrossed in one of his games as usual, but they all looked up when she entered and stood behind Maurice with her hands on his shoulders. "Er, guys. This is ... Maurice ... he'll be staying with us tonight."

"Hey."

"Hi."

"Cool."

Sherryn squeezed the child's shoulder and turned him toward the passage. Thank God she'd raised her children right. Otherwise, some awkward questions would have been asked in front of Maurice. They'd probably gang up on her at the first opportunity, but right now, she had time to make up a story.

Resentment surfaced again, twisting her stomach. Why should she be the one to come up with lies to pacify their children?

Since Reece was the one who'd created this problem, he'd have to explain how and where he'd gotten the boy.

In the smaller of the bedrooms on the ground floor, she pulled back the sheet on one of the double beds. "You can sleep here."

"Me alone?" Maurice asked, stifling a yawn.

"Yes. Something wrong?"

With a jerky shake of the head, he sat on the edge of the bed, searching every corner of the room in a sweeping pass.

"I'll be back in a moment, okay?"

He nodded and put a thumb in his mouth. Sherryn went upstairs to the laundry closet where she kept new items for the children. She got a pair of pajamas and hurried back to Maurice, who hadn't moved from where she left him. He glanced around the room again when he changed and slid onto the mattress.

"There's nothing to be afraid of," Sherryn said, laying his clothes on a chair. "I'll leave the door open, okay?"

He curled on his side in the middle of the bed. "Okay."

She hit the switch and left a crack of light pouring in through the doorjamb, suspecting she'd have to check on Maurice before the night was over.

She slipped into the living room where the children were still glued to the television set. All except Justin, whose body language told her he wasn't his usual relaxed self. He examined her, his eyes questioning.

But what could she say? She had no answers, so she used the excuse of prying Kyle away from the set to avoid Justin, but shot him a glance on her way out.

He still had his eyes on her as if waiting for her to confess that something had gone haywire. He was closer to his father than to her, but always sensed when things were not normal between them.

She and Reece had had many tiffs during their eighteen years together, but nothing as serious or with the potential for disastrous consequences as this situation.

She refused to think about the future. If she made it through this hour, then she'd deal with the next one when it came.

Seven

Reece sank backward on the bed, the whimper in his throat making a mockery of his manhood. Since this afternoon, peace eluded him. But if he cared to examine his conscience, his peace of mind had been missing for more than five years. He'd simply learned to live each day, keeping an uneasy truce with the worry that had become part of his existence.

Ordinarily, his bedroom was a sanctuary. Now he was sure the room where he spent much of his time with Sherryn would be a threshing floor where he'd be tried again and again.

Eyes shut, he thanked God for blessing him with Sherryn. Another woman might have chucked both him and the boy into the street, but not his wife.

Her slanted eyes, which usually lit with affection at the sight of him, were now reddened, and her lips slightly swollen from crying. Though hurt and striking out at him, she still cared enough to help the boy. Pity his mother refused to do as much for him.

Gloria's actions made him mad all over again. If Miss Ivy's version of events was accurate, Gloria planned to start a new life. But how could she start afresh without the tools of her trade? Her children were the means by which she earned her living. The only thing Gloria ever did was tend bar and live off the men who fathered her children. Having given them up, what did she plan to do now?

He sucked his teeth and sat up. Why should he care what Gloria planned to do with herself, when all she wanted was to mess up his life?

Sherryn had been gone for some time now, which meant she was going to reappear soon. He didn't need to plan what to say to her. She'd lock herself down until she could cope with whatever explanation he offered. She'd always been like that and Lord, she knew where to stab him so it hurt like the dickens.

He didn't understand it himself, but after leaving the depressed Waterhouse community so many years ago, he was still sensitive about growing up there. All the same, he continued to visit for reasons he had difficulty explaining to himself. He didn't want to be known as one of those who forgot where they had come from, but the irony was, that very sentiment had put him in scalding water. If he had avoided the area, Gloria wouldn't have gotten the opportunity to put him on her budding list of baby fathers.

He shuddered at all the challenges and uncertainties to come, for he had no future until his family got past this disaster.

He waited, but Sherryn didn't come back.

Hunger pangs squeezed his stomach, but the coward in him dreaded facing whatever had happened downstairs. He worried most about Justin, who worshipped him. He loved his eldest child just as much, and didn't want to think about how Justin's knowledge of Maurice's existence would affect their relationship.

Had Sherryn said anything to the children? Did they suspect anything? What had she done with the boy? The unanswered questions rattled around his brain, threatening to unhinge him.

The weight of his agony took its toll, and he slept.

He stirred to find Sherryn standing over him. Her expression flickered from grief to disgust. Then a blank wall fell over her features, leaving indifference.

He sat up and rubbed his eyes to clear them. Sherryn jerked and turned toward the bathroom. On a regular night, he'd follow her in, since neither of them had showered yet. Instead, he stretched and headed downstairs, breathing easy after a glance at his watch. Twenty past ten. All the kids would have gone to bed.

He opened the pots on the stovetop. Sherryn had prepared his favorite meal—curried goat with white rice. She'd seasoned the mutton with her special mixture of spices, including garlic, ginger, chutney, Scotch Bonnet pepper, and then simmered it over a low flame until it was tender. But of course, he had no appetite for dinner. He poured the food into plastic containers and put them in the fridge. Then he placed the pots in the sink and watched the water swirl in from the pipe.

He took a bag of banana chips from the biscuit bin, got some of Kyle's apple juice, and sat at the table, munching on automatic. Should he spend the night in one of the bedrooms on the ground floor? Sherryn wouldn't welcome him in her bed tonight. He pushed aside the 'maybe never again' that tormented his mind.

He rested his forehead on his folded hands, trying to empty his brain, but it was impossible not to think. Pictures floated behind his eyelids—images of himself playing in the squalor of a yard in Waterhouse, nose running, torn shirt hanging open over tattered shorts, and bare feet itchy with ringworm sores.

The picture shifted and his heart pounded, just as it had when he was ten years old and a police Jeep drove up and stopped on the street corner. At the time, he was pretending to belong to the group of gunmen hanging out on the 'ends'. One of them flung a gun into his hands and said, "Hold dis and gimme back later."

Reece's age allowed him to melt away in the crowd of women and children who gathered to heckle the police. He hitched the weapon in the waistband of his shorts like he watched the men around him do many times. Then, he walked away on shaky legs, sure that a policeman's hand would grab his shoulder at any minute. It didn't happen that day, but he never forgot the experience and decided a life of crime wasn't for him.

The sketch changed again, and he saw himself at thirteen years old in high school. He'd grown used to washing and ironing his two uniforms every evening to keep himself neat and clean because the boys in his class were merciless with their teasing when they found a weakling. Though he was poor, Reece was not prepared to be the object of anyone's meanness. Only he knew how his temper smoldered and became a relentless force that demanded release when it was roused. Therefore, he kept to himself and avoided the altercations that rose so often among the teenage boys.

During that time, hunger was his constant companion. His mother always 'forgot' to give him lunch money. Looking back, Reece wondered how he learned anything. Every dollar his father gave his mother for his care was frittered away on cigarettes and rum. When there was a dance in the area, Cynthia, his mother, outfitted herself and had her hair done. Now, as he sifted through his memories, he found that she took care of her needs in other ways.

Countless times he was forced to wait outside their house while she entertained. He kept his distance from her partners, who abused him if they caught him sneering. Waves of shame still crawled over his skin as he recalled standing behind the zinc fence in their yard and hearing two of the area men talking about her as they stood outside on the street.

"Who, Cynthia? A everybody woman dat. She give you anyt'ing you want for a few bills and some cigarette.'

Reece shook with anger and tears had stung his eyes while he was forced to listen to the details of what else his mother did for the right price. Moving from his position would have meant discovery and a few cuffs around the head for listening to a conversation between adults.

Years later, he realized his mother was an alcoholic. Through observation, he learned more about human nature than he should have at his age. He knew which criminals to avoid if he didn't want to be hit for no other reason than being in the wrong place at the wrong time. He also learned to avoid his mother when she was drunk. He risked going near her only to steal the money his father provided.

As he matured, he swore never to associate with low-class women like his mother, and he kept his word to himself, until Gloria.

Cynthia—she insisted he call her that—nearly killed him when she found out he had intercepted the maintenance money.

Reece waylaid his father one Friday evening and stated his case. His father hadn't said much, but agreed to give him the money instead.

When she found out, Cynthia said nothing to Reece. She bided her time and attacked him one night while he slept. A leather belt woke him, and Cynthia chased him around their house, destroying chipped figurines and glassware in her rage.

Reece escaped by diving through a window, earning himself dozens of cuts and bruises. He also lost a patch of flesh on a broken soda bottle.

Another woman in the yard, who had a vacant room because her son had recently moved out, gave him refuge. Miss Millicent allowed him to stay with her and continued to hide him for several more nights.

After Cynthia's temper cooled, he negotiated with Miss Millicent, and she let him live with her for a small fee.

His mother threw threats at him, but never hit him again.

The room he stayed in was ill lit and cramped, but clean. It contained a cot, a dresser, and a straight-backed chair, which was all he needed. He did his homework on the bed, or the table in the cluttered living-cum-dining room.

In exchange for his meals—and as she termed it, 'the little bit he paid for rent', Miss Millicent taught him to take care of her sexual needs.

By then, Reece was fifteen and found her demands too much for his growing body. No matter how early he went to bed, he could barely stay awake in school.

His mother's death freed him from having to perform nearly every night.

He was desperate to get out from under Miss Millicent's roof, and so when another woman stabbed and killed his mother in a fight at a dance, he seized the opportunity that came to him.

Reece persuaded his mother's landlord to rent him the two-room shack. He didn't disclose where the payments would come from, but ended the man's objections by paying two months' rent up front.

Miss Millicent stopped talking to him when he told her he was moving out.

Since Miss Millicent turned him on to sex, Reece gathered experience not only from the wealth of things she taught him, but widened his reach among the females in the neighborhood. He wasn't handsome, but the combined package of his athletic body, golden-honey eyes, and sculpted lips stirred something carnal in the women around him.

Reece used his physical attributes to get what he wanted, conscious that he was no better than his mother.

Miss Millicent had schooled him in the wisdom of using condoms, and he never went anywhere without them. He worked his body until he was in a position to stop. Then he turned his efforts to using his brain to earn his keep and gather wealth.

Sherryn came into his life when he'd established his business. She helped him with its gradual expansion and stuck with him until now. With so much history between them, living without her was not something he cared to contemplate.

His hand caught the cold surface of the glass, which brought him back to the kitchen. He ate another handful of chips, finished the juice, and plodded upstairs, prepared for a sleepless night.

Eight

Sherryn lay still until Reece turned the water on in the shower. A glance at the clock told her it was after eleven. She pulled on a dressing gown, stuffed her feet into the slippers next to the bed and went to check on the little boy who refused to stay out of her head.

With the flat of her hand, she pushed the door open.

Maurice was not in the bed.

She touched the switch, flooding the room with light. A thankful sigh escaped when she saw him.

He crouched across from the cupboard, where he could see the entire bedroom, hands clasped around his legs, chin on his knees. Terror faded from his eyes that lit up at the sight of her.

Sherryn stooped before him. "Something frightened you?"

His hoarse voice was low. "Ah not used to sleeping by miself and di light from di window ... "

She had forgotten to close the drapes, so he had a full view of the moonlit back yard, where the wind ruffled the trees. From her childhood experiences, plant life took on monstrous shapes on a moonshine night, so she could only imagine how frightened he'd been.

"Nothing's going to hurt you. Come lie down in the bed."

He rocked back and forth on his heels. "I-I want to stay here so."

Sherryn sucked her bottom lip, wondering what to do. She closed the drapes while he sat watching her. "I'll be back in a minute," she said.

She climbed the stairs and tapped Justin's door, relieved his light was still on, though it shouldn't have been.

"Come," he grunted.

He slouched in front of his laptop, wearing a tee-shirt and sweat bottoms. He stretched, sat up, and eyed her over his shoulder. Again, it struck Sherryn how closely he resembled his father, both in height and physique.

"Don't you have school tomorrow?" she asked.

He removed his reading glasses. "Yes, but I couldn't sleep, so I started researching some stuff for my Biology project."

Out of habit, Sherryn got a quick eyeful of his surroundings. His beige-themed room was neat, except for the desk piled with papers, textbooks, and notepads. The rumpled double bed bore evidence of him tossing around in it. The cot opposite had his backpack on it.

"Maurice is afraid down there by himself. Can ... would you let him sleep here?"

His brows closed in on each other, and she thought he would refuse. He tapped a pencil against the desk in a rapid beat before answering. "I suppose."

"Thanks."

He stopped her before she could escape. "Mommy?"

She kept her gaze on his chest. "Uh-huh?"

"Who exactly is that little boy?"

Sherryn cleared her throat while strangling the doorknob in her fist. "Your father's relative."

"What relative, Mommy? You said the same thing in the van, but Daddy has no family that we know about."

She looked at him then, confirming that he was more than halfway to guessing the truth.

"Why don't you ask him?"

His mouth opened, and she dreaded what he was about to say. However, he sprawled in the chair and stared at the screen instead.

Sherryn went on her way.

The rippling currents now in motion hinted at a tidal wave set to sweep over their family. She hoped the backwash wouldn't destroy them.

After she settled Maurice in Justin's room, Sherryn went back to her bedroom. She slipped into bed and turned off the lamp, leaving a dim glow on Reece's side. Immediately, she faced the wall and closed her eyes.

Seconds later, Reece came out of the bathroom and switched off the light.

With a tiny sigh, she admitted she'd been silly to shut him up when he was willing to explain what had happened.

Anything would have been better than the bad movie unwinding in her head. Try as she might, she couldn't dislodge the image of Reece doing to that woman everything he did to her. Did he make love to her as often? Did he find her more attractive? Was she better in bed?

Sherryn wriggled in discomfort each time Reece kissed and stroked the stretch marks on her breasts and belly, declaring that he loved every one of them. For him, they represented her commitment to giving him the family he craved.

Her questions continued in an unending reel. Did he do the same to her when she had his baby? What happened to make her drop Maurice off on their doorstep? Did she get tired of waiting for Reece to leave his family for her? Did he refuse to make more babies? She chided herself because it was obvious the woman had no use for the boy.

But that didn't matter, did it? What mattered was that for the five or so years of Maurice's existence, she had lived in a fragile bubble, on borrowed time, because Reece's lover could have walked in at any time and burst it with one pinprick.

Why today of all days? Why me? Why my husband?

In another moment, she questioned her reasoning. Why not him? They came from the same place. It made sense that they'd understand and be attracted to each other.

A sudden need came over her to do something drastic, but what?

After turning this question over in her mind for minutes on end, she told herself to stop. If anybody had anything to decide, it was him. He needed to sort out where he was going to live and what he was going to do with his love child.

Tears she didn't realize she'd shed formed a moist patch under her cheek. She sniffed quietly, in case Reece was awake.

He sighed and spoke in the darkness. "Sher, I can't take this. Please talk to me."

She allowed some time to pass before she responded. "I have only one question. Why?"

She had to listen hard to hear his words. "It only happened once, and I was drunk at the time."

She sprang on that. "And I suppose that makes it okay?"

"You know I'm not saying that."

"So what are you saying?"

"That I really wish you'd give me a chance to explain."

She stifled the urge to blast him with the obscenities twitching to escape her lips. Instead, she folded an arm under her cheek and said, "You can't possibly say anything to make this right, but you want to talk, so I'm going to listen."

After a few beats, he asked, "D'you remember our last big quarrel?"

"We don't have them often, so yes, I remember."

"Seven years ago, almost."

She wondered where he was heading. "Yeah?"

"Remember when I ... "

"Groped me until I had sex with you?"

"I was going to say, got you pregnant with Brandon."

"Well, if I recall correctly, you came into the office downstairs, questioned me about my motives for saving my own money, and took what you wanted."

Sherryn preferred to forget that she hadn't resisted him for long. Even now, she still grew flustered at how well Reece knew her body and the ease with which she submitted to his lovemaking. Every. Single. Time.

He shifted on the mattress. "We did argue about that account you had. Then, *that* happened and you refused me for months afterwards."

While connecting dots in her head, Sherryn stayed silent, refusing to acknowledge his words or validate his reason for cheating. She fought not to release pent up tears, but the cream valance and drapes wobbled in the darkness cut by the streetlight.

"During that time, I ... uh ... "

Her words were a savage whisper. "Screwed that boy's mother?"

"I was in Waterhouse, had too much liquor and ... "

"Fell into her bed?"

He sighed. "Yes."

Reece shifted again, as though unable to find a comfortable position. "Sher, I didn't mean for it to happen, and I haven't done anything like that since then."

She rolled to confront him. "Like I'm supposed to believe anything you say. You lied, Reece, and you've been lying for six years!"

He lay on his back, unmoving, his words muffled. "How was I supposed to tell you I not only cheated on you, but had a baby coming? I asked her to abort it, even gave her the money, but she didn't."

Sherryn understood why, but she wasn't about to explain that as a woman, she knew how those things worked. The easiest way for that woman to get Reece to take care of her for at least eighteen years was to get pregnant. That was the way of the sly ghetto woman, and he was savvy enough to understand. Play with fire and you must get burned, as old folks would say.

Sometimes plans backfired, and the victim disappeared not long after the trap slammed shut. When the man was married, like Reece, and could be held to ransom, a wily female capitalized on his misfortune.

Sherryn didn't want to imagine how much money that woman had sucked out of him in the intervening years. The money-grubbing sow!

She wasn't going to swallow his story whole, but had to admit based on the boy's age, the timing was right.

Shunted firmly into the present by the warmth of Reece's hand on her shoulder, Sherryn shrugged away his touch. Her chest was compressed as though Kyle was lying on it during one of their roughhousing sessions. She needed to relax somehow and release the uncomfortable tightness gripping her upper body. Another sigh escaped into the darkness. Would she have done anything differently had she known he'd wander into someone else's bed?

Crossing her hands over her stomach, Sherryn allowed her mind to travel to where their troubles started.

Theirs was an interdependent relationship. She loved Reece passionately, understood the emotional needs which sprang from years of neglect, and catered to them. Reece, in turn, adored and pampered her and used all his sexual skills to keep her addicted to him.

Both of them accepted their intense, unhealthy jealousy of anything that stood between them.

Sherryn recalled how in the early days she had to coax him out of anger after he found her hanging on to the arm of an old schoolmate, who was also an invited guest at a cocktail party thrown by her girlfriend Barbara.

She dealt with Reece's misgivings as they arose, knowing how her insides got stirred up when another woman so much as glanced at him.

Their children came early in their marriage and when their third child, Celia, started pre-school, Sherryn decided to turn her baking and cake-decorating hobby into a business.

Reece converted one room on the bottom floor of the house into an office, and took a day off from work to drive her around Kingston while she bought all the additional equipment she needed.

Apart from opening an account for the business, she'd already started a savings account years before in her name only.

Referrals from other mothers for whom she did birthday cakes brought her a steady income. Then Reece began pressuring her for another baby, for which she wasn't ready. Sherryn now had a little space and wanted to savor her freedom.

They argued over it, and Reece was unwilling or unable to understand why she didn't want to be pregnant again so soon. He repeatedly hunted down and threw out her birth control pills, which led to more arguments.

Though Sherryn grew up in a small household, she enjoyed their growing family and didn't think the end of the world was imminent if she didn't have another child right away. She assumed Reece was threatened by her success, not that he said anything. She knew he was insecure and had reservations about not being her sole means of support. With that in mind, he conditioned himself to providing generously for the family, and refused to acknowledge her desire for independence.

Since starting the business, she drew less on the money he provided, preferring to contribute to their household expenses because Reece had taken care of the family since the start of their marriage. Over time, he chose to forget their agreement that Sherryn would return to work when the children were somewhat independent.

As her business expanded, Reece found reasons to interrupt her work, using sex as the main diversion. She was patient with him, understanding the uncertainty that plagued him. He was needy and unsure of himself, though he presented the opposite picture to those around him. The family was no longer at the center of Sherryn's world, and he couldn't handle it. But Reece was nothing, if not smart. He used the physical hold he had over her to his advantage.

On the day of their big fallout, he came home in the afternoon and tried to entice her to leave the office and the quotation she was preparing for a set of wedding cakes. He'd hung over her shoulder nuzzling her neck, when she reached into the desk drawer for something or other. He went still, and when her gaze fell on the passbook, she knew he'd seen it too. Reece picked it up, opened it, and moved to stand beside her.

She held her breath while his mouth puckered and his eyes darkened. He threw the book on the desk next to her hand. It fell with a thwack that made her flinch.

In the seconds before he spoke, she held her breath.

"Apparently, you have a plan I don't know about," he said.

She hastened to soothe his fears. "That account is simply a place to put the excess funds from the business. The bank doesn't pay interest on checking accounts, so I opened this one."

He folded his arms across his chest, staring her in the eyes. "We have an investment account."

"Come on, Reece," she said, "don't make a big deal out of this."

She cursed herself for leaving the book in plain sight and getting caught. Though she allowed Reece to take care of her, Sherryn held strong views about having her own money—just in case.

When they started having children, she'd been delighted to give up her job at the car dealership but she was never comfortable depending on Reece for all of her needs, even though he made good money from his trucking business.

Her mother and father had drilled the value of independence into her head, and she knew how fickle men could be, so each week she saved a little from the money she withdrew for shopping.

While she tried to find words to appease Reece, she also hoped he hadn't noticed how long ago the account was opened.

He pulled her to a standing position and spoke close to her ear. "When you do things like this, you make me think you don't need me."

She struggled to ignore his warm breath and concentrate on his words. "You know it's not like that."

Now he was breathing in her space. "Isn't it?"

She pushed him away, but he grabbed her arms. "Why are you keeping that account a secret? You planning to leave me?"

"N-nothing like that. I just ... "

"Need to have money of your own. Why?"

"Reece, it's nothing. Trust me. I-I ... what if something happens to you, and I'm left alone with the kids?"

His expressionless stare said he wasn't going to accept that explanation. "Don't think for a minute that I'll ever allow you to leave. I love you and need you." His hands dropped to her hips, tracing light patterns. "Just like you need me."

He kissed her despite her protests. "We want the same things, don't we?"

She leaned into him, about to groan yes. Then she pulled her scrambled senses together. "No! You do this every time. You're not going to sidetrack me with sex."

"I'm not trying to sidetrack you, but I do want to find out what you're up to."

She pushed against his chest. "You have a nerve. Like you're my father or something. I don't report to you, Reece Allbright. If I have money you don't know about, it's my choice."

"I'm your husband. Why you want to hide anything from me? That's not how our marriage works!"

She turned away from him, calming herself to prevent a pointless argument. Measuring her words, she said, "Your problem is that you want to control me. You don't own me, Reece."

He stood behind her, crossing his hands over her breasts. "I'm not trying to control you. You're my wife. I don't expect to have secrets between us. What would you think if you found out I had funds saved away that you didn't know about?"

She stayed quiet, forcing him to walk around to face her. "Sherryn, I asked you a question."

She shrugged. "You're your own man. What could I do about it?"

He pursed his lips and stared into her eyes. "Now I'm wondering what other secrets you have."

In an attempt to lighten his mood, she softened her voice. "Don't be silly. Maybe you should go back to work and leave me to do what I was doing before you started annoying me."

He raised his brows. "So, I'm annoying you?"

"Yes, you are." She fanned him away. "Go back to your office."

"Not before I kiss you goodbye."

He crowded her again, and she rolled her eyes and tilted her head. "Okay, fine."

Reece avoided her lips, placing a string of kisses along her neck and over her cheek. She wanted to ease away, but the tip of his tongue traced the shell of her ear while he undid her bra. She opened her mouth, and he stifled her words with a heady kiss.

"Reece," she protested, as he nibbled her neck. "Not now, I have things to do."

He ignored her words, but Sherryn didn't blame him. Her heated body was sending opposing signals.

"They can wait."

Her temper stirred at his arrogance. "No, they can't."

Twisting in his grip, she tried to re-hitch her bra.

"I don't see what's so important that it can't wait," he said, slipping his hands around her waist.

"Reece, I can't. Not now."

He went still. Then one hand slid down the front of her shorts and inside her panties, swiftly reducing her to white-hot shivers.

"Yes, you can," he growled in her ear.

Slowly, he undid her clothing while kissing her flesh and whispering against her skin.

Sherryn cursed her weakness as Reece's warmth surrounded her, his chest pressing against her back while she braced against the cool filing cabinet.

She let out a cry of fulfillment at the pinnacle of their coupling and grabbed the cabinet to keep from collapsing as he groaned his satisfaction. Reece leaned against her, hands splayed on her belly, chin on her shoulder. "See, Sherryn, I might not own your mind, but I own your body."

Shock held her still for countless seconds. When she could stand properly, she pushed him away. "So, that's what this was for you, some sort of self-affirmation?"

His mouth opened, but she didn't allow him to speak.

"We'll see how well you do the next time you want some sex and it isn't available. From now on just keep your hands to yourself."

He closed the space between them, but she wagged a finger at him. "Don't touch me! Don't you dare."

She'd held firm for two and a half months, outraged that he'd make love to her just to prove he was in control. By then, she was pregnant again, and Brandon arrived promptly within nine months.

Reece's gentle snore intruded on her thoughts. She glowered at him in the dark and flopped onto her side, hoping he'd wake up. It did the trick.

He touched her arm. "Sherryn?"

"Take your hand off me. I don't want to talk anymore."

He muffled an anguished groan. It should have made her feel better, but only made her pain worse.

Nine

Sherryn rose early, after a restless night during which they dozed in snatches.

Reece got up every so often to do God only knew what downstairs. The last time he returned was after four a.m., and Sherryn felt him poised next to her, wanting to speak but not knowing what to say.

She slowed her breathing, reveling in his discomfort.

He wouldn't risk approaching her after her last words to him during the night, and eventually fell asleep just before she gave up on getting any rest.

She satisfied herself with glaring at him. While she showered, she daydreamed about the many painful ways she could find to kill him. As she toweled off, she recognized the stages people went through when they lost a loved one. Yesterday's shock still hung over her, but with facts and evidence in her face, grief closed in fast. Reality hit hardest during the night, when she couldn't stop seeing Reece with Maurice's mother. Sure, he told her 'it' only happened once, but it was one time too many and could she really believe him, considering how intimately she knew him?

Sometimes she wondered how she kept up with his sex drive and concluded long ago that he used sex as a way to avoid dealing with unresolved issues. There were places within him she had never reached, experiences he never shared.

He claimed she didn't have the capacity to understand, saying they came from two separate worlds.

Sometimes his secrecy disturbed her, but being a dutiful and loving wife, she accommodated and eventually got used to his voracious appetite for sex, which she also enjoyed.

As she relived the scene on her doorstep, she mourned the loss of her familiar and comfortable world. She had long ago accepted that neither of them was perfect, but they loved each other and were raising reasonably behaved children, which was a lot more than some of her friends could say.

Judith, her closest girlfriend, was well-off financially, but wasn't happy. She kept a smile in place and resigned herself to pretending not to know that her husband, Barry, had one affair after another.

Barbara, her other bestie, claimed the life had gone from her marriage. Added to that, her husband, Winston, aided and abetted their out-of-control, fifteen-year-old daughter, whom he believed could do no wrong.

Sherryn always had a sympathetic ear for her friends' problems, but personal experience was different from sitting on the sidelines. Now she could relate to Judith's disillusionment, but unlike her friend, was not prepared to accept what Reece had done.

To Sherryn's mind, her own situation was worse. She not only had knowledge of her husband's outside son, but he was in her face because nobody else wanted him. How was her pain supposed to get better if she had to see the result of Reece's cheating? What was Reece going to do with the boy? What would her children think? What would her friends think?

Everybody would soon know Reece had cheated.

"Hold on a second! Why am I stressing myself over this?" she asked her reflection in the bathroom mirror. "I'm the victim here and Maurice isn't my responsibility."

She replaced her toothbrush in the cup, avoiding the question forming in her mind.

What's going to happen to him?

Meeting her gaze, she said emphatically, "I don't care."

Moving on automatic pilot, she marched to the kitchen where she prepared breakfast. Then, she moved to her office to start some of the day's tasks. She sat at her desk, a cup of coffee within reach, but it went cold. The sheet detailing the orders she had for the week lay untouched while her mind rested on the boy in her son's room upstairs.

A sound came from the doorway and she stirred, unable to restrain the smile that broke over her face when her precocious six year old peeked around the office door, before coming in to hug her.

"G'mornin', Mommy, can I watch some cartoons before breakfast?"

"No way. I won't be able to get you to budge if you don't bathe first."

He perched on the arm of the couch close to where she sat.

"What if—"

"The answer is no. Go find the bathroom. I'm coming."

"Okay, but can I—"

"No, Brandon. We'll talk after you have a shower."

He jumped to the floor, sighing. "All right, but I was only going to ask if I could get ice cream money today."

She put aside the open folder in her lap and got up. "Yes, I'll give you the money. Now go."

Smiling, she trailed him upstairs.

Brandon made life interesting and ironically, was her favorite child. He questioned everything, negotiated even when it wasn't necessary, and as young as he was, his faith was strong. Her mother said he had an old soul, which Sherryn believed, for on occasion she caught herself about to tell him things she shouldn't. Brandon argued with such maturity, she sometimes forgot his age.

He also had a tendency to ask awkward questions.

A lump forced its way to her throat, for Brandon would want the details of how a stranger came to be in their home. The questions hadn't started because Maurice was still in Justin's room, and Sherryn was sure he wouldn't come out, unless she went to get him.

Her reprieve didn't last long.

Brandon began the inquisition while she dried his slender body. "Mommy, who is the boy that stayed with us last night?"

Her hands stilled, and she was thankful she held him close while rubbing him with the towel. He'd know something was wrong if he looked at her.

"Um, your father's relative."

"What's a relative? You used that word yesterday, but I didn't hear what you told Justin about it."

"It means he's related to your father. You know, like you and I are mother and son?"

"So, how is he Daddy's relative?"

She squeezed his narrow shoulders. "Ask your dad."

"Why can't you tell me? You don't know?"

"Brandon, your father will talk to you about it."

"But Mommy—"

"It's time to get dressed. Put on your brief and socks. I'll be there in a minute, okay?

"Okay, but there's still stuff I need to know."

She wanted to laugh at the picture he made, hands outstretched, palms turned upward like a wise old man—missing front teeth and all—but the things he wanted to find out were not at all funny.

"Fine. Ask me later."

"One more thing," he said, unmindful of his nakedness. "Can I play with him when I come home?"

"I doubt he'll be here."

"But if he is, can I play with him?"

"Brandon!"

"I'm on my way."

She refused to consider Brandon's request as a possibility, and to her relief, the semi-chaos that ruled their house during early morning hours saved her from fielding any more questions.

Working quickly, she dished plates of corned beef and cabbage and green bananas and set them on the table.

She cocked a brow at Justin when he sat, taking the slight shake of his head to mean the boy wasn't yet awake.

"I want you all ready by the time I come back down," she said on her way out of the sunny kitchen.

Maurice lay in bed, sucking his thumb and plucking at the edge of the pillow. When he saw her, he pulled his legs closer to his body, forming a tight comma.

"Morning, Maurice. You okay?"

He nodded.

"You hungry yet?"

He nodded again, and she turned away, distracted by the sound of the front grille opening. Miss Emelyn was the only person expected that early.

Maurice's face was now scrunched up, as though he had much on his mind. Sherryn blinked, cleared her throat, and muttered. "I'll be back."

In the passage outside, she leaned against the wall, stunned by her reaction to the boy. She tilted her head upward, willing the tears to go away. A moment later, she stared at the veined tiles, sighing at the idea of a five-and-a-half-year-old boy having to worry about his future. Teary and miserable, she re-entered the room.

Maurice sat up, finger in his mouth, while he picked at a scab on his knee.

Sherryn watched him, imagining that she was seeing Reece in the past he preferred not to talk about. Had he been haunted by the same concerns at Maurice's age? No. She recalled that he'd lived with his mother almost up to her death. She put aside her thoughts and focused on the child.

"Did you sleep all right?"

He spoke around his finger. "Yes."

"I'll be leaving in a little while, but—"

She swallowed hard when his eyes clouded with anxiety.

"I won't be out for long," she added, rushing her words.

Under the crumpled tee-shirt, his shoulders relaxed, thin and delicate as the wings of a hummingbird, making her want to cry again. Instead, she concentrated on making him comfortable.

"Miss Emelyn is downstairs. I'm going to ask her to come up to give you a bath and something to eat until I come back, okay?"

He apparently decided he could trust her, so he nodded.

"Catch you later," she said with a smile.

His lips curved, and Sherryn's tears threatened again, because it wasn't the smile of one of her happy I've-had-a-privileged-life children. It was the tentative approach of one who had seen abuse, like a dog who hoped for kindness, but had been kicked too many times.

She waved at him from the door, and he gave her a funny little wiggle of the hand that warmed her heart and an instant later, made her want to murder her worthless husband.

Downstairs, she greeted Miss Emelyn and asked her to take care of Maurice, adding that they would talk more when she got back. While rounding up the children and their assorted bags, lunch kits and folders, she wondered what explanation she'd give Miss Emelyn, who was like a mother to her and Reece.

She rushed outside after the children, dreading the ride she had to take with them.

The silence didn't last long inside the van. Brandon, strapped in beside her, waited until she hit the major road to ask, "So, Mommy, you know yet if he'll be there when we get home?"

"It's not later yet," she said, looking straight ahead.

"Why him not going to school?"

"'Cause he's not old enough yet." She turned her head for a second. "And speak properly."

"Okay. So, how old is he?"

"Almost six."

"So how come Kyle and I have to go to school?"

"Because some people send their kids to school early."

"Why? When we could just stay at home and play all day?"

Sherryn relaxed at the direction the conversation was taking. Giving Brandon a quick smile, she teased him, "But then you wouldn't get to do some of the fun stuff you do at school."

Melaine leaned over Sherryn's shoulder and she glanced at her in the mirror. Her fringe needed attention; it flopped over her brow and into her eyes. She leaned in closer, tickling Sherryn's neck with her processed hair. "Seriously though, Mommy, who is he and why's he staying with us?"

"Melly, your hair needs cutting," Sherryn mumbled, and pretended to be distracted by a group of children crossing the street. "And you need to sit down."

Melaine, or Melly as everybody called her, rested on the seat, but continued to seek answers. "Oh, and when is he leaving?"

A line of vehicles built up behind the van, but Sherryn let another cluster of students cross the street. Her children were fortunate not to have to brave the traffic on foot in the growing heat. Nor did they know what it was to use the public transportation system, with its packed buses that everybody complained about. Horns beeped behind her while Brandon prompted her. "Melly asked you a question, Mommy. Three, as a matter of fact."

Sherryn adjusted the rearview mirror and inched forward, desperate to escape the unrelenting questions.

Justin stared out of the side window, but that didn't fool Sherryn. He was too still not to be listening.

"Can I get a minute to focus on the road?" Sherryn snapped.

As if Sherryn wasn't already under pressure, Celia stuck a finger in the book she was reading and edged forward.

Sherryn cupped Celia's cheek for a second, making a mental note to take her back to the hairdresser they found recently, who specialized in natural styles. Celia had tamed her crop of spiral twists into two thick plaits that were now fuzzy.

She spoke into Sherryn's ear, "I can see he's related to us, but I can't figure out how, since Daddy doesn't have any family."

"He does have a cousin somewhere or other," Sheryn said, embarrassed by her cowardice. All her delaying tactics were a waste of time and effort, because the truth was bound to come out.

Another peek in the mirror at her eldest child worried her. If she didn't know better, she'd think Justin disapproved of what she was doing. He resembled his father even more when he was being stubborn.

Anxiety tightened her chest and for a nanosecond Sherryn sympathized with Reece. He'd have the devil of a time explaining Maurice to their firstborn, and she wouldn't escape either, for like Brandon, Justin needed an explanation for everything.

Justin, as their first child, used to act as if he owned his parents, but his attitude changed as his siblings were born. He was their natural leader and used his authority to keep them in line, but more often he horsed around with them, particularly Melly to whom he was closest. The affection among her children was something that made Sherryn proud. Glancing at Justin again, she glimpsed the formidable man lying beneath the surface. He'd confront her when she least expected it. He was like his father that way.

He surprised her when he spoke. "Give Mommy a break, man. Remember what happen' yesterday with the police?"

Melly and Celia grumbled, but went back to their activities and left Sherryn to her driving.

Justin was the last drop-off, as usual. When he stood outside the van, he slung his knapsack over one shoulder, slid the door closed and said, "Hold on, Mommy."

He walked around the front of the vehicle and stood beside the driver's window.

"I know," he said.

She tried smiling. "What d'you think you know, Justin?"

"That boy is Daddy's son."

He moved the knapsack to his other shoulder. "He looks too much like us not to be. Plus, both of you are acting weird, which tells me something big is up."

Sherryn gripped the wheel and waited for her throat to open up, but what could she say? She couldn't deny the truth, and refused to lie to her son. Not that he'd asked a question. Justin had made a simple statement of fact.

He hugged her around the neck and kissed her cheek, right there in the driveway with students passing them both ways. Then, he murmured something in her ear that he hadn't told her in a long time. "I love you, Mommy."

Tears stung her eyes and wet her cheeks, but she answered. "I love you too, baby."

She lowered her head, ashamed of breaking down in front of him.

Smiling despite the sorrow in his eyes, Justin patted her shoulder. "Things'll work out. You'll see."

She cupped the side of his face, blinking to clear her vision. "Thanks for being my bestest son."

He grinned at their oldest, corniest joke from when he was her only child. "And you're still the bestest Mommy in the whole of Jamaica."

He walked away, reminding her so much of Reece it hurt to look at him. Justin liked to consider himself a roughneck, which made him cool among his friends, but Sherryn was acutely aware that the little boy in their home had experienced the harshness of life firsthand, having lived in the ghetto.

Justin knew nothing of that life and probably couldn't imagine the hardships that came with living hand-to-mouth. Still, his attitude told her he had matured and would someday be a considerate and sensitive man.

She rested her head on her hands, working out her next move. It didn't take long before she found a stopgap that would clear her mind for a while.

Ten

For the first time in her married life, Sherryn didn't want to go home. Inside that house, there would be too much time to think about what Reece had done.

Judith lived around the corner from Justin's school, and Sherryn desperately needed to talk to someone. Who better than another woman, and more to the point, one who understood what she was going through? For the umpteenth time, she wondered how her friends dealt with the pain of knowing their husbands cheated time and again.

On the way over, Sherryn called ahead. "'Morning, Judy. I just dropped Justin off and wanted to swing by. You busy?"

"No, I was tending my flowers. Everything all right?"

"We'll talk when I get there."

"I'll tell the guard to look out for you."

"Thanks."

Sherryn sucked her lip into her mouth and swallowed to dislodge the painful lump in her throat. She rarely visited Judith this early, hence her question.

Justin's gesture still rested on Sherryn's mind and she tried not to think about the scene that had played out between them, in case she started crying again.

Though she felt better than she did yesterday, her heart still weighed a ton. She suspected the gnawing emptiness in her middle would remain for some time. Tears welled in her eyes, but instead of having the luxury of a good cry, she cleared her throat and blinked several times. At the gated entrance to Judith's country-club-style community, the guard who knew her by sight waved her inside.

Would she be able to talk to Judith without falling apart? It didn't matter. They had known each other long enough to be totally honest about their problems. Sherryn, Judith and Barbara had grown up in the same neighborhood and attended the same schools. Though the other two women were older than Sherryn, they remained friends, and the three of them had shared many troubles.

While she cruised past chateau-style houses, Sherryn thought about how much to share with Judith. For once, their situation was reversed. She was the one having man troubles. She hadn't anticipated anything destroying what some folks considered a boring day-to-day existence. She enjoyed her life and found satisfaction in taking care of her family.

A sigh deflated her chest. Reece was a man, so she should have expected this at some point. Somehow, she credited him with super-human qualities and remained wrapped up in their life together, like a child in a never-ending fairytale. She should have known better.

Judith met her at the door, wearing a sweat suit. Her hair was swept up in a ponytail, which made her look younger than her forty-six years. They hugged and exchanged greetings, but Sherryn was uncomfortable with the way Judith studied her as she stood on the doorstep.

"Come. I put the kettle on for coffee."

Sherryn followed Judith through the sitting room, which opened into a larger living area. They crossed to the octagon-shaped kitchen, where blinding light flowed in through the bay windows. The smell of percolating coffee wafted through the room.

Judith drank nothing else, but made instant whenever Sherryn visited. She couldn't stand the taste of percolated coffee. It was something Judith ribbed her about regularly, saying she had crass taste buds.

Sherryn sat at the table, nestled against one wall and stared into the garden, paying little attention to Judith's movements between the counter and cupboard. Judith set a coffee mug in front of her and sat, mixing sugar into her own cup. Closing her eyes, Sherryn inhaled steam from the Blue Mountain instant coffee.

"What's bothering you, Sher?"

A hot rush of tears accompanied Sherryn's words. "Reece cheated on me. He has a son. He's five plus."

Judith's spoon clanged against the cup; her mouth opened, but no words came out. She covered Sherryn's hand with one of hers. "I don't know what to say. This is going to sound dumb, but are you sure?"

Sherryn got up, snagged a piece of hand towel off the roll and blew her nose. She flung the paper in the bin and plopped into the seat. "The boy's mother dropped him off yesterday. He's the spitting image of Reece."

"What did Reece say?"

Sherryn's eyes welled again. Her voice was harsh when she spoke. "He told me some rubbish about being drunk and having sex 'cause of some argument we had."

A line settled between Judith's brows. "What?"

"The year before Brandon was born, we had a disagreement. I refused to have sex with him for a while, and ... " She sobbed, pressing both hands to her head.

Judith pressed more paper towel into Sherryn's hand, while making comforting sounds.

"He's not still seeing the woman, is he?"

"He says no, but how can I believe him?"

"You have to admit, he's always been a devoted husband and—"

Sherryn glared at Judith. "Devoted my behind. All this time, he's probably been with her, hoping I'd never find out."

"Come on, Sherryn. You know better than that. How many times have Barb and I wished for just a fraction of what you and Reece have together?"

Everything inside Sherryn had turned upside down and she was tired of acting as if she had it all together. She laid her head on her arms and howled, while Judith patted her back.

What had Reece been thinking about? Things would never be the same between them. Sherryn knew that much because her biggest pet peeve was cheating men. Her two best friends suffered unspeakable humiliation in their marriages, and their experience had colored Sherryn's views on fidelity.

Judith allowed her to cry and when her tears stopped, Sherryn went to the bathroom and washed her face. In the mirror, she cracked a smile. If she continued breaking down like this, she'd have to stay at home, hiding her ugliness.

She stared herself in the eyes, standing straighter. Reece would not see her in this condition. Her pride wouldn't let her, even if he was living it up while she was playing the role of faithful wife. She might be devastated, but she refused to lie down and behave as if her life had ended. She had her children to think about. He could blow away in the wind for all she cared.

She looked up at the ceiling to stop another round of tears from falling. Who was she fooling? She loved that man—maybe more than she loved herself.

"That doesn't mean I'm prepared to put up with slackness," she muttered, turning away from her reflection.

When she returned to the kitchen, Judith asked, "So, the boy's at the house?"

Sherryn nodded and eased into the chair. "There was nowhere for him to go. His mother took off somewhere."

Judith spun the cup on the table before meeting Sherryn's gaze. "I'm gonna say something but don't take it the wrong way, okay?"

A nod and a sniffle made up Sherryn's response.

"This sounds like Reece walked into an unfortunate situation." She held up her hands. "Not that I'm excusing him. But have you stopped to consider that this woman might just be making a play for him? Dropping the boy off would be the perfect way to wreck his home life."

"Why now?"

"I don't know, but you forget I've seen it with Barry's women. Remember the time that woman sent a text to my phone to tell me she was pregnant by him?"

Sherryn nodded.

"It's the same thing," Judith continued, "Reece is a great husband and father. She might just be trying to back him into a corner."

"It doesn't take away from the fact that he slept with her."

"I know that. And if I know you well, you haven't given him a chance to explain the circumstances."

"I listened for a bit, but after a while I shut him up."

The flicker of impatience on Judith's face made Sherryn want to pout and justify her action, but she stayed quiet.

"This is going to be a trying time for both of you," Judith said. "It can't be business as usual. You like to turn him off like a light switch when you're upset, but that's not going to work. You need to get to the bottom of this and stop being childish."

Sherryn's narrowed her eyes and opened her mouth to butt in, but Judith held up a hand to stop her. "And don't ask me what gives me the right to talk to you this way. Thirty-odd years of putting up with you gives me the right. Now, you're going to have to focus your energy if you expect your marriage to survive."

"I don't know, Judy." Sherryn cupped her forehead in her hands, wanting to cry again. "I don't see how I'm going to get past this."

"Think about your children for a second. You're not the only one in for a rough time. Do they know?"

"Justin's figured it out. The others ... "

"Just remember you're not the only one affected by this situation. I can only imagine the state Reece is in, not to mention that boy who's been thrown off at your house like a can of garbage." She squeezed Sherryn's shoulder. "You're a strong one. Take it one day at a time. That's how I cope."

Sherryn looked away from Judith, unwilling to admit that she understood the message.

Judith's speech was easy to make, but she didn't have to go home to face a child that her husband had fathered during a night on the town. She got up to leave, ignoring the weight that pressed down on her, sapping her energy.

If God was on her side, Reece would be out of the house when she got back.

Eleven

God hadn't answered her prayer because Reece's van was still in the driveway.

Since she was on her own, she'd do the next best thing, which was to avoid seeing or talking to him. She entered the house, intending to lock herself in her office until she remembered Maurice. She had to check on him first.

The surface of the Mahoe table at the center of the living room shone and the room was neat.

Miss Em had already worked her magic.

Maurice was watching cartoons. His spindly feet stuck over the edge of the children's favorite sofa, and a cushion rested in his lap. Sherryn acted as if she didn't see him hurrying to stuff it back where it belonged, behind him.

He struck her as lost, sitting in a corner of the couch trying to take up as little space as possible. From the corners of his eyes, he watched her.

A change of clothing didn't improve his appearance. The dingy white tee-shirt was spotted, the neck frayed. Sherryn couldn't determine the original color of his faded shorts and couldn't help thinking his mother certainly kept herself in better condition.

Trying not to make the boy more uncomfortable than he was, she turned toward the television, making up her mind to get some things for him. Before that, she wanted to talk to him so she sat on the other end of the sofa.

"You okay?"

"Yeah."

"You're not hungry?"

He thought about it, then shook his head. "No."

"What d'you usually do when you're at home?"

"Play in di yard."

"You do that all day?"

"Yeah."

"Does you mother work?"

His shoulders lifted and fell, suggesting he wasn't sure.

Guilty over prying information from a child, Sherryn kept an eye on the doorway. "So she stays home and takes care of you?"

"No."

"So what does she do during the day?"

"Mi don' know."

Sherryn positioned herself so she could see Miss Em approaching. "Does your father come to see you often?"

Maurice's thumb crept into his mouth. The fingers of his other hand picked at the half-healed cut on his knee. He shook his head. "Him don' come at all."

This left the question of where Reece dropped off money for him. "He doesn't visit you, ever?"

Slowly, his head went from side to side. "Only when him ca'an find mi madda at di bar."

She thought about that for a few seconds, while they watched each other. She cocked her head to the side, recognizing that he was observant and had as much potential to learn as any of Reece's other children.

Anger warred with disgust inside her over Reece's neglect, but she had to admit, she understood his position. The man she knew would not be prepared to deal with an ongoing problem he'd tried to solve at the outset. But what about the boy? Surely, Reece understood he was hurting the child by pretending he didn't exist.

She stared across the room and out the window when tears flooded her eyes. The emotions swirling inside confused her all over again. Why should she be concerned whether Reece cared about this child or not? She looked at Maurice and her throat tightened because his earnest eyes sought something from her.

"Miss?" His hoarse voice startled her.

"Hmm?"

"Miss, why nobody don' want me?"

Pain gripped her throat and she couldn't swallow, but she also couldn't cry. He'd never understand what was wrong with her. Instead she sighed, and tried to come up with something that would make sense.

"I can't answer that, Maurice." She leaned in close as if she were about to share a secret.

He, in turn, tilted toward her. "Except to say that I know you're special. They just don't know it yet."

A frown conveyed his doubt. "Really?"

"Yes, you are," she said, touching his bony shoulder. "Don't move. I'll be back in a little bit."

She hurried into Brandon's room, picked out a set of his clothing she thought might fit well enough, along with socks and footwear, and left them downstairs in the room where Maurice had first gone to sleep the previous night.

Miss Emelyn was in one of the bathrooms tidying up, but Sherryn asked her to get Maurice ready to go out. The older woman didn't hide her curiosity, but Sherryn had little time to explain anything. She had a mission to complete first and so she headed upstairs to find Reece, who was running late.

She closed the door behind her when he emerged naked from the bathroom. She looked him in the eyes. "Your son needs some things. I want money to get them."

A range of emotions flickered over his face and was gone before Sherryn could identify all of them. However, she suspected the main one was shame at the boy's condition, and gratitude for what she intended to do.

"Yes, you should be ashamed and no, there's no need to be grateful. I'm not doing it for you."

When he winced, Sherryn realized she'd spoken her thoughts. Reece got his wallet off the dresser, took some bills out of it and counted off six of them, then put the last one back.

"What is this?" she asked, holding up the six thousand dollars he'd handed her. "Things are expensive on this island. The boy has next to nothing. This is not enough."

"That's almost all the cash I have," he said, "use your credit card."

"Fine, you're paying the bill."

Sherryn made sure she left Reece a little something to remind him that she wasn't going to make life easy. "While we're gone, you need to decide what you're going to do with him."

Before she shut the door, her gaze went back to him.

He sat on the bed, clasping his head between his hands. A perfect picture of despair.

She smiled—a grimace of spite rather than anything close to amusement. A sense of shame pushed her to ease his distress, but she hardened her stance. The need for revenge was stronger.

With the early morning activities out of the way, she had time to think. Her energy was low, as if she'd gotten a bad cut that was now stale, but throbbed with pain and demanded her attention at the expense of everything else. How was she supposed to get past something like this? She'd been lulled into false security because of Reece's continued devotion, when all the while he'd been enjoying himself outside their home.

Even as she told herself his pain and regret were evident, another part of her insisted on making him suffer. Their time together taught her all the things that affected him most. She hoped she'd have the willpower to resist the desire to make his life hell.

Twelve

Maurice's closed eyelids trembled and tiny moans escaped from him as he licked mango ice cream.

Sherryn was shocked when he told her he'd never eaten ice cream before, and had gone inside the parlor because he was fascinated by the giant cone on the wall and the assortment of cakes on display through the plate glass showcase.

First, she had taken him to one of the shopping malls in Half-Way-Tree and gotten him several sets of clothing. She also bought underwear, socks, shoes, and sneakers. Until Reece found a permanent place for him, she figured she might as well get all Maurice needed. She let her eyes roam her surroundings, and shied away from any further thoughts about his future.

She sucked the last of the ice cream from the spoon and grinned at him, taking pleasure in his enjoyment. His bright smile revealed signs of decay around his front teeth. He needed to see the dentist.

She caught herself—those were milk teeth and would be a waste of time and money to fix. Her thoughts chattered on unabated, but she returned his smile wondering when he became her responsibility.

When you started to care.

Maurice stopped moving when yellow liquid ran down his fingers. He shot a glance at her, as though expecting her to scold him. She searched her bag and pulled out a container of wipes. "It's okay. You can clean up when you're finished."

He beamed at her, and she scanned the pastel-painted shop to escape his open adoration. It made her uncomfortable. He was like a young animal latching on to the first person who showed him kindness. What kind of life had he lived to be so grateful for a little attention from a stranger?

It saddened her that through no fault of his own, Maurice faced such difficult circumstances. She eyed the boy, but her focus was on his father, who didn't have a clue what a mess he had created. Reece had no doubt been too busy throwing money at the boy's mother, hoping the problem would go away.

Guilt had stopped Sherryn from picking up where she left off earlier, but she had a right to as much information as she could gather, and this time away from home gave her the opportunity to find out what she wanted to know.

"Um, so Maurice, when was the last time you saw your father before yesterday?"

He hiked one shoulder and let it fall.

"You don't know?"

Resentment tinged his words. "Don' 'member."

"Don't you like him?"

Maurice crunched the waffle cone, frowned and wobbled his head. "No."

"Why not?"

"'Cause him don' like me."

"I'm sure that's not true, Maurice," Sherryn said, then cursed herself for a fraud, for she had no idea how Reece felt about him.

Maurice's drew his brows together and pouted. "Mi madda tell me so."

Only good sense held Sherryn back from rolling her eyes. What kind of woman would tell a child his father didn't like him?

The answer came to her in seconds. One who's resentful and takes it out on the only victim at hand.

"Then why did she bring you to our house?" Sherryn asked.

"She say she tired of raisin' pickney and want a fresh start." He finished the cone before continuing. "She give mi bredda and sista to dem fadda and then she bring me to your yard."

Sherryn hunched toward him. "So your mother has three of you?"

Nodding, he said, "Yeah. Mi is di younges' one."

Chin in hand, she asked, "You miss her?"

While he examined his messy hands, another pout claimed his mouth. Slowly, he shook his head. "No."

Sherryn opened the plastic pouch between them and wiped his mouth and hands.

After a well-needed trip to the barber, she took him home. He was asleep in the seat behind her when she drove into the yard. She shook him gently, and he sat up, blinking a few times before his eyes closed and his head drooped to one side.

Sighing, she got the things she'd bought out of the van before she attempted to wake him again. For a moment, she studied him, his face relaxed in sleep. If she didn't know differently, he could be one of her children.

She bit her lip, then picked him up.

He was lighter than he should have been for a boy his age and was malnourished in comparison to Brandon, who was a few months older. Her son was not only taller, but much heavier.

She stood in the driveway, getting used to Maurice's weight when he opened his eyes, smiled, and snuggled into her neck.

What would happen to him and what would life be like for him anywhere Reece took him?

No doubt, he'd continue to be neglected, perhaps one among many. Sometimes she heard horror stories on the news of children being abused in places of safety. She frowned, disturbed at the thought of Maurice being left in any such facility.

His head shifted against her neck as he made himself comfortable, sucking his thumb. He has so little, she thought. Tears burned her eyes as she looked at him, admitting she had lost the fight.

After she put Maurice down to continue his nap, Sherryn sat in the dining room with Miss Emelyn, who nodded and peered into her eyes.

"Yes, I did know the boy belong to Mr. Reece from I see him," the older woman said.

Sherryn spun the glass on the table. Lemonade surged up the sides and the ice cubes tinkled in the silence. Miss Emelyn patted her hand. "Never mind, mi dear. Is so man behave. No matter what you give dem at home, dem still find excuse to stray all over di place."

"You know life is weird, Miss Em? If I'd done that, you'd think I was barefaced and wicked, but Reece does it, and you brush it off as if it's nothing."

Miss Emelyn's unruly eyebrows lifted. "No, Miss Sher, you know is not so. Is jus' dat man is man, and dem goin' to stray even if you give dem what dem want seven days for di week. Is jus' a fact of life." Miss Emelyn nattered on. "But you is a good woman. 'Cause nobody else me know woulda mek di pickey stay inna dem marital home. But him seem like a nice likkle bwoy."

"Yes, he is," Sherryn agreed.

Cocking her head toward the room where Maurice slept, the older woman asked, "So what you goin' do wid him?"

"I don't know," Sherryn said, opting to keep her own counsel.

Miss Emelyn gripped her arm tight. "You don' plan to leave Mr. Reece?"

Shrugging, Sherryn got up from the table.

"Miss Sher, mi begging yuh, consider long and hard before yuh do anythin'. Mr. Reece mek a mistake, but him is a good man. T'ink about yuh children. You know dem love dem fadda."

"Mmm."

Sherryn regretted confiding in their helper. She didn't need the additional pressure. Miss Em had worked for them over ten years and was part of their family, and though Sherryn respected her opinion, this situation was something she would have to figure out for herself.

She headed for the bedroom where she had laid Maurice, surprised to find she had gone halfway through day two of her ordeal and hadn't disintegrated. Thank goodness she had the kids and work to keep her occupied, otherwise she might have gone crazy.

When Maurice woke up, Sherryn kept him occupied watching television. After an hour, she gave him a pencil and paper to draw with while she worked.

He drew cars and buses, and when he grew bored, came over to watch her flip through cake decorating magazines. She gave him one with birthday cakes, and he sat on the couch, ogling the different creations, refusing to believe they were edible.

When she got ready to leave, Maurice didn't ask to come with her but watched from the verandah with a fixed stare as she drove out, his finger wedged in his mouth. Sherryn left him at home to avoid an awkward situation, since Maurice and her children were still not properly introduced.

Brandon was delighted to find Maurice still in residence, but Sherryn dreaded leaving them alone together. She feared what Brandon might ask, as well as what Maurice would say.

Thrilled by the fact that Maurice was as fascinated with motorized toys as he, Brandon put curiosity aside during their playtime.

While she worked out a cake design for an anniversary party, Sherryn kept an eye and ear on the boys, in case she needed to provide a distraction. But she had to bring her mind back to her task repeatedly as her thoughts kept straying to Reece.

She glanced at the digital clock on the desk, hoping he remembered to pick up Justin after football practice. But he wasn't likely to forget since Justin usually called to remind him. She asked herself whether her son would be as quick to tackle his father as he was to take her to task for what he saw as violations. She shook her head. Sometimes Justin could be as controlling and demanding as Reece.

Thirteen

Reece rubbed his forehead, trying to stave off a headache. He waited for Justin, who joked with his friends before telling them goodbye in terms Reece was too old to understand.

On his way to the Land Cruiser, Justin's body went stiff and the friendly grin disappeared. He got in, strapped on his seat belt and spoke deep in his throat. "Afternoon."

"How was practice?"

"Fine."

"Want to get some wings and fries before we head home?"

"No."

Reece started the van, acknowledging that things were going further downhill. Justin never refused food.

"D'you want to talk about whatever is bothering you?" Reece asked once he left the school premises.

"No. But something's bothering you."

Reece masked his surprise and allowed Justin to talk.

"Yuh not acting the same since yesterday. I wonder if it have to do with that little relative of yours."

Reece decided to tackle Justin head on. "Yes, it does have to do with him, and it also affects you, but I'm warning you not to pass your place with me."

Reece understood Justin's reaction stemmed from hurt, but he never allowed him to forget that before everything else, theirs was a father/son relationship.

Justin's stare was intense and disapproving.

"You're almost an adult, so you understand that we make mistakes," Reece continued.

"How you can make that kind of mistake when you always tellin' me what to do and what to avoid?"

Reece shrugged. "I don't know, son. One more thing I could add to that list of do's and don'ts is to stay away from alcohol. It dulls your senses. Makes you do stupid things you wouldn't do otherwise."

"So, he's your son?"

Reece sucked in a deep breath and let it out with his answer. "Yes."

Justin twisted in the seat, and the smell of sweat and fabric softener drifted over Reece. "Daddy, yuh such a hypocrite! Always lecturin' me to be careful, treat girls with respec', and look what yuh do to Mommy!"

The heat of Justin's words and his disappointment made Reece flinch.

"What her friends goin' to think, and what about our friends? The whole world goin' to know you cheat on her, and yet the two of you always so lovey-dovey. What you goin' to do if Mommy don't want to stay married to you? What goin' to happen to our family?"

"Justin, this is between your mother and me."

Breathing hard, Justin yelled, "But this goin' to affect all of us. You just said it yourself! He turned his head away, forcing Reece to listen closely to hear his words. "If anybody did tell me you would disrespect Mommy like this, I'd say it was a lie ... "

"That's enough, Justin."

"No," Justin shouted, "it's not enough! This morning she cry! She cry, Daddy! What you goin' say to the others? You know how Brandon ask questions. You let me down. Jah know!"

Reece studied the bumper of the station wagon in front of him, conscious of the throbbing in his head. "I know it's cool to speak that way with your friends, and I don't give you a hard time over it, but don't confuse me with them, okay? You will speak to me with respect—"

"Daddy, you're just avoiding the subject."

Reece held on to his temper, gripping the steering wheel hard. "And you will address me properly."

Justin leaned against the door, sulking.

Reece didn't continue the conversation because Justin had his mother's ability to stay mad, close to forever. He'd ignore Reece and continue to do so as long as he felt justified.

The evening traffic stretched ahead of them, which meant inching toward Queensborough in strained silence would be torture. Reece eyed the jumble of vendors and their makeshift stalls along the sidewalk. The women sat with their thighs spread wide and skirt tails lapped behind cut-off cartons crammed with small items, including hair ornaments, combs, and make-up. How many of those women were single mothers juggling between the care of their children and trying to make enough to survive? Why couldn't Gloria do the responsible thing and take care of her own child? Why use Maurice to destroy his life?

Reece ran a hand over his hair, thinking about his children.

Melly kept everything inside, so she'd pretend nothing was wrong while she suffered.

Celia let her body language convey her disapproval, but she'd also give him the silent treatment.

Brandon might throw a host of questions at him for which he wouldn't have answers, and then he'd pray for everything to be okay.

Maurice would continue to feel rejected, and his resentment would blossom.

Kyle would remain happy and oblivious to the havoc around him, or so Reece hoped because he'd heard somewhere that young children were attuned to their parents' moods.

He sighed into his palm. Sherryn would continue to distance herself from him. This forced Reece to assess whether he could deal with everything she'd send his way. He didn't know how to survive another bout like their fall out seven years ago. He'd barely made it then and had been nursing guilt ever since.

Justin startled Reece by hopping out of the van the moment he stopped in the yard.

Exhaustion like he hadn't known in years crept up on Reece. Instead of getting out of the vehicle, he leaned against the headrest and allowed his thoughts to drift.

Fourteen

If ever a woman was made for a man, Sherryn was created especially for him. Reece knew it the moment she walked into the showroom of the Toyota dealership where he had gone to purchase a car. She crossed the floor to a desk where another woman sat. After a moment's conversation, she handed over a sheaf of yellow paper.

Reece admired her slim, yet curvaceous body, dressed up in a business suit. In his mind, he stripped the outfit off her, but what he imagined lay underneath was not the only thing that fascinated him. It was something he couldn't quite touch. Whatever 'it' was, lay in her spirit—the way she gave the other female her full attention, the interested light in her eyes, her soft laugh. He conjured up a picture of that concentration turned on him and the resulting daydream pleased him.

When she walked away, he excused himself from the salesperson and rushed to catch up with her. He didn't think about what he was going to say, he simply had to get her attention.

She was striking up close. Her dark-brown hair had golden highlights, and the layered haircut complemented her oval face. Her small mouth hinted that she was amused and many times during the coming years, she'd turn up her little nose at what she called his antiquated ideas.

She studied him, head tilted back, eyebrows elevated. "Yes, you needed something?"

"Uh, yes." He felt foolish for not thinking about what to say to her, now that he had her attention. "I'm Maurice Allbright."

He fished out his wallet and handed her a business card. "And it would make my day if you'd agree to go out with me."

A dimple made a brief appearance beside her mouth. "Just like that?"

"Uh-huh. I couldn't help it. I looked up and uh ... "

A full-fledged smile lifted her lips. "There I was?"

"Yeah." He slid his hands into his pockets to disguise the effect her closeness had on him. "Somethin' like that."

She scanned the card and eased a step away, depriving him of the fruity aroma of her perfume. "Give me a good reason why I should go out with you, especially since I have a boyfriend and you're a stranger."

"'Cause I love you?"

A hand covered her mouth too late to muffle the loud chime of laughter. "Well, at least you made me laugh. She folded her arms. "So, you're a comedian?"

Embarrassed, Reece tried to cover his gaffe by shrugging and giving a casual reply. "No, but I did make an impact. Seriously though, there's something about you I like. Would you give me the chance to find out what it is?"

For several moments, they observed each other. She removed the pen stuck on the pocket of his shirt, wrote something on his card and said, "Call me."

She walked away, and Reece knew without a doubt, here was the woman who'd share his future. At the thought of his earlier bout of idiocy, he wanted to cup his forehead and say a swearword, but he was still standing in the display area. Instead, he cursed his stupidity and hoped she hadn't wondered if he shouldn't be in Bellevue with the other disturbed people.

He wasn't a hundred percent in love with her yet, but expected to be soon. She had something he wanted in his wife. It was a quality not every women possessed—class. It was there in the way she dressed, carried herself, and spoke. Even her laughter was cultured and though she was younger than he—or so he assumed—she had the maturity of an older woman.

He slipped the card into his pocket, but not before noting her name. After he concluded his business with the sales representative, he returned to his office to think about how to win Sherryn Jones.

It was no easy task. He allowed a day to pass and called her at home the following evening. They started a flirtatious, yet frustrating exercise where they got acquainted through daily telephone conversations.

He sensed she wanted to know more about him before committing to seeing him, so he didn't push. She'd soon have an important decision to make—remain with her current boyfriend, or go out with him. He used every tactic available to him, and two weeks later, Sherryn agreed to a date.

He made the most of the opportunity by taking her to an upscale restaurant and after dinner, they went dancing at a popular nightclub. As the days went by, they spent more time together. Reece had already made up his mind about Sherryn, so he set himself the task of convincing her that he was the man she wanted, even though she had reservations about settling down so early in her twenties.

Fearing he'd lose her, he stepped up the pace, and Sherryn agreed to marry him within six months. He hadn't regretted a day of their marriage.

Reece's foot hit the pedals, and he yawned and stretched in the cramped space, aware that he couldn't sit in the vehicle all evening. He had to face his family sometime, plus he still hadn't worked out what to do with Maurice. Sighing, he turned the windows up and got out of the van.

Once inside, Reece made his regular rounds through the house. He'd developed that habit as the family grew. In the living room, Brandon and Maurice played with a police station house and squad cars. Brandon rushed over to give him a waist hug.

"Hey, Daddy. We're playing police and gunmen car chase."

Maurice continued to play with a miniature police car as if his father wasn't standing in the doorway.

Reece understood why the boy pretended not to see him. He'd always ignored Maurice whenever he happened to see him on his visits to drop off maintenance money.

"Gonna have a shower, kid. See you at dinner."

"'K," Brandon said, before running back to grab a car and flop down on his belly.

Reece moved upstairs when he found the kitchen empty.

"Come in," Melly yelled in reply to his knock on the door.

Both girls were doing homework. Celia curled over the desk reading a textbook, and Melly lay belly-down on the floor, feet waving in the air.

He forced a smile. "How are my girls?"

"Good."

"Fine."

Neither of them looked up from their books, tried to hug him, or wheedle anything out of him. Something was off, and Reece was all too conscious of what it was. He sighed for the umpteenth time. "Later, girls."

Their reply was somber. "Later, Dad."

He pulled the door shut behind him.

Dad. He really was out of favor. His children only called him that when they were upset with him.

Justin's attention was divided between his homework and keeping an eye on Kyle.

At the sight of Reece, Kyle ran over and grabbed him by the legs.

Reece lifted him into the air, making him squeal. After putting Kyle back on his feet, Reece faced Justin, disturbed by the need to explain his visit.

"I know we just got in, but I was checkin' on everybody, as usual."

Justin's tone was spiteful. "Actually it's been more than an hour, but when you have things on your mind, you don't notice time passin'."

Rubbing a hand over his aching forehead, Reece withdrew and went to find Sherryn.

She lay staring at the ceiling when he entered their room. Her sniffles and the way she turned her head into the pillow told him she was crying again.

The now-familiar compression gripped his chest and he breathed deeply, not that it helped him feel any better.

He had no words to make things better between them, but he had to try. He went into the bathroom, and the extra minutes he spent in the shower were nothing more than an attempt to give Sherryn time to compose herself. His inability to find something constructive to say frustrated him. Since his secret was exposed, his mind had stopped working. He couldn't concentrate and when he did focus, it was to think about what he'd do if Sherryn left him. Then his brain would freeze again, and he'd wake up to find he'd been staring into space, wasting time.

He put on some clothes, sat on the bed and touched her arm. "Hon?"

She turned, looked at his hand on her arm, and he pulled away.

"What you want, Reece?"

"To know how you are."

She hissed air through her teeth and rolled away from him. "Just leave me alone."

"But we need to talk."

She flipped onto her back to score him with her eyes. "Talk 'bout what? We've said all there is to say, and I don't want to hear anything else, except maybe what you're going to do with that boy downstairs."

Slapped with his biggest problem, Reece turned away.

"Yeah, thought so, for you don't know what to do with the son you don't want. I'd think you'd know better than to treat him like the garbage you put on the side of the road for the truck to collect, after the way your mother treated you."

Stung by guilt, Reece went to stand by the window. Sherryn continued to pelt him with her words. "That's all men do, create problems they can't solve."

"Sherryn, I explained what happened. I didn't—"

"Yeah, you didn't plan for all of this. I'm askin' you for the last time, what you goin' to do with that child?"

Reece said the only thing he could think of, a plan which had to suffice until he could make other arrangements. "I'll put him in a home."

The bed rustled and an outraged Sherryn spat at him. "What you just say?"

He slipped both hands into his shorts and faced her. "I'll have to put him in a home."

Sherryn's voice turned icy. "In all this time, I never realized I married a monster."

He waited for her to explain, and she didn't disappoint him.

"Only a monster would consider putting his child in a home. That's the place for kids who have no—"

"What d'you expect me to do?" He walked from one end of the bedroom to the other. "I'd be out of my tree to ask you to keep him. I don't have anyone else I can ask, and I don't know where his mother went." He stopped and rubbed both hands over his face. "I can't ask that of you, Sherryn. I just can't."

"So you plan to just take him and drop him off at some children's home, eh?"

He shrugged. "I don't see that I have another choice."

"Did it occur to you that the State needs a good reason to provide shelter for your child? What you goin' to tell the authorities? You ca'an bother with him, like his mother?"

"It's not exactly like that."

She stood inches away, staring up at him. "What is it like, Reece?"

The curling texture of her hair distracted him from the intense energy surrounding her.

"It's ... I ... don't know what to do with him. I told her not to have him." He met her eyes then. "I give her money for him every month, but she ... "

Reece's composure deserted him, and he slipped into Patois. "She deliberately gone lef' him. She know I ca'an take care of him. What di hell must I do wid him?"

"Reece, what you're suggesting is heartless and wicked. I hate you for even thinking it. Have you ever been inside one of those homes? Huh?"

She spun away from him, crying but he gripped her arms while she struggled to escape.

Reece held firm and eventually, she turned and rested her head against his chest, still shedding tears.

"Sherryn, you have to understand. I know every time you see him, you're going to remember and I've done enough to hurt you already. I just can't ask you to take care of him. It isn't right or fair."

While he patted her back, she sobbed into his chest and then slid her arms around his waist. Her tears wet his tee-shirt, and Reece was staggered at her outpouring of pain. As her sobbing continued, he too broke down and wept, something he hadn't done in more than thirty years.

Fifteen

They talked, but nothing was settled. Sherryn made sure Reece understood that. They decided to level with the children. They'd never hidden things from them before and didn't want to start, despite this embarrassing and bizarre situation. Based on Justin's guess as to Maurice's relationship to them, Sherryn assumed he'd probably discussed the matter with Melly, if not Celia too.

Sherryn took Maurice to one of the downstairs bedrooms, gave him some toys, and explained that they were going to have a discussion with the kids. She left him staring at the fire engine in his hand as if trying to decide what to do with it. His thumb again found its way to his mouth. Clearly, he guessed their talk had to do with him being in their home.

His anxiety pulled at her, weighing her down and sucking her energy. Stiffening her spine, Sherryn prepared for what she had to do next.

The boys watched television on the ground floor, while they waited for dinner.

Sherryn got Celia and Melly out of their bedroom. In the living room, Sherryn sat beside Reece on the sofa meant for two, and the children sat wherever they were comfortable.

Feeling the unease radiating from their children, Sherryn went straight to the matter on their minds. Her gaze rested briefly on each child. "Um, your father has something to say to you all."

Reece clasped his hands before he spoke. "Uh, Maurice ... the boy who came last night ... " He cleared his throat and whispered. "Maurice is more than a relative. He's my son."

In the silence following his announcement, nobody moved. Then Brandon spoke. "Cool! Does that mean I have a brother my own age to play with?"

Justin killed Brandon's outburst with a glare.

Celia and Melly exchanged a quick look. They'd obviously had some discussion and arrived at their own conclusion. Celia fixed Reece with a disapproving stare, and Melly sunk inward on herself, playing with the frayed edge of her shorts.

Justin spoke on their behalf. "What does this mean, Mommy?"

"Uh, your father and I haven't made any decision as to where we go from here. We have a lot of stuff to consider."

Justin sat forward. "Yeah, like isn't it wrong for you to have a child that Mommy doesn't know about? Isn't that cheating, Dad?"

Reece spoke in what Sherryn recognized as a deliberate monotone. "Yes, I cheated on your mother and yes, what I did was wrong. I ... never mind."

From his abruptness, Sherryn understood Reece held something back, which she figured were words to the effect of, *There, you've said it. You happy?*

But Justin wasn't finished. He joined his fingers and examined them before continuing his attack. "So why you bring him here? Why you never leave him where you get him?"

"I didn't bring him here. I wouldn't do that to your—"

Justin face twisted as he spoke. "Yeah, which means you'd have lied to Mommy forever if you hadn't been caught."

Sherryn raised her hand and did her best not to let her gaze stray toward Reece. "Justin, I understand how you feel, but there's something I need to ask all of you."

They waited while she glanced at Reece and then back at them. "Maurice's mother left him here, and there's no one to take care of him. D'you mind if he stays here in the meantime?"

"Cool!" Brandon said from the floor.

The two girls shared a glance and shrugged. "It's okay with us," Melly said, "since he's here already."

Justin got up, sucked his teeth, and left the room.

Reece attempted to go after him, but Sherryn held on to his arm. "I'll do it."

Justin refused to answer when she knocked at his door. She rapped a second time, entering when the stubborn hush continued. He sprawled across the bed, chin on his folded hands.

"I'm sure you heard me knocking," she said gently.

"Thought it was him."

"Doesn't matter. He's still your father, and you owe him respect."

He turned to eye her, defiance in every movement of his body.

Without words, Sherryn let him know she was still in control. She stared him down with her don't-make-me-have-to-show-you-who's-in-charge expression.

Justin shifted his gaze first.

"Yes," she said, "he's done something terrible, but that doesn't mean you step out of line."

He nodded when he realized she was serious and rolled over on his back. "You know what I don't understand?"

She lifted a shoulder to encourage him to continue.

"He disrespected you, has nowhere to put his—"

"Careful, Justin."

"—son, and now he wants us to take him in?"

She pushed his leg aside and sat on the bed. "He didn't ask me to do it, Justin. That request came from me."

He sat up frowning. "But Mommy, why would you do something like that? It's not going to hurt every time you see him?"

"Yes, it will, but I don't have a choice. Maurice has nobody, and I wouldn't feel right knowing I turned him out on the street."

Justin's frown told her he didn't agree with her reasoning. She took one of his hands, forcing him to look at her. "You see those boys we pass at the stoplights every day, wanting to clean our windscreen and always asking for money?"

"Yeah?"

"Would you want Maurice to end up sleeping on the street and begging for something to fill his belly, especially knowing he's your brother?"

Some time passed before he answered. "No."

"Then you have to understand why I'm asking this of all of you. You have so much." She let that sink in. "He has nothing."

"But where's his mother? Why she leave him here? Why she can't take care of him?"

Seeing the wisdom of saying as little as possible, Sherryn held her peace. "I don't have all the answers, but d'you think she'd leave him here if she wanted him?"

"Mommy, I don' understand di whole t'ing. How you can just bring over somebody like a package and leave him? And how Daddy get mixed up wid dat kind of woman?"

"Again, Justin, I don't know. But what I do know is that your father is confused and distressed over it. Don't make this any harder on him."

He gazed at her, his disbelief plain. "Mommy, when I'm ready to get married, I want a woman like you for my wife."

She smiled. "I'm not a pushover, in case that's what you're thinking. When a child's future is in question and I can do something about it, I don't have much of a choice, do I? And you know what? I'm proud of you for understanding that I can't throw out Maurice. One thing I want you to remember as you go through life is this—what goes around, comes around."

When he nodded, she poked him in the chest. "By the way, don't think I don't notice you letting loose with the Patois. You know what I always say."

He grinned, fanned her away, and mimicked words she'd spoken for years. "Yeah, yeah ... practice makes perfect and you need to set a good example for your brothers and sisters."

She walked to the door, where he stopped her with a question. "Mommy, tell me the truth. You goin' to leave Daddy?"

A moment went by before she responded. "I don't know."

She looked in on Reece and the children before going to talk with Maurice. Kyle bounced on Reece's lap, and the girls seemed to have him under pressure as they talked. Reece flung her a desperate glance, which she ignored and went on her way.

Maurice stood by the window facing the backyard when she entered the room. He spied her over his shoulder and turned, honey-colored eyes huge in his face. White tracks marked the path tears had taken down his cheeks and snot clotted under his nose.

Sherryn guessed his finger hadn't come out of his mouth since she left. Taking him by the hand, she pulled him over to sit on the bed. "Maurice, d'you like it here?"

His head bobbed up and down and he sniffed. "Yes, Miss."

"You guessed we were talking about you, right?"

His head lowered, and his shoulders drooped. "Yeah."

"We just had a family meeting, and the kids agreed you could stay if you want to."

His chin lifted and his lips parted. "Fi real, Miss?"

She ran a hand up his back and around his shoulder. "Yes, Maurice, you can stay with us."

He peeked up at her. "What him say?"

The irony of the situation brought a tiny smile to her lips. "He's fine with it."

"Thanks, Miss," Maurice whispered and closed his eyes. They flicked open in seconds. "I can go to school too, Miss?"

She nodded, though she hadn't thought that far ahead. "We ... I'll have to get your records."

Curiosity contracted his brows. "Records?"

She squeezed his skinny body to her side. "Don't worry 'bout it, Maurice. Your dad and I will work it out."

The finger that had slipped out headed back to his mouth. She intercepted it at midpoint and gave him what she hoped was a reassuring smile. "What's worrying you now?"

He waited a while before answering, as if he understood the magnitude of what he was about to ask. "Miss, if mi madda come back for mi, please don' send mi back wid her."

Anger stirred against Gloria for using Maurice as leverage with Reece. Conscious of the fact that she shouldn't make promises she might not be able to keep, Sherryn gave him the best stopgap she could come up with at the moment. "I can't guarantee you that, only your father can. But if she does try, I'll do my best to see she doesn't get you."

That was enough for Maurice, who closed his eyes. "Thanks, Miss."

She turned his face up to hers. "Remember how I told you that you're special?"

His head bobbed in response.

"You need to remember that, no matter what, okay?"

Though his expression said he was doubtful, he nodded.

Sherryn hugged him again and then pulled him to his feet. She led him to the bathroom and prepared him for a proper introduction to the family.

Justin was good enough to let Maurice sleep with him until she could make more permanent arrangements. She had an idea, but needed to convince Justin to vacate his space. Brandon, Maurice, and Kyle could share the room Justin now occupied if he moved downstairs. She'd give him the larger of the two rooms to pacify him, but she'd organize that tomorrow. For now, exhaustion seeped into her bones, and her earlier tears left a dull throbbing at her temples.

In bed, she lay on her back, allowing the tension to drain out of her body. Reece lay on his side, but he wasn't asleep. He'd tried to say thanks earlier, but she brushed him off, acknowledging the wounded stare he gave her before going into his office, where he got nothing done.

Brandon had blabbed that he had gone in there and found him staring at the television, which was off at the time.

She'd smirked, satisfied with the knowledge that she wasn't the only badly disturbed soul in the Allbright household. Staring into the darkness, she followed the path that had brought them together.

Reece had taken her by storm from the moment they met, because as he later claimed, he knew she was going to be his wife from early on out. Conversely, she'd known no such thing and teased him for years about declaring his love at their first meeting. Involved at the time, Sherryn knew she couldn't see both men, but Reece had been persuasive. He hadn't pressured her at the start, but as their daily conversations heated up, he had smooth-talked her into seeing him.

After their first date, there was no question of her retreating to her safe world.

Reece treated her well, and she found him funny, intelligent, and down to earth. Though he tried to hide the way he felt about her, Sherryn soon found out he was smitten. His passion for her wasn't the only thing Reece kept under wraps. He was reluctant to discuss his past.

All she knew was that he ran a business, had almost no family, and came from Waterhouse. He was hypersensitive about it, not that it bothered her. What mattered was that he was strong enough to survive his rough childhood and the death of his mother during his teens. He also revealed that a female employer gave him the start he needed to get in business.

Sherryn guessed, but never confirmed, that Reece had provided the woman with sexual favors. His experience clued her in to the fact that he was either older than he was saying, which he wasn't, or he had lived a lot in his short life. Sherryn supposed it was the latter.

Her affection and regard for him grew in a short time, forcing her to break up with her boyfriend, Robert. Her parents approved of him, as they had known him since he was a boy, but in comparison to Reece, he was boring. When Reece touched her, her nerve endings tingled. When Robert did, she felt nothing. Besides, they had never gone beyond the chaste kisses that defined their relationship. Robert was old-fashioned, which was what Sherryn suspected her parents liked most about him.

But she had doubts about settling down at twenty-two years old. She had little experience with men and had lived a sheltered life, but didn't question Reece's love for her.

Her parents had doubts about his suitability, based on where he grew up, but put them aside once they knew he adored her and had the money to care for her.

She fell in love with him and once Reece got her into his bed, any ideas she had about gathering more experience in the romance department disappeared. The things Reece did to her body and the sexual desire he aroused in her reassured Sherryn that she wouldn't be missing anything if she committed to him.

They married, had children, and he had lived up to his promise to adore, provide for, and protect her—until now.

She shifted, sighing. Why was it impossible for a man not to stray? Her friends told her that all the time, and she had admitted that more often than not, men did wander. Countless times she wondered if Reece had cheated even once during their marriage, but hadn't given it serious thought because they still loved each other as much as they did in their earlier years.

Propping her cheek on her hand, she asked herself whether she hadn't sent him out with a permission slip by refusing to have intercourse with him for over two months. If she'd known a baby would be the result, she might not have been so quick to deprive him of his marital rights.

Her parents always said discussion was better than silence, but she didn't operate that way. Reece liked to talk things over, but she preferred to stew on any perceived wrong he'd done to her and make him suffer. And suffer he did, for he hated being at odds with her and was uneasy until they made up their differences.

Why hadn't she listened to her mother, the eternal peacemaker, instead of using spite to settle her problems?

Even now, anger flickered to life inside her. Why was she blaming herself? He was the one who had done something wrong. She didn't send him out to get drunk and screw anybody.

Another sigh parted her lips. If she allowed it, resentment would keep her awake for most of the night. She curled on her side and concentrated on the adjustments she had to make to include Maurice in their family.

Now, if only it were as easy to kick his dog of a father to the curb.

Sixteen

In the filtered light seeping into the room, Sherryn watched Reece as he slept. Hatred seared everything inside her and she folded both hands into fists.

How dare he lay there so peacefully when she hadn't closed her eyes for more than a few hours during the night? She had a mind to wake him up for no other reason than to be cruel. In a moment, she changed her mind. He had gotten as little sleep as she did.

Looking at him, she realized she had absorbed some of his misery on top of her own. That's how much she loved him.

A slight smile curved her lips. He'd told her many times that if other people knew their habits they'd think them obsessed, for he too watched her sleep.

He had matured well and didn't look much different from when they met. His forehead now carried more lines and a few strands of gray glinted in his hair. The sharp outline of his mouth relaxed in slumber, and his thick eyebrows met in a faint line. He frowned, and Sherryn recalled how she'd found his strong features altogether intimidating, particularly his piercing honey-gold eyes.

He stirred and his lids lifted, forcing her to change position and stare at a spot on the wall across from the bed. No way did she want him to think she was longing for reconciliation—not when she was still bruised and battered by his betrayal.

He rolled over and sat up, shifting the mattress.

She pictured him scrubbing his hands over his eyes, which he did each time he woke, and allowed the tension to seep out of her body when he padded away from the bed and into the bathroom.

The unaccustomed silence and the loss of their early morning rituals saddened her. Morning breath and all, Reece enjoyed their playful tussling before getting out of bed. He often continued until he drew uncontrolled laughter from her. On many occasions when they got too loud, Justin told them their behavior was unbecoming and they should act their age. They'd simply reminded him that not too long ago, he enjoyed horsing around with them. They also told him to mind his own business.

Reece emerged from the bathroom after his shower, went to the closet and picked out something to wear. Force of habit made her disclose her plans to relocate the boys. "I'm going to move Justin downstairs and put Maurice in with Brandon and Kyle."

He questioned her reflection in the mirror. "Won't they be crowded in one room?"

"I don't think they'll have a problem."

He shrugged. "If you're sure."

She wanted to scream over his indifference to Maurice, who clearly needed him. He paid so little attention to the boy, she was forced to do everything for him whether she wanted to or not.

Reece was too wrapped up in feeling sorry for himself to notice.

She threw him a killing glare, which he caught in the mirror. He stopped in the middle of slipping his shirt into his pants. She didn't react to his wordless plea, but flounced away to check what was going on downstairs.

Pleading a headache when she first got up, she'd asked Justin to lend a hand with breakfast.

The kitchen was a mess. Justin had made bologna and egg sandwiches for himself and Brandon, and both girls sat munching from bowls of corn flakes.

Sherryn guessed Kyle was still asleep and that Maurice was too shy to mingle with the others. She made a mug of coffee for Reece, which she placed on the table and covered with a saucer.

"I expect all of you to be ready by the time I come back down," she said on her way out of the kitchen.

Miss Emelyn had not come as yet, and if Sherryn was late leaving home, Reece and she would have to split the drop-offs for the kids to be at school on time. She stopped by their room to give him advance notice that she was running late, but didn't find him. She hurried toward the boys' room, footsteps slowing as she unraveled Reece's forceful words. "... too old for that. When you want to piss, you get up. Decent people don't piss in their bed. That is for animals."

When he marched past her, dragging the sheets with him, Sherryn wanted to kick him.

"Reece?"

He turned, holding the bunched-up cloth.

"I need to talk to you in our bedroom. I'll be there in a minute."

From Reece's words, she knew what she'd find when she walked into Justin's room. She struggled to maintain a neutral expression, while Reece's insensitivity sent the blood pounding through her head.

Maurice's damp clothes clung to him and he stood by the stripped twin bed, wiping his eyes on his sleeves.

Kyle came to her, wagging a finger. "Mommy, Mauree piss in the bed."

"Kyle, that's not a good word. You mustn't use it."

His face crumpled. "Daddy said it."

"I don't care. Don't let me hear you use it again."

Taking Maurice by the shoulder, she turned him toward the end of the corridor. "Go to the bathroom. Soon come," she said. "Kyle, stay here until I come back, okay?"

He nodded, picked up a racing car off the floor, and ran it along the edge of the cot. She definitely wouldn't make it out of the house on time.

Serve Reece right—he'd have to drop off the kids and then get to work.

He faced their bedroom window, navy pants pulled tight across his butt. She shifted her gaze to the white pin stripe shirt. He removed his hands from his pockets and turned at the sound of her footsteps. She closed the door and stood behind it.

"What the heck is wrong with you?" she asked.

He frowned. "He's old enough to know better. None of our kids—"

"Totally different situation, Reece. The boy is in a strange house, knows he's unwanted, so what d'you expect?" She rubbed her forehead. "I'm trying to make the best of a bad situation, so do me a favor and get off your high horse. That boy out there hasn't got anybody and he darn well knows it."

She walked toward him and halted at midpoint, fearful she would hit him. "You're the only familiar, or should I say, slightly familiar thing left in his world. He needs you—"

"But he has to learn—"

"I don't want to hear anything from you. The way you look at him tells me all I need to know. Wake up, Reece! You had a hand in creating him. The least you can do is be a man, and a father to him."

She marched to the door and dropped her mini-bomb. "I'm running late, and Miss Emelyn's not here, so you have to take the kids to school. All of them, except Kyle."

His pained expression amused Sherryn, but she kept a straight face.

Although Reece wasn't pleased, he didn't dare moan about how he hated battling the traffic to the different schools their children attended.

She leaned into the room. "By the way, you know better than to use bad language in front of the kids, worst of all Kyle. Get a grip, Baby-Father. I'm the only one around here who has any excuse for that kind of behavior, and you don't hear me using coarse language with our children."

Maurice sat on the edge of the tub waiting for her. She gave him a bright smile. "Take off your clothes and get in the shower, I'll be right back. Going to check if Miss Em has come yet."

She scooped Kyle up and hustled downstairs with him. On her way through the living room, she met Miss Emelyn. "Miss Em, wonderful, you're here. Keep an eye on Kyle for me. I'm seeing to Maurice upstairs."

"Fine, Ma'am." Miss Emelyn took Kyle out of her arms. "What happen little man? You getting weighty, you know."

Sherryn left Kyle babbling with Miss Emelyn and went to give Maurice his bath.

He stopped poking the dangling showerhead, petrified when he saw her.

She smiled and rubbed his head. "It's all right, Maurice."

He relaxed and gave her a tentative smile.

"I know you might be ashamed about wetting the bed, but I understand. You're in a strange place, and you're not comfortable yet. Would you like me to leave a nightlight on for you?"

Shamefaced, he asked, "What is a nightlight?

"It's a small light that we plug into the wall so that if you need to use the bathroom in the night, you can see in the darkness." She smiled, hoping to ease his mind. "Sooo, you want me to plug one in later?"

"Yes, Miss. T'anks."

While she soaped and washed him, she sang as she did for Kyle.

He stared at her, transfixed until she came to the end of the song. He murmured something too low for her to hear.

"What did you say?"

"You can sing that for me again?"

She started over.

"Do your ears hang low, do they wobble to and fro? Can you tie 'em in a knot, can you tie 'em in a bow? Can you throw 'em over your shoulder like a Continental soldier? Do your ears hang low?"

He laughed when she finished. "Dat's a funny song."

She laughed along with him. "Kyle thinks so too."

"You can sing another one?"

"Sure."

As she sang, Sherryn marveled at Maurice's delight with a simple nursery rhyme, something that formed a daily part of her children's early years. Out of curiosity, she questioned him. "Nobody ever sang you a nursery rhyme?"

"No."

"Not even Itsy Bitsy Spider?"

He seemed intrigued by the sound of that, so she sang it too.

When Kyle and Maurice sat at the table eating eggs and sausages, Sherryn went to prepare herself for the workday, but first she had to drop Kyle off at pre-school. Maurice gladly came along for the ride and when they returned home, was disappointed when she said she had to work.

She gave in to his doe eyes and allowed him to sit on the couch, where he flipped through some of Brandon's books, stopping to examine all the pictures. She watched him for a while, perplexed that his mother kept him out of school. Most Jamaican children were in school by the time they were two and a half years old. At six, Brandon was reading proficiently, even surprising her with some of the words he used. She sank in her chair, daunted by the mammoth task she had taken on herself.

"Maurice?"

"Yes, Miss?"

"Did your mother put any papers in your knapsack?"

"What kind o' papers?"

"Never mind. Think you can bring it for me?"

Maurice jumped off the couch and swept through the door. He came back with the black bag clutched to his chest, then held it out to her.

She put it on her lap. "You didn't take anything out of it, did you?"

He frowned and shook his head.

Sherryn made a quick and thorough search and came up with what she expected to find. Nothing. She ran her teeth over her lip, mystified as to why his mother gave him away without bringing along a birth certificate—something he'd need if she intended that Reece keep him. Unwilling to go where her mind was headed, Sherryn decided to deal with what she could and avoid worrying about things that weren't yet a problem. She'd let Reece apply for copies of any documents they needed for Maurice.

One more thing to add to the mental list she was keeping.

Then her mind strayed where she was determined it wouldn't. She snorted at his mother's thinking. No doubt, she hadn't sent the birth certificate because she intended to use it for her own ends.

That ghetto rat thought she was slick, but she'd soon realize Sherryn was no pushover. They'd also see who was smarter.

Seventeen

Someday soon, Reece was sure he'd lose his mind. The children kept up a lively banter as he drove, however, none of them spoke directly to him—not even Brandon. He punched relentlessly at the keypad on the video game.

Justin only turned his head to make mock-threatening remarks to Melly, and whenever his eyes met Reece's by accident in the mirror, Justin looked away.

Unwilling to believe his children were closing ranks on him, Reece waited until the two girls got out of the vehicle in the school's driveway and walked away before calling them back.

"Nothing for Daddy this morning?"

They half-grinned sheepishly at each other before pressing a kiss to his cheek, but their eyes avoided his.

He grabbed Celia's hand, knowing vexation lurked behind her blank expression. "I know it mightn't mean much to you right now, but I *am* sorry for all that's happened."

She pulled her hand out of his and her plaits lifted and fell as she spun away. With a touch to the shoulder, she got Melly moving. They trudged away in identical pale blue uniforms, tilting forward as if carrying too many books in their knapsacks.

Justin snorted in the back seat, but when Reece eyed him in the mirror, he stayed motionless as if that made him invisible.

Brandon leaned over from the passenger seat to grasp Reece's shoulder. Flicking a glance at Justin, Brandon whispered, "I know you did something wrong, but since you said you're sorry, I'm going to forgive you."

Reece patted his son's knee, wishing his other children viewed things as simply. With a smile, Reece acknowledged that while Brandon's generosity stemmed from having a new playmate, his older siblings were no doubt worried about their parents' relationship.

Guilt coiled inside Reece at the memory of how he'd spoken to Maurice for peeing in the bed. He wanted to deny that his treatment of the boy stemmed from the fact that he couldn't confront Gloria and have it out with her, but he couldn't. All the bitterness within him over Gloria's actions was transferred to her son. The rational part of his brain told him that he was being unreasonable, but he couldn't help taking out his anger and frustration on the ready target Maurice provided. Sherryn's generosity only deepened his shame.

Justin cut in on his reflection. "My school is still down that road, and you shoulda drop off Brandon first. That's how Mommy always does it."

Reece stared at Justin, but didn't reveal his anger.

Justin wore a smirk that told Reece he'd deliberately waited for him to pass the side road before letting him know.

Reece rubbed the back of his neck. It would be a nightmare to go around the block again in the stalled traffic. A glance in the mirror confirmed that the motorist behind him was too close for him to attempt a U-turn and he was all too aware that Justin relished his dilemma.

After they sat in the unmoving line of vehicles for two minutes, Justin swung the door open and got out. "Is all right, I'll walk it back to school."

He slammed the door, rocking the vehicle.

Brandon leaned out to yell, "You going to pop off the door?"

Justin's glower had Brandon sitting back in his seat, puzzled. "Daddy, you know what's wrong with Justin?"

While massaging his forehead, Reece spared him a glance. "He's angry with me, and I don't blame him."

"Is he angry 'cause you got a new son?"

"Something like that."

"Well, I don't mind."

Love for his second to last child pulled a smile from him, and Reece patted Brandon's hand. "I know you don't, but it's causing some problems, which I hope we can work out."

"I'm going to pray about it, okay?"

"Thank you."

Brandon closed his eyes, clasped his hands in front of his chest, and was silent for a moment. When he finished, he said, "I've talked to God about it, so it's going to be okay."

Reece hoped all he'd heard about God's special care for women and children was true.

Maybe He'd intervene and let Reece keep his family, but from everything happening around him, it seemed nothing would go in his favor. He had serious doubts his family would forgive him anytime soon.

Eighteen

Three weeks passed and they settled into an uncomfortable truce. Sherryn asked Reece to drop off the children more often, and he didn't dare complain for fear of upsetting her.

Maurice blossomed under her care and started learning to read with Sherryn's guidance, and unsolicited help from Brandon.

Brandon and Kyle were the only ones who talked to Reece without restraint.

Miss Emelyn only expressed sympathy for Reece whenever Sherryn wasn't around. "Never mind, mi dear, things soon get better," she'd say and pat his hand whenever she passed him in the house.

Maurice did such a good job with reading and writing his letters that Sherryn ordered Reece to apply for a copy of his son's birth certificate as she planned to enroll him in school after the Christmas term.

The stress caused Reece to lose weight. If Miss Emelyn didn't get to work early enough to fix breakfast, he didn't eat until lunchtime and even then, he had no appetite.

He stopped going home during the day and used the time to work, or so he convinced himself. He didn't achieve much while staring at the television screen or the monitor in his office. How much longer could he go on living in limbo? he asked himself while slicing his mind to shreds on the painful scalpel their marriage had become.

His biggest problem was his inability to right the wrong done to Sherryn. The irony, as he saw it, was how well Maurice was getting along with the family. Gradually, Justin took him under his wing, showing him 'boy stuff' that Maurice hadn't done before, like shooting marbles and mastering the yo-yo.

Only Reece stood still on the outside, while they all continued their regular activities.

His relationship with Maurice improved by a slight degree. He didn't talk to him much, but never cursed or shouted at him.

Sherryn made sure of that.

He began to feel like a criminal in his own house. Whenever Maurice was in the same room with him, Sherryn appeared, as if anticipating the need to act as a buffer between them.

Several times while playing with Brandon, Reece caught Maurice peeking at them. Considering they were living under the same roof, Reece grew impatient with himself for not being able to provide what the little boy needed. Something kept him from connecting with Maurice.

With each passing day, he appeared healthier. Reece accepted that he had been malnourished, which again raised the question of what Gloria did with the money he provided for Maurice's care.

Reece daydreamed about the many and varied ways he could find to take revenge on Gloria. As small as the amount was, for five hundred dollars he could have her beaten up by some crack head. He considered tracking her down and forcing her to take her son back. That fantasy he cast aside because Gloria had already done the damage she intended to do. He'd be lying to himself if he didn't admit he was thankful that Maurice had escaped growing up to become another criminal in the breeding ground of Waterhouse.

In some ways, it was a relief to have his secret out in the open. From the outset, Maurice's existence was a colossal burden which Gloria used to threaten him, usually when she wanted to gouge more money from him. When she started dropping threats to leave Maurice at his house, Reece wondered how she knew his address. It didn't take him long to figure out that she must have searched his pockets while he was sleeping off the liquor he'd sucked up on the night he had sex with her. Everything she wanted to know was on his driver's license.

A thousand times, he berated himself over his stupidity. Then he resigned himself to being extorted, within reason.

Sherryn wouldn't condone cheating, worse he had a child to show for his transgression. His problem had worsened and then exploded when he refused to give in to Gloria's demand for a lump sum. He'd planned to drop off money for Maurice and went to the bar where she sometimes worked.

Right away, he knew something was up from the way she fluttered her false eyelashes at him and asked that he walk with her outside. On the dusty sidewalk, she leaned against his vehicle, one knee bent and her foot resting on the wheel. "I want to do some business, and I need a start. Yuh can lend mi some money?"

"What kind of business, and how much money?"

"Yuh don' have to know what mi goin' to do. All yuh need to know is dat yuh wi' get back di money. Mi need twenty thousand dollars."

Her level stare and the outrageous request silenced him. When he found his voice, he laughed. "Yuh drinking some of that rum yuh selling? While the dollar not worth much, mi still not giving yuh twenty thousand dollars without knowing what yuh using it for."

She'd straightened up off the Jeep and pressed her hands to her sides. "I shouldn't even be asking yuh to lend mi money, you should be givin' it to me because I have a pickney for you."

He knew the madness signaling his rising temper had leapt into his eyes when she eased away from him.

"Yuh know what?" she asked. "Yuh better mek up yuh mind and gimme di money or else I goin' bring Maurice to yuh house an' lef him."

He took a step toward her then. "Yuh must be mad to ra—"

"Don't tell mi no bad word."

"If yuh ever pass yuh place an' bring dat boy to mi house, yuh goin' to be sorry."

"Den gimme di money. I know yuh can afford it."

Mad as hell, Reece lowered his voice and spat out each word. "Don't t'ink yuh can dictate anything to me where it concerns my money. I owe you nothing, but to take care of your son, and I give you more than enough money to do that."

She backed down and went back to flicking her eyelids at him. "So yuh nah gimme di money?"

"Is like yuh deaf or somethin'. You're not getting any more of my money, especially since yuh son always look like him starving. I work too hard to waste money on you."

"I wonder what yuh wife woulda do if she see what yuh been keeping a secret."

"Interfere wid my wife, Gloria, and you're a dead woman."

She stepped back, staring at him wide-eyed.

He hoped his words were enough to intimidate her but obviously she regrouped, because within a week, Gloria dropped Maurice at his door and did her disappearing act, leaving his life in tatters.

He roused himself from the sofa, where he'd been resting with his feet up, and moved to stand by the window. Sherryn's rows of pink and white mini ixora, and the greenery smothering the fence, always calmed him.

Brandon and Maurice dashed by, shouting and laughing. With a half-smile, Reece thought about how different his own childhood was from theirs, or more specifically Brandon's life. Neither he, nor any of his siblings ever experienced hunger with nothing available to fill their bellies nor had they lived in squalor with parents who didn't care about their welfare.

Brandon zipped by again, and when the blur representing Maurice whipped by, Reece altered the line of his thoughts. None of his children had lacked anything, except Maurice. Reece suddenly woke up to the fact that Maurice had lived his own experience, or came closest. That in itself made him more unique, more resilient, more like him than all the others. Another wave of shame crept over Reece, and he couldn't bear to look at the child he'd been persecuting. He was about to turn from the window, when Brandon skidded to a stop and yelled, "Hi, Daddy."

Unable to halt in time, Maurice ran into him, and the two of them fell to the flagstones dotting the side of the yard. Reece stepped forward to see the two boys laughing in a heap. He chuckled as they picked themselves up, rubbing their knees and elbows.

"You saw that, Daddy?" Brandon asked.

Reece nodded and grinned at him, including Maurice in his laughter.

The boy frowned for a second, angled his head to one side, and stole a glance at Brandon. His attention crept back to Reece, who had smiled at him for the first time in his life. A small answering smile lit his eyes and traveled to include his mouth. Soon, a grin covered his face. Brandon tugged at his tee-shirt, but Maurice didn't budge right away.

"Come nuh, man."

Maurice winced at Brandon's direct cry in his ear, but it got him moving. He gave Reece the parting gift of a smile before they ran off again. Reece leaned on the ledge, blinking to clear his vision. A simple smile from Maurice, and he didn't know his ears from his ass. In the few seconds he looked at Maurice, he saw himself reflected in the desperate longing that shone from the boy's eyes.

The fear of rejection still tormented Reece's soul, for as much as Sherryn loved him, his past continued to haunt him, convincing him that one day she'd leave him. Unlike Maurice, his mother hadn't left him, but she might as well have, for all the attention she had given him.

Rousing himself from his depressing memories, Reece went to sit behind the desk. He picked up a framed picture of Sherryn, wishing life was as simple as in days gone by. His head flopped against the back of the chair, and a groan escaped from his throat. He also spent too much time thinking about what he didn't have with Sherryn anymore—sex.

In the aftermath of Gloria's bombshell, he didn't try to touch Sherryn, and didn't see her melting in the near future. Sherryn enjoyed his loving, but when she made up her mind to deny him, nothing changed her mind. He scratched his chin, wondering when, if ever, things would be normal between them. He had to find a way to make it happen, but how?

Deep in thought, he stroked Sherryn's cheek through the glass. He frowned when she appeared in front of him.

How had she entered the room without him hearing or noticing? He laid the picture on the corner of the desk, self-conscious that she'd caught him caressing it. She drew a chair from one corner and sat, her thighs exposed by cut-off jeans. His imagination took off at a gallop beneath her red cotton shirt.

Sherryn rebuked him with narrow-eyed silence.

He stared back, unblinking, refusing to be chastised for laying his desire out in the open.

Her gaze fled his and made a leisurely circuit around the office.

He waited, understanding that as soon as she composed herself, she'd talk to him.

The seconds ticked by, and he wondered whether she was going to keep him in suspense forever. She licked her lips twice in quick succession, something she did only when she was nervous. What reason did she have to be edgy?

She shifted and addressed his hands folded under his chin. "Did you get the birth certificate for Maurice?"

He nodded, opened the drawer, and handed her a manila envelope. She took it and slid the copies out. She was silent for a stretch and he sensed that apart from wanting to be certain he'd done what she told him, Sherryn needed details about Gloria, so again he waited.

She scanned the certificate and went frosty on him. "Any problems getting it?"

"No, they just needed as much information as I could provide to process the certificates from the hospital records submitted after his birth. His mother never applied for his birth certificate."

Sherryn wet her lips and replaced the documents. "There's something I need to know."

"What's that?"

"Actually, there are lots of things I need to know."

"I imagine so." Reece said, trying not to get knotted up with anxiety.

"Are you still seeing that ... Gloria?"

Reece rubbed his forehead and shook his head. "No, I only saw her when I left money for Maurice."

"And how often was that?"

"Once per month."

"How many times did you say you slept with her?"

"Once, Sherryn, only once, and I never—"

She waved at him. "Yeah, yeah, I get it. You never meant to do anything."

She turned pained eyes on him. "You know, I've thought about this from every possible angle, and I still don't get it. The one thing I know is that I don't see myself ever forgiving you."

"Sherryn, I—"

Her hand went up to stop him. "I trusted you, and you took that away. Worst of all, the children are hurting. They aren't saying much, but I know they're hurting."

"I know, Sherryn, but what can I do?"

She studied him, and sadness tinged her words. "There's nothing you can do to fix this, Reece, and I don't know where we go from here. I've been thinking, but I just can't make a decision."

At pains not to alarm her, or allow his panic to show, Reece knelt beside her and gripped her hand. "Please, Sherryn, I don't know what I'll do if you leave me. Please don't even think about it."

Her hand lay limp in his and she said nothing.

Reece panicked, the blood hammering in his veins. "Please say you won't leave me. We said for better or worse. Don't—"

She cupped his cheek, stroking his skin, giving him hope. "I can't promise you anything. I'm still hurt and confused, and then there's Maurice."

"Sher, please don't let him stand between us."

She took her hand away, but continued to stare into his eyes. "You've changed, Reece."

He tilted his head, not understanding the point she was making. "What d'you mean?"

Her shoulders lifted and settled as she drew a deep breath and looked away from him. "In all the years I've known you, I never expected this from you. And to make matters worse, apart from hurting our family, you're showing us a side of your character we've never seen. How you treat that boy … it's not good for your children to watch.

"From where they sit, you not only betrayed me, but you're taking out what that woman did on Maurice, and it makes you look bad."

He jostled her hand so she'd give him her full attention. "It might surprise you, but I think we connected today."

Sherryn tried tugging her hand away, but he held firm. "You think I'm telling you this because of what you just said, but that's not it."

He got up, pulled her to her feet, and led her across the room. "Today, I was standing by the window. Here. They were playing outside, and Brandon stopped to say hi. Maurice ran into him, and they fell down. When they got up, I smiled at them."

Her puckered brow showed her confusion over where his story was going.

"He looked at Brandon and back at me to be sure I was actually smiling at him. The smile he gave me brightened his whole face. I'm ashamed to admit I've never seen him smile like that before today."

Sherryn spoke softly. "I bet he was thinking the same thing about you."

Reece folded her hand between his. "Sherryn, I know this is hard for you to deal with, but I'm asking you, please, don't give up on me. I don't know how, or what I'm going to do, but I'll do anything to make this up to you. Anything."

She rubbed her eyelids. "There's really nothing you can do," she said. "What can you do when you've ripped a hole in the fabric of our marriage? How d'you fix the fact that your children think they weren't enough to keep you from starting another family? How d'you fix all that, Reece?"

He dropped her hand and whispered, "I don't know."

She lifted a hand as if she were going to touch him, but let it fall. A few more seconds passed before she crossed the room and closed the door softly behind her.

Nineteen

Reece woke to find himself in use as a bounce-about. Kyle's hands and elbows abused Reece's ribs and groin. He shielded the area between his legs as the blows continued.

"Kyle, stop."

His youngest wriggled his way to the floor, laughing at Brandon and Maurice who popped up from behind the sofa making faces at him.

"What you all up to?" Reece asked.

"We're playing hide-and-seek." Brandon showed his gap in a sly grin. "We're hiding from Kyle, but he keeps finding us. It's his turn to hide, but he's hiding on top of you—right Maurice?"

Maurice nodded, but remained silent.

Reece swung his legs off the sofa to make space for Brandon, who made a beeline for him and settled on the seat, dragging Maurice down beside him. "Daddy, we want to ask you a question."

"What d'you want to know?"

"Can we get a fish tank and fish?"

Reece wondered where the request had come from. When he looked past Brandon, Maurice's lowered head supplied the answer.

"I don't see why not, but what d'you know about fish-keeping?"

"Nothing," Brandon chirped. "But Maurice knows all 'bout it."

Maurice's thumb was halfway to his mouth by this time.

Clearing his throat, Reece asked, "Maurice, how d'you know about fish keeping?"

While Brandon nattered on, Maurice's head sank lower.

"He knows 'cause the man on the corner who sells fish and fish tanks showed him how."

"Is that true, Maurice?"

The boy nodded while stealing glances at Reece.

"Him sell everyt'ing reasonable?"

Maurice nodded. "And him wi' even get somebody to build a stand for the tank if you ask him."

Aiming a tentative smile at Maurice, Reece said, "Then I guess we're getting a fish tank."

Brandon whooped and gave Maurice an energetic high five, which all but pitched him off the seat. Once his excitement subsided a bit, Brandon peppered Reece with questions.

Reece held up a hand to stop the eager flow of words. "We'll do it on Saturday, but at the pet shop. We'll get more of a variety there."

"Cool," Brandon shouted and hopped off the settee. "Come, Maurice, let's tell everybody."

They raced out of the room, leaving Reece shaking his head. He needed some of their unlimited energy. He yawned, conscious that his energy was at an all-time low. While he stretched, his next thought caught him by surprise.

While Maurice's life had improved, it was ironic that Reece's had taken a serious turn for the worse.

Twenty

Sherryn leaned against the headboard with the phone pinned between her ear and shoulder. The late afternoon sun painted the cream walls a warm gold. She reminded herself it was time to change the drapes and then tuned in to Judith, who had slipped into lecture mode.

"After living through what I have, you can deal with this. I know it's hard to forgive, but Reece loves you, and you love him. You two are not like Barry and me—together because we can't bother with the hassle of getting a divorce."

"Judith, I'm not sure I can live like that. I—"

"You don't have to. He made a mistake, a terrible one too, but at least he's sorry. Not like my butt plug of a husband, who acts like he's the best thing since sliced bread.

"Your life will take time to settle down again, but if you want your marriage to last, you have to come to grips with the fact that Reece dropped the ball, and help him move on from there. Otherwise, you might as well pack up and move out now."

Sherryn scooted to the end of the bed, picked up the remote, and muted the television. "I understand what you're saying, but I didn't know this would be so hard to deal with. How d'you live with Barry doing this over and over?"

"I survive the humiliation by telling myself this too shall pass. That's how I stay sane. I've been through too much with him to walk out and allow some young gyal to take what I've worked for all these years. Why should I make things easy for him?"

"But don't you ever want some loving?"

Judith chuckled, and Sherryn pictured her curling soft hair around one finger, which was her habit. "Who said I'm not getting any? You and Reece are so wrapped up in each other, sometimes you can't even see past the nose on your face. I guess because we haven't seen each other as often, you wouldn't know how energized and fresh I am these days. I got myself a diversion, my dear."

"Judith, you must be joking! You did look different last time, but I thought it was the ponytail."

"I sound like I jokin' to you? I know it's wrong, but I'm only human, Sherryn. I haven't let Barry touch me in years, and rather than allow my t'ings to shrivel up and drop off, I'm makin' use of them."

"You're somethin' else, you know that?"

"Yeah and knowing you, you're doing the opposite—starving yourself and Reece too."

"You don't think he deserves it?"

"Yeah. To a point. But if that man is as much of a sex-machine as you say, then hellooo, don't you think you're takin' things to the extreme? You might just be sending him into some other woman's bed again."

"You know it's not that simple. How d'you make love to a man you know has been in someone else's bed, and got a son on top of everything?"

"Sher, if it only happened one deggey-deggey time and so long ago, can't you let go of that?"

"It's not as easy as you're making out, Judy."

"My point is this. You need to decide what you're doing, but you ca'an hang him out in the wind indefinitely. Some women in this country have a thing for married men.

"They make love to them and send them home to wifey. Them don't want responsibility, them only want money, so you better think long and hard about what you're doing to Reece. Next thing you know you'll be sharing him with some greedy young woman."

Sherryn worried her scalp with her fingers and shook her head. "I have to wonder about you. Reece disrespected me, and you're saying I'm to be careful what I do to him? He should wash my feet and drink the water for not putting him and his son out on the road."

"I agree, but the reality of the situation is that you have to do one of two things. Either you make up with him, or kick him out of your life. Otherwise, the whole thing is just going to fester like a diabetic sore, not getting better, until one day you realize everything's rotten all the way through, and you have to amputate a limb.

"That limb will be your marriage, if you're not careful. It's your choice how you deal with the situation. Decide your mind, and talk to Reece about where you plan to go from here."

Sherryn scratched at a mosquito bite while she gathered her thoughts. "I suppose you have a point, and I'd be lying if I said I'm not missing what we used to share, but I won't make anything easy for him."

"You'd be a saint if you did, girl. You hang in there, and don't let that man get away. Otherwise, I might snap him up myself."

"Yeah, that is just talk. You know how possessive and jealous he can be. Could you live with a man like that?"

"But you knew that before you married him, and you're a fine one to talk, because you're not much better than him when it comes on to jealousy."

Sherryn didn't waste time denying the truth. "All right. Talk to you later, and thanks, I can always count on you to reduce things to brass tacks."

"Don't mention it. You always have to listen to me whine about my no-good husband, so it's no big deal to return the favor."

Sherryn dropped the phone into the cradle, turned up the sound on the television, and laid back on the bed to try and unravel her thoughts.

Twenty-One

The dim interior of the bar matched Reece's gloom. Sighing, he placed the bottle of Malta on the counter and spun it between his hands.

"If you lose any more weight, people going to think you have AIDS or somethin'," Ronald said.

One side of Reece's mouth lifted in a half smile. "I'm all right, man."

"You're far from all right, if you ask me. From the way you look, it's kinda obvious you don't patch up things with Sherryn yet."

"No, and stress going to kill me meantime."

"I always know dat gyal Gloria was trouble. You wa'an mi to arrange something nasty to shake her up a likkle bit?"

Reece shook his head. "No, I'll deal with her myself."

"All di same, if you need any help, you only have to ask."

"Thanks, man, but everything cool."

Taking a sip from his malt drink, Reece thought Sherryn had good reason not to like Ronald. She'd always viewed him as a criminal, and she was right. Ronald was unemployed and survived on odd jobs that ranged from driving a taxi to being a thug-for-hire.

Reece focused on the bottle, seeing his friend's diamond knob, scruffy cane rows, and untidy clothes. Once again, he wondered why he still hung on to the old connections. His refusal to cut the cord to the neighborhood had facilitated the encounter with Gloria. What did he have in this grim neighborhood of zinc fences, potholes, and dirt-poor, unemployed, and in some cases, unemployable people?

Nothing, except a misguided sense of loyalty. He hadn't received many favors during his struggle to rise above his depressing start in life, but he'd been smart enough to use his brain and body to drag himself out of the ghetto. He was no different from other ghetto youths, but for the drive to succeed.

For some reason he couldn't pinpoint, he felt obligated to hang around, almost apologizing for being successful. If he stopped visiting, he'd miss nothing, and wouldn't lose anything. His place was with his family, not in some frowsy bar sipping drinks with a man of questionable character.

Reece chugged the rest of the Malta, told Ronald good-bye, and paid for the drinks. His home situation needed sorting out, and it couldn't wait any longer.

Twenty-Two

The door opened, and Reece entered the bedroom.

Sherryn had counted off barely two minutes since his arrival.

He'd come straight to her after parking the van. What was on his mind?

"Uh, Sherryn, can I talk to you for a second?"

What a coincidence that he should appear so soon after her talk with Judith. Was it a sign that she should try to fix this mess before things went too far downhill? Her answer came out on a sigh. "Sure."

She studied him from where she sat, leaning against the pile of pillows.

He sat on the side of the bed, running a hand over the sheet. He needed a shower. She could close her eyes and differentiate his smell in a crowd. At the end of the workday, his cologne lingered, along with a bit of sweat, and the musk that was his alone.

She breathed deeply of him, missing their close contact once more.

He got up, walked to the window, and began his speech. "Um, I was thinking. I haven't done anything to make you think ... uh, Sherryn, please have dinner with me tonight."

Struggling to hide her surprise, she raised one eyebrow. "Why?"

"I want to talk to you, away from home and the kids."

She allowed the silence to linger, then sat up and placed her feet on the floor.

Reece was taking a different tack, and she didn't quite know how to deal with him. For more than a month, he'd lived with her silence instead of tackling matters head-on. By asking her out, he was putting the ball in her court.

She smiled inside, but showed him a stoic expression. "Fine, but can it be tomorrow? Tonight's a school night."

"Oh, yes, stupid of me. Tomorrow then."

He stood, poised as if wanting to say something else, but not knowing how to begin.

She put him out of his misery. "I'm going down to my office now."

He touched her arm as she walked by him. "Sherryn?"

"Mmm-hmm?"

"I'm sorry. For everything—hurting you, the children, the embarrassment ... "

Regret sat heavy on his features, and while tempted to give in and end his suffering, Sherryn closed the door on her sympathy. A little more pain wouldn't do the cheating fart any harm.

She locked herself in the office with paperwork to take her mind off Reece. That didn't work for long, so she turned to cleaning.

A knock sounded on the door soon after she sat on the floor rooting through a box of cake decorating magazines. "Come."

Justin leaned around the door. "We can talk?"

"Sure, come, and how many times do I have to ask you to—"

"Speak properly," he finished. "Mommy, you know how it go already."

Sherryn gave him her don't-talk-crap look, which didn't disturb Justin in the least. Hiding a smile, she pulled out a handful of magazines. "Help me sort these according to years. Oldest ones at the bottom."

"You had to give me some work to do, right?"

"Well, you *are* interrupting what I'm doing."

"Fine. Um ... about Daddy and you. You decide anything yet?"

Another rap at the door interrupted her answer. Half of Melly's body appeared in the doorway. Celia pushed Melly inside, came in behind her, and shut the door. Sherryn stared at Justin, who grinned at her.

"Well, we were talking and figured it was best to come to the source." He threw a long-suffering glance at his sisters. "I was supposed to get details from you, but apparently I can't be trusted with information."

"It's not that," Melly said, squatting between them on the floor. "You're going to take all evening, and then tell us what you think we can handle, so we might as well get the info firsthand."

Sherryn pushed the coffee table out of the way and moved over to make room for Celia, while Justin flipped through an old Wilton Yearbook.

Melly crossed her legs and faced Sherryn. "So, what are you and Daddy gonna do?"

Tempted to avoid the issue, Sherryn neatened a stack of glossy journals before speaking.

"We haven't made any decision yet."

Celia put in a question, her golden eyes anxious. "Are the two of you staying together?"

"Like I said, we haven't—"

"Come on, Mommy," Justin said. "You mean to say you and Daddy don't siddown and talk about this situation yet? I find that hard to believe."

Despite the gravity of the subject matter, laughter bubbled out of Sherryn's chest. "Justin, have you spoken to your father, really talked to him since Maurice came to live here?"

He shook his head, but didn't give up. "That's different. Your side is more complicated, and it involves us. If the two of you break up, who we goin' to live with?"

"Me, of course."

"And what about Maurice? You surely not goin' to keep him?"

"Naturally, he'd be with Reece."

Melly's voice carried the anxiety mirrored on her sister's face. "But we don't want you to break up. Things just won't be the same."

"But they're not the same now, are they, hon?"

"No, they're not," Celia said, "but at least all of us are still in the same house. I can't imagine living without Daddy."

"Hon, if we were to break up, your father would be able to visit."

Melly sighed and brushed the hair away from her eyes. "Mommy, you're not hearing us. We don't want you to break up."

Sherryn grasped her thirteen-year-old's hand. "I'm not saying we're splitting up, but at the same time I can't make any promises. You understand that, don't you?"

"Mommy, if you don't gone yet, what's the sense in leaving at all, or kicking Daddy out?" Justin asked.

A slight smile crossed Sherryn's mouth. "Make up your mind, Justin. Wasn't it you who wanted me to kick him out in the first place?"

"Yeah, that was then, this is now." He scratched his head, bit his lip and sighed. "You know what I don't understand?"

Sherryn shook her head.

"Why do men have to cheat? It's like it's something we must do, whether we like it or not. Most of my friends have more than one girlfriend."

Sherryn's glance flicked to the two girls, but Justin flapped a hand in his sisters' direction. "It's all right, Mommy. Melly and I talk about this stuff sometimes, and Celia reads so much, she must know 'bout all them things already."

Celia's lowered lashes and sudden stillness confirmed that what he said was true.

Sherryn made a mental note to keep a closer eye on her eleven-year-old's reading material, and then tried to give an explanation. "I wouldn't say men have to cheat. It happens for a variety of reasons."

"We know that, Mommy, but what makes me mad is that Daddy told me a year ago, when I turned fifteen, that I shouldn't play with people's emotions. He said only a fool messes around with more than one woman at a time. He also said not to do to any girl what I wouldn't want someone else to do to them." He pointed to Melly and Celia with his chin. "And yet him do the same thing."

Before she spoke, Sherryn included all of them in her gaze. "Sadly, it's part of our culture, and somewhat accepted. But that's not to say it's okay. There's nothing right about it."

"I know," Justin said, "but I still wonder what Daddy was thinking."

Sherryn studied Justin. When had the feathery hairs appeared over his lip? And when had he put on the muscles that rippled on his arms as he moved. He was turning into a man right before her eyes.

She broke the quiet spell that descended on the room. "All the same, Justin, this is between your father and me. I need to remind you all of that. You remain respectful to your father, or you answer to me, okay?"

"Trust your dad and me to work out our differences and make the best decision for both of us, and the family, okay?"

They nodded, and she smiled, proud of their maturity. Both she and Reece had done something right in raising these children. She hoped somehow they'd be able to resolve their differences and keep the family together.

The following afternoon, on her way to pick up a set of cake-toppers, Sherryn put the final touches on the cake in her mind. She'd picked up Brandon from school and paid scant attention to him and Maurice yakking non-stop in the seat behind her.

She smiled, admitting how similar the two boys were. They could be full siblings for all anybody knew. Their lips were shaped the same, and they had Reece's distinctive eye color. The only difference in their physical appearance was what both their mothers had passed on to them. Brandon was slender and had her high cheekbones, while Maurice was filling out and would be plump, like the woman who'd left him on her doorstep. He also had her caramel complexion.

Sherryn focused on the subject of their discussion, reminding herself she needed to do something about Maurice's speech. "What are you two going on about back there?"

Brandon grinned at her. "The fish tank we're gonna get."

"What fish tank?"

"The one Daddy's gonna buy this weekend."

Amused by her son's excitement that had him bouncing in the seat, she asked, "How come I don't know anything about it?"

"'Cause it's man stuff, that's why."

Wondering if Reece understood what he was taking on, she asked another question. "When did Reece agree to this, and who convinced him?"

"Two days ago, and we did. He said okay. We're going to the pet shop tomorrow."

Sherryn laughed, shaking her head.

Brandon sat forward, frowning. "What's so funny?"

"Reece must have forgotten the last few pet disasters we've had."

"We'll take care of the fish, won't we, Maurice?"

Maurice nodded, shifting on the seat.

"Okay, son, if you say so."

They went back to their discussion about how many kinds of fish they'd get.

Sherryn shook her head again, recalling how Melly and Celia had begged and pleaded for a dog that Reece had ended up taking care of on his own. No doubt, the same thing would happen again, as it had with the guinea pigs that Justin absolutely had to have when he was ten.

Eventually, her parents had taken the dog out of pity when Sherryn explained that Reece was burdened with being its sole caretaker. He'd had more trouble getting rid of the guinea pigs, but eventually found a home for them with a friend of his, who also had children. The fish needed less care, but Reece would be responsible for cleaning the tank.

She spared another glance at the eager twosome, hoping their enthusiasm would keep them focused on helping Reece care for the fish they'd soon have. Turning another doting gaze on them, she reminded herself to drop off the application form for Maurice's entry to school in January, surprised to find she didn't resent him at all. What she felt was sympathy and growing affection.

Pity she couldn't say the same for Reece. She loved and hated him by turns, which was frustrating and made her wonder whether she'd ever settle in one direction. His neediness used to madden her, but now the hate she carried inside frightened her, more so when she harbored thoughts of killing him while he slept.

Burdened by her disturbing thoughts, she turned her mind to adding more items to her shopping list. In the back of her mind, she hoped they would reach a decision on their future that evening. The strain of living with the unresolved problems between them was taking a toll on her mental health.

Twenty-Three

Sherryn picked at the last of the spicy crab on her plate, telling herself she wasn't affected by the way Reece's black shirt intensified the color of his eyes. Neither did it matter that he'd been to the barber and looked as well put together as the day she met him.

He had said nothing about their stand-off since they sat down to eat.

She scanned the brickwork encircling the small courtyard, and admired the olde-worlde ambience created by the rusted cannon perched on an outcrop above them. The waitresses, in sweeping bandana dresses and kerchiefs tied around their heads, added to the olden days atmosphere.

Sherryn sniffed and turned her head toward a nearby bed of roses, closing her eyes to enjoy their perfume.

Reece was watching her when she let out her breath and pushed the plate away. For a moment, he let his gaze wander to the three other couples sharing the intimate space.

Now, he stared at the table, frown lines marking his forehead.

The waiter arrived to remove their dinnerware and cutlery. Thankfully, he was back within a minute with her ice cream dessert.

Sherryn rolled her thumbs over each other, chiding herself for the tension settling between them. A smile crept across her face and she relaxed, recalling how Maurice enjoyed the ice cream she'd bought him on the day she took him shopping.

Reece cut into the memory. "Mind telling me what's making you smile?"

"Maurice. I'm remembering when I took him for ice cream."

"Oh."

His fingers drummed on the tabletop while he searched her gaze. Sherryn was startled to find that Reece didn't have a clue where to begin trying to repair the damage he had done. She understood that was what this intimate dinner was about, but wasn't going to help him. He'd made this bed of thorns, so it was up to him to find his way out of it.

To her surprise, he didn't rush to say anything else, but watched her eat the ice cream with his lips parted, and a familiar expression in place. Her neck and face grew hot when she realized how much watching her had affected him. Subconsciously, she'd been teasing him with her slow suction of the spoon, and the lazy flicking of her tongue as she cleaned her lips of the last traces of ice cream.

He shifted, and one of his hands left the table. She watched it return, and guessed what he'd been doing in those seconds it hadn't been visible.

His faint smile was an acknowledgement of her unease at his discomfort.

"You've said there's really nothing I can say to make this any easier or better for you, but I wanted to give you this."

He leaned sideways, pulled something out of his pocket, and handed it to her.

She opened the tiny gold box and removed the ring inside from its velvet cushion. A cluster of diamonds surrounded baguettes of varying lengths that winked at her. The design was exquisite, like nothing she'd seen before.

When she looked at him, Reece spoke in a husky voice. "I had it designed specially for you. Sherryn, I broke my vows to you, but with this ring … " He took it from her and slid it on the ring finger of her right hand. "I recommit myself to loving you, and will spend the rest of my life adoring only you."

"Reece, I don't … "

"Don't say anything. Please. All I ask is that you let me do all I can to make you love me again."

She opened her mouth to say she had never stopped loving him, but changed her mind. He didn't need to know that right now.

Judith's words echoed in her head. " … if that man is as much of a sex-machine as you say … you might just be sending him into some other woman's bed again."

"Pay the bill and let's go."

Her mind wandered on the drive home. Was Reece confused by the signals she was sending? She hadn't said she was willing to work things out, but he had to know she had reached a turning point and was going to make love with him that night. He'd always been good at reading her.

At home, she checked on the children, and he made the rounds, securing the house.

They met in the bathroom, where she stood in front of the mirror, hoping she was doing the right thing.

He clasped her around the waist.

They exchanged no words, but communicated through the huge pane of gilt-edged glass.

He turned her into his arms and kissed her, taking his time. Eventually, he slipped the black dress over her head, and they stepped into the shower to rediscover each other.

She hid the tears she shed as Reece made love to her because she could do nothing about the images of him and Gloria that scrolled behind her closed lids. She wanted to reject him, but perhaps sensing what was going on in her mind, Reece continued his adoration of her body until she gave in to her passion and clung to him, sobbing as waves of pleasure crashed over her.

They satisfied their hunger for each other several times during the night, however, Sherryn did not respond when Reece told her he loved her. Despite knowing he wanted to hear the words, Sherryn refused to speak them. After he fell asleep, clasping her to him, she cried again, afraid her emotional scars would never heal.

Twenty-Four

On Saturday morning, Reece woke early, battling the disappointment and optimism fighting inside him. While Sherryn let him make love to her, she hadn't told him she loved him, but he refused to entertain the thought that maybe her love had died.

He brushed his fingers over her cheek where the sun slanted across her skin. She moaned and rolled away from him to snuggle into her pillow. He rose and went to shower, reminding himself he hadn't won her eighteen years ago by being faint-hearted.

As early as he got up, Brandon and Maurice waited for him downstairs. He fried bacon, which they had with thick slices of hardough bread, and cups of warm Ovaltine. He cleaned up, not wanting to leave a mess for Sherryn, and took both boys upstairs where they laid out what they planned to wear. He bathed Brandon first and sent him to his room with a smack on his narrow butt. While he soaped Maurice, he studied him. The boy resembled him as closely as his other children did. He told Maurice to turn around and got ready to rinse him.

The child peered over his shoulder. "We really goin' to buy di fish tank and everythin'?"

He frowned, wondering why Maurice would doubt his word. "Yeah, right after both of you put on your clothes."

"And it goin' be my own too?"

Reece nodded, understanding his need for reassurance. "Yes, just as much as it will belong to Brandon."

Instead of slapping Maurice as he had Brandon, Reece asked him something. "Yuh never own anything yet?"

Maurice shook his head and jammed his finger into his mouth. Reece resisted the need to tell him he was too old to be sucking his finger. "Yuh mother never buy you any toys, or things like that?"

Another shake of the head gave Reece his answer. "So what you play with?"

"Juice box and bokkle stoppers," Maurice said around his thumb.

Anger clogged Reece's throat. Not only had Gloria starved the boy and barely kept clothes on his back, she never bothered to give him anything to make up for her neglect.

He rubbed a hand over his forehead, cursing himself for being a hypocrite. Justin was right. He was angry over what Gloria hadn't done for his son, but what had he done? He was just as bad, maybe worse than she was since he had never made an effort to see Maurice or find out how he was doing, knowing the sort of woman Gloria had turned out to be. He raised his head and caught the child watching him.

"Go put on your clothes," Reece said.

About to turn away, Maurice continued to stare at Reece, who gently pulled the finger out of his mouth. "You need to stop sucking your finger. You goin' to spoil your teeth, okay?"

Maurice nodded and walked away.

Seconds later, Reece chuckled and shook his head.

The boy held his finger at the ready to stick back in his mouth the minute he was out of sight.

By the time Reece got dressed, Brandon and Maurice were hopping about with excitement. They scrambled into the Land Cruiser behind him, talking at the same time.

It took them ten minutes to get to the pet store, and an hour and a half to decide on what they wanted to buy.

Reece found it difficult to convince them that they couldn't get at least thirty fish for the three foot tank they bought.

The owner of the shop who saw his plight, explained that some of the fish were natural enemies, and could not live together in that small space. They settled on two pairs of goldfish and two pairs of angelfish. They also bought enough equipment to open a mini store, because Reece couldn't resist buying the stuff Maurice asked questions about, but would not admit to wanting, like an ugly extra-terrestrial creature wearing scuba equipment.

At home, Reece gave himself a crash course on setting up the tank.

Brandon hung over his shoulder, reading aloud from the book he bought on fish keeping. Then the two boys expressed so many opinions and suggestions that he couldn't concentrate. He stopped his mind from swirling in confused circles by asking them to decide where they wanted to set up the tank.

They both agreed to put it in a corner of the living room, and Sherryn gave permission.

She rescued Reece by taking them out of the house with her for a quick trip to the supermarket, promising to buy icicles.

Reece had to swear not to start setting up without them, and with a few minutes of quiet, wondered if he'd gone mad to undertake another pet project with his children.

He laughed, realizing he'd included Maurice unconsciously, and forced his attention back to the book because he needed to understand what he was doing before Brandon and Maurice descended on him again.

By the time they returned, Reece had set up the filter, attached the hose, and put them out of the way. He also screwed the bulb to the socket in the hood of the tank.

While they decided the color of the pebbles they wanted on the bottom, Reece unrolled the adhesive plastic simulating the sea floor, and stuck it to the back of the tank. They reached a compromise, and Brandon spread a layer of aquamarine stones to cover half of the bottom of the tank, while Maurice spread black ones on the other side. After helping them place and anchor the ornaments and plastic aquatic plants, Reece filled the tank with water he had set aside overnight. After releasing the fish into their new home, the two children fed their pets, watched them eat, and kept vigil in front of the tank until Sherryn dragged them away for food.

While Reece packed their excess purchases in a carton, Justin walked into the living room. His footsteps stalled, and Reece suspected Justin would have left again if he thought his father hadn't seen him. Instead, Justin hesitated before picking up the remote and flopping into one of the sofas. His greeting was a sullen word. "Dad."

Reece was peeved, so his response came out harsher than he intended. "Is that the way we raised you?"

"Sorry," Justin muttered, switching on the television.

Reece folded the flaps over the box and got ready to move it. Justin's voice stopped him from getting up. "Daddy?"

Reece raised his brow, encouraging him to continue.

"Um ... you and Mom ... have you fixed things yet?"

"Not really, but we're making some progress. Things are a bit better than they were a few weeks ago as you can see."

"So you guys not splitting up?"

"Who told you that might happen?"

Justin shrugged. "Nobody, but neither of you is saying anything concrete, so we wondered."

"You know we wouldn't do anything without discussing it with all of you."

"I know that, but like I said, nobody's saying anything."

Now Reece shrugged. "Son, you can't rush these things. I hurt your mother badly, so I have to be patient while she works through her emotions. If—"

"Speaking of emotions." Justin glanced toward the living room entrance. "What d'you have to say about all the stuff you told me a year ago—you know, about women and not messing with their emotions?"

Reece kept his expression neutral while thinking Justin was his mother's emotional twin. He forgave and forgot nothing.

"All of that still stands," Reece said. "The fact that I made a mistake doesn't change things one way or another."

A sneaky expression stole over Justin's face. "Daddy, tell me somethin'. If you could take back everything, make it go away, what would you do?"

Reece took a deep breath and lifted the box. "None of what I did this time around."

"So you're saying you'd even give up Maurice?"

"Even him."

That seemed to satisfy Justin, who asked no more questions.

Reece, however, was disturbed and wondered about Justin's state of mind. At sixteen, he shouldn't be asking questions like that, as if Maurice and he were in a popularity contest.

Then Reece examined himself. Yes, he regretted what he'd done, but what kind of answer had he just given his son? He'd admitted Maurice's life was worthless, which struck him as cruel, not to mention blasphemous.

He rubbed a hand along his jaw. In the past month, he had discovered things about himself he wasn't sure he liked at all. Sherryn was right; he had changed. Hissing softly with self-disgust, he plodded from the room to chuck the carton in the storage space.

His thoughts bothered him for the rest of the afternoon and into the evening.

In the cool of the falling dusk, he lay unmoving beside Sherryn in bed, hands folded under his head, conscious of her concern each time she flipped a page.

Eventually, she turned the book face down in her lap. "Are you going to stare at the ceiling all night?"

"Uh, no, I'm all right."

"I didn't ask if you were all right. What's eating you?"

He turned his head and looked up at her.

She, in turn, cocked her brow. "You've been like this all evening."

"I've been thinking."

"That's fairly obvious."

"I feel bad about Maurice."

She gave him her 'oh really' expression."

"Don't look at me like that, Sher. Please. I feel awful enough already."

"Okay, fine. Talk to me."

He gazed at her, mesmerized—struck once more by his good fortune. Sherryn had always understood his need to clarify his thoughts by talking things through—at least those things he could talk to her about. She became his confidante early on in their relationship and used to listen to him reason out business proposals and his plans for the future. She even tolerated him while he spouted political opinions in which she had no interest. Now, she waited patiently for him to speak.

"It's Justin. We talked a bit today and I'm not comfortable with something he asked me." Reece avoided connecting with Sherryn while he spoke. "He wanted to know if I'd take everything back if I could. I told him yes ... and then he asked if that included Maurice."

The intensity of her stare forced him to look at her.

He wasn't sure what he saw in her eyes when she spoke. "And what did you say?"

"I told him yes."

Reece waited for her to say something, but she didn't. The heavy chirping of crickets in the darkness outside distracted him, and he sat up, rubbing both hands over his eyes.

"What exactly is bothering you? The fact that you told him you'd make

Maurice disappear if you could, or the fact that he asked the question?"

"Both," he said, clasping his hands. "It's disturbing that he'd ask something like that. Makes me think he has too much of me in him." He sighed. "You know, that need for validation."

The mattress moved as she changed position behind him. "It's not such a strange question, Reece. Think about it. His world has shifted, and all he's searching for is reassurance. His age doesn't mean he's less immune to hurt than a ten or eleven year old. Before Maurice came on the scene, he was the center of your world. The two of you did everything together and just as I felt ... feel let down, so does he."

Reece frowned over his shoulder. "You think that's what it is?"

She nodded, her expression sober.

"But he knows he doesn't have any reason to be jealous."

"Does he? All he knows is that you did something that's put a wedge between the two of you. When was the last time you rapped like you used to?"

A shrug moved Reece's shoulders. "He hasn't exactly welcomed any conversation from me. Your son is like you in that respect."

She ignored that comment and moved closer. "Now that you've had a chance to think about what you said to him, would you actually prefer if Maurice didn't exist?"

He thought a while before expressing his feelings. "At first, I'd have loved if he had somehow disappeared, but now I see so much of myself in him and I blamed him for disrupting my life, when none of this is his fault.

"His mother chose to have him, not caring that she was doing it for the wrong reasons. I sometimes wonder what would have happened to him if you hadn't decided to help."

"In spite of what you did, I couldn't live with myself knowing my children were well provided for and Maurice was out there somewhere, needing care. It might be different if I didn't know him, but I do."

"Sherryn?"

"Hmm?"

"I know you didn't do it for me, but ... thanks."

She got off the bed, walked away and closed the bathroom door between them.

Staring after her, Reece cursed himself for making her cry.

Twenty-Five

On Sunday mornings, Sherryn ensured that everybody went to church.

Nobody dared rebel openly, but Reece tugged continuously at the sleeves of his jacket, and Justin insisted his was getting too tight.

Sherryn always assured them they could stand an hour and a half of discomfort if they concentrated on what they were supposed to. She focused on the pastor speaking at the raised podium and ignored the sighs, low hisses, and rustling beside her. Above the altar, biblical scenes etched in colored glass captured her attention while she listened. She tuned her family out, and soon they resigned themselves to their time on the wooden bench.

She smothered a grin as Reece shifted beside her a few minutes later and ran a finger around the edge of his collar. Then, she pretended not to see when he gave up and loosened his tie.

Brandon and Maurice wore identical white shirts, black ties, and trousers. Consoled by having Maurice's company to stifle his boredom, Brandon reconciled himself to being there. He glanced at his father, whispered to Maurice, and the two of them giggled. At Sherryn's warning frown, they quashed their laughter and stared straight ahead.

She poked Reece in the side. "Keep an eye on them. They're having too much fun."

He shifted Kyle on his leg and placed a restraining hand on Brandon's arm. Subdued, Brandon sat back for a few moments, before leaning over to say something else to his brother.

This time, Sherryn widened her eyes at Justin. He rolled his, sighed noisily, and prodded Maurice until he got up. Scooting over, Justin then moved him to the other side, away from Brandon. Melly and Celia turned to investigate the shuffling going on behind them.

Uh, oh. Sherryn spotted Maurice's finger edging toward his mouth, while he peeked at Justin. She cleared her throat and leaned forward until she caught Justin's eye.

What now? his said.

A chuckle nearly escaped her at Justin's impatient expression. She inclined her head toward Maurice, and Justin's brow cleared.

He understood her unvoiced request and said something to Maurice.

She smiled when Maurice's finger slipped from between his lips, and he held back laughter with a hand placed over his mouth. After a quick smile of thanks to Justin, she faced forward, satisfied.

Maurice's excitement over his first trip to church with them surprised her. He couldn't remember ever having been inside a church.

She'd laughed quietly, knowing he'd be bored eventually. None of the others was eager to go, however, she believed in doing her best to ensure they were rounded individuals, and so she took them to church.

After another look at them, she hid a tiny smile. Each child would make her proud in the future, she was sure of it. Maurice needed a bit of steering and love to make him forget his rough start in life, but she had no doubt he would do well, based on his current progress. He had his father's temperament where it concerned learning how to do new things. He was stubborn and worked consistently until he had mastery of his task.

Though he came to them under painful circumstances, he fit in well. They smiled at each other, and shock slid through her. As short as his time with them had been, Sherryn admitted she loved this boy as much as the children she had carried inside her body.

She looked up at their father, distinguished in his formal wear. How she adored him. She stopped herself from leaning against him and stroking his skin.

They got some curious glances that first Sunday when they walked into church with Maurice in tow.

Someone was bound to ask a question at some point, and as soon as she formed that thought, one of the elderly ladies in the pew behind them tapped her shoulder and whispered, "And who is dis likkle boy?"

In a second, embarrassment twisted her insides and tears sprang to her eyes. She tried to reply, but couldn't get her mouth to form a single word. Even if she said the boy's name, the woman would know their secret.

How she resented what Reece had done to their relationship. Minutes ago, she'd been thinking how much she loved him, and with a single question she now hated him with equal ferocity. God help her. She felt like a child on a seesaw—up this minute and the next, depressed. When would her emotions settle?

Deciding to stick with partial truth, she said, "He's a relative of ours."

The woman chuckled and tugged on Maurice's ear before touching his cheek. "Him is a handsome likkle t'ing."

Sherryn sank against the back of the pew, relieved, but it hadn't gotten any easier.

She wished she wasn't such a stickler for things concerning her family because it was what kept her showing up each Sunday. Despite regular attendance and more time spent in prayer, she wasn't at peace. It pained her to realize that deep inside, she didn't believe she'd ever be happy again.

Twenty-Six

With the coffee mug in one hand, Sherryn picked up the mail with the other. A loud knock at the door startled her, and she spilled the coffee. She sucked her teeth and set the cup on the table near the front door. Before she opened it, she dropped the napkin she carried over the spreading coffee. A couple of dogs in the yard would have stopped the intruder from getting to her doorstep, and causing the resulting mess. She yanked the door open, beating back annoyance.

Gloria stood outside, a determined expression in place.

Sherryn's heart rate doubled, and she went into battle mode. Taking her time, she scanned Gloria from head to feet and didn't give her the satisfaction of speaking first.

This time, Gloria wore a pair of jeans and her belly fought to stay inside a skin-tight, sleeveless shirt. Today's wig carried burgundy highlights and hung past her shoulders. An assortment of jewelry hung from her ears, neck and wrist.

Under Sherryn's silent appraisal, Gloria lost her sneer. She shifted, thumbs stuck in the loop of her jeans. "Mi come fi mi pickney," she said.

Sheryn leaned on the doorframe and raised her brows in mock horror. "You mean the one you left here more than a month ago, like garbage?"

"Nuh gimme no argument. Mi come fi Maurice." Gloria craned her neck and leaned to one side. "Maurice, is you dat? Come 'ere."

Angling her body sideways, Sherryn saw that Maurice stood behind her.

The kindergarten workbook and pencil fell to the floor and his mouth hung open. He hid behind Sherryn and stuck his thumb in his mouth.

Gloria shouted, "Maurice, yuh don' hear mi calling you?"

He burrowed further behind the door, shaking.

Gloria stepped forward, and Sherryn closed the gap in the doorway. "You'll have to talk to his father before Maurice goes anywhere."

Sherryn slammed the door and turned the lock, too disturbed to revel in the fact that she nearly caught the other woman's fingers in the opening.

She knelt before the trembling boy and folded him to her chest. Both his arms crept around her neck, and his small frame shook as his mother banged the door and continued to call for him.

"It's all right," she whispered, stroking his head. "I won't let her get you, okay?"

He nodded, and she held him away from her. Liquid pooled in his eyes, ran from his nostrils and around his thumb.

Sherryn took him by the hand and led him to her office. She grabbed the roll of hand towels off her desk, dried his face, and made him blow his nose. On her way out the door, she ran into Miss Emlyn's squat figure.

"Is who makin' dat racket outside?" she asked.

"Maurice's mother," Sherryn said, sidestepping the older woman.

"What she want?"

Sherryn peeked over her shoulder at Maurice before murmuring, "She came back for him."

Miss Emlyn placed her hands on her hips while a frown contracted her brows. "You not goin' give him to her?"

"'Course not. If she wanted him, she wouldn't have left him here. I have to call Reece."

Tipping her head toward the front of the house, Miss Emlyn spoke. "She out-of-order to come makin' all dis noise outside yuh door. You want me go t'row her out of di yard for yuh?"

Sherryn surprised herself by laughing. She patted the woman on the shoulder. "No, Miss Em. It's all right. Reece will know what to do. You just keep Maurice company."

Nodding, Miss Emlyn entered the room. Sherryn went upstairs, confident that the housekeeper would take the child's mind off what had just happened.

Sherryn sat on the edge of the bed and dialed Reece's cell number. He answered after a couple of rings.

"Reece, that woman is here, and she wants Maurice back."

"Where is she exactly?"

"At the front door, making a lot of noise and banging on it."

"Don't give him to her, okay?"

"You don't need to tell me that."

"Sorry, I know. I'm coming."

Sherryn hung up the phone, wondering if she really wanted Reece to see Gloria. She shrugged away her doubt. It wasn't as if he couldn't have seen her anywhere else if he chose to, and the woman was making a nuisance of herself. Thankfully, few people were at home at that hour of the morning to hear the ruckus on her doorstep. She rubbed a hand across her brow, then plodded downstairs past the front door, where Gloria continued her one-sided shouting match.

Sherryn picked up the abandoned workbook in which Maurice had started doing math exercises. A quick look confirmed that he'd gotten all his sums right. It would be a pity to give him back to his mother, but could they keep him against Gloria's wishes? Only Reece had any real power and would probably win if the matter went to court.

Sherryn pushed away her worry and disgust at the vulgar words reaching her through the heavy wood. She closed the book and walked away, thankful that Maurice couldn't hear the noise from her office.

She had a mind to get a bucket of water and wet the Jezebel outside. A good dunking would cool Gloria down, but it was better to avoid a brawl. There was no way she'd be getting in a fight with the likes of Gloria, so she put the wicked, but appealing idea aside. Out of spite, she wished Reece would be angry enough to give Gloria a good smack when he got home.

Twenty-Seven

Reece sped through the streets with rage surging in his bloodstream.

How dare that slut turn up at his house demanding Maurice? She had to be mad, after leaving the boy the way she did.

Slowing his breathing, Reece forced himself to think past the madness trying to claw its way to the surface. If he didn't get hold of himself, he'd do something stupid which he couldn't afford.

Gloria had come back for one reason. The new life she wanted hadn't materialized. If it had, she wouldn't be at his door demanding her cash cow. Reece didn't intend to hand the boy over. Maybe he would have, if she'd turned up a day or so after she dropped him off, but not now that he understood what Maurice's life had been like with her. As far as he was concerned, Gloria wasn't fit to raise a pig, and he wondered if she'd gone to her other children's father, demanding them back as well.

He skidded into the corner, raising his foot off the gas, and pulled up behind the marked taxi idling at his gate. Throwing the driver a glare, he stalked across the cement walkway.

The engine fired up, and Reece curled his lips into a sour smile. Good, he thought, get ready to leave with this bit of rubbish that's hell-bent on destroying my life.

At his approach, Gloria did a backward shuffle. He smirked, watching her deflate under his stare. "What you want, Gloria? 'Cause surely yuh don't think mi goin' give Maurice to yuh."

"Is my pickney. Dat mean I can tek him anytime I want."

"Funny how you never realize Maurice was hungry and next to naked when him was living at your yard."

He moved closer to her, staring her in the eyes. "Is what you do wid mi money, Gloria? Why Maurice don't have no clothes, or anything else?"

She sassed him, laying her hands on her hips. "Dat is not your business. Your business is to provide for him."

Fearing he'd lose control and hit her, Reese barked, "Gloria, get off my property before I have to call the police."

"See how yuh like it when I report to dem how yuh kidnap mi son!"

"You t'ink the police stupid? One look at you and them goin' to know you're nothing but a careless slut."

Her hand came up and she blindsided him with a stinging blow to the face.

Only willpower kept Reece from slapping her and while his ear rang from the blow, he hauled her down to the gate, yanked open the door of the taxi, and stuffed her inside.

She griped at the undignified treatment and shimmied across the seat out of his grip.

He bent over and hung on to the window, his words slow and deliberate. "If you ever come back to my house, I swear on my mother's grave I'll kill you."

He glared at the man behind the wheel. "Driver, carry her back to whichever garbage heap yuh pick her up from."

The man drove off with Gloria screaming expletives from the back seat.

Reece straightened the sleeves of his shirt before walking into the yard, doing his best to ignore one of their neighbors, who stood on the sidewalk a few houses down.

Sherryn stood in the doorway waiting for him. Her faint smile disappeared and left disappointment behind. "Reece, how you get mixed up with a woman like that?"

He shrugged, wanting to find somewhere to hide. "Where's Maurice?"

"In my office."

"Him know she was here?"

Sherryn turned away nodding. "Yeah, she was calling him to come to her. He's upset. I'm sure he's thinking we might send him back."

Reece flexed restless fingers, unsure of what to do.

"I think you should talk to him," Sherryn said, as she moved down the passage.

He locked the door and followed her to the office, where Maurice curled up in one corner of the couch, his head on the armrest, and his thumb in its usual place. His eyes were red and weepy.

Sherryn sat beside him and rested a hand on his shoulder. "She's gone, okay?"

He nodded and lifted his head. "She goin' to come back?"

Sherryn stared at Reece. Silently, she told him to ensure that whatever action he took backed up her words. "I don't think so, Maurice. We'll do our best to see that doesn't happen."

The boy turned to his father, seeking confirmation. Reece walked over, lifted Maurice, and sat with him on his lap.

Maurice was either too worried or distraught to remember to be afraid of him. His small shape folded into Reece's, a disturbing reminder of the limited contact they had with each other. He ran a hand over Maurice's back. "I won't let her take you away."

Only a quiver of his body told Reece that the boy heard him.

"I mean it," he continued. "I won't send you back."

Maurice sat up and stared at his spotted legs. "She say she goin' come back wid di police. I did hear her."

"I don't care what she said. Not even the police can force me to give you to her." Reece pasted a smile on the tail end of his sentence when Maurice trembled. He patted the boy's shoulder as further reassurance. "Don't worry about it."

Maurice nodded, but Reece understood that his anxiety wouldn't disappear on command. Exchanging a helpless look with Sherryn, he wondered what else to say to stop him from worrying. Now, he felt even worse about his role in making Maurice's life a nightmare. Reece touched him again and found that he'd fallen asleep.

Sherryn tried to pick him up, but Reece waved her away.

"I'll do it," he said and got up with Maurice in his arms. After he laid him on the bed upstairs, Reece watched him sleep. He'd been far from happy to see Maurice lying on his couch a month ago, but every time he studied him, Maurice tugged at something inside him.

It wasn't Gloria's intention for him to fall in love with his child, but Reece accepted that he was more than half way to that point. Gloria would know soon enough that he wasn't about to let her disrupt either of their lives again—no matter what he had to do to ensure their peace of mind.

Uttering something like a snarl, Reece turned on his heels and left the room.

Sherryn called to him from their bedroom when he stalked past.

He turned back, rubbing a hand over his face. When he sank on the end of the bed, he rolled his shoulders to relieve the tension gripping his muscles.

Sherryn stood by the dresser, rifling through a plastic document envelope. She slipped a finger between the sheets of paper inside and faced him. "What're you gonna do? You know this isn't the end of it."

"No, but I'm not sure what to do yet. She made threats about the police, not that she has a leg to stand on, 'cause nobody forced her to leave him here."

Sherryn laid the envelope aside, folded her arms, and stared him in the eyes. "How does she know where we live?"

"I never brought her here, if that's what you're thinking." He cleared his throat and met her gaze. "I was drunk when I, when we ... so, I guess she must have gone through my wallet. My driver's license has our address."

Glaring at him, Sherryn lifted the envelope and snapped the button shut, muttering, "Well, if you lie down with a dog, you must rise with fleas. Bad enough you had sex with that piece of trash, but you had to fall asleep too, leaving your family open to all sorts of embarrassment." She came to stand in front of him. "You know you have to do something, don't you? I refuse to have that woman coming here whenever she feels like. I'm not putting up with it, and my children shouldn't have to deal with your mistake, so you better sort this out quickly."

He said nothing, but got up and left the bedroom, wondering if his life would ever return to normal.

Twenty-Eight

She followed Reece downstairs and went to her office where she transferred her orders to a spreadsheet on the computer. When the office door opened a while later, she was double-checking her order book.

Maurice peeked in on her with sleep still clouding his eyes.

She beckoned him inside with a smile and a wave.

"Had a good nap?" she asked when he sat on the padded chair nearby.

He nodded, and his hand edged up to his mouth. Sherryn shook her head slightly, and he placed his hand on his knee, shamefaced.

She rewarded him with a smile. "Wanna see some of my work?"

He nodded again and came to stand beside the desk. She opened up a folder with pictures of cakes she had done in recent months. He moved in closer to scrutinize each picture. After a moment, he pointed to one. "You sure that can eat?"

"Why?"

"'Cause it look too good to eat."

"Why, thank you, Maurice."

"I can watch you do the next one?"

"Sure, but wouldn't you rather be playing with Brandon?" she teased.

"Yeah, but this is interestin'."

"Maurice, you ever had cake?"

A slow shake of the head was his response.

She was careful to hide her shock. "Want some?"

He bobbed his head and a grin spread over his face. "Yes, please."

"I have to go out later, so we'll get some cake and ice cream, okay?"

"When we goin'?"

"Don't worry your head about that. We're going in the afternoon before I pick up the others from school." She looked sideways at him. "Tell me something. Is there any way you'd want to go back to your mother?"

He gawked at her as if she had suggested that he stand in the middle of a busy street. "Please, Miss, don' send me back. She goin' to beat me, and mi goin' to be hungry all di time."

Tears shone in his eyes, making Sherryn regret her question. She put an arm around him. "Your father and I promised not to give you to her, remember?"

He sniffed and dipped his head.

"I'm glad you do, 'cause your father always keeps his promises."

She forced herself not to think about the one Reece had broken, which brought her this child.

"Always?" Maurice asked.

"Mmm-hmm, no matter what he has to do to keep them."

"Even for me?" Maurice asked, a hopeful gleam in his eyes.

Sherryn hugged him then, wishing she had it in her power to make everything better. "Especially for you."

His tremulous sigh softened her resolve to stick to her day's schedule. She held him away from her. "You know what? Why wait until later for ice cream and cake? Come, let's find something for you to wear."

He slipped his hand in hers, and they left the office.

She raced him up the stairs, allowing him to beat her, and was delighted to hear him laughing freely for the first time since he moved in.

His good humor slipped away when he caught her watching him.

She reassured him with a pat on the shoulder and a squeeze to his chin. "It's okay to have fun, you know."

"Mi madda used to say mi mek too much noise."

Turning from the cupboard with a pair of jeans and a tee-shirt in hand, Sherryn gave them to him. "Noise is not a bad thing all the time. I think little boys would go mad if they weren't allowed to make some."

He reminded her of an old man when he spoke, nodding. "Mi think so too."

"I think so too," she said softly.

He repeated her words, smiling.

"Good boy."

She pulled the shirt down over his head once he'd cast off the one he was wearing.

He smiled again, and Sherryn saw in his face the affection she was sure shone from hers. Her answering smile widened, and she chucked him under the chin. "Come on, let's go treat ourselves."

Sherryn made a disgusted face. "Eeew."

"It tastes nice," Maurice said, waving his spoon in the air.

Sherryn grimaced a second time. "I don't know about that."

Maurice laughed when he looked at her. "Yes, it does."

She eyed the mess in front of him.

He had broken up bits of cake on top of the ice cream, allowed it to melt, after which he mixed it all together. He slurped another spoonful, his mouth surrounded by pink goo.

"Anything you say. I bet you'd think milk and … "

He wasn't listening to her, but had his head angled toward the window. When he turned back to her, he laid the spoon in the bowl and put a hand on his tummy, as if it hurt. He swallowed convulsively, and Sherryn expected him to vomit.

She was about to ask if he was feeling sick, when she saw what ailed him.

His mother stood akimbo outside on the aisle. Her posture and the tight frock did little to disguise the mound of her belly. The smirk she wore confirmed that Gloria thought she had them at a disadvantage. How did she find time to change clothing and be in the same place as them so soon after their run-in? Something wasn't right.

Sherryn's heart bumped against her ribcage and she expected to be sweaty in a minute. Glaring at the woman, she reached for the handbag squashed between Maurice and her on the seat. In seconds, she had the phone in hand.

"Reece, we're at Penny's Eatery in Half-Way-Tree. Maurice's mother is going to cause a scene."

By the time she put the cellular back in her bag, the woman had parked herself by their table. "Maurice," she said, "you comin' wid me now."

He hunched in on himself, chin tucked into his neck.

In a quiet, but emphatic tone, Sherryn said, "Maurice is not going anywhere."

"Me is him madda," Gloria said, fists planted on her sides.

Sherryn kept her voice even and cocked her head upward. "You never knew that when you left him at my house?"

"Mi lef' him at him fadda yard," Gloria replied, wriggling her neck and shoulders.

"And that is where he's staying, 'cause I'm not giving him to you."

"How you goin' stop me from taking my pickney?"

It was not quite lunchtime, but a fair number of early eaters occupied tables in the fast food restaurant. Sherryn squirmed, but quickly forgot the heads turned in their direction when Gloria eased in closer.

"How you know where to find us?" Sherryn asked, knowing Gloria's appearance was too much of a coincidence.

Something flashed in the other woman's eyes and was gone within seconds.

"You know it's against the law to stalk people?" Sherryn asked.

"Who say I stalkin' you? What reason I have?"

Sherryn allowed her eyes to land on Maurice. Then she eyeballed Gloria and cocked one brow.

Gloria huffed before shouting, "Mi ca'an stalk mi own pickney."

By now, people were looking at them and Sherryn wished by some miracle the woman would vanish.

Maurice sat unmoving, his attention fixed on the fiberglass tabletop as if he'd go unnoticed if he stayed still. Sherryn squeezed his shoulder, hoping he wouldn't start crying.

Gloria bellowed. "You t'ink you is him madda? Maurice, come 'ere now."

His shoulder jerked under her hand, and Sherryn murmured, "Stay right where you are. Your father's coming."

He slumped further and let his breath out.

Despite the air conditioning, Sherryn's body heat climbed. She'd be darned if she let Gloria intimidate her. Squaring her shoulders, she said, "You're going have a long wait, 'cause you're not getting him."

Seeing an opportunity to further her cause, Gloria scanned the crowd and flung her voice up by a few decibels. "You better gimme mi pickney or else! You know dat kidnappin' is 'gainst di law? People tell mi if dis right."

Sherryn wanted to melt to a puddle and slide away as Gloria launched into her tale of kidnapping, and the wrongs committed against her. A crowd gathered near their table while Sherryn stared into the melting cup of ice cream. Her head snapped up when Maurice sniffled. She couldn't sit and wait for Reece to save her, especially when Gloria was trying to convince everybody that Sherryn had stolen her child.

"Kidnapping? Kidnapping?" Sherryn got to her feet, waving a hand at Maurice. "You threw him off on my doorstep, and now you're accusing me of child stealing? You better get a grip."

Gloria opened her mouth, but a man wearing a shirt with the restaurant's logo interrupted her. "Excuse me, ladies. I'm sorry, but I'm going to have to ask you to—"

Gloria spun on him. "To do what?"

"Leave. This sort of thing cannot be condoned inside—"

"You ca'an force me to leave before mi ready." Gloria yelled.

The man slipped into silence and waited to speak while Gloria continued yelling.

A pair of policemen on patrol paused outside the window. The male employee beckoned to the officers and seconds later, they cut through the people gathered at Sherryn's table.

"Is there a problem?" one of them asked.

"Offica, dis woman kidnap mi pickney," Gloria said.

The policeman frowned at Sherryn, glanced at Maurice, and then spoke to Gloria. "Have you made a report?"

"No, not yet."

"Instead of disturbing the peace here, I'd suggest you do that. Come with me."

Gloria folded her arms across her chest. "But she might escape wid him."

The taller of the two officers spoke. "Doesn't seem to me like she's trying to make a getaway. My partner will keep her here."

Reece walked up behind the policeman speaking to Gloria. When she spotted Reece, her mouth opened and closed but no words escaped.

Having got the policemen's attention, Reece explained the situation. While he talked to them, Gloria raked Sherryn with hate-filled eyes. She pointed at Reece. "You t'ink him can stop mi from getting back mi pickney?"

A vein throbbed in Reece's forehead, and his eyes narrowed at Gloria's words.

Sherryn's pulse sped up at the thought of his fury unleashed on Gloria and grabbed his arm.

"Reece!" She waited until she had his full attention before speaking again. "We should get out of here."

The officers escorted them outside, but that didn't stop Gloria from positioning herself where Sherryn had to pass her.

Maurice cried openly and refused to get up. Though sympathetic, Sherryn was also impatient to get out of the store and away from the crowd. She squeezed Maurice's hand and eased him out of the bench behind her and to her other side where Gloria couldn't get at him. Reece picked up Maurice, who sobbed into his shoulder.

From where she stood, Sherryn couldn't see Reece's expression, but could almost touch the waves of anger rolling off him. His voice erupted over his shoulder. "Gloria, I swear, if you don't leave my family alone, I'm goin' to make you sorry you ever see the light of day."

"You t'ink is me goin' to be sorry? You watch what I goin' to do next."

"Don't test me, Gloria. Apparently, you don't remember that I come from the same place as you."

Sherryn had no idea what they meant, but his words worked magic. Gloria stood aside and allowed them to pass.

As they left the store, she shouted, "Don't t'ink dis is di end. Mi want back mi son!"

With trembling fingers, Sherryn opened the van.

Reece strapped Maurice down while she wiped tears from his cheeks with a napkin.

"It's all right," she whispered while blinking away tears.

Maurice leaned his head against the door and sucked his thumb.

She sighed, wishing as she had frequently in the past month, that Reece had considered the consequences of his actions before stepping outside of their marriage.

Gloria came out of the store and sauntered up to the van, arms folded in front of her.

"Maurice, don' forget where you live, 'cause you comin' right back."

That started him sobbing again. Reece's shoulders heaved, and from the tightness in his jaw, he had his teeth clamped together. "Gloria, if you know what's good for you, leave right now."

Sherryn fired up the van to get away from the people staring at them through the plate-glass window. The officers walked toward Gloria as if to intercept her at the same time as Reece approached her.

She backed away, shouting abuse.

Reece moved to follow her, but Sherryn stopped him with a plea. "Please, Reece, don't do anything to get yourself in trouble."

He stared after Gloria, his gaze intense.

Gloria was now in conversation with the policemen, who looked to be passing on a stern warning.

Sherryn gripped Reece's arm through the window to get him to look at her. "Promise me you won't do anything about her just now."

"I won't," he said, turning his head to where Gloria still stood.

Sherryn didn't believe him.

Twenty-Nine

Later that evening, Sherryn watched Maurice from a corner of the living room.

Justin sat on the arm of the sofa where she sat and pointed with his chin. "Is what happen to him?"

Pausing to see if Maurice was listening, she murmured, "We saw his mother today. She wants him back."

Maurice occupied the same position he had for the last hour. He sat in front of the television, staring at the cartoon characters that chased each other across the screen. He neither smiled, nor laughed, as normal.

If anyone had told her that children worried to the extent he did, she'd have said it was a lie, but he had done nothing else since they got home earlier in the afternoon. Brandon gave up, after begging him endlessly to go outside, and went upstairs to play games on the computer.

Maurice hadn't moved since—not even when Sherryn, in desperation and against what she knew to be healthy, offered him the day's second serving of ice cream. He'd shaken his head and leaned against the sofa, feet stretched out, sucking incessantly at his finger. Unwilling to take away the comfort he derived from the act, she left him to it.

Justin's outrage pulled her back into the living room. "She want him back? Mommy, is what kind of woman dat?"

Smoothing out a page in the magazine she was flipping through, Sherryn frowned. "You know I don't like it when you talk that way."

"Yeah, but all the same, she lick her head or somethin'?"

Despite her annoyance with him, Sherryn chuckled. "I really wouldn't know if she hit her head, but I do know she's not helping him."

They eyed Maurice's still figure before Justin eased off the sofa arm, tying together the strings in the waistband of his sweat bottoms. "Lemme see what I can do."

Her lips twitched as Justin hung over the chair with his bottom in the air and the tee-shirt half way up his back while he spoke to Maurice. Doubting he'd be successful, she continued turning pages in the magazine. Her brows lifted when Justin passed her with Maurice in tow. Her sixteen-year-old responded with a smug smile.

She was still wondering how Justin had convinced Maurice to leave the room when Reece walked in and sat across from her. He wore work clothes, but had pulled his shirt free of his pants. His forehead bore lines of concern.

"You okay?" he asked.

"Apart from what happened earlier, I'm quite all right."

With his fingers folded together between his knees, Reece asked, "Is Maurice any better?"

She shrugged with one shoulder. "He's been sitting in front of the television since we got home. Dunno what Justin said to get him to move, but they just left."

A strained sigh came out of Reece.

We seem to be doing that a lot lately, she thought, as he scratched his scalp.

When he lifted his head, she concentrated on the magazine.

"I'm sorry about that," he said. "You shouldn't have to be entangled with, uh, Gloria."

Sherryn took her time closing the magazine while she gathered her thoughts. "If this is how she plans to continue, then I think you need to call in the police."

"The police?"

"Yes. What she did today is against the law. She denied it, but I know she followed us. Her turning up there was too convenient to be an accident, and she obviously knows Maurice is terrified of her. If I wasn't sitting where I was, he'd have gotten up and gone to her."

Reece hung his head and rolled his thumbs around each other, deep in thought. Another sigh left his lips before he shared what was going on in his head. "D'you think I need to tell him again that she won't get him?"

"It can't hurt. I tried telling him, but it had no effect. He's not talking, so I gave him some space."

She wasn't sure how to broach the idea that had come to her while she fretted over Maurice, but figured now was the best time. "With all the changes in his life over the past month, it might be a good idea to arrange counseling for Maurice. What d'you think?"

He frowned, and she expected some resistance, knowing that the idea might sound strange. In their culture, few people took their mental health seriously, sometimes with disastrous results. A year ago, a friend of Justin's had suffered anxiety attacks and then fell into deep depression, which was the result of unresolved feelings over his parents' separation and eventual divorce.

"I have no objections if you think it will help."

"I'm sure it will," she said. "I'll make a call to the Family Services Ministry and see what they recommend."

Folding his hands behind his head, Reece sucked his bottom lip and stared at the ceiling. The only sound in the room was the ticking of the wall-clock, and as time crept by, Sherryn grew more uncomfortable.

Something was going on with Reece. She confirmed it when he put on a blank expression after he caught her watching him.

Meeting his eyes, she warned him not to be foolish. To quell her anxiety, she said a prayer for him and the family.

In one movement, Reece rose from the seat and then walked past her. His body language made her uncomfortable and she hoped he'd do the sensible thing and forget whatever he was planning.

Thirty

Reece stopped at Justin's half-open door. He and Maurice hovered in front of the computer screen while Justin maneuvered the joystick to his right. The younger child sat still, wincing when the figures on the screen collided in a shower of sparks and booming noise from the speaker boxes. Reece left, relieved that Justin was not so mad at him that he'd ignore Maurice. He swallowed hard, humbled by Justin's helpfulness in the face of his personal distress.

The laughter coming from his daughters' room stopped when they spotted him in the doorway. Both of them stared at the open books in front of them, despite their carefree giggling a moment ago.

"May I come in?" he asked.

They nodded, and he crossed the room to sit on one of the beds.

A current of air lifted the tangerine fabric of the curtains and he followed its movement.

Melly flipped a page, which moved Reece's focus to where she lay. He cleared his throat and dragged his attention away from the carpet in the center of the room. The peach and mint green fabric had never been so fascinating before. "You're doing homework, right?"

Melly and Celia nodded—a study in absorption. Melly's head sank between her shoulders as she lay propped on her elbows on the rug. At any other time, their solidarity might have amused him, but the situation was serious. Reece rubbed his palms together while he braced himself. "Um, I know that apart from our family meeting, we haven't talked about Maurice."

They looked at him then. Melly sat up and crossed her spindly legs, while Celia observed him through her glasses.

"What more is there to talk about?" Melly asked.

Celia raised her brow in agreement with her sister's question.

Reece ignored Melly's rudeness and pressed on with an explanation. "We haven't been talking much since everything happened, and I wanted to find out how you're both doing."

His two daughters were aware that Melly was the child who could wheedle almost anything out of him. Although Justin was the eldest, when they all wanted something from him, they used Melly to get it.

Celia wielded much power over him, as well. She was quiet by nature, and in Reece's opinion, was the most mature of his children. Like Brandon, she had an old soul. She was also much like her mother. When she withdrew from him, she did so completely. If he could reach her, then he stood a chance of salvaging their relationship.

The complexity of his children's character awed him. While they resembled each other closely, each had their unique quirks, which made them distinct individuals. He awoke from his reverie to catch them staring at him.

"We're doing okay," Melly pronounced dryly. "The only problem we have is whether you and Mom are going to stay together or not."

He cocked his head, brows puckered. "You're still on that?"

Celia remained silent while Melly continued talking, her palms spread wide. "Both of you keep skirting around what's happened and the only person who's happy is Maurice, and of course, Brandon.

"I don't want to speak for your mother, but we haven't discussed splitting up as an option."

He gave them his undivided attention before speaking again. "Your mother's a strong woman and can do anything she sets her mind to, but if I had to live apart from all of you, I don't know what I'd do."

Melly watched him, her slender fingers cupped around her jaw while her elbows rested on her crossed legs. Sympathy shone from her eyes, but Celia continued to stare at him, unimpressed.

"I know I've let you all down." He appealed directly to his younger daughter. "But haven't you ever done something you wished you hadn't?"

Celia's gaze faltered, and he guessed what she was thinking. Six months before, she and Melly had gone into his office to leave him a surprise birthday present. What they had done, by accident, was tip over one of his two-drawer file cabinets. He'd left a glass of water on top and the result was a mass of wet papers, which they had stuffed back into whichever files came handy. Some of the documents, printed on an inkjet printer, were ruined. The rest reminded him of accordion files—they were wrinkled that badly. Both girls had stayed mum on what happened and by a process of elimination, Reece got around to them.

He grilled each girl separately when neither admitted to creating the mess.

After he asked Celia why she refused to look at him, she confessed and admitted everything in one breath. He hadn't punished them because he understood what they had been trying to do but had spoken to them about breaking his trust, particularly when their mother lectured them all the time about speaking the truth, whatever the cost.

Now, Celia avoided making eye contact. When she did, he knew she understood his position. Her body lost its stiffness and she lowered her head. Fiddling with the tail of her tee-shirt, she answered, "You know I have."

"Then, isn't it possible that you can forgive me?"

Still, she resisted him. "It's not the same thing."

"I know that." Dreading her answer, he asked, "What could I do to make things better?"

Celia glanced at Melly. "Like she said, we want to know what's going to happen."

"And like I've said before, these things take time. We all have to be patient and you have to trust me to work out things with your mom."

They consulted without speaking, made a decision he was not privy to, and then nodded at him.

"Now," he said, getting to his feet. "Can I get a hug?"

Reece sighed as they enfolded him in a waist hug. Nothing the world had to offer was better than what he had at home. As long as he had the power, nothing would disrupt his family's peace again.

Thirty-One

In the living room, Sherryn sat in front of the television, listening to the news with one ear.

"And on the crime blotters, thirty-six-year-old Gloria Wedderburn was found bludgeoned in her two room house in the Waterhouse community. There was no sign of forced entry, and based on information received, the police theorize that Miss Wedderburn may have been attacked by someone close to her. Miss Wedderburn remains in critical condition at the Kingston Public Hospital. Investigations will continue..."

With nausea knotting her stomach, she stumbled to her feet and hurried to Reece's office. She slammed the door behind her and marched to the desk. Despite trying to calm herself, her breathing was uneven. "Tell me you didn't do it."

Brows raised, Reece stared at her, but she wasn't fooled. She remembered his silence, and the deadpan expression he wore two days earlier, after they talked about Gloria and Maurice. His eyebrows drew together. "Do what?"

"Hurt Gloria," she whispered.

With one hand, she gripped her neck, the other hugged her waist. How was it possible to go from normal body temperature to freezing within minutes? She shivered, shook her head, and tried to form a rational thought.

Please, God, don't let him have anything to do with this. I can't bear this on top of everything.

Reece broke in on her prayer. "Hurt her how?"

"It was just on the news. She's in hospital in critical condition. Please say you don't know anything about it."

"I don't. No doubt she got what she was working for, but I didn't do it."

He spun the chair as she walked around the desk. Gripping him by the shoulders and bending to stare into his eyes, she begged him, "Promise me you didn't do this."

"Sher, it had nothing to do with me. I haven't seen her since the day before yesterday. Besides, she moved. I wouldn't know where to find her."

She cupped her forehead in one hand. "Jesus, Reece, the police are going to come."

He nodded. "Yes, of course, but I'm sure I'm not the only person who'd love to see her suffer."

"You know this will cause more problems, don't you?"

His shoulders heaved as if he was trying to control his breathing. "Unfortunately, yes."

"What do I tell the children if the police come here?"

"I hope they don't." His earnest stare helped reassure her. "Maybe I should go to the station, rather than wait for them to come to me."

"I dunno, Reece, if you didn't do anything then—"

"You're right," he said, "but I don't want the children frightened if the police turn up here."

"Oh, God," she whispered.

He got up and held on to her arm. "What's wrong now?"

"Maurice, how do we tell him his mother's been hurt?"

"I don't think we should say anything. Let's see what happens first. I don't want to scare him. Not after what she did."

"Okay. Yes. That's the best thing to do."

He pulled her into his arms, and she allowed him to hug her. She whispered into his shoulder, "I hope this doesn't turn into a bigger nightmare for us."

Gently, he rubbed her back and then kissed her forehead. "I hope not. Sher?"

"Mmm?"

"I wish I had the words to say how sorry I am about all this."

Sherryn had no words to comfort him.

The police didn't take long to find them. They came a day later while Sherryn watered the plants on the veranda. Reece was away and Miss Emelyn and Maurice were both upstairs. When Maurice was not with Sherryn, he tagged along with the older woman, asking her to tell him tales of Anansi—a crafty spider from West African and Caribbean folklore.

They knocked on the wrought iron gate before entering the yard. She beckoned the two men forward, thankful they had arrived in an unmarked car. Immediately, she recognized them as police officers. They had the look—clean-shaven, low hair, dark glasses.

"Good morning, Ma'am. Is this where we find Mr. Maurice Allbright?"

Sherryn nodded.

The taller of the two removed his glasses before he spoke. "Is he at home?"

"No. He should be at the office, or if not, somewhere on the road."

The second officer had an unbelievably thin moustache, which Sherryn caught herself watching. "D'you have a number where we can reach him?"

Water splashed over her foot from the watering can. "Uh, yes."

She told him Reece's mobile number, which he wrote down. Then Sherryn asked the inevitable. "I'm his wife. D'you care to say what it's about?"

The men exchanged the briefest of glances before the taller one slipped his glasses back on. His vague reply was deliberate. "It has to do with a case we're investigating."

Annoyed for no reason she could define, Sherryn snapped, "You mean it has to do with Gloria Wedderburn."

Her direct approach startled the officers, who looked at each other again. Small wonder their necks didn't snap, she thought sourly. She almost smiled at their surprise. "I watch the news too."

Both men walked away from her. "Okay, thanks, we'll catch up with Mr. Allbright."

Her stomach cramped, and then churned. She wanted to believe in Reece's innocence, but knowing how deep his passions ran, she had her doubts.

Thirty-Two

Reece motioned the policemen toward the visitor's chairs facing his desk.

Sherryn told him about their visit to the house, so he expected them to turn up at some point.

"Please, have a seat."

The plainclothes officers grunted and sat down, giving the sparsely furnished office a thorough once over with sharp eyes.

Reece's assistant shut the door and left.

The cop with the moustache pulled out a notebook and a pen. "Your wife called you?"

"Yes, she did."

"That was good of her, considering ... "

Warning himself not to jump to any conclusions, Reece asked, "Considering what?"

The second officer, who had a beer belly, leaned forward. "The fact that you're a suspect in this case."

"Am I? My wife knows I didn't do anything."

They ignored that and moved on. "How d'you know Gloria Wedderburn?"

Reece answered promptly, "She has a son for me."

"Where is the child now?"

"At my house."

Pencil Moustache's eyebrows climbed up his forehead. "You mean to say, with your wife?"

Nodding, Reece answered. "Yes, she's an exceptional woman."

The other officer laced his fingers together over his stomach. "So, your wife is raising your sweetheart's child."

Not liking the sound of that, Reece took time over his answer. "Yes and no. Gloria brought him to my house more than a month ago and left him there. She didn't want him anymore."

"And your wife allowed him to stay there?"

"Yes. There was no other place for him to go."

"She's really a good woman."

"Without a doubt."

The man with the strange moustache took over the questioning. "Didn't this cause some friction in your home?"

"Of course, that's partly why Gloria took him there."

"What other reason did she have to do that?"

"She told the boy, Maurice, that she was starting a new life, and that he and brother and sister would have to live with their fathers."

"D'you know how many other children she has?"

"If you know about me, how come you don't know about her other baby-father?"

"You know him, or where we can find him?"

"No."

"Please remind me of the last time you saw Miss Wedderburn."

"The day she tried to bully my wife into giving her the boy."

"Did she say why she wanted him?"

"No, but knowing Gloria, she probably wanted to dig more money out of me."

"Did you threaten her?"

"I told her she'd be sorry she was born if she didn't stop fooling with my family."

The officer shifted position and peered at his notebook, giving Reece the chance to stare at his ridiculously thin excuse for a moustache.

"We'll be tracking your movements during the morning in question, however, that doesn't cancel the fact that you could have paid someone to beat up Miss Wedderburn."

"I had no reason to do that."

"But isn't that the way of dealing with things where you come from?"

The old sensitivity reared its head, which annoyed Reece. "Officer, you know how long ago I left Waterhouse?"

The officer smirked. "Have you? From what I hear, you still frequent the neighborhood."

"I have friends there. That's not a crime."

"But a lot of what goes on there is."

"Be that as it may, officer, I had nothing to do with Gloria's beating."

"That's not what she thinks."

Reece put his elbows on the desk. "She woke up?"

"Yes, and we spoke to her." He flipped a page in the notebook. "Miss Wedderburn said you threatened her and further, she thinks you're the culprit."

Reece sucked his teeth. "Gloria is trouble with a big T. I wouldn't waste my time on her."

"She doesn't think that at all. In fact, you're the only person she suspects."

"That doesn't surprise me. Gloria seems to think she means something to me. I don't care whether she's alive or dead, much less to waste time and money to beat her up. The only thing I'm sorry about ... "

He stopped talking before he said too much.

"What are you sorry about, Mr. Allbright?"

"That whoever beat her up didn't kill her too. How on earth Gloria can accuse me when she moved out after she left Maurice at my house? I didn't even know she was still living in Waterhouse."

Reece didn't know what to make of the policeman's silence and was too incensed to care. He placed both hands flat on the desk. "Officer, you have any more questions?"

"Not right now, but we'll be in touch."

"Fine, and please ensure that when you catch the man who did this, I get the chance to shake his hand."

Both officers exchanged a glance before the paunchy one rose and shook Reece's hand. "Thank you, Mr. Allbright. Remember we'll need to speak with you again."

"Sure." Reece walked them to the door.

Hesitating, as if he had forgotten something, Pencil Moustache stopped, facing him. "Where were you yesterday morning, between nine and eleven o' clock?"

"Here, then I had a meeting out of the office at ten. After that, I was on the road. I move around a lot."

"Hmm."

They left, and Reece went back to the desk and dropped in his seat, conscious that the situation could deteriorate. He picked up the family portrait and studied it, hoping Gloria didn't cause any more trouble by kicking the bucket. If she died, he'd obviously be the main suspect.

The police visit tainted his previous good mood. Things were settling down at home and he was hopeful they would soon return to normal, but running true to form, Gloria now posed another problem.

She certainly knew how to aggravate him. On what might be her deathbed, she still managed to make him angry. Again, he cursed himself for his involvement with her. He leaned his head against the chair, disgusted that he had allowed Gloria's accusations to rattle him. No doubt the police would think him cruel and insensitive, but they didn't know Gloria and the depths of deviousness to which she would descend. The woman was lower than a snake's belly.

He saw himself like it was yesterday, sitting at the bar with Ronald, growing more miserable as he had shot after shot of Appleton Gold and Pepsi. Like every other man who drank alcohol, he understood the danger, but knowledge hadn't stopped him that night, more than six years ago.

Unable to make any progress with Sherryn, he had taken his latest bout of depression to the bar for one drink that turned into an alcohol orgy.

At midnight, after slurping up as much Guinness as he could on Reece's tab, Ronald had given up on consoling Reece and left him slouched at the bar.

Reece had some sort of conversation with Gloria. He remembered her soft murmurs as she listened to him whine about Sherryn, while she leaned on the counter. Only the good Lord knew what he told her as he blubbered about his misfortune. He remembered her helping him outside and leaning him up against the wall on one side of the door when it was time to lock up. Somehow, she got him into the vehicle. He had no memory of driving the van, even after searching every crevice of his mind.

Shudders shook him each time he thought about how he could have killed them, or someone else driving drunk, because to the best of his knowledge Gloria couldn't drive. He wondered about her sanity for putting herself at risk like that, but in hindsight, she obviously had a plan.

Reece also had no recollection of what they did when they got to her house, but Gloria made sure he understood when he woke, that they had had sex. As he had worked saliva into his mouth, which was as dry as sandpaper, Reece tried to figure out how he had gotten into Gloria's bed, had sex and couldn't call to mind a single detail.

When he could form a sensible thought, he resigned himself to the fact that Sherryn was going to kill him. What explanation could he give for being out all night? That was something he'd never done before. After dragging his clothes on, he sniffed his body in a frenzy, hoping Gloria hadn't left any scent on him. Edging back to sit on the untidy bed, he clutched his thudding head, trying to get his mind to work.

Then horror had sent him bouncing to his feet. He had cheated on his wife and worse, he hadn't worn a condom. He didn't carry them because he didn't need them. Realizing the magnitude of his dilemma, he collapsed on the bed, massaging his pulsing forehead and groaning in distress.

At first Gloria appeared sympathetic, rubbing his back, urging him not to worry, but he couldn't rid himself of the idea that she was only saying what he wanted to hear.

He lived in an agony of guilt, shame and remorse until Gloria declared she was pregnant.

Then, life took on a hellish quality. He begged Gloria to have an abortion, but she refused. He appealed to her on the grounds that she already had two children she couldn't take care of properly, but that hadn't helped. After many heated conversations, Reece discovered why she had taken him home.

Although aware of Gloria, he had never been attracted to her, and despite his frequent visits to Waterhouse, he stuck by the promise he'd made to himself not to get entangled with a ghetto woman. Once he realized she was interested in him, Reece had been gentle, but firm in his refusal to spend time with her. He hadn't forgotten his mother's bad reputation, and Gloria's was even worse. She worked in the bar almost every night of the week and all the barflies in the neighborhood flocked there because of her.

The day after he slept with her, Reece got himself tested for STDs. A week later, he repeated the process. To his relief, Gloria was clean, but his problem was just beginning to grow. As her pregnancy advanced, so did her demands on his pocket. She also threatened him repeatedly with revealing her pregnancy to his wife.

His hatred grew and festered as her belly did, and he detested her for various reasons. Apart from holding him to ransom, she was destroying his mental stability. He spent too much time distracted by her threats and tantrums when she didn't get her way and to make matters much worse, his moodiness puzzled Sherryn.

By that time, Reece had apologized for his stupid behavior and told Sherryn he was drunk and had slept it off in the van the night he hadn't come home. His stink when he got home that morning had backed up his lie.

She had gradually warmed to him again, which made his mood swings inexplicable. As time passed, he relaxed and was grateful that Gloria didn't follow through on her threats, but he should have known her greed was a time bomb, waiting to explode.

His gaze caught the family portrait, still in his hand, and he told himself to stop wasting time rehashing bad memories. He decided to work from his home office, but lost more time painting disturbing mental pictures concerning Gloria, and what might happen if she died.

Thirty-Three

At home, Reece had a snack and sat down to complete the haulage log. Later on, he caught himself staring into space, tapping the paper under his fingers. It was close to the end of the day, and he was still sitting behind a desk. Bracing his feet on the floor, he rolled the chair to face the window. He hated being deskbound, but had learned to discipline himself to complete sit-down tasks when they cropped up. Now, he needed a break. A knock at the door cut into his thoughts. "Come."

Justin popped his head round the office door. "We can talk?"

"Yeah, sure," Reece said, turning the chair back to its original position.

Justin sat, hooked his leg over the arm of the chair, and got comfortable.

Reece hid his delight that Justin had come to chat. It was something they used to do before he found out about Maurice.

Justin gulped a bottle of cherry Tru-Juice, his Adam's apple bobbing. He grinned and wiped a hand across his mouth. "Boy, I was really thirsty."

"How was training?"

"Good, good."

"So what's up?"

"I've been thinking." Justin tried crushing the plastic bottle. "You remember the conversation we had the other day? About Maurice?"

"I remember."

"Well, you know when I asked what you'd do to have things back like before?"

"Yeah?"

"I shouldn't have asked you that." Justin skimmed the room before focusing on Reece. "I mean all of this isn't his fault."

"I know, and I shouldn't have said what I did. That was wrong." A sigh worked its way from deep inside him. "I agree with you. Maurice isn't responsible for what happened between me and his mother, and while he wasn't planned, his life isn't worth any less than yours or mine."

Justin nodded his understanding. "You know what though?"

"What?"

"At first I hated having him around, but he kind of grows on you, and he's far less annoying than the other little game-boy geek you have for a son. Maurice been acting kinda strange since yesterday, but for the most part, he's all right."

They exchanged a grin, after which Justin got up, sharing his intention to eat anything on the loose in the kitchen.

With his chin cupped in his hand, Reece watched Justin leave, noting how much he'd filled out in the last few months.

Reece went back to checking off the haulage trips for the week, which kept him busy for a while. When the door opened again, he yawned and raised his head.

Sherryn stepped inside and pressed the door shut behind her.

"Reece," she said, "we might need to change our plans."

‖ She perched on the edge of the chair in which Justin had sat. "You wanted to hold off talking to Maurice, but I think you better do it now."

"Why? What's he done?"

"It's what he's not doing. He's still not eating, and you know he likes his food."

Reece stopped scrolling down the list and concentrated on Sherryn.

"I can't get him to do anything, and he hasn't stopped sucking his thumb since our run-in with that woman."

Slumped against the chair, Reece rubbed his eyes. "So, he's back where he started?"

"Yeah. I'm worried about him. He was doing so well, and now he won't even look at any of the workbooks I bought him."

Reece folded his fingers together over his lips. "Where is he now?"

"Where he's been for most of the day—in front of the television, but he's not watching. As stupid as it sounds, I didn't think it was possible for worry to affect a child this way."

"I know what you mean. I was thinking the same thing while I watched him yesterday. His mother has a strong hold over him, and in spite of what we said, he still believes she'll get him." He drummed his fingers against the desk, then rolled away and got to his feet. "I'll take him for a drive."

"Okay, good. I hope it helps."

"Me too."

"I'm gonna make that call and get the earliest appointment I can to see a counselor."

"Yeah. Thanks." He held on to her arm. "By the way, the police came to see me today. I'll tell you about it when I come back."

She nodded, and they walked to the living room together where Maurice sat alone, in front of the television. An air of gloom hung around him, which led Reece to curse his own helplessness.

"Maurice?" Caught up in his world, the child didn't respond. Reece called louder and Maurice jerked and turned his head. Forcing a smile, Reece asked, "Want to go for a ride? Just you and me."

Suspicion fell over the boy's features. No doubt he was remembering that first ride he'd taken with Reece.

Ignoring Maurice's narrowed eyes and wrinkled brow, Reece put what he thought was an inviting expression on his face and held out one hand. "Come on, it's all right."

Clearly reluctant, Maurice looked from Sherryn to him and back again before getting up. His small hand slipped into Reece's, and they walked toward the front door.

When they drove away from the house, Reece's concern turned into worry.

Strapped into his seat, Maurice kept his head turned to the side, but not far enough to hide his tears. He blotted them using his shoulder and without asking any questions, Reece was certain he remembered their trip back to Waterhouse that day more than a month ago.

Deciding against saying anything just yet, Reece drove into the parking lot of a fast food restaurant and stopped.

Having dried his face when he thought Reece wasn't paying attention, Maurice examined his surroundings. If he wondered why they were parked up against a ficus hedge, he didn't ask.

Reece unlocked their seatbelts and turned toward Maurice. "You want to tell me what's wrong?"

Maurice lowered his head and sniffled. Examining his newly-cut fingernails, he refused to answer.

"I can't fix the problem if I don't know what's troubling you," Reece said.

Maurice's finger edged back into his mouth, and he spoke around it. "She say mi goin' back to live wid her."

Although he sympathized with Maurice, Reece was annoyed that the boy preferred to believe what Gloria told him over Sherryn and his promises.

"And I told you," Reece said, "that you weren't going back." He lowered his voice when Maurice looked at him with the old fear. "Didn't your mother tell you she was moving on?"

"Yeah, she say she startin' over."

"And didn't Sherryn and I explain that you'll be staying with us?"

"Yes, but mi madda want mi back."

Reece shifted, stretched his arms out before him, and gripped the wheel. What could he say to get the child to believe that he wasn't going back to some disgusting tenement yard in Waterhouse? He didn't know how many minutes passed before he got a clue as to what was going on in Maurice's mind. Small wonder he didn't think of it before, coming from the same situation as his son. He loosened his fingers from the steering and leaned closer to the boy.

"Maurice, is it that you think we don't want you, and that we're going to get rid of you the first chance we get?"

He waited, and waited some more, then listened keenly while Maurice stated his case.

"Mi madda always say you never want mi. When she get vex, she say if you coulda kill mi you woulda do it."

Shame held Reece still. Of course, Gloria knew he wouldn't have done anything like that, but the boy didn't. It explained the fear the child had of him. He hadn't wanted another child—not with her at any rate, but she refused to listen. Now he discovered her callousness went way beyond anything he expected.

How could she say something as awful as that to her child? And how could he explain to a five-and-a-half-year-old boy the reason he kept his distance? No wonder the boy felt unwanted.

Maurice interrupted this thoughts with more words. "She say she did give mi to you already, and you never want mi."

Reece couldn't help his passionate response. "That's a lie! Gloria never offered to give you up before."

He held back words he ached to speak because Maurice gaped at him, frightened. When he had his emotions reigned in, Reece continued talking. "Your mother is the one God gave you, so I'm not going to try to turn you against her, but what I will say is that I won't ever send you back to her, not even if she begs."

Maurice pulled a glistening finger out of his mouth. "Really?"

"Really." Reece smiled. "Not even if she pays me a million dollars for you."

"Not even for a trillion, million, hundred thousand dollars?"

Clearly, Brandon had taught Maurice his skewed currency values, which made Reece laugh. "Not even for that."

Maurice's laughter made Reece's eyes water for a few seconds. I must be getting soft, he told himself.

"Since we have that sorted out, would you like a hamburger?" Reece asked.

Maurice's loud giggle and bobbing head told Reece things were right again in his world.

Reece opened the door and stepped out of the van. "Come on, let's go get that burger."

Thirty-Four

A smile teased Sherryn's mouth when she looked at Maurice, who hummed Do Your Ears Hang Low while he worked at Phonics. It was his favorite song, and though Brandon made fun of him, Maurice continued to sing the nursery rhymes he'd learned from Sherryn.

"You're almost done?" she asked.

"Yep." His feet wriggled in the air. "What we doin' next?"

"I dunno. Maybe we can take an ice cream break. What d'you think?"

His smile dimmed, and Sherryn chided herself. Since the day Gloria turned up at the restaurant, ice cream didn't hold the same thrill for Maurice.

She backpedaled quickly. "Okay, what if we have some banana chips and drinks instead?"

"Can I have Kola Champagne?"

"You know soda's not good for you."

He sat up, and his shoulders drooped.

Holding back a sigh over her weakness, Sherryn gave in. "Just this once, and no more for the week, okay?"

His smile reappeared. "Yes, thanks."

Sitting at the counter in the kitchen, Maurice swung his legs from the high stool while they crunched their way through a bag of chips. Brushing salt from his cheek, she gave him a gentle reminder. "Dinner's not too far off, so you should leave some space."

He withdrew his hand from the bag. "Okay."

With her chin propped on her palm, she watched him slurp up the tangerine colored soda.

"You really like that stuff don't you?"

He nodded and showed teeth stained a light orange.

"Your mother gave it to you all the time?"

"Most o' the time."

"The sugar is bad for you, plus it rots your teeth."

Concern flooded his features. "It will rotten mi teeth fi true?"

"Yes, Maurice, and remember what I told you about speaking properly?"

"It kinda hard, Miss, because nobody talk like that in my yard."

"You don't live in that yard anymore, do you?"

He sighed. "No."

"It's not that hard, and you're a quick learner."

That raised a smile out of him. "When I go to school, I goin' do good like Brandon."

"I expect nothing less from you."

While she cleared the bag and cups off the counter, Maurice watched her, frowning. "Miss, I really not goin' back to mi madda, I mean my mother's yard?"

"Didn't Reece say you're not going back?"

Shamefaced, Maurice moved his head up and down. "Yes, but mi don'—"

"What's that you said?"

"I don't want to go back. I told him, but ... "

"But what?"

"What if she come and tief me away when you not here?"

Laughter overrode Sherryn's concerns about his speech. "Nobody comes to someone's house to steal their children."

"Yes, them do it," he said. "It name kidnapping."

Trying hard to hide her amusement, Sherryn said, "Nobody's going to kidnap you, okay?"

He seemed set to argue, so she jumped in before he got a word out. "Okay?"

"All right, but—"

"Neither your father or myself is going to allow you to be stolen. Matter of fact, we won't let you out of our sight, so take that off your mind. Your only worry should be how well you do on the next set of exercises in your workbook."

She led the way out of the kitchen. "I have to pick up the kids soon. You staying with Miss Em or coming?"

"I'm goin' to put on my sandals."

"Meet me in the living room."

"Yes, Miss."

Sherryn stopped him as he prepared to dash down the corridor. "Uh, Maurice?"

"Yes, Miss?"

"Can you call me Aunt Sherryn? Miss' makes me feel like a schoolteacher."

"Okay, Miss."

Both of them giggled and went their separate ways.

When she stood in her bedroom, she smiled at her reflection in the mirror pleased to find they were getting over each hurdle. Since living with them, Maurice had never addressed Reece by any name, which she understood. She supposed he didn't think he had the right, or perhaps was waiting for an invitation from Reece. Hearing Maurice call Reece Daddy would be painful each time she heard it, but Sherryn guessed the day was coming. She needed to prepare herself for it.

Gloria's condition came to mind and she prayed again that her fear about Reece's involvement in the attack was just the product of her overactive imagination.

Thirty-Five

Sherryn and Judith sat in Barbara's parlor, a clustered room she had decorated in a cloying shade of peach. The whoosh of the overhead fan intruded on the silence, but made the heat of the afternoon bearable.

Their host entered the room, carrying a tray of drinks. She set it on a circular table, which stood on monstrous brass feet. Barbara gave Sherryn a frosty glass of lemonade and handed Judith a Lite Beer.

They had these get-togethers once every couple of weeks, where they relaxed and caught up with the happenings in each other's lives. Barbara walked backward, holding a tumbler of her usual drink—vodka and orange juice—and sat when her calves hit the edge of the sofa. After a small sip, she pulled her sundress over her legs and flipped her hair back. "Sher, you certainly keep your business a secret."

Tired already by the explanation she was expected to give, Sherryn raised one shoulder in a casual gesture. "It's not exactly a secret, and you were in Miami. We haven't seen each other for close to a month, remember?"

"You could have told me when we spoke last week."

Shuffling her feet for something to do, Sherrryn said, "It's not exactly my favorite thing to talk about. It's hard enough to deal with."

Judith pleated the leg of her shorts and let off a pained sound that represented laughter. "Don't start me off on that subject. Anyway, Barb, I told Sher not to cut off her nose to spite her face and make matters worse. I wouldn't run that risk with a man like Reece."

Sherryn wanted to slap her. "No matter what Reece does, you defend him. You on his cheering squad or something?"

"You're still doing the nasty regularly with each other after eighteen years, and that makes him all right in my book."

"Is that all you think about?"

Barbara butted in. "Is 'cause she not getting any. Speaking of which, what's going on with Barry these days? Is he still as busy as ever?"

Judith snorted. "Is there ever a time when he's not busy trying to climb on anything in a skirt?"

Sherryn was about to comment that she didn't know how they dealt with the constant turmoil, but kept her mouth shut. She was no longer in that exclusive club where couples were faithful to each other.

"Judith says you got a new son," Barbara said, eyeing Sherryn over the rim of her glass.

"Mmm. The poor little thing doesn't know whether he's coming or going."

"So how are the kids taking it?"

"Like all kids do, they adapt."

"And your parents?"

Sherryn allowed the ice to clink together in her glass. "That's a whole other story. They've kind of withdrawn, you know like clams in a shell. They adore Reece, but they're having a hard time with this, especially Mom. Dad's not so bad, but you know how conservative they are."

Judith took another slug of beer and squinted at her. "Are they speaking to him at all?"

"Of course. My mother believes in keeping the peace, but she thinks me having Maurice is a bit much, so they haven't been to the house since he's been living there."

"I understand." Barbara nodded slowly. "I'd stay out of the way if I was in their position. It's best not to take sides in a situation like this."

Sherryn waved in Judith's direction. "Only Reece's main cheerleader over here finds it necessary to champion his cause."

Daintily, Judith drank the last of the beer and set the bottle on the table. "I'm just saving you from yourself, Sher. Left alone, you'd starve the man for the next year, which isn't helping anybody. By the way, have you given him any during the past month?"

"You know that's none of your business."

"All the same, I have to look out for both of you, not to mention talk some sense into you."

Sherryn's words were emphatic. "Reece and I are fine."

"Don't get defensive on me. You know I care about the two of you."

"Yeah, I know you do." Sherryn sipped her drink, and then tried changing the subject. "How's Pam? she asked Barbara."

"Pamela," Barbara said, "is out of control, as always. Her father is also in denial—as usual. How I ended up with such a promiscuous child is beyond me. I finally gave up and got her some birth control pills. The last thing I want is for her to bring home some pickney for me to raise in my old age. I bet yours are as well behaved, as ever."

"Yeah, lucky for me. They get up to the usual stuff, but thankfully nothing too far out of the ordinary."

"So," Judith asked, "how are they taking this whole thing between you and Reece?"

"You need to cut back on that stuff." Sherryn gestured toward the Lite Beer. "Barbara asked the same thing not five minutes ago. They're all dealing with it in their own way. 'Course, everybody gave Reece a hard time. I was almost sorry for him."

"I saw him on the road about a week ago," Barbara said. "He seemed a little thin."

Sherryn couldn't curb her glee. "He looks a lot thinner to me. Serve him right. Bet he'll think twice about dropping into anybody's bed next time."

Judith's tone was hopeful when she addressed Sherryn. "So, you guys are working things out then?"

"I guess."

Barbara frowned at her over the table. "You don't know?"

Sherryn shrugged and got up to stretch. "The kids sure don't want the family to split up and truthfully, I never gave Reece the impression that I planned to leave him. But one thing I do know is that if he does it again, I won't think twice about kicking him out the door."

"Life should be that simple," Judith grumbled.

"What d'you mean?" Sherryn asked, easing back onto the patterned seat.

"I should leave Barry and start over, but I've waited too long, and put up with too much crap to walk away now."

Giving Judith a sympathetic glance, Sherryn said, "If you want to salvage anything, it's never too late to walk away. Why postpone your happiness if all you're getting from him is grief?"

Wearing a sly expression, Judith crossed her legs. "As you well know, I've found a way to compensate."

Barbara stared at Judith, goggle-eyed. "You mean to say—"

"Yes, I'm seeing someone."

Sherryn shared her disapproval. "I think you're doing a little more than just seeing him."

"Yes, party pooper, I *am* doing more than seeing Troy, and what a world of good it's done me."

"What am I going to do with her?" Sherryn moaned. "What would Barry think of you seeing someone almost young enough to be your son?"

"He doesn't have a right to think anything. He lost any privileges he had with me years ago."

"But still—"

Judith uncrossed her legs and sat forward. "But still, what Sherryn? Wake up, will you? Not all of us have anything near as special as you and Reece.

"It took me a long time, but I finally opened my eyes. I won't allow myself to be dragged down by Barry and his affairs. I'll just do what I want, when I want, and I couldn't care less if he finds out."

"I can't say I blame you," Barbara said. "I've put up with the same foolishness for years. The only difference is that Winston has been a little more discreet than Barry. He actually thinks I don't know when he's seeing someone new." Sighing, she shook her head. "These men are pitiful. But I have my own life, and I'm financially independent, so I refuse to worry about the stuff I can't change."

"Amen to that," Judith cheered. "I think it's time for another beer."

While she spun the ice cubes in the lemonade, it occurred to Sherryn that her life was nowhere as complicated as her friends'. Yes, she'd been cheated on and her trust destroyed, but at least Reece hadn't thrown it in her face, expecting her to live with it. And thankfully, the tests done at the gynecologist and the lab had come back negative.

When Judith returned clutching another beer, Sherryn stretched her legs and smiled.

"You know what, Judy? Unlike most people, when you drink, you do make some sort of sense—even if your hearing suffers a little."

Judith smirked and held up the bottle. "I wouldn't be so sure of that after I've had another one of these."

Sherryn allowed her friends' banter to pass over her while she considered the things that had happened during the past month. Her life had turned upside down, but she still loved her husband, and he was trying to make amends.

Overall, life was good.

Thirty-Six

The breeze on his skin cooled the sun's heat, but Reece longed to be on his way. He'd stopped at an automotive shop on Hagley Park Road to get a part that needed changing on the van. While there, he ran into Ronald, who was leaving after purchasing wipers for the banged-up Toyota he was using as a taxi.

Reece glanced around, conscious that Ronald could be mistaken for a criminal. Not that Reece had any details, but Ronald was always in the know when certain things went down in Waterhouse. It was one thing to keep company with him there, and another to be seen with him outside the community.

Reece asked himself why Ronald hadn't tried harder to better his life, but why worry about him when he seemed content with barely getting by? If he wanted better for himself, he'd have taken up Reece's offer years ago to find employment for him. Reece supposed pride held Ronald back, not that it stopped him from asking for money now and then.

Another look at his watch had Reece shuffling to get away, and despite his warning that he had to get back to work, Ronald showed no sign of leaving the parking lot. Hiding his impatience, Reece made another attempt to get away. He glanced at his watch and opened the door of the van. "I have to get back, so ... "

"And we jus' start talkin'?"

"I have to earn some bread, Ronald."

Traffic passed back and forth on the roadway, their horns blaring, which irritated Reece more.

Ronald hitched his dark glasses up on his nose and ran a hand over his freshly-done cornrows. "I don' see you around anymore. You abandon di ol' neighborhood?"

Reece shifted from one foot to the other. "Not really, been busy. It comin' on to Christmas, so businesspeople have a whole heap o' things to move around the island."

"Oh, mi think you forget mi."

Reece opened the door and put a leg inside. "Naw, man. Nothin' like dat."

Ronald folded his arms, and a line appeared between his brows. "By the way, how Gloria son fittin' in at home?"

"Him all right. Doin' well," Reece said while edging behind the wheel. "You hear Gloria in hospital?"

Ronald nodded. "Somebody did tell me."

"Look like she get a bad beatin'."

Ronald pulled up the baggy jeans hanging around his hips and patted his waist. "Den you business?"

"Not really, because she was makin' mischief between me and Sherryn, but she is a woman and a human bein'. I wouldn't want nobody to beat up my wife like dat."

"Some gyal deserve beatin'."

Reece looked hard at him. Was there more to Ronald's words than he was saying? When Ronald continued speaking, Reece shook off his thoughts.

"Don' waste your sympathy. Gloria only business wid herself, as you well know."

"True dat, but like mi say, she's a woman, and mi kinda sorry it happen to her, even if she mek mi mad just by seeing her."

Ronald spat on the asphalt. "You obviously have time to waste. Anyway, somebody from our ends visit her, but she did still knock out."

Reece frowned and wiped the sweat off his brow. "You mean she still unconscious?"

"Yeah, mi wonder if she wi' live. Is a good t'ing she did give up di pickney dem. Wha' woulda happen if she did still have dem?"

Shrugging, Reece answered, "I don' know."

Now he was puzzled. Had the police lied to him about Gloria's condition to force a confession, or was she still out of it?

Ronald tapped the door and drew back, not quite meeting his eyes. "All right brethren, see you later."

"Yes, Ronald, take care."

Reece drove away, grateful he had escaped. How could Ronald be so callous about Gloria's beating? It wasn't as if Gloria had done anything to him. But then, Ronald lived a tough life and didn't have a steady woman to take the edge off his coarseness. That made his uncaring attitude understandable.

That same evening, Sherryn sought Reece in his office, easing into the seat across from him. "You haven't said anything about Gloria. D'you know how she is?"

He told himself to be careful. While Sherryn wanted information, she'd be suspicious if he seemed too involved. Injured or not, Gloria was responsible for the discord in their home. Ronald had at least provided information which would come in useful now.

"She's still unconscious."

Her gaze settled on him, and he wanted to squirm for no reason he could pinpoint. Still, he decided to withhold the information the police gave him. No need to worry Sherryn with Gloria's accusation—that's if the police hadn't lied.

"How do you know? Did you visit?"

Even if he had gone to the hospital, he couldn't have admitted going anywhere near Gloria. He could have found out her condition without seeing her, Sherryn would say. He also imagined Sherryn telling him that his weakness was not being able to see trouble and stay away from it. Laying his hands on the desk, he answered, "No, I saw Ronald today."

Sherryn's face went sour. "Is where you see him?"

"In the auto parts store."

"What him was doing there, lookin' somethin' to thief?"

He couldn't help the laughter that shook his body. "He was buying a pair of wiper blades."

Sherryn made a dismissive gesture with her hand. "Which no doubt, he stole the money to buy. So he said anything else?"

Had he imagined Ronald's evasiveness? Perhaps he wanted to be in the clear so badly, he was seeing shadows where none existed.

"No, that's all he said, and I didn't ask any questions."

She slouched in the seat to stare at him. "I really wonder who'd do a thing like that. Once upon a time, it was unheard of for a man to attack a woman, much less put her in a coma. What's going to become of this country of ours?"

"I wonder myself."

She sat up, pressing her knees together. "I'm wondering if we made a mistake not telling Maurice what happened.

"What you mean?"

"I was thinking that if she dies, he might be upset. She is his mother, after all."

"Somehow, I don't think he'll be devastated. Like I told you, the only person Gloria loves is herself. She has nothin' left over for Maurice, except to use him as a tool to dig money out of me."

"I was only thinking that if she dies, it'll be easier to explain if Maurice knows she's ill."

Reece smiled, knowing his adoration was plain to see. Sherryn was always thinking ahead. He was sure his emotions were still plastered on his face when she spoke. "You know I'm right, don't you?"

"Yeah, like you are most of the time."

She smiled while she preened. "Just as long as you understand that I'm the brains of this operation."

He responded to her teasing with another grin. "Oh, that's one thing I never doubt, Mrs. Allbright."

Their humor faded, and Reece soaked up the affection in her gaze, hoping things would continue to improve between them.

"By the way," she said, "remember we went to see the counselor today?"

At his nod, she continued. "It went well. She spoke to Maurice, with and without me. She thinks he's adjusting pretty well, and mentioned it would be good if you could keep the link between him and his other siblings."

Reece nodded. "I'll see what I can do, but they went to live with their father's mother, so it'll be kind of tricky to arrange for him to see them."

She bit her lip. "I'm sure we can do something at some point."

Shortly after she left his office, Reece went searching for Maurice. Brandon, Kyle, and he camped out near the tank, in a corner of the living room. Reece had cleaned the tank once already, because Brandon and

Maurice had gone overboard with the fish food. Since then, they were under strict instructions not to feed the fish without supervision. Barred from doing that, they entertained themselves by hovering in front of the tank, watching the fish lining up and hoping to be fed.

Kyle saw him first and clung to his legs. "Daddy, we watching the fish."

Reece lifted him and blew on his neck, which made him giggle. Peals of laughter escaped from his youngest when Reece hoisted him into the air.

"Mommy's coming," Justin said from the couch.

Reece threw him a grateful glance. Sherryn hated when he flung Kyle in the air, protesting that he'd vomit, or worse, slip out of his hands and crash to the floor.

"More, Daddy! More!" Kyle screamed as Sherryn walked into the room.

"Uh-oh," Justin said, giving his father an I-told-you-so look.

Sherryn took Kyle out of his grip. "Weren't you supposed to be talking to Maurice? You're just as bad as the children."

"Maurice, I need to talk to you for a minute," Reece said.

Sensing his reluctance, Reece walked over and gripped his shoulder. "Come on, there's nothing to be afraid of."

Maurice's wide eyes said otherwise, so Reece hoisted him onto his side. "This won't take long. I promise."

He plunked him on the sofa in his office and sat beside him.

Maurice waited, with his thumb twitching, for Reece to speak.

"Um, your mother, Gloria. She's in the hospital."

Expecting him to ask a question, Reece paused, but the silence continued.

"She's unconscious. You know what that is?"

Nodding, the boy asked, "Like when you sleeping, right?"

"Yeah."

"Why she uncon-sleeping?"

"Someone hit her, and hurt her head."

"She goin' to dead?"

"You know what that is?"

Maurice's cocked eyebrow conveyed outrage. "'Course, people dead every day in Waterhouse."

Fascinated, Reece followed up with a question. "How?"

"Police kill dem, gunman kill dem, sickness kill dem."

"How d'you know so much about death?"

Maurice's shoulders lifted and fell. "Everybody talk 'bout it and I hear, so I know."

Reece viewed him with new respect. Had he known so much at his age? He concluded that he might have, since he had learned much by listening to the adults around him. Ghetto residents talked about most subjects in the presence of their children, no matter how young, forgetting that they had functional ears and curious brains. His children were much more sheltered when they were Maurice's age, because both he and Sherryn were careful about what they said in front of them.

One corner of Reece's mouth turned up in a smile. Sherryn was much better, of course, and didn't hesitate to tear chunks out of him for careless statements like the one he made when Maurice had wet the bed. Turning his mind back to the conversation, he asked, "Would you be sad if your mother died?"

Reece wondered why he even asked when the boy wiggled his head from side to side with more energy than necessary.

Puzzled, Reece asked, "Not even a little bit?"

Maurice's finger went into his mouth while his other hand plucked at the collar of his polo shirt.

"Why not?"

"Gloria don' care 'bout me."

"That's what you call your mother?"

"Yeah, she say mi mus' call her so."

Reece shook his head, thinking Gloria was just as bad as his mother. While he wondered if he knew what he was doing, Reece continued asking questions.

"How d'you know she don't care about you?"

Maurice rolled his eyes before answering, as if he was talking to someone younger than himself. "'Cause she only happy when you bring money."

"Tell me something else," Reece said. "Does—did Gloria leave you and your brother and sister with anybody else when she wasn't at home?"

"Naw. She jus' ask Miss Ivy to give a eye on us, but we take care of weself."

Horrified once more that he had allowed the boy to live the kind of life he'd determined none of his children would have, Reece willed himself to continue. "Nobody ever trouble any of you?"

Cocking his head upward, the child frowned. "How you mean?"

"Nobody ever touch you in a way they shouldn't?"

A knowing expression crept over Maurice's face. "Oh, you mean like when a man and woman do dat t'ing without clothes on?"

Distracted, Reece asked, "What you know about that?"

"One time I did see—"

"Never mind that. Answer my first question."

"No, nobody ever do anyt'ing to me. Me and Kemar and Shakira always stay together."

Reece assumed those were the names of Maurice's siblings.

Sherryn's words came back to him. "I'm glad you mentioned them. Don't you miss them?"

Bottom lip pulled into his mouth, Maurice nodded. "Sometimes, but I don' 'member dem all di time."

"If you want to see them sometimes, I could talk to their grandmother," Reece said.

Maurice nodded again. "Dat sound good."

Reece slipped an arm around Maurice. "Anyway, to get back to your mother, I wanted you to know about her being in the hospital, just in case of anything."

Maurice sat up straight and asked a question. "Jus' in case she dead, you mean?"

"Yeah."

"Well, I hope she dead then," Maurice said in a matter-of-fact tone.

Reece's mouth popped open and seconds passed before he could come up with a sensible comment. "You shouldn't say things like that, Maurice. It's not nice."

"I don' mean anythin' bad. Just that if she dead, she won't come for me."

"Don't tell me you still have that on your mind?"

Maurice folded his arms and pressed his lips together, which pulled a sigh from Reece.

He stared at the clutter on the desk across from where they sat and decided against rehashing that old conversation. Verbal reinforcement was not working, so he'd have to find another way to convince Maurice that he had a permanent place in their home. But how?

Thirty-Seven

While Brandon, Kyle and Maurice played in the living room, Sherryn and her mother talked over glasses of June plum juice in the kitchen. Veronica Jones's puckered mouth and crumpled brows gave away her disapproval.

Sherryn's attention wandered to the glass-fronted cupboards, which held stoneware sets her mother only used on special occasions. When she spoke again, Sherryn tried to make sense of her words.

"I can't get over how much that boy looks like Reece. Talk about strong genes."

Sherryn's mouth quirked in a semi-smile. "You say that nearly every time you see your grandchildren."

"True." She studied Sherryn with questions in her eyes. "How are things at home?"

"As well as can be expected, I suppose."

Veronica's chin lifted and she moved her head toward the living room. "I see he's fitting in."

"His name is Maurice."

"Yes, yes, I know."

"He's not the enemy you know, Mom. Maurice is just a small boy who needs our help. Reece is the one I sometimes want to hurt."

"I understand, and I commend you for what you've done for the boy. You surprised me by how well you've handled this."

Sherryn laughed. "Me too, actually. It's something I have to live with, and I'm learning to deal with it. What makes it less painful is that Reece is trying to make it up to me." Her humor disappeared. "I'm having some terrible mood swings that worry me though."

She wondered whether there was any other contributing factor to her awful moods.

Her mother laid a hand on top of hers. "I'm surprised you're even speaking to him, knowing you."

"Put it this way, Maurice is what happened the last time I ... you know."

Her mother's thin lips twitched. "Thank God, you've learned your lesson."

"Why am I always chastised for being who I am, and yet you make allowance for Reece when he fouls up? Even my friends do it."

Her mother spread her hands, all innocence. "I don't know. Could be because Reece is more laid-back and willing to do what it takes to make up, unlike someone who shall remain nameless."

Sherryn's lips curved, but she wasn't amused. "I don't think I'm gonna ask who that is."

"I'd advise you not to think too much on the situation. Your energy will be better spent trying to repair your marriage." Her mother cocked an ear in the direction of the living room. "Any minute now they're going to drive your father mad with the noise."

Sherryn got up and pushed the chair back under the table. "I better go rescue him."

When she asked the children to be quiet, her father waved her aside. The three boys had squished themselves together on the sofa with him, listening to a story. They laughed at his dramatization of the various roles.

Since everything was under control, Sherryn took a seat in one of the sofas and watched them, waiting for the story to end.

Her father was more accepting of Maurice, and hadn't hesitated to treat him as one of the gang. Another burst of laughter came from the sofa across from Sherryn.

Maurice was participating as much as his brothers. Not long ago, he'd have watched while they had fun, unsure of himself. Now he was in the middle of the action.

Sherryn hoped he continued to thrive and forget about his life before he came to them.

When it was time to go, her father handed out the sugar-dipped, gelatin Ju-Ju's he kept for the younger kids whenever they visited.

His moustache tickled her ear while they hugged. "I know your mother's not too keen on Maurice, but she'll come around," he said close to her ear.

"I hope so," Sherryn murmured.

He stroked her cheek. "Men more readily understand and accept these things. Women take more time to deal with the whys and wherefores."

"Thanks, Dad. Mom and I spoke, so I guess maybe, with time—"

"Don't worry your head. She'll get there. Your mother doesn't hold grudges."

"I know. We'll talk," Sherryn said.

In the van, while Brandon protested, they sang Maurice's favorite songs, off key and at the top of their lungs. They tumbled into the house, still singing, and Justin begged Sherryn to take the trio upstairs so the older kids could finish watching a movie.

She got the younger boys bathed, changed, and settled in their room. After that, she plodded to her bedroom, her brain engaged in an emotional battle that was now a daily occurrence.

Reece opened sleep-hazed eyes and greeted her from the bed.

Feeling drained, Sherryn removed the emerald and gold necklace and earrings he'd given her last Christmas. For a few seconds, she stood in front of the mirror with her eyes closed. Then, she yawned and rubbed the back of her neck.

"You all right, hon?" Reece asked.

"I'm okay. I just never realized how exhausting little boys can be. Brandon and Kyle were a handful before. With Maurice added to the mix, I have a hard time keeping up with them. Dad had a ball, of course."

"Maurice is misbehaving?"

"Why d'you ask that?"

"Just what you said about them being a handful."

She shook her head. "I only meant we'll have to monitor Brandon and Maurice. When they put their mind to it, they get up to all sorts of trouble."

A question popped into her head as Reece blinked and rubbed sleep from him eyes.

"By the way, who's caring for the fish?" she asked.

He yawned. "That's a low blow, Sherryn. You know I am. They're all enthusiasm, but have no practical use. All they want to do is feed the fish."

"It's not like you didn't know it was going to happen."

"Yeah, but I still fall for it every time."

"At least it made Maurice happy and that's worth something. 'Course I hope you remember that when you're emptying pails of stale fish water."

"Remind me to come find you, Mrs. Allbright. You won't have so much talk then."

Sherryn fell on top of Reece and kissed him on the mouth, to which he responded by tickling her sides.

When he'd had enough, he turned over, so he snuggled against her and they lay that way, not talking. It was something they did unconsciously, enjoying each other's company, without making conversational demands.

Disturbing pictures flitted through Sherryn's mind and she forced her mind in another direction to avoid the resentment rearing its head.

Their door opened after a few sharp raps. Justin, Celia, and Melly poured into the room.

"Didn't you say you wanted to be left alone?" Sherryn asked.

"We did," Justin said, eyeing them with approval, "but the movie ended, so now we want to go out for something to eat."

Yawning, Reece asked, "Didn't you have dinner?"

Melly crawled on the bed with them. "Yeah, but we want a little something extra."

Sherryn rolled her head toward Reece, stretching in the meantime. "You up for this?"

He sat up and put his feet on the floor. "I suppose. We'll never hear the end of it if we don't go. Up, Melly."

She got off the bed grumbling, but the smile on her face said she was far from upset.

"All right, I'll get the boys dressed," Sherryn said. "We'll meet the rest of you downstairs in twenty minutes."

Despite their excitement, Sherryn got the three youngest dressed within ten minutes and used the other ten to make herself presentable. She applied lipstick in the mirror, recalling times in the past when they had the same impromptu activity, suggested by one of the children. Now they had one more child.

Downstairs, the children organized themselves according to which parent they wanted to drive them. The younger ones stuck with Sherryn, and the older set rode with Reece. Basking in the cool of the evening, Sherryn enjoyed the drive, following the Land Cruiser until it pulled into the parking lot of Fiona's, an ice cream parlor. Reece had obviously made the decision for the teenagers, otherwise they would have gone to a fast food restaurant.

They occupied one of the largest booth, slurping an assortment of ice cream and cake. Sherryn studied her children, not surprised to find that she counted Maurice among them.

He leaned against Brandon and said something, which made him giggle. Maurice caught her watching him and offered a smile.

She teased him with a funny face, and he cocked his head at her as Reece did sometimes.

Another glance around the table confirmed that she had made the right decision in having Reece's children. They were not perfect, but each of them had their own special qualities that enriched her life. When she realized Reece was watching her, she decided not to hide her feelings from him. Without speaking, she let him know that she still loved him.

For now, he had to be content with that.

The frequency with which they made love had decreased, but Reece put no pressure on her, which she appreciated. With time, she'd perhaps forget he'd been in Gloria's bed, and maybe she wouldn't see them together whenever he touched her.

Justin tilted his head toward her and then looked at his father. Whatever he saw must have satisfied him, because he grinned at the two of them.

If only she still had the confidence in Reece that his children did.

A sharp burst of anger seared her happiness, forcing her to fight away tears. She lowered her head and concentrated on slowing her breathing, hoping none of them noticed she was out of sorts. She gripped her spoon, anxious for her rage to fizzle and die before she somehow ruined the evening for all of them.

Thirty-Eight

Sherryn gripped the counter, more as a means of grounding herself than anything else. The policeman's sympathy unnerved her and she barely heard his words.

"I'm sorry, Mrs. Allbright. You can't see your husband now. He's still being questioned."

"In relation to what?"

"I'm not at liberty to say."

Coaxing herself to stay pleasant, Sherryn asked, "Can you at least let him know I'm here?"

"When the interrogation is over."

She held her jaw together to prevent any excess words from spilling out. "D'you have any idea how long that'll be?"

"Sorry, no."

Seething with frustration, she moved to the wooden bench. After resting there for endless minutes, her breathing condensed into stuttering puffs. She struggled to stop herself from zeroing in on something she didn't want to think about: Reece in jail.

She leaned forward, pressed her hands to her forehead and warned herself not to fall apart. Then she glanced at her watch, thankful she had already dropped off her cake orders and picked up the children.

She had called Reece to ask him to pick up several items at the supermarket near his office and was puzzled by his response. "Let me call you back."

"Why? Where are you?" she asked as suspicion clouded her thoughts.

"Police station."

"What you doin' at the station?"

He paused before he answered. "Talking to the police."

"'Bout what?"

"I'll call you as soon as I'm finished."

His vague answers had served to alarm rather than reassure her. Without delay, she had left Miss Em in charge and came down to the stationhouse.

Now, she wasn't sure when she'd be leaving. Thankfully, Justin was old enough to supervise his younger siblings if Miss Em had to go before Sherryn returned home. Despite her anxiety, she smiled, recalling the conversation she had with Justin before she left the house.

At the end of her call to Reece, she caught movement behind her and spun around.

Justin had moved from the doorway to the desk and rubbed her head. "How's my bestest old girl?"

"Who you calling an old girl? How many boys your age have a mother as young and fit as I am?"

Justin laughed raucously. "Mommy, it's so easy to wind you up."

She hid her anxiety with a smile. "What d'you want Justin Allbright?"

"Just checking up on you."

"Isn't that your father's job?"

"Yeah, well, he isn't at home, so I'm filling in."

"Mmm-hmm, what d'you really want?"

"Nothing," he protested. "Well, actually, I heard you talking. Who's getting locked up?"

"Nobody."

"So what Daddy doing at the station?"

"How d'you know I was talking to your father, and by the way, didn't your mother teach you not to eavesdrop on people?"

"You have that special thing in your voice when you're talking to Daddy, and I wasn't eavesdropping, I was in the room already."

"So how come I didn't know you were here?"

Running his thumbs under the waist of his sweatpants, Justin grinned. "All right, you caught me. Sorry, I shouldn't have listened, but why is Daddy at the station?"

Sherryn pressed a hand to her cheek, debating how much to tell Justin.

She used her judgment and decided on the truth. If Reece was arrested, it was better that Justin heard it from her rather than on the news. Reece would understand why she told Justin what was happening. He was old enough to deal with the knowledge. "Someone beat up Maurice's mother and she's in the hospital."

Justin furrowed his brow and nodded. "So the police think Daddy did it."

"Mmm-hmm."

"Daddy wouldn't do anythin' like that."

"Man, you're sure of your father."

"That's not in him. He'd beat up a man maybe, but not a woman."

"Well, he said he didn't do it."

Justin nodded. "I believe him."

"Okay, but how d'you know what your father is capable of doing?"

"We reason like grown men, and I know my father. I have no reason to doubt him. If he said he didn't do it, then it wasn't him."

Sherryn waved him away. "All right, big man, go keep an eye on the kids and give me a minute to organize myself."

A mischievous glint lit his eyes as he backed away. "Anything for you, old girl."

With a half-hearted smile and a twitch of the wrist, she had dismissed him and prepared to leave home. Hours later, she was still sitting inside the station having learned nothing.

Suddenly conscious of the stocky officer who sat at the counter eyeing her now and then, Sherryn crossed her legs and looked away from him. When next she raised her head, Reece was walking toward her, escorted by one of the officers who had come to the house. She couldn't read Reece's body language. He could be sparse with his emotions when he chose to be and yet, he often talked about her ability to lock her feelings away from him.

He stepped through the gate in the counter, surprised to see her.

Sherryn's heart plunged to her stomach. Reece's lawyer was with him. She recognized James Minott from earlier days when she helped Reece with the business. Although, they hadn't seen each other in ages, James smiled and took her hand. "Long time, Sherryn."

She looked at Reece, trying to gauge his mood when he stood next to her, but his eyes revealed nothing.

"Sorry we couldn't meet again under better circumstances, James," she said.

As though he understood what was going on in her mind, he said, "I wouldn't start worrying just yet."

She let his words wash over her and reassure her. Then she threw a dirty look at the officer manning the desk before sliding both arms around Reece's waist.

He held her close and rubbed her hair.

When she eased back, he kept both hands at her waist.

"Is it Gloria?" she asked.

He nodded. "Yeah."

"Is she dead?"

His doting expression went sour. "Yeah."

"Jesus," she whispered. Frowning at him, she said. "They really think you did it."

James touched Reece's shoulder to get his attention. "Sorry. I'll talk to you tomorrow morning. Try not to worry. It doesn't help."

"Thanks, my friend," Reece said, while they shook hands.

With a wave to her, James left the building and crossed the parking lot.

Reece slipped one arm around her shoulder and guided her down the steps toward the van. At the door, she slipped the key out of her jeans, impatient for answers. "How come they picked you up so fast?"

"Apparently, she regained consciousness long enough to accuse me of trying to kill her, so they called me in for preliminary questioning."

Reece took the key from her fingers and opened the van.

Sherryn shook her head. "I don't like this at all, Reece. What if—"

"Sher, don't worry about it. I didn't do anything."

"I know, but sometimes the wrong people get locked up."

"Trust me, they have no reason—other than Gloria's lies—to put me in jail."

"I agree, but I hope you see what happens when you get mixed up with the wrong people."

"Believe me, I know. The only thing keeping me out of lock-up is the fact that James knows what he's about, and I can account for my movements on the day she got hurt."

Sherryn bit at the tiny skin fragments sloughing from her lip, noting absently that she was dehydrated. Gripping the wheel with both hands, she willed her mind away from the picture forming in her head. Reece standing over Gloria, hands bloodied, clutching some obscure object.

She closed her eyes, and when she opened them, turned her head toward Reece, trying to clear any trace of suspicion from her mind, but couldn't avoid one obvious question. Why would Gloria say Reece had attacked her if he hadn't? Surely, she couldn't be that wicked. Was the man Sherryn loved capable of assaulting a woman? She had no reason to think he did, but Gloria had threatened everything Reece valued most.

He touched her shoulder. "I'll be behind you."

She moved her head up and down in slow motion, overcome by the sensation of being held underwater. Everything conspired to make her feel as if she were drowning and had little hope of survival.

She waited for Reece to get into the van, her mind still wrapped around Gloria's death. Would they be able to live down the impending accusation, as well as the firestorm of gossip poised to hit their family? At the thought of her wounds being ripped open again, resentment held Sherryn in a chokehold.

While she adjusted the rearview mirror, she glared at the Land Cruiser and held back the sob hurting her throat. Why did Reece have to stray and tarnish their family name with his nastiness?

Tossing her head to clear away her bitter thoughts, Sherryn drove off faster than intended. When she got to the end of the street and realized she'd left Reece behind, she slowed the vehicle.

After that, he stayed close to her bumper.

The ten-minute drive gave Sherryn time to sort through her emotions, for which she was grateful. Fear gripped her at the thought of what she might do if she yielded to the ideas taking root inside her.

At home, the two of them held a mini-conference in the kitchen. Reece rubbed the back of her hand where it rested on the dining table.

She slid a glance at him, certain he knew she was unhappy. She needed to start somewhere, no matter that what she wanted to do was slap him senseless. Instead, she took the sensible course. "Um, what did James say?"

His deep exhale washed over both their hands. "According to him, what

Gloria did was to make a dying declaration, which is considered legally binding. Based on what she said, the police have started an investigation. If this goes to court, her words will be used against me."

"So that's why you called James?"

He nodded. "It was the wise thing to do."

Her hand twitched and she made a fist while trying to keep her voice even. "So now they'll be investigating you for murder?"

Again, his breath warmed her skin. "Yeah. They'll check everything I told them before they do anything else."

His words chilled Sherryn. What if he didn't have a good enough alibi and they locked him up? Her throat constricted around the question she had long avoided, but now needed to ask. Reece would be resentful, but she had a right to some answers. She let her breath escape through her lips. "And where were you when Gloria was attacked?"

A frown descended on Reece's brows, his eyes went dark and his lips pressed together. Sherryn read disappointment in his gaze. But what did he expect? That she would continue to be compliant and devoted after what he had done to their marriage? His silence and wounded expression roused her sympathy, which she pushed away and waited for his answer.

He explained his movements in a monotone, staring at the tabletop. His activities sounded like that of any normal day, but Sherryn didn't fool herself into thinking he couldn't have included additional stops along his route. God knew he made enough time to and from work to hang out with that worthless Ronald whenever he felt the urge to visit.

She rubbed her forehead. What would it take for Reece to abandon that cursed ghetto?

Her thoughts turned to Maurice, and she met Reece's eyes, conscious of the way his mouth

drooped.

"You have to tell Maurice," she said.

"I know, but I'm not sure how to handle it."

"He won't be hysterical, so it shouldn't be hard."

"His mother wasn't his favorite person for sure."

Sherryn raised a half-smile, while Reece's thumb moved over her skin.

"Could you stay while I talk to him?" he asked.

"Sure," she said.

She sank in the seat and watched Reece leave the room, walking as if he'd aged by thirty years in the last few hours. With one hand, she massaged her forehead, wondering how she'd get through the coming storm.

Thirty-Nine

Reece walked out of the kitchen feeling as if his life had imploded. His energy was low and he was in no mood for the job that had to be done with Maurice. He held on to the doorframe before entering the living room. The children gathered there, draped over the furniture, each doing their own thing.

How did Celia concentrate on the book she was reading while Justin had the television turned up so high? He wasn't watching it, but was playing Checkers with Melly, who waved at Reece when she noticed him. A stray truck rolled toward Reece, and he stopped in time to avoid stepping on the bright yellow toy. Kyle grabbed the truck, zoomed by him again, and ran straight to where Brandon and Maurice knelt together, viewing their fish. He ran between them, bounced against the tank, and fell on his bottom, laughing. The water sloshed about, and the fish danced on the wave. The two older boys turned, heads close together, to glare at him.

Their expressions changed when Reece walked into their line of sight.

"Hey, Daddy," Brandon said, getting up to give Reece a quick hug.

Maurice turned away to stare at the fish all lined up, tails swishing expectantly.

Reece understood exactly what Maurice was feeling—a part of things, yet apart. He continued calling Sherryn 'Miss', never addressed Reece by any name, and aside from the times he'd held him when Gloria upset him, they had no further physical contact.

"What are you lot up to?"

"Nothing," Brandon said, "Kyle won't behave himself."

"He's a baby. He's entitled."

Brandon rolled his eyes. "Everybody says that when he does something silly."

"C'mon," Reece said, poking him in the side. "Give him a break. You used to do silly stuff too. Still do, when you want to."

"Dad," Brandon said, stretching out the word to two syllables while edging away to avoid being tickled.

Maurice stared into the water, hands resting above his bent knees. Reece tapped him on the shoulder. "I need to talk to you in the kitchen."

The boy straightened, but unlike every other time Reece asked to speak with him, Maurice simply wore a questioning expression. Reece guided him from the room to the sound of Brandon's protests, and curiosity from Justin, who watched them leave.

Sherryn pulled out the chair beside her. "Sit here."

Maurice sat, placing his hands in his lap.

Reece sat across from him, and for a moment, said nothing. Weighing his words, he spoke. "Maurice, your mother … your mother… "

Maurice frowned and shifted. His face grew sullen.

Reece sucked in a deep breath, but didn't say anything else.

Just do it! Sherryn urged in her mind.

Another sigh and swallow overtook Reece before he said, "Maurice, Gloria's dead. She died in hospital."

Maurice's chest caved in and he slumped in the chair, relief written all over him. He offered Sherryn a tentative smile, then turned his attention on Reece. "She dead fi true?"

"Yeah, she was conscious for a while, but she relapsed and died."

"What you call a relapse?"

"She got worse."

The boy put both hands on the table, clasped together. He included Sherryn in his next question. "She really, really dead?"

Reece nodded, now used to Maurice's habit of repeating questions until he was satisfied.

"Okay," Maurice muttered to his hands.

Sherryn tapped his chin to get him to look at her. "Aren't you even a teensy bit sad?"

His head swung from side to side as he answered, "No. Gloria never love me." Staring into her eyes, he whispered, "Not like you."

Sherryn met Reece's eyes across the table. She wanted to cry, but blinked several times and dipped her head.

Reece tore his attention away from Sherryn and looked back at his son. "Um, I might as well tell you—the police think I beat her up."

Maurice frowned. "Why them t'ink that?"

"Because Gloria told them I had something to do with it."

"I don't know why she did t'ink that." Maurice shrugged, and his voice dropped. "She lie like what."

Reece peered at him, unsure of what he'd heard. "What you said?"

"I say, she lie like what! She tell mi you hate mi and that wasn't true. Mi glad she dead."

In the hush that followed his words, Maurice sprang off the seat and ran out of the kitchen, sobbing.

Sherryn stared after him, and when her eyes fastened on Reece, he let his breath out on a heavy sigh. "No, give him some time to himself. In spite of what he said, she's the only mother he had—until recently. I'll talk to him later."

Sherryn drew her fingers over the polished surface of the table. "Fine, but I have to wonder if Gloria understood the damage she was doing when she filled his head with nonsense."

"Trust me, she knew what she was doing. That woman did everything to get back at me for not giving in to her demands."

"If you had kept your pants zipped—"

Melly appeared in the doorway, breathing hard. "Mommy, Brandon and Maurice are fighting upstairs."

Forty

Sherryn raced up the steps, leaving Melly and Reece behind. In the boys' room, Justin held on to a flailing Brandon, who had tears pouring down his cheeks.

Maurice sniffled on the edge of his bed beside Celia, who clasped a paperback between her legs. Kyle was doing his best to remove the book.

"What is going on?" Sherryn asked, standing akimbo.

Justin shrugged, while Brandon spoke up. "I came up behind him, and all I did was ask what was wrong, and he hit me."

Disappointed, Sherryn turned to Maurice. "Is that true?"

Maurice nodded. "Him was asking mi over and over, but I never mean to hit him."

"Did you hit him back, Brandon?"

Brandon lowered his head and looped his thumbs around each other. "Yeah, a few times."

"Come on, Brandon," Celia said. "It was more than a few times. I had to pull you off him."

He glared at his older sister. "Okay, so I hit him, but I—"

Sherryn clapped her hands twice. "Okay, we need time alone with Brandon, and then you're next." She pointed to Maurice. "After that, we'll talk to both of you together."

When the room was clear, she sat beside Brandon on the bed. Reece took the chair by the desk.

"Hon, what's the problem?" she asked. "You and Maurice were getting along so well."

Brandon hunched over his hands. "I don't know what's wrong with him. He won't talk and he doesn't want to play. I only hit him because he hit me first, and I was angry with him 'cause he didn't want to play with me."

Sherryn slipped an arm around him. "It's not that he doesn't want to play with you. His mother died, and Reece just told him, so he's a little blue."

"I don't think so. He hates her."

"He's a little boy, hon, and right now he's confused. When bad things happen, you have to give people time to work out their feelings, okay? It sounds to me like you were nagging him, and that's why he hit you. Now go outside and send him in."

Maurice entered as if he were facing a prison sentence. With a lift of her chin toward Reece, Sherryn let him know she wanted him to speak to the boy. Reece waved Maurice over and sat him on his leg.

"I know you're not feeling so good right now," he said, "and that Brandon can be overpowering, but you shouldn't hit out at people because you're upset—especially not your family. D'you understand?"

"Yes."

"I won't punish you this time, but if you do it again, I can't promise to be as patient with you. Okay?"

"Yes," Maurice whispered.

Reece patted him on the back. "Good, now call Brandon."

When both boys stood in front of them, Sherryn spoke. "Before anything else, the two of you are brothers. I want you to remember that, always. Families have their disagreements, but we do not fight each other. D'you understand that?"

Two nods greeted her question.

"Now say you're sorry and make sure you mean it."

Both boys mumbled their apologies.

Satisfied, Sherryn held on to Reece's arm as they left the bedroom. She turned at the doorway.

Brandon and Maurice watched each other from their individual beds. They would be fine in a few minutes.

"I think we should talk to the children now," she said, when she stood outside the door.

"What about?"

Her mouth pulled down at the corners. "That woman's death."

Reece closed his eyes and let out his breath. "Yeah. I guess we should."

She got the boys out of their room and assembled the others downstairs.

With her hand in Reece's, she outlined the reason for the sudden gathering. "We thought you should hear this from us, rather than anyone else. We told Maurice earlier that his mother died today."

The children looked at Maurice, who sat cross-legged on the floor staring at his feet. Kyle played with the cleft in Reece's chin, oblivious to the serious nature of the discussion.

"That's not all," Sherryn added, squeezing Reece's fingers.

He cleared his throat and took over from her. "The police think I did it. Someone hit her over the head, and she was in hospital before she passed away."

Melly and Celia gasped and their eyes opened wide.

Brandon sat on the floor next to Justin's legs gazing at his father with his mouth hanging open.

Justin's eyes went wide, but he said nothing.

From Melly and Celia's reaction, it was clear he hadn't told them anything, which pleased Sherryn. Her son knew how to keep things in confidence when necessary.

"Why do they think you did it?" Brandon asked.

"She told them I was the one who hit her."

Head tipped toward his father, Justin frowned. "I still don't get why she woulda do something like that."

Reece spread his hands. "Hard to say, but I didn't do it."

Justin nodded along with his sisters and made a dismissive gesture with one hand. "We know you didn't." Looking sideways at Maurice, he said, "She's one strange woman, that's for sure."

Sherryn couldn't help but admire the faith her children had in their father and wished she was as sure of his innocence. Putting her disloyal thoughts aside, she said, "We hadn't spoken about this before, but Maurice is here to stay. We never planned to send him back to his mother, so this is now his permanent home. We're hoping this will be okay with everybody."

A wordless exchange took place among the children before they let Sherryn know—again without speaking—they were all right with that decision. It was as much a surprise to her as it was to them. She hadn't known she was going to say that.

Reece crushed her fingers in his, no doubt overcome by her announcement. When she flinched, he loosened his hold and offered her an unspoken apology to which she smiled in response.

Maurice wrapped his hands around his knees and hid his face, but not before Sherryn saw his tears. She let him be for the moment, not wanting to embarrass him in front of the others.

"That's it," she said, trying to sound cheerful. "If you have any questions, you know where to find us."

She went and stood by the doorway. "Maurice, come here."

He got to his feet, head lowered, and shuffled over to her. She bent to his eye level and murmured in his ear. "Go wash your face, okay?"

He nodded and slipped past her.

She beckoned to Reece, and when he came to her, Sherryn looped her arm through his and they left the living room together. It was important that the children understood they were united, although facing a tough situation. Behind their bedroom door, Reece embraced her, kissing her neck.

"I love you," he murmured. "Don't know what I'd do without you."

She closed her eyes while his thumb caressed her cheek, and although her skin warmed under his close study, Sherryn held her silence. She tried turning off her thoughts, but couldn't. What would they do if the police charged him with Gloria's murder? All their problems could have been avoided if he had kept their marriage vows sacred.

Once the gnawing root of bitterness found its way into her mind, Sherryn turned cold and stiff in Reece's embrace.

He gazed down at her, still holding her by both arms. Disappointment clouded his eyes, but she couldn't find the voice to tell him what he so desperately wanted to hear.

Forty-One

Barbara leaned forward, frowning at Judith. "Please don't drop any cake in that chair."

Shaking her head, Judith picked bits of chocolate crumbs out of the folds of her skirt. "You and this chair. You're the only woman I know who'd decorate in peach, give me something to eat, and then hound me about sitting on the furniture."

"Say what you want. This is my space, and I don't want any rats carrying me away."

Sherryn stopped their exchange by clapping her hands. "Before the two of you start fighting over foolishness, can we get back to what we were talking about? We don't have all afternoon."

Barbara kept her eyes on Judith while speaking to Sherryn. "Like I was saying before Judy started turning my chair into a roach motel, you can order your stuff on Ebay and pay with a US credit card. You have one of those?"

Sherryn shook her head.

"You already have a local dollar card, so it won't take long. Just apply for a US currency card, and you can shop online for all those fancy cake tins you want to buy."

Judith spoke around a mouthful of cake. "Better yet, why don't we take a trip, just the three of us? No husbands, no children, no worries."

"There is the small matter of a US Visa," Sherryn pointed out.

Eyeing her as if she'd admitted having a third breast, Judith asked, "You mean you don't have a Visa?"

Sherryn giggled. "Don't need one. Most everything I want is right here."

Her smile faded as a vision of Reece reminded her that although things appeared normal on the surface, she was an emotional mess.

During the last few days, her older children had skirted around her, fearing a blow up might come with little provocation. Her latest rage had occurred because Justin made a light supper for everybody and left a sink full of dirty dishes. When she confronted him, his mouth had sagged at the corners and he'd been careful not to make eye contact while she ranted about his untidiness.

Tears of remorse had burned her, but Sherryn refused to call him back and apologize.

He plodded down the stairs to the kitchen, and she went to her room, clicked the door shut and wept with frustration over how she'd handled the situation.

It hadn't ended there. She'd paced the bedroom, seething with anger and blaming Reece for her mood swings. When he got home fifteen minutes later, she fed him a generous serving of her rage because he forgot to pick up her order of cake fat, flavoring, and icing sugar.

She'd ranted, stalking from one end of their room to the other, willing him to say something to justify the fury bubbling inside her like steam from an overheated radiator.

His refusal to engage in an argument maddened her, and she screeched at him, "Why'd you have to ruin our lives by sleeping with that whore?"

She stomped toward him. A crack vibrated up her arm, and his head jerked sideways.

Hiding from the accusation she expected to find in his eyes, Sherryn gawked at the blood trickling from his lip. Shock propelled her toward the bed, where she lay down working through what she'd done. In backhanding Reece across the mouth, the ring on her finger had twisted and the diamond setting had cut his lip.

Worse than that, she couldn't remember the last time she had occasion to slap any of her children, and never with such violence. Unable to bear what she'd done, she screamed at him. "Get out! Get out, and don't come back! "

His eyes went dark, and he tried reasoning with her, but she covered her ears and shouted, "How many times do I have to tell you? Get out!"

Someone knocked at the door and it opened before either of them gave permission. Justin stood outside, his chest heaving. "Is what happen?"

Reece tried blotting the blood using the sleeve of his dark-blue shirt, but Justin caught the movement. His gaze turned reproachful, but he didn't say anything.

Maurice appeared next.

Then Brandon poked his head around Justin, looking from Reece to her before asking, "Mommy, you're all right?"

On catching Maurice's stricken expression, she nodded, unable to say anything.

Maurice looked back and forth between Reece and her, before he turned and ran away.

A flurry of hurried steps took her into the bathroom to stare in the mirror.

What's wrong with me? She asked her reflection. She couldn't continue like this. It wasn't fair to herself or anybody else.

They left her alone after that, and she pretended to be asleep when Reece slipped into bed in the early hours of the morning and touched his lips to her cheek. Hot tears had trickled into her pillow while she wondered how it was possible to love him more, although he'd destroyed her trust. And how was he capable of such tenderness after the way she'd treated him?

The thought brought tears to her eyes again. She squeezed back the tears and sat up, her attention captured by something Barbara had said. "What was that?"

"I was asking whether you saw the newspaper today. There's a story about Reece's, um, the murder, along with the fact that the crime has not yet been solved. It, ah—"

Barbara shook her glass, raising a tinkle from the ice cubes, which did little to disguise her discomfort.

Smoothing a hand over her linen pants, Sherryn asked, "What else did it say?"

"Not much." Barbara slipped on her sandals and got up, shaking out the folds of her dress.

"Since it's *not much*, bring the paper with you when you're coming back."

Barbara's delicate features contracted in a frown. "You sure? It's not that important."

"Well, you mentioned it."

After sipping her drink, Barbara murmured, "Me and my big mouth."

"Yeah," Judith agreed. "And it gets even bigger after you've had a few of those."

After throwing Judith a glare, Barbara left the room.

"Seriously though," Judith continued. "You don't think Barb's drinking too much Vodka?"

"I'm sure she can handle her stuff," Sherryn said.

Her comment was disproved when Barbara returned with a fresh drink, tossed the paper to her, missed, and came close to toppling into the chair.

"Careful." Judith cocked a brow at her. "You might hurt yourself."

"Thanks. I'm okay."

Sherryn found the article and scanned it, wanting to scream when she read about Reece's 'involvement with the deceased'. The paper reported that Gloria's murder might have resulted from her part in a love triangle with Reece and another man whom the police were seeking.

Sherryn flung the paper aside after sucking her teeth. "Where they get all this trash? Do they even care that he has a family?"

"Of course not," Judith said. "They're only interested in selling papers."

Sherryn tracked back and forth across the carpet, her arms folded. "Sometimes I could just kill Reece. I don't know how much more of this I can take."

Judith put out a hand to stop her. "Sherryn, I understand, believe me, but you have to calm down. You also need to remember that all of this will come up because of the murder, which is an extraordinary factor. I'm sure Reece—"

"Don't even mention his name to me, Judith. Right now, I'm so mad I could—"

"Judy's right," Barbara added. "You're not doing yourself any good. The best thing to do is—"

"Don't presume to tell me the best thing to do, Barbara. I'm not in the mood for it."

Judith spoke up, fixing Sherryn with a stare. "Your problem is that you're too spoilt. Don't think I'm trying to downplay what Reece did, but you need to remember that others have it much worse than you. 'Could be Reece was a womanizer like our husbands, but he's not. For heaven's sake, get a grip and hold it together."

Sherryn couldn't believe what she'd heard. "You don't know what I'm going through, and maybe I'm not prepared to settle, like both of you."

Sherryn's words were factual. All of them understood that, but Barbara and Judith stared at her, clearly insulted. Rubbing a hand over her forehead, Sherryn dropped into the sofa. "I'm sorry. I shouldn't have said that."

"It's what you meant," Judith said and allowed her hair to fall forward to hide her expression, but her flushed skin gave away her embarrassment.

"Yes, well. That's true." Sherryn touched Judith's arm. "But still, I shouldn't have said it. I understand all the reasons you've both stayed with your husbands, but this whole thing has me confused, and I really don't know what I want to do."

"It's your decision of course," Barbara said. "Just don't take too long to make up your mind. It's not impossible for Reece to get fed up and—"

"Don't go there Barbara."

The older woman held up both hands. "Fine. I rest my case. But in the event—"

"Give it up, Barb. This is my marriage." Sherryn lifted her handbag from the floor and got up. "Can I take the paper?"

"Sure."

"I'll catch you girls later."

"Try not to be too hard on Reece," Judith called after her.

"Yeah, yeah," Sherryn muttered on her way to the front door. "Let's see who can stop me."

Forty-Two

Sherryn's decision to put Reece through hell followed her into the evening while the rational side of her brain urged her to stand down. Something alien egged her on, over which she had little control.

Reece was late getting home, which made things worse. She stewed over the paper, reading and re-reading the article until she could recite the words. The van's engine alerted her to Reece's arrival. A few short months ago, she'd have looked forward to him coming in to mess with her.

Lately, his greeting was cautious until he knew what kind of mood she was having.

Rebellion sprang to life at that thought. She wasn't the one at fault.

She straightened trinkets on the furniture that didn't need fixing, knowing it would take him a while to get to the bedroom. He'd move through the house, checking on the children's activities before coming to her. It took him twelve minutes to reach their room, which was average.

He walked in, undoing his cuffs, and sat on his side of the bed. "Hey, Sherryn."

She was ready for him, shaking the paper. "Don't 'hey, Sherryn' me. Did you see today's paper?"

He closed his eyes instead of answering.

"So you did, huh? My husband, Maurice Allbright—involved in a love triangle!"

He turned so he could see her better. "What I did with Gloria had nothing to do with love."

"Oh really? So what was it you had with her all this time?"

He got up, and his unbuttoned shirt revealed the wiry hair covering his chest. "I told you, Sherryn. It only happened one time."

"It was one time too many! I just can't get past it, Reece. I wish I could, but I can't."

As sobs shook her body, Reece's arms enfolded her. She inhaled the lingering scent of his musky cologne, listening to his heart thudding in his chest. For the briefest of moments, she clung to him before antagonism took over, and she jerked away, slapping at him with both hands.

"How can I forget when every time I turn around, there's something to remind me of it? I can't do this anymore, Reece. I can't."

He grabbed her arms and squeezed, cutting off her circulation. "No, Sherryn. Don't."

Wriggling away from him, she screamed, "I can't live with it. Please go, Reece. Just go."

His brows drew together, and he took rapid steps toward her. "Sherryn, what are you saying?"

"I want you to go." A painful ball expanded in her throat, but she forced the last word around it. "Tonight."

Her resolution wavered when Reece's eyes watered.

He blinked, licked his lips, and walked away. At the door, he gazed at her for a long moment, drew his shirt together, and then he was gone.

Sherryn gulped, but the swelling in her throat wouldn't go away. She swiped her face with the sleeve of her shirt and went to the window.

In the driveway, Reece approached the van. When he tilted his head upward, she stumbled backward, sobbing. She curled on the bed, listening to the engine fire up. The usual annoying beeps indicated he was reversing from their driveway. A sharp screech sounded from the road below, and the van roared away, taking what little composure she had left. She sobbed into Reece's pillow, certain she needed to see a therapist because she had now done her worst.

Where had Reece gone? He hadn't stopped to take anything with him. What if he did something stupid? What was she going to say to the children if he didn't come back?

She rolled onto her back to stare at the blank television screen, fighting the sea of self-pity in which she was about to drown. She'd talk to the children in a few minutes. Right now, she didn't know what to say, so she gave herself time by thinking back to happier days with Reece.

Some time later she stirred, under the impression she was being watched.

Justin sat at the foot of her bed. Celia and Melly stood over him, and all three spoke in whispers.

Sherryn hadn't heard them enter the room. Her heart ached as she eased up against the carved headboard, wondering if she'd be able to find words to tell them what she had done.

Justin turned away, and she supposed he wanted to hide the disapproval written all over his handsome features. He stared at the yellow drapes brushing the floor.

Melly nudged him before he faced Sherryn, piercing her with his father's eyes. "Mommy, you put out Daddy?"

Was there any significance to the fact that all of them wore white? Shaking her head, Sherryn put aside her flight of fancy that white was a symbol of purity and her children, in their innocence, were ready to find her guilty although their father was the one who had done her wrong. Dragging her attention from the white tee-shirts, she looked at each child, seeing their father in their steady gazes.

Nodding, she said, "Yes, I asked him to go."

Justin spoke to his clasped hands, his voice low. "But why, Mommy? You said you wouldn't do anything without telling us."

"Sometimes it's just not possible to consult. I know I promised, but it just happened. Did your father tell you he was leaving?"

Justin put his head in his hands. "Him just say him leaving for a while."

How could he be gone for a while, and he didn't take any personal items?

Sherryn's eyes smarted and her throat tightened when reality hit again. She'd told Reece to go. The shock had probably stopped him from taking anything.

Her lips took on a petulant curl. Why make excuses for him? She had to do what was best for her. But if she had done the right thing, why did she feel this was the worst day she had ever lived? She rubbed her forehead and reminded herself the children came first. She owed it to them not to fall to pieces, though her insides felt as if Reece had taken a vital part of her when he left.

Curling the end of one of her plaits around her finger, Celia blinked hard and asked, "Where did he go?"

"I don't know. We didn't discuss it."

"It's all right, Mommy. We'll call him and find out," Melly said.

Trying not to cry, Sherryn stilled her trembling hands while her children hugged and kissed her. They filed out of the room and when he got to the doorway, Justin said he'd check on her later.

She assumed he was coming back to talk, but she still had no explanation for the bout of hysteria, which made her force Reece out of their home.

Exhaustion threatened to hold her down in bed, but Sherryn had a job to do, so about an hour later, she went in search of Maurice.

He went still when he looked up from the puzzle Brandon and he were arranging in their bedroom.

"Can I talk to you for a little bit?" she asked, putting on a facsimile of a smile.

Maurice got up and moved toward her, while Brandon begged him not to take too long to come back.

Sherryn walked ahead of him to her bedroom, where she paused outside before deciding to go down to the office. There, she sat on the small sofa, patted the seat beside her, and pretended not to see how Maurice hesitated before settling at the other end. She positioned herself so she faced him, but didn't try to touch him.

"Um, about what happened this evening. Your father and I had a disagreement which had nothing to do with you."

He didn't say anything, but squinted at her. It was clear he thought she was lying. She put out her hand, and he edged away, hunching in on himself.

"Maurice, have I ever hit you?" she whispered.

He rested one arm on the sofa, leaning away from her. "No."

"So why are you shifting as if you think I'm going to slap you?"

He spoke so quietly, she barely caught his words. "Because you did lick him." He scratched at the ridges on his shorts. "Just like how Gloria used to lick me."

Upset at being likened to his mother, Sherryn sprang from the seat, startling them both.

Maurice cowered in the corner of the chair, staring at her.

Sighing, she dropped onto the sofa and patted his knee. "I'm not going to hit you, okay? Your dad and I have some things to work through, and then we'll be fine."

"So, why him not here?"

"I, uh, he'll be back in due course."

He frowned. "What that mean?"

"It means he'll be back soon."

Maurice's frown stayed in place. "Tonight?"

"Not exactly," she mumbled. "Maybe tomorrow, or the day after."

"What goin' to happen to me if him don' come back?"

A smile lifted one corner of her mouth, and she squeezed his shoulder. "Anybody ever told you, you worry too much?"

He shook his head, bit his lip, and then sighed. "Is just dat mi madda dead, and if him gone ... "

She started to correct his speech, but changed her mind. Language could wait until this crisis was past. "Maurice, trust me, you'll be fine. Reece will come home, and things will go back to normal."

His honey-colored eyes warned her not to fool him. "You promise?"

Suppressing her doubts, Sherryn pulled him close. "Yes, Maurice. I promise."

After he left, Sherryn stared across the room, swamped by guilt. What good would their sessions with the counselor do if she caused more upheaval in Maurice's life? As it was, she'd probably undone the psychiatrist's work by her actions this evening.

She got to her feet, rubbing her forehead. She'd solve that problem later. Now, she had to figure out where Reece had gone.

Forty-Three

"Anything more for you?" the bartender asked, sounding cheerful.

Reece shook his head and drained the remaining amber liquid from the tumbler. Wisdom dictated that two drinks were more than enough.

His phone rang when he set the glass down. He unhitched the cellular from his belt and squinted at the display. Someone was calling from home.

Striding out of the open-air bar, he headed to the room he'd rented for the night. His heart pumped with anticipation, as he hoped the caller was Sherryn, but instinct said it wouldn't be her. Justin, more likely than not.

"Daddy?" Celia's echoing voice let him know immediately he was on speakerphone.

The fact that Justin hadn't taken the lead surprised him, but Reece didn't have time to figure that one out.

"Yes, hon, I know why you're calling. I'm okay."

"Mommy ... we ... when you coming home, Daddy?"

"When Mommy says I can."

The plastic card from his pocket opened the lock. He walked into the room and flicked the light on before kicking the door shut. Massaging his forehead, he trudged past the pocket-sized bathroom and into the compact space where the drapes matched the gold and green comforter on the bed.

"And when is that going to be?" Celia asked.

"Honey, I don't know."

"Which hotel you staying at?" Justin asked.

"Resthaven Inn."

"Since you never take anything, what you goin' to wear?"

Justin's question stopped Reece in the middle of peeling off his socks. "It won't be hard to get a few things. I can do that in the morning."

"Daddy? Make sure you get something to eat," Melaine said, her distress plain to hear. "And please make up with Mommy as soon as you can." Her voice dropped a few notches. He frowned, concentrating hard to follow her words. "We miss you already."

Reece stiffened and pressed the phone closer to his ear.

One of them sobbed in the background. He groaned, fairly certain it was his younger daughter.

"Celia, please don't cry." He pinched the flesh between his brows, wishing he could go back and change the past. "Honey, pick up the phone."

She did, sniffling into the earpiece. He spoke as if she were an adult, knowing she would understand the intent of his words. "I know how this is affecting all of you, but it can't be undone. I'll do everything I can to fix things between your mother and me. I won't rest until I do, okay?"

She didn't answer, but her continuing sobs twisted his gut and made him feel useless.

"Okay, hon?"

She whispered yes, but the soft cries continued.

Justin came on the line. "We're gonna go now."

He cleared his throat, but Reece heard the threat of tears in his son's voice. "Come home soon, Daddy."

"I'll do my best," Reece said.

He wanted to throw the phone against the wall. The violence might have relieved his frustration, but the underlying problem wouldn't be solved. On the way into the shower, he tried to figure out what had prompted Sherryn to tell him to leave. Though he was aware of her mood swings, he'd had no alternative but to be patient since he was the root cause of her unhappiness. He'd waited for the next bout, but hadn't anticipated her throwing him out.

His anxiety got worse when he remembered Maurice, who had to be going through one of his withdrawal episodes now that Reece wasn't at home. The boy would wonder if he'd be sent away next.

Reece slipped out of his work clothes, dropping them on the bath mat while calming his fears. He didn't need to worry. Sherryn would do everything to ensure Maurice was comfortable; he could depend on her for that.

He washed his hair for want of something to do. Wearing a towel, he sat on the side of the double bed, working out how to fill the rest of the evening. It didn't make sense to sit around doing nothing.

He eyed his discarded clothing with distaste, but decided to put them on, minus his boxers. He might as well purchase the things he'd need for the next few days. With depression weighing him down, he got the keys off the bureau, and headed into the night.

Close to Half-Way-Tree, he visited the store where Sherryn bought much of their children's clothing. The winking lights in the shop windows reminded him that Christmas was just over a month away. He shut away doubts as to whether he'd be home by then and purchased a few suits of clothing and personal items from the men's department.

On his way back to the hotel, a spark of defiance encouraged him to swing the van around and head toward Waterhouse. Nobody there would reject him.

The resident band of mongrels put up a din when he hammered on a zinc gate, reinforced by a wooden frame and capped nails that had long turned rusty.

"Comin'!"

Ronald's aggravated expression matched the irritation in his voice, when he yanked the gate open. "A wha' happen, man? Why you beatin' down di gate?"

He squinted at Reece under the streetlight. "Oh, is you. Wha' happen?"

"Nothing. We goin' for a drink."

Ronald let go of the gate, and spoke grudgingly. "All right den. Gimme a minute. Mi soon come."

He reentered the yard, squeezing past a brown and white dog trying to escape into the street. Reece didn't care that Ronald wasn't happy to see him; he simply needed company. So much for thinking he wouldn't be rejected. These days, he couldn't do anything right, it seemed.

He pushed away the warning in the back of his head that this was exactly how the incident with Gloria had started. He leaned against the van, assuring himself he had things under control.

A young woman went past him, wearing a tiny pair of shorts and a tank top that revealed more than it concealed.

"Big man," she called, with a hopeful glint in her eyes.

Reece raised a hand in silent acknowledgement because she'd take anything else as encouragement.

When he didn't respond to her unspoken invitation, she threw him a last look over her shoulder and continued down the rutted sidewalk.

Ronald came back wearing a black football jersey and three-quarter jeans.

Reece reminded himself not to have too much to drink, and set off down the sidewalk to the bar on the corner.

They'd be safe there as Miss Sylvia, the barmaid, was a lumpy woman in her fifties.

"Why you choose to stop 'ere, man? Who wan' to see Miss Sylvia hairy chin?" Ronald asked.

Swallowing laughter, Reece chucked his friend on the shoulder. "Jus' calm down. We not stayin' long."

They greeted two old men slumped over tumblers of clear liquid—most likely, white rum—and sat on the high stools lining the bar. Under the soft light, Reece examined the opened bottles of liquor on the counter behind the bar. A dusty display of beer and wine bottles stood on buckling semi-circular shelves. Reminding himself again not to go overboard, Reece tuned in to Ronald's bad-tempered muttering.

His grumbling stopped only when a woman came through the bamboo curtain and greeted them with a smile. A gold filling glinted from the side of her mouth. She was attractive in a common sort of way—the usual weave, and tight tank top and jeans fitted on a plump, shapely body. Easing closer to the counter, Ronald returned her smile.

"What happen, Baby-love?"

Light bounced off her gold tooth. "Good evening. How you do?"

"Me all right," Ronald said. "Weh Miss Sylvia?"

"Is her night off tonight." The woman batted super-long lashes at both men. "So what you havin'?"

Ronald hunched on the edge of the Formica-covered counter. "What you name?"

She glanced over at Reece. "Kimisha."

"Well, Kimisha, I want a bottle of Guinness. Reece wha' you havin'?"

"Lite Beer."

The barmaid frowned at him. "Lite Beer? A big man like you?"

"Jus' bring di beer."

She flounced away to yank the fridge door open. The thump of the bottles on the counter conveyed her displeasure.

Reece hoped she didn't get any splinters in his beer from her heavy-handed use of the metal opener.

"Is wha' wrong, baby?" Ronald asked. "Mine you sour mi Guinness wid dat face."

Her nostrils flared and she cut her eyes at Ronald, to Reece's amusement.

Ronald took objection and his quick temper ignited. "Eh, mind you manners. You is here to serve di customas, not to run dem out di bar!"

With an extended hiss of the teeth and a flash of synthetic hair, she disappeared into the darkness beyond the clicking bamboo curtain.

"Some a dem barmaid ya don' have no manners," Ronald declared, before sipping his stout.

"Mmm."

"So, how you and di wife?"

Reece placed the beer on the counter. "Not so good. Sherryn still upset, and now that Gloria dead, t'ings kinda up in di air."

"Boy, Sherryn did always too sensitive." Ronald scratched his ear and then looked at Reece. "Jus' mek she understan' dat Gloria was a mistake. Now dat she dead, di problem solve, don't it?"

Reece stopped short of shaking his head. "It don' matter dat she dead. Sherryn still have a problem wid di whole t'ing."

Ronald pursed his lips, and then smirked. "Woman sure complicated. If Sherryn was my wife, you know what mi woulda do?"

"Mmm." Reece didn't continue the conversation simply to avoid getting into an unnecessary argument. Ronald's answer to any disagreement with women was to beat them into submission.

That wasn't Reece's style and never would be. He chuckled at the image of him trying something like that with Sherryn. She'd call the police to lock him up, after she castrated him.

Following on Ronald's six Guinnesses, his five beers, three shots of Appleton, plus a whole lot of the barmaid's attitude, Reece paid the bill. Despite the advice he'd given himself, he'd still had too much to drink. Another bit of defiance that wouldn't hurt anybody but him.

He walked with Ronald up the street, where he had left the van, and at forty miles per hour, followed the white lines back to the hotel to crash for the night. He didn't take off his clothes, nor did he turn out the light.

Ignoring the lightheadedness that came from drinking on an empty stomach, he flung a hand over the pillow next to him and fell into a deep sleep, filled with images of skimpily clad women grinding under him in bed.

Forty-Four

The throbbing behind his eyelids woke Reece. He groaned, wondering what day it was. Tuesday? Wednesday? Who cared? He twisted his head to one side, and in the shadows, a woman lay beside him in bed.

He turned away to curl on his side and rub his pounding forehead. He must have died and gone to hell because someone continued to beat the inside of his head with a gong and his mouth was as dry as a desert.

Then he remembered the woman beside him.

Oh, God!

He hurled himself off the bed, unwilling to rely on the light from the lamp, or his mixed up brain. Scrambling across the floor, he grabbed the plastic handle controlling the drapes and twisted it hard, then turned to confront his destruction.

His breath deserted him, and he sagged against the wall. Thank God. The bed was empty, save for the pillows and the rumpled sheets.

Head bent low, he searched for the phone, and when he found it, flopped onto the mattress to sit. The display on the phone read eight-thirty.

He called the office, wincing when the younger of the two clerks answered, "Allbright Haulage," in a chirpy voice.

Oh, to be his age and without a care in the world.

"Good morning. Is Maureen in as yet?"

"No, sir. Should I give her a message?"

"Sure. I won't be in today. If she needs me, she can reach me on my cell phone."

A long shower and a few mouthfuls of tap water didn't improve his condition. Back in bed, his stomach kept up its rumbling, but he ignored it, hands folded behind his head.

The children were all in school by this time, except for Maurice, who would be at home with Sherryn.

How was she coping? Was she thinking about him at all? Did she even care that for the first time in eighteen years, they hadn't spoken for more than twelve hours? What was she doing? Maybe setting exercises for Maurice before she settled down to work at her desk.

Miss Em would be bustling about the house tidying up, and he should be at work.

But what was the point of going there to sit around staring into space? Maureen, his assistant, had stopped asking what was wrong, but continued to keep a concerned eye on him, when she thought he couldn't see her. Would he even feel like going to work tomorrow? Right now, if he didn't have to get up, he'd stay put.

At noon, when the stirring in his belly turned to a less-than-subtle roar with accompanying nausea, he got up and ventured to the restaurant attached to the main building. Under different circumstances, the small terrace might have been a pleasant place to pass some time. A tangle of red, white, and tangerine bougainvillea surrounded the white latticework enclosure, but Reece barely noticed. He sipped hot coffee and with workman-like determination, ate the pumpkin-rice, steamed fish, and vegetables set before him.

After he signed the chit, he strolled back to the room, hung the Do Not Disturb sign outside the door, and locked it. The nausea he'd fought off returned in full force, sending him to the bathroom to retch until everything he had eaten swirled together in a multi-colored mess in the toilet.

After rinsing his mouth, he stretched out on the bed and picked up the phone to check if perhaps Sherryn had called.

No dice.

He checked the battery level and found that the phone needed charging. Later, he'd buy a charger.

For now, he didn't have anything pressing to do or any place else to be.

He closed his eyes, accepting the relief that sleep offered.

Forty-Five

Maurice smiled at her, but his eyes gave away his anxiety. He turned his head toward the window, but Sherryn guessed he saw nothing as they drove past the houses built on sprawling lots of land.

The gloomy silence earlier on hadn't done anything to lessen his fears. While Brandon had concentrated on getting to the next level of the game on his PS Vita, which now rested inside the dashboard, Justin and Melly stared out the window, and Celia pretended to read. Kyle nattered to himself, but every so often asked "Where Daddy?"

Living in the same space as Reece didn't give her enough time or space to work through her feelings. She hated disrupting their lives, but what choice did she have?

The ring, the bottles of perfume she didn't need, and the flowers all boxed her in. Reece even gave her a silly musical card, knowing the gifts did nothing to change the situation. Why did men think material things had any effect when they fouled up? Maybe they could pacify other women, but not her.

She glanced at Maurice, who now slouched in the seat, staring ahead.

Maybe with time apart, she could figure out a way forward. The trouble was, being away from Reece wasn't what she wanted. The coldness of the king size bed was proof of that. She'd lain in one position all night, acutely aware of his absence. No matter that their bed was huge, Reece surrounded her when they slept.

She frowned, wondering whether the children had spoken to him before they left home, but she forgot to ask and it was too late now since they were all in school. After she pulled into the yard and parked the van, she stopped Maurice before he jumped down.

"Would you like to talk to your father?" she asked.

He answered yes after narrowing his eyes and looking hard at her.

Leaving him in her office after she dialed Reece's number, Sherryn went to get them both a drink. On her return, she handed him a glass of orange juice and placed the other on her desk. "You got him?"

"No, it say, please leave your name and a message."

Nibbling her lower lip, she dialed the number again, ready to hand the phone to Maurice if Reece answered. She too got the standard recording. Maybe his phone was off, or maybe the battery had run down, since his usage was heavy. After weighing her options, she called the office and was relieved it wasn't Maureen who answered.

"May I speak with Mr. Allbright, please?"

"I'm sorry, Ma'am, he won't be in today."

"Thank you."

Where on earth was Reece? Why wasn't he at work? Had something happened to him?

Her thoughts churned and her stomach knotted, preventing her from thinking straight. Where had Justin said his father was staying? Seconds later, the name of the hotel came back to her and she spun through the phone book to find the telephone number.

"Hello, can you connect me to Mr. Allbright's room, please?"

She forgot to hand the phone back to Maurice, who hadn't taken his eyes off her. Instead, she paced, keeping the phone to her ear until the voicemail kicked in. Stifling the need to howl with frustration, Sherryn dropped the phone on the desk and sat down.

Maurice's question broke her absorption. "You ca'an find him?"

Her first reaction was to snap at him, but she couldn't. Rather than upset him further, she simply shook her head. When she reached for the phone again, her elbow butted the glass she had rested on the desk. Quickly, she righted it, but not before orange liquid splashed across the wood and onto a notepad.

Maurice moved the pencil cup out of the way, and she snagged a roll of hand towels to mop up, cursing beneath her breath. She dropped the sodden lump into the garbage bin. Though she wanted to get rid of the stickiness on her fingers, she was too upset to leave the room.

Maurice watched her from the side of the desk, but she didn't have the energy to try and comfort him. Instead, she sat with both hands cupping her cheeks while fighting back tears.

It wasn't like Reece to be absent from work, so where on earth was he?

Forty-Six

By four-thirty Reece roused himself and left the hotel premises. He was back by five-thirty with a new charger. By five forty-five, he was scrolling through his messages with the phone connected to the plug.

The office had called twice, and his home number appeared more than a dozen times, starting at nine-fifteen. He figured Sherryn had made some of the calls, and was tempted to ring her, but he wasn't sure how she would respond. Ignoring the other listed numbers, he called home.

The first genuine smile for the past twenty-four hours crossed his face when Brandon yelled hello in his ear.

"Hey, Brandon. You all right? Where's Justin?"

"Daddy, Maurice said—"

Brandon's words ended in mid-sentence as Justin took Reece to task. "Daddy, what happened to your phone? I've been calling you since I got home from school."

"Sorry, the phone went dead. Let me talk back to Brandon for a second."

Brandon aired his grouse right away. "Daddy? Justin grabbed the phone out of my hand—"

"I know. I hope you and Maurice haven't been driving your mother crazy."

"Noooo. When you coming home?"

"Soon. Now put Justin on the line."

A bit of a shuffle took place before Justin got the phone.

"How's your mother and your sisters?"

"Mommy kinda spaced out. She here, but she not here. She prob'ly missing you. Melly and Celia are all right. Dem helping me keep an eye on the boys." A few seconds of silence fell between them before Justin asked, "You want me to see if Mommy will talk to you?"

"Yeah."

Seconds turned into minutes before another round of shuffling went on.

"Hello?"

"Sherryn. I was checking on the kids and—"

"I tried calling this morning, but, um, you didn't answer the phone."

"The battery was dead."

"Okay."

"Justin says he's taking care of things."

"Yes, he is."

Disappointment curled in Reece's belly. Obviously, Sherryn had nothing to say to him so he figured he'd put them both out of their misery. "Is Maurice close by?"

"Hold a second."

"Hello?" Maurice said, his voice low and tentative.

"You hanging in there?"

"Yeah, but when you comin' back?"

Conscious that he had no grounds on which to speak, Reece said, "Soon."

"You sure?"

Reece crawled out on a shaky limb, hoping he wouldn't fall off and be proven a liar. "Before you even start to miss me, I'll be home."

"Jus' make sure."

"I will. Lemme talk to Justin, please."

Reece stared at the tiles, agonizing over the stilted conversation he'd just had with the woman he loved.

"Yeah, Daddy."

"When you hang up, please tell your mother I love her."

 "Why you never say it to her when she was on the phone?"

"The time wasn't right. Ensure you check all the windows and doors before you go to bed, you hear?

"Yes, Dad. Take care of yourself. I'll call before school tomorrow."

Reece imagined Justin shaking his head. He was Dad again, which wasn't good.

Neither of them hung up. On Reece's part, he didn't want to be disconnected from them, but as he breathed out and got ready to cut the connection, Justin spoke.

"When you goin' to try and talk to Mommy?"

"Soon."

The teenager's sigh hinted at his impatience. "Don't leave it too long."

On his own again, Reece switched on the television and scrolled through the cable channels, desperate to stay occupied. He was hungry, but wary of eating anything in case he vomited again. To take his mind off food, he looked around the small space he'd now lived in for a day. The room was a poor substitute for the rambling house he shared with Sherryn and the children. Funny how he'd always taken his office for granted. Now, he missed sitting at his desk, never mind that all he'd done there lately was reflect on the mess his life had become.

His thoughts turned to Maurice, but he reassured himself once more that Sherryn would see to it he was all right.

Reece moved to the window to stare at the peach blooms on the hibiscus hedge. He settled his weight on the ledge, facing something he had avoided for a long time. His irrational jealousy over the years had led him to his current disaster. The explanation he'd given Sherryn for how he ended up sleeping with Gloria was, at best, stupid.

His inability to deal with Sherryn's desire for independence had blinded him, and his insecurity was such that he wanted Sherryn to need him. Well, so much for that. Finding that bankbook had shocked him to the core. Sherryn had enough money saved to do without him and still provide for herself and their kids.

The sexual assault on her that day more than six years ago, and his comment about owning her body if not her mind, was more of a way to prove to himself that he still had some measure of control over her than anything else.

But bolstering his self-esteem had come at too high a cost. He'd shot his mouth off, not realizing their marriage wasn't about one-upmanship, or his sexual prowess. It was an alliance of mutual love and trust. Sherryn could have left him any time, if she'd intended to—only he was too tangled up in his need for reassurance to see it.

Groaning with disgust, he scratched his head, contemplating his next move. He couldn't sit around waiting for Sherryn to allow him to come home. He had to do something to save their marriage and, at the same time, prove he'd learned his lesson. But would that be enough, considering she was now at the point where she couldn't live with how he'd hurt her?

Forty-Seven

Reece flipped through the mail from the previous day, scratching the stubble around his chin. Self-conscious in his creased shirt, he hoped Maureen hadn't noticed it was fresh from a wrapper, and that he hadn't shaved.

In his new quarters, he'd been too sluggish to do anything about his appearance, and when he stood in front of the mirror trying in vain to straighten the folds in both his shirt and pants, he understood the magnitude of what had happened to him.

After many changes in his life, he owned a house, had the family he wanted ever since he could remember, but had now ended up without both. A flash of hatred for Gloria blinded him, and he crushed the envelope in his hand.

Maureen's open curiosity alerted him to his lapse, so he loosened his grip and sat to allow her to bring him up to date on what had happened in the office yesterday.

Glancing toward the open door, she spoke close to a whisper. "The police called yesterday afternoon. I said you were out and told them to get you on the cell. Did they call?"

He shrugged. "They might have, but the phone was dead. I suppose someone will be in touch today."

Her neatly arched brows edged together as she took a seat opposite him. "How's Sherryn dealing with all this?"

"Not very well."

Maureen scanned the stubborn creases across his chest before meeting his eyes. "You're not at home, are you?"

"You're a detective or something, Maureen?"

She showed her uneven teeth in an apologetic grin. "No, boss man, just observant."

Rubbing his chin, Reece smiled. She definitely saw too much, which was part of what made her good at her job.

She picked up the file she'd placed on the desk earlier. "I know you didn't kill that woman."

"Thanks for your faith in me." He grimaced and rested both arms on the desk. "I just hope the police find who they're looking for soon."

"I'm sure they will. Now here's a list of your calls, including the message left by the police."

Reece took the documents, and when Maureen left, shunted aimlessly around the office. He paced to the window and dragged a hand over his hair while he stared at the shiny leaves of the lush spathiphyllum Maureen had insisted he needed to brighten the office. Should he wait for the police to call, or was it better to satisfy his curiosity by calling them first?

He sat, spread his hands on the desk pad, and stared at them. In life, he'd never waited for things to happen, but created his own opportunities. The present situation was no different.

Taking slow, deliberate breaths, he flipped through the messages and then picked up the phone. His lawyer complained about the short notice, but agreed to meet him at the station. He called the police next. When the conversation ended, he palmed his key, told Maureen he'd be back, and left the office.

Inside the station, an officer immediately showed him to a room. The officers who had questioned Reece last time soon joined James and himself, and they exchanged greetings.

"My client is here because you called, but we're not sure why you needed to speak with him," James said.

"We've been checking the information he provided, but we have a few gray areas we'd like to clear up."

James opened both hands in invitation. "Go ahead."

The officer consulted a pad on the table. "You told us that on the day Miss Wedderburn was attacked, you had a meeting out of office with Fidelity Trading."

"Yes, that is so."

Eyes narrowed, the policeman scratched his ear. "Where exactly did you go after that?"

James nodded at Reece, who swallowed his annoyance. He had given them that information the day Gloria died. Why did they need him to rehash it? Inhaling deeply, he recalled his activities that morning. "I had another meeting. I went to the bank after that. From there, I stopped at the garage.

You have all those addresses. I had lunch and then went back to my office."

"So you'd say you were out of office for how many hours?"

"Two and a half, maybe three."

The guy with the pencil moustache stared at him, trying to intimidate.

Keen to end the questioning, Reece said what was on his mind. "I don't understand why you're not after anybody else. I can't possibly be the only person who wanted to hurt Gloria."

James stopped him by laying a hand on his arm.

With his gaze still fixed on Reece, the officer laid his hands on the open file jacket between them. "We tracked down a woman she had a feud with, as well as her other baby-father."

Reece raised his brows. "Was he missing?"

"No, but he was out of town for a while on a construction site, which is why it took us a while to locate him. Besides, he doesn't have a relationship for her to disrupt."

Smoothing a hand down his sleeve, Reece shook his head. "So, of course, you're now back to me."

The taller of the two officers—whom Reece recognized by his beer belly—spoke for the first time, aiming a glance at Reece's shirt, before he stared him in the eyes. "You had serious motivating factors. I imagine your life can't be a bed of roses right now."

Shrugging, Reece refused to comment.

"Your wife can't be a happy woman either," the officer continued, leaning forward. "And being a married man myself, I'd certainly do anything to preserve peace in my home."

"I dunno what you're suggesting, officer, but in spite of what Gloria did, I wouldn't have killed her."

The man studied Reece, his head cocked to one side. "That leaves the question of what you would do to get rid of a troublesome sweetheart."

Reece rubbed his fingers back and forth on his forehead. "Gloria was *not* my sweetheart."

The officer continued as though Reece hadn't spoken. "We have good reason to suspect you had something to do with Gloria Wedderburn's murder."

Frowning, Reece leaned in close to the table. "What d'you mean?"

"You have to come better than that," James said, in response. "Reece, let me ask the questions."

"Any of your friends knew Miss Wedderburn?" the officer continued.

Reece nodded. "Nearly everybody in Waterhouse knows Gloria has a child for me."

The two officers exchanged a glance. "Well, one Mr. Ronald Vincent, otherwise called Crusher, was seen with Miss Wedderburn on the day of her assault. A little bird told us they had an argument."

"That's not strange," Reece said. "The only person Gloria never had a quarrel with was her mother, and that's 'cause it's not possible to argue with the dead. That woman disagreed with everybody in the bar where she used to work."

"Isn't it possible, knowing how volatile Mr. Vincent is, that he'd take it upon himself to attack her?"

"I don't know of them having any big falling out for Ronald to do anything like that."

"But he is capable of violence, isn't he, Mr. Allbright?"

Reece wanted to squirm, but looked at James, who indicated with a nod that he should answer. After too long an interval, Reece said, "I suppose he is."

"And you never solicited his help in taking care of the problem you had with Gloria Wedderburn?"

"No, I didn't."

"As far as we know, nobody else had a serious enough grouse with Miss Wedderburn to want her dead, which makes you our prime suspect."

"Gentlemen, if you have no more questions, I'm going to ask that we end this interview," James said and picked up his briefcase.

Fighting the chill seeping into his bones, Reece stared the policeman down. "I had nothing to do with Gloria's death, and unless you can prove otherwise, we're leaving."

The two officers made eye contact once more, and the younger man said, "If you did kill her, rest assured, you won't get away with it."

Reece leaned back in the metal chair. "Then I won't have a problem, since I didn't kill her."

"That remains to be seen, doesn't it, Mr. Allbright?"

Despite James's comment that the police had no evidence against him, and therefore couldn't charge him, Reece left the station even more worried.

On his way back to the office, he made a call.

"Ronald, the police questioned me again about Gloria, and them say you had a fight with her. What happen between the two o' you?"

"You know how she did love fly off her mouth. She disrespec' mi in front of mi friends. Mi couldn't mek dat pass."

"So, you go to her house?"

Reece noted the brief pause before Ronald answered. "Yeah, mi did go to her yard inna di evenin', but she never deh home."

"So you never go back?"

"Mi don' like how you a question mi. Is what happen?"

"The police investigating both of us for Gloria's murder."

"Dem have no reason to involve me." Ronald uttered enough bad words to blister Reece's ear. "Even inna death, dat gyal still a cause problems."

Mindful of Ronald's short temper and that he would likely go on cursing forever, Reece ended the call. The fact that Ronald hadn't denied murdering Gloria left him uneasy. Or could he take that to mean Ronald really didn't know about the whole incident?

He prayed Ronald hadn't done anything foolish to try to help the situation with Sherryn. Ronald could be loyal to a fault, as Reece had already discovered.

Two years earlier, Reece had had a minor run-in with another man in the neighborhood. The guy had put a dent in Reece's vehicle with a handcart and refused to accept responsibility, claiming a car going in the opposite direction had forced him into the parked Jeep. Ronald had walked up and heard the two of them arguing.

Months later, Reece saw the guy while standing at the entrance to a bar in Waterhouse.

On spotting Reece, he crossed to the other side of the road, rather than going past him on the sidewalk.

When Ronald grinned and remarked that the man was under manners, Reece had asked what he meant. Ronald had been delighted to tell him he'd beaten up the man.

Based on that incident, it wasn't impossible that Ronald had a hand in

Gloria's death. If Ronald had attacked her, as disgusted as Reece was with himself over being a coward, he didn't want to know.

Forty-Eight

The seventy-two hours since she had kicked Reece out were the worst in Sherryn's life. She swung between depression and despair, acting normal only for the sake of her children, but she wasn't fooling anybody.

She had no answers for Brandon's insistent questions, and no way to end Maurice's reproachful silence because she had promised him Reece's quick return. Snapping at Brandon only depressed her more, and to avoid Maurice's gloominess, she stayed in her room, occupied by the whorls on the ceiling panels.

She had too much on her mind to continue acting as if everything was the same.

Now, more than ever, she appreciated Justin's role in keeping his siblings under control.

Miss Em was a godsend, and took care of their physical needs. She volunteered to stay overnight when Sherryn withdrew from all her regular activities, but Sherryn was tempted to tell her to go home on the second night, when she started a petition for Reece to return.

"Miss Sher, the children need dem father," she begged. "Yuh don' see likkle Maurice 'fraid and confuse. Him not even eat a slice of the pineapple-upside down cake I bake, and you know how him love dat. The girls dem lookin' sick." She shook her head. "You losin' weight. Yuh realize yuh don' eat anyt'ing since Tuesday?"

Sherryn turned away and headed down the passage. "I'm fine, Miss Em."

Her words followed Sherryn. "Yuh not fine at all, and I ca'an even imagine Mr. Reece condition. I know him mus' want to come home."

Sherryn escaped to her bedroom, where she spent most of the past three days. The buzzing from Reece's pillow forced her to pick up the cordless phone. "Yes?"

Her mother spoke in one breath. "Sherryn? You watching the news?"

"No, what's on it?"

"This whole business with Reece. The police arrested some man—

Ronald Vincent."

Anxiety wormed its way through Sherryn's fog. Her brows scrunched up while she worked out who Ronald Vincent was supposed to be. "Really?"

"Yes, the news said the man is Reece's friend from Waterhouse. Seems like he had some argument with the woman who died. The news said someone saw him near her house on the day she was attacked." Her mother paused and the background noise from the television filtered to Sherryn.

"The last time it was on, one of the neighbors asked me if the Maurice Allbright in the news was your husband. I hope this ends soon. What on earth was Reece thinking to take up with that woman?"

"I don't have the faintest clue. Only he knows."

"This whole business is distasteful. While I don't believe he did it, think about what the scandal will do to the family, and to make matters worse, you've kicked him out as if he's guilty. I don't know how you can put the man out of his own house."

"Easy. It's my house too, and I couldn't stand the sight of him. Reece had to know he was playing with fire."

Her energy was non-existent and listening to her mother was too much work, so Sherryn ended the conversation. "I'm in the middle of something now," she lied. "I'll talk to you later."

She understood her mother's concerns, but wasn't in the mood to comfort anybody. She had her own wounds that needed tending.

Soon Barbara and Judith would call to ask if she'd heard—as if it was possible for her not to know.

Sherryn wanted to weep over her plight, but had no tears left. The shame was a living, germinating thing that occupied a corner of her mind, making her hate Reece. It kept her company during every waking hour and it mocked her with every interaction she had.

Had the new client connected her with Reece? Did the other mothers dropping off their kids know her husband had cheated on her? Did they snicker behind her back? Did they know her husband was being questioned by the police for murder?

When she didn't hate Reece, she was eaten up with self-disgust over how she missed him, as though he were dead. Which in a way, she wanted him to be. She wanted him dead to be able to move past the hurt, the bitterness, the disappointment, the soul-searing anguish.

Why should she want him to come home when the sight of him would make her angry all over again? Why have him return when he had destroyed their children's trust and brought ugliness into their home? Why should she let him back into her life? Simply because she missed him and could sense his distress at the separation from them?

Those weren't good enough reasons.

Their conversation on the previous evening was brief and nonsensical, but she had nothing to say to him. She needed him, and deep in her heart she wanted him to come home, but what was the point when she still hadn't made a decision about their marriage?

The door swung open, and Justin hovered above her. Anger contorted his features.

"Mommy, Rodney, just called to ask if Daddy involved with some woman's murder."

Sherryn sat up and pulled Justin toward her. At first he resisted, then allowed her to drag him to sit beside her. "Losing your cool won't help. Remember we discussed it the day she died?"

He gripped the sides of his head, resting both elbows on his thighs. "You have any idea how shame goin' to kill me tomorrow?"

Annoyed by the combination of her mother's concerns about gossip, and now Justin's ego, Sherryn sighed. "Of course I do. I've had to face the neighbors and everybody who knows us."

"What if dem lock him up? What we goin' to do then, Mommy?"

"Justin, don't go buying trouble we don't need, okay?"

Clearly dissatisfied with her reaction, he got up and walked away, grumbling, "Mi goin' to call Daddy now."

"Good luck to both of you," Sherryn muttered.

Another sigh escaped at her callousness.

Justin had done his best to help her keep things together. For that alone, she should have been more sympathetic since her son was obviously hurting.

God, she was pitiful! Crumbling because of a stupid man. She swallowed self-pity and forced herself to stand.

What had possessed her to act as if she was responsible only for herself? While she was locked away, sinking in the doldrums, her children were suffering, and their home was in shambles. She dragged a hand across her dripping nose and shuffled to the bathroom.

After she made herself look less like her world had ended, she'd take up where she left off three days ago, when she stopped being a mother. No matter what Reece had done, she had no excuse for ignoring their children when they needed her most.

Forty-Nine

Rubbing a hand over the spot on his forehead where a headache threatened to start, Reece did his best to comfort his firstborn. "Justin, you know how badly I feel about all this. Rest assured I didn't murder anybody."

"Daddy, me know you never murder anybody. Is just the shame of having your name all over the news that mi ca'an deal wid. Plus, you need to settle things wid Mommy and come home."

"I can't do that until—"

Justin's protest drowned him out. "I don't care what you have to do, Daddy. You need to come home—the sooner, the better."

"All right, son, I hear you."

Justin lowered his voice to its normal pitch when he spoke again. "I'm goin' to do my homework, and I have to check on everybody after that, so later."

While massaging his chin, Reece stared at the blank computer screen. Justin had been on the edge of tears when he hung up. He was trying, that much was clear, but the situation at home was too complex for a sixteen-year-old boy to manage.

Inactivity was not an option, but apart from one idea, Reece was no closer to a solution than he'd been since he left home. He could beg Sherryn to take him back, but what use was begging when she was likely to say no? Nothing had happened to change her mind. Considering that his name was splashed over the airwaves and in print, she had no reason to take him back.

Buying himself back into her good graces wasn't going to work. Sherryn was not, and never had been, moved by guilt-motivated gifts—throwing him out had more than proven that. But she had to know he was sorry for what he'd done.

His inability to figure out how he could earn her forgiveness dogged him into the night. At ten-thirty, he left the office for the hotel, with a glimmer of an idea to win her back.

By nine o' clock the following morning, Reece posted bail for Ronald, who had to check in at the station every day, according to the terms of his release. Reece suspected the police had allowed Ronald bail because they had no evidence he killed Gloria. Ronald was unfortunate to be in the wrong place at the wrong time. Locking him up was a way to rattle him, and no doubt, the police didn't have a reliable witness who could say Ronald was at Gloria's house at the time of the attack. If they did, he would have been held without bail for as long as it took to bring his case to trial.

Reece reminded himself he had nothing to do with the argument between Ronald and Gloria and hoped his friend had not committed murder.

Ronald was grateful, but unruffled. It wasn't the first time he had spent a night in lock-up. After dropping him off at his yard, Reece visited the bank and the investment company. Then, he went home.

He hid his discomfort with a smile when Miss Em opened the door and saw him standing outside, hesitating to use his key, because technically, he wasn't living there.

"Missa Reece," she bellowed and grabbed his arm. The broom she held when she opened the door lay forgotten on the floor. "It feel like is a long time mi nuh see you. Come inside, man."

"Can you get Sherryn for me?"

"Of course."

She grabbed the broom, hurried away, and returned in no time, beckoning to him. "She in her office. She say to come. Mek sure yuh don' leave again, yuh hear."

The furniture hadn't been moved, but everything seemed unfamiliar, as if he hadn't been inside the house for months. The cream walls made the living room seem larger, and his glassed-in entertainment center didn't have any fingerprints, but he wasn't fooled. It fascinated Justin, who he was sure had entertained himself using it while Reece was away.

The water in the fish tank was still clear. After counting the fish, he smiled. Neither Brandon nor Maurice had succeeded in killing any of them. A pile of books on the mahogany table in the corner represented Celia's reading material. She insisted on leaving them there, claiming Melaine's junk had a life of its own and swallowed unsuspecting items left in their room.

Kyle's neon toy box occupied another corner—a measure Sherryn put in place to keep his things together and prevent everybody else from injuring themselves falling over his toys.

He inhaled the familiar scent of lemon furniture polish, which Miss Em used as if they got the stuff free. He trod down the passage toward the back of the house, his footsteps loud on the parquet. At Sherryn's office door, he paused, filled his chest with air and rapped on the wood.

"Come in."

Though muted, her voice made the blood rush faster through his veins.

He clasped the doorknob as if he was in danger of falling, should he let go.

Sherryn had never looked better or worse. The white, cotton shirt left her arms bare, and jeans covered her long legs. Her close-cropped hair showed off the high cheekbones and oriental slant to her eyes that had first seduced him. She wore no make-up, but a hint of pink touched her lower lip where she'd caught it between her teeth. She had lost weight.

He wanted to kiss her, but her blank expression held him back.

Only her eyes revealed her torment.

He asked no questions and didn't need to, because the same distress burdened his spirit. He approached her and stopped where she stood by the desk, crumpling several sheets of paper. Over her shoulder, he met his own gaze in the framed mirror hanging across the room. The deep color of his eyes echoed his dark mood, and for the first time since he left home, Reece realized how his appearance had changed.

Sherryn shifted, recapturing his attention. Not wanting her to guess his intention, he dropped a kiss on her mouth in a swift move and stepped away.

She pressed her lips together and sat down, scanning his new shirt in the process.

"Where's Maurice?" he asked.

"Miss Em's supposed to be bathing him."

"The others—how are they?"

She shrugged and moved sideways to grip the edge of the desk, leaving him with a view of her profile. "Trying to cope."

Reaching into his shirt pocket, Reece pulled out a folded envelope and put in front of her.

Sliding a glance his way, Sherryn opened the flap and read the statement inside. "Why?"

He crossed the room to stand in front of the window. "This problem started all those years ago, because I wanted to own you—body and soul. If you needed me, you'd never leave me. That's what I thought, but I was wrong."

He walked over and stopped beside her. "I've moved half of everything in our accounts to one in your name. I don't know what else to do to show you that I'm trying to change my attitude. It doesn't solve what's happening between us now, but there won't be a better time to do this."

Sherryn kept him out of eyeshot, refusing to turn her head. "Why are you here?"

"Because I want to come home, Sherryn. I don't want to be away from you. I miss you. I miss our children. I can't stay another night in that hotel."

She got to her feet and studied him, her face expressionless. Only the ticking clock cut the silence between them. Her words, when they came, were a mere whisper. "You're free to come home, Reece." Arms folded across her chest, she continued in a monotone, "I'm still having trouble dealing with our situation, but the children are unhappy, so I'm willing to try to work things out."

She lifted her face to his. "Sometimes I hate you and it's killing me. That's why I asked you to leave. I don't want our problems to poison our family. D'you understand?"

He nodded, disturbed by her admission, but unwilling to stop the flow of her communication. At least she was talking to him, rather than doing things the usual way, which was to punish him with silence.

He angled his head toward the passage.

A pair of fast-moving feet squeaked to a stop in the doorway. Maurice stood there with a glimmer of a smile lighting his face. Half his collar was tucked inside his polo shirt and the tail of it puddled around the waist of his shorts. The boy walked forward, wearing a wide grin, and Reece surprised himself by picking him up for a hug.

Maurice gripped him tight around the neck.

"You all right?" he asked.

Maurice nodded and leaned his head toward Sherryn. "Yeah, and she wi' feel better now that you come back. Since you gone, she sad every day."

Reece held Sherryn's gaze over Maurice's head while lowering him to the floor, and caught the shadow that passed over her features.

Maurice pulled at Reece's shirt, forcing him to look away from her. "You not leavin' again?"

"No," Reece said, after Sherryn shook her head.

He squeezed Maurice's shoulder and returned the adoring smile the child gave him, now certain of what had affected Sherryn a moment ago.

Although she had cursed him over his initial reaction to Maurice, witnessing their interaction had to be difficult for her. Reece understood it was a natural reaction because his world had revolved around their children, until now. Still, he was one hundred percent certain she didn't resent Maurice for the growing bond with him.

She picked up an empty glass off the corner of her desk. "Maurice, could you put this in the sink?"

"Okay." He wrapped both hands around it, lifted it with care and made for the doorway.

Sherryn sat sideways before the computer, looking up at Reece. "So, you're going to work today, or d'you plan to be here when the kids get home?"

"I'll go back to the office and give you a chance to talk with them. I also have to check out of the hotel."

"Okay, I'll explain to Maurice—"

The child sped into the room. "What you goin' to explain to me?"

"Reece is going out again." She took Maurice's hand, and rushed to continue when his head jerked toward his father. "But he'll be back later in the evening."

"Is true?" Maurice asked.

Nodding, Reece rubbed the boy's head. "Yeah, I have some things to do, so I'll see you later."

Maurice searched Reece's face as if he didn't believe him. "You sure?"

"'Course I'm sure." He got down to the child's level. "If I don't come back by six o' clock, ask Sherryn to call me, okay?"

Maurice tilted his head to one side, staring hard at Reece. He looked at Sherryn for a few seconds and then said, "Okay."

Reece got to his feet, tapping Maurice on the arm. "I need to talk to Sherryn. Can you give us a minute?"

"Miss Em have something for me in the kitchen. I goin' to get it."

At Sherryn's lifting of her eyebrows, Maurice corrected himself. "I'm going to get it."

An awkward pause descended when he left. Ill at ease, Reece focused on Sherryn's hands that were shuffling papers on the desk. "See you later. I'll call before I come."

"Fine," she said, placing her arm along the back of the chair. "One more thing. It's not about the money."

"What?"

"The money isn't why I agreed you could come home."

"I know that."

After another wordless exchange with her, he left the room, admitting they had lost something precious. No longer could he gauge her reaction to him by looking at her. She'd now closed away a part of herself that used to be accessible to him. She only showed him affection in brief snatches, and once she suspected he could read her, a protective mask slid into place, locking him out.

He sighed, thinking about the amount of ground he had to make up, wondering when, if ever, Sherryn might forgive him.

By the time he arrived at the office, he'd drummed up a bit of optimism. He had captured Sherryn's heart through patience and dedication, and they'd been through much together. If she was willing to have him around, it meant she didn't totally hate him despite what she'd said.

He could live with that until he won her again.

Fifty

"Sorry, Judith." Sherryn moved the phone to her other ear. "I won't make it this afternoon." Reece will be back this evening, and I want to prepare something special for dinner. Nobody around here has been eating right since he left."

"You mean since you put him out. Anyway, I'm happy you've come to your senses."

"You come to yours yet?"

"How d'you mean?"

"I'm talking about Troy, of course."

"I haven't had this much excitement in years, and I'm not likely to give it up. Matter of fact, I'm thinking of leaving Barry."

That stopped Sherryn from flipping through the order book. "Not for this twenty-odd-year-old boy?"

"I'm my own woman."

"You mean you're really serious?"

"Of course. I'm thinking of moving out and getting my own place. Troy is all for it."

Sherryn rolled her eyes and wedged a pen inside the book. "But of course, Judy. He's a young man looking for somebody to take care of him, and by the sound of things—"

"Don't say it, Sherryn. This is the best I've felt in years, and Troy's directly responsible. There's nothing wrong with me giving him a few material things in exchange for some good loving."

"I wonder what Barry will say about that, since the material things will be coming out of his pocket."

"He can afford it. If he was taking care of business at home instead of chasing tail, things would be different."

"Anyway, Judith, I gotta go. Just be careful. Men don't handle this sort of thing well."

Sherryn was certain Judith had not considered all the complications that could come from her actions, but was too preoccupied with work and planning the family reunion to dwell on Judith's decision.

Dinner was a bittersweet affair for Sherryn.

The children filled Reece in on their activities and doted on him as if he'd gone missing for a year. When he arrived home, Brandon hugged him around the waist, declaring that God had answered his prayers.

After dinner, Kyle refused to get off Reece's lap, and Justin stayed next to him for most of the evening. Melly and Celia hung around his neck over the back of the sofa, while Maurice, content to be in the same room, lifted his head occasionally to ensure Reece was still there.

Sherryn questioned whether she'd be missed if she left for a time, and admitted she was jealous. Sometimes she thought Maurice appreciated her more than all of them put together. However, that was because she was perhaps the first person who had shown him affection.

She listened to them jabbering, relieved their home hadn't turned into a battleground. She suspected whose side their children might take if that happened. Justin would support his father for the mere fact that she had sent him packing.

She might have the girls' sympathy for a time, but despite everything, they had pined for their father. As young as he was, Brandon was possibly the only one she could depend on not to blame her. As with everything he wanted, he was sure God listened to him when he prayed.

A soft smile took her unawares, and she laid the magazine in her lap.

Maurice relaxed on the floor, with his arms behind his head. He had now positioned himself so he could see Reece without moving.

He's such a low-maintenance child, Sherryn thought. He asks for so little and is happy just being around us. I wish I were as easily satisfied.

Reece laughed at something Justin said, dragging Sherryn back to her original thoughts. She focused on Maurice's swinging leg while bitterness seeped over her at the evidence of the happiness around her. All of them were behaving as if their time together had never been interrupted.

Reece included her in his laughter, and she dredged up a lukewarm smile, ashamed of the acidic thoughts that were at odds with the relaxed front she presented. She got to her feet and turned away, but not before looking at Reece.

His knitted brows gave away his concern.

She could fool everybody else, but not him. Reece knew she was upset.

Sherryn kept going until she reached her office. She sat at the desk and rested her head on her folded hands.

Jesus, what's wrong with me? she thought. I should be glad Reece still wants to be with me after the way I've treated him, but instead I resent him.

No longer could she avoid the reality of their situation. She had to rein in her emotions before she wrecked her marriage. How could she tell Reece in one moment she wanted to work things out, and then not be able to control her desire to make his life hell?

She hadn't made any sense of her state of mind and her mood hadn't improved when the phone buzzed in her ear later that night. She was cold, and her arm was cramped from lying on it too long.

Try as she might, she couldn't make head or tail of Barbara's garbled words.

"Barb, slow down. I don't understand a word you're saying."

She yawned and squinted at the glowing numbers on the digital clock before sitting up. It was after eleven. Reece was not in bed, but she had no time to think on his whereabouts because Barbara nattered on, keeping her voice low.

Why was she whispering?

"...and she's refusing to go to the hospital."

And what on earth was she going on about? "Barb, please. Did something happen to Judith?

"Yes, Barry beat her up." Barbara's voice rose to just above a whisper. "She's over here now, and she wants to wait 'til mornin' and see her own doctor."

Heart racing, Sherryn asked, "She have any broken bones?"

"How me goin' to know dat? I'm not a doctor. Her eyes look real bad though. She's one big bruise, if you ask me. Barry must have gone mad."

"Lemme talk to her."

The sniffling on the line told Sherryn that Barbara had passed the phone to the other woman."

"Judy, I'm so sorry. You okay?"

A heavy sob was Judith's answer.

"I assume he found out about Troy, but how did that happen?"

Through broken sobs, she said, "When I was talking to you earlier, he was on the other line."

"Oh, boy. You're gonna stay the night with Barbara, right?"

Judith's breath stuttered down the line, her response faint. "Yes."

Sherryn sighed. "Judy, you sure you don't want to see a doctor? What if you have internal bleeding?"

Judith bawled into the phone while Sherryn tried to comfort her, conscious of her uselessness. "Hon, don't cry. Barb will take care of you, and I'll come by in the morning, okay? If the pain gets too bad, you have to call a doctor right away, you hear?"

She stretched to put the phone back and caught Reece on the edge of her vision.

He stood in the doorway, holding on to the knob, but made no move to enter the lamp-lit room.

"Something wrong?" he asked.

She nodded. "Barbara just called. Barry beat up Judith. He crossed the tiles to sit on the bed, facing her. "Why?"

"She has a lover."

Frown lines appeared in his forehead, and his expression shifted before she could define his feelings. "So, she's with Barbara? How badly is she hurt?"

"I guess she can't be all that bad if she's refusing to see a doctor tonight."

His fingers tangled with hers. "Let's hope so."

She remembered hitting Reece, and him trying to protect her and their children by wiping away the evidence of what she'd done. Another man might have hit her back, but not him.

She didn't know if he had cheated on her before Gloria, but considered herself lucky his passion for her hadn't died. Unlike her friends, she had a husband who cared about what she did and whom she did it with. She couldn't imagine herself living as Barbara and Judith did, with men who cared little about how their affairs affected their wives. Reece knew of their challenges, but she never explained the depth to which Barry and Winston had hurt her friends.

A tiny gasp parted her lips when she understood what had gone on in Reece's mind when she told him Judith had a lover. The old Reece would have jumped on that bit of information and gone possessive on her, but the man before her now had chosen not to give it more than a passing thought. She admired him for his restraint.

Giving him the first genuine smile since he arrived home, she held on to his hand. "Reece, come to bed. I need you right here."

He obliged her, climbing into bed in his sweats and tee-shirt to cuddle with her. His warmth comforted her, and above everything, she missed the way he cocooned her in bed, holding her gently like she was something precious.

And she was precious to him. He didn't have to tell her, because his actions always supported his loving words.

He murmured in her ear, "Sherryn?"

"Hmm?"

"I love you."

She blinked away tears, wishing she could get past the stubbornness that kept her from healing.

Fifty-One

A kaleidoscope of bruises covered Judith's pale skin. The rings around her eyes ranged from deep pink to purple, and her black shirt emphasized the cuts and scrapes on her upper arms. She brushed her fingers over swollen lips, calling attention to her broken acrylic tips.

Barry and she must have had a whopper of a fight.

Sherryn laid her bag on the sofa and leaned toward Judith. "He knows where you are?"

Judith mumbled and shook her head. "No, but he's been calling the cell phone."

"No doubt he'll get around to calling one or the other of us soon," Sherryn said.

Barbara lips curled. "He'd have some nerve. You should let the police deal with him."

Judith's hair bounced as she waggled her head. "No way. Can you imagine seeing hints about it in the gossip columns? I'd just die. I won't call the police."

"So what are you going to do?" Sherryn asked. "It's a matter of time before he finds you."

"I'd go to a hotel, but ... "

"But what? Barbara asked.

Anger flashed in Judith's bloodshot eyes. "He cut up my bank cards and took all the money I had."

Barbara rubbed Judith's back, speaking softly. "Never mind. We'll help until you get back the cards."

"But he's going to close the accounts. He said so." Judith dabbed away tears with a crumpled hanky.

"Calm down, Judy. Money is something you don't need to worry about. You're forgetting how much of it your family has? Don't you have a savings account somewhere?" Sherryn asked.

Judith laid trembling hands in her lap. "That's all well and good, but he said he'd kill me rather than let me leave. I only got away because I called a taxi and snuck out when he fell asleep—the drunken shit."

Barbara grumbled, a sour expression in place. "I suppose this is a case of a cow never knowing the use of him tail 'til him lose it."

"Mmm. But you have to take the threat seriously. We need an out-of-the-way place where he won't think to look for you, and we have to move fast, because he'll check our houses first." Sherryn used a finger to indicate Barbara and herself. "Since the doctor examined you already, let's leave now."

Sherryn frowned and raised a hand. "Wait a minute. Barb, where's your digital camera?"

Barbara got up from beside Judith. "Gimme a sec."

She returned within a minute, and Sherryn urged Judith to stand against a wall. Barb took several frontal shots of her face and arms, before snapping pictures of her profile from both sides.

"I'm not going to the police," Judith warned, keeping her gaze on the tiles.

"You never know when you might need these," Sherryn said. "Barb, make sure you keep those pictures safe."

"Sure. I'll save a set to my hard drive and also print them, just in case."

Judith went to sit on the edge of the sofa. Her voice cracked when she asked, "What am I going to do with those? Why would I want to even look at them?"

Sherryn sighed and sank on the cushion beside Judith. "Since you won't make a report to the police, this, along with your doctor's report, is good evidence if you ever need it.

With a wave of the arm, Judith said, "Fine, do what you want, but remember I won't be pressing charges. I can't. It's just too embarrassing."

"What you should do is get the police to lock up that worthless husband of yours. That would give him something to think about. What if he had killed you?"

Judith refused to answer, and after a moment Barbara shook her head and stalked across the room. "Let me change and get my handbag. Judy, you and I are the same size, so I'll grab some stuff, and we can get the rest on the way."

They waited without talking, and Sherryn did her best to avoid looking at

Judith's battered face. Barbara's living room was decorated exclusively with mahogany furniture and sculpted accent pieces.

After she skimmed the room and her gaze went back to Judith, Sherryn wondered what Barry's reaction would be if he saw the result of his anger. How could he do this to the woman he'd sworn to love and protect for better or worse?

Barbara returned to the living room within ten minutes, all business-like in a linen suit, and carrying a duffel bag. "There's a guesthouse in Barbican, where my cousin had her reception. You can stay there until Barry cools off."

"Who say I'm going back to him?"

"Well, I'm glad you're using your head," Sherryn said, scanning the seat to make sure she wasn't leaving anything behind.

Before they went through the front door, Barbara stopped to wrap a chiffon scarf around Judith's head and face.

Sherryn followed Barbara's Camry to the plaza in Manor Park and waited with Judith, while Barbara purchased underwear and personal care items.

At the guesthouse, Sherryn used her credit card to pay for two nights' accommodation and when Judith was settled in a cozy room with elegant rattan furniture, they warned her against talking to Barry in his current mood.

Sherryn left to pick up cake-making supplies and told them both to call if they needed anything.

Again, she was grateful for the man she had chosen to share her life with and couldn't imagine Reece hitting her.

Although she wasn't complaining, Judith had to be in a lot of pain from the punches and slaps she'd taken.

Sherryn said a prayer for both her friends and their marriages, and then said one for herself. The three of them needed all the help they could get.

Fifty-Two

Ronald's casual stance—leaning against the Jeep, arms and legs crossed—was at odds with his frown. "Mi don' understand what di police up to. Now mi sorry mi did go to Gloria yard. Next t'ing mi know dem arrest me for murder."

Reece stared at the zinc fence in front of him, his mind in turmoil.

If the police charged Ronald, Reece couldn't convince anybody that he hadn't asked him to kill Gloria. Everybody in the community knew Ronald was fiercely loyal to him, and they all were accustomed to Ronald's hair-trigger temper and violence.

"Ronald, you know is about time you learn how to control yuhself?"

Ronald turned toward him, eyes flashing under the orange bandana tied around his forehead. "Wha' you mean?"

"The police only swoop down on you because of how you behave," Reece said, hoping Ronald would calm down.

Slapping himself on the chest, Ronald shouted, "Dat nuh give dem no right to harass mi."

"Unfortunately, is so life go," Reece said. "By the way, you have the number?"

"Yeah, man." Ronald scrolled through his phone and reeled off a number, which Reece added to his cellular.

He'd put Maurice in contact with his siblings later.

After a few seconds of tense silence, Reece asked, "When Gloria goin' bury?"

"Her sister come down from foreign to mek arrangements. Supposed to be next week, mi hear."

Reece straightened up from the vehicle. "Take care and link me, if anything happen."

"Cool, mi bredren," Ronald said as they knocked fists.

Reece drove away, easing around the patchwork of potholes, wishing he was more disciplined about avoiding Waterhouse.

Sherryn wouldn't be pleased to find out he was still hanging around Ronald.

He went back to the office with the intention of staying there until a decent hour, but gave in and went home after lunch.

Sherryn lay across their bed napping, and when he wandered back downstairs, disappointed, he found Maurice in the kitchen helping Miss Em with dinner.

He didn't want to be alone in his office, so he sat in the living room tapping the remote against his leg. A deep breath lifted his chest, and he caught the scent of curried goat.

Miss Em was ecstatic that he was home and promised she'd cook him something special when he left that morning.

He got comfortable on the kids' sofa, inhaling its slight musty odor. No matter how often Miss Em washed the cushions, or what deodorizer Sherryn sprayed on it, it retained its smell because of the children. They loved its comfort and piled together on it in the evenings to snack and watch television.

Sherry tried replacing it several times, but was always outvoted and had to satisfy herself with changing the fabric, which rapidly smelled lived-in again. She compromised by never allowing guests to sit on it. To Reece, it smelled like family.

A sound from the doorway interrupted his thoughts and his finger hit the remote, switching on the television.

Maurice stopped when he saw him, but Reece tried to put him at ease, knowing Maurice was more comfortable with him when they were with the rest of the family.

"Come sit over here."

The boy sat at the other end of the sofa, with his hand resting on the arm.

For want of something to say, Reece asked, "You and Brandon still getting along all right?"

Maurice nodded. "Yes, and him show me how to play the computer game."

"Would you like one for yourself?"

Maurice's mouth fell open. "You would buy one for me?"

Smothering a smile, Reece put a hand on the child's shoulder. "Yes. That's why I asked."

"Dat woulda nice," Maurice said, his pitch high with excitement.

"We can deal with it on the weekend." Reece paused, made a quick decision and squeezed Maurice's arm. "Tell me something. Did Gloria and her other baby-father get along all right?"

Maurice rolled the hem of his shorts and squinted like someone thinking hard. "No, them used to fight all the time."

"Why?"

"Gloria always say the money him bring never enough for Kemar and Shakira, and then him would tell her she love money too much. After that, them would cuss bad words."

Reece could well imagine that scenario because Gloria hated being denied money she felt was her due. He supposed her other children's father had the same mindset as he. Why give her money to waste when the children were in need? He also understood how she could drive someone to murder. No doubt, she had provoked her attacker. Gloria was that kind of woman.

He channeled his attention to the child beside him, reminding himself that Gloria was beyond help.

"Would you like to talk to your brother and sister now?"

"What you mean?"

"I got their grandmother's number. You could talk to them right now, if you want."

"Really?" A smile spread over Maurice's face.

"Go get the cell phone off the desk in my office," Reece said.

Maurice jumped off the seat and sped from the room. In less than a minute he returned, holding the phone out to Reece.

He took it, found the number and dialed. After he explained to the children's grandmother why he was calling, she put Maurice's brother on the phone.

Sherryn occupied Reece's mind, which made him forget to listen to Maurice's side of the conversation.

Without a doubt, Gloria's murderer had left the burden of her children's care on their grandmother. It was the way of things in Jamaica. In the absence of parents, grandmothers were often left to care for kids. Thankfully, that wouldn't be his son's lot—not that Gloria had any relatives in Jamaica that he knew about.

Reece motioned to Maurice that he wanted to speak to the woman again. When he had her on the line, he asked whether she had any objection to him bringing Maurice to see Kemar and Shakira. She didn't, so he promised to take Maurice at some point, and ended the call.

Maurice stared at Reece, his mouth opening and closing within seconds.

"You wanted to ask a question?"

"Yeah." He squirmed before facing Reece. "Why mi madda tell me you never like me? I always wonder is what mi do to cause that."

Moving closer to the boy, Reece said, "Your mother was a strange woman. I never told her I didn't like you, and you never did anything for me not to like you."

"Then why you always cross when you see mi?"

"One day I'll explain, but the short answer is that your mother always made me angry."

"Oh, so it really wasn't me that mek you vex?"

Reece shook his head slowly. "No, Maurice, it was never you."

The boy leaned back, processing the information.

Reece didn't offer any additional explanation. Instead, he concentrated on the football match on the television. He sensed rather than saw Maurice's movement beside him and turned his head.

Maurice's features relaxed. "Mi glad it wasn't me."

Another moment passed, during which he pouted. "Mi did tell you how mi madda like to tell lie."

Reece pursed his lips to hide a smile and with a solemn nod, said, "Yes, you did tell me. By the way, her funeral is next week. D'you want to go?"

Slowly, Maurice shook his head. "Mi don' like funerals. Dem mek mi feel sad."

Though he had no intention of attending, Reece continued the conversation. "Your brother and sister will probably be there."

"Mi still don' want to go."

"Fine. I won't force you to go."

Reece's decision not to attend the funeral had everything to do with self-preservation. Firstly, he had gone to countless burials. He'd also had enough of crying women and dry-eyed children left behind, both by friends and acquaintances over the years.

Secondly, the case was still unsolved and he was sure some thought him guilty of Gloria's murder. He had threatened her often enough for people to believe he would do her some damage, given the opportunity, but his threats had served their purpose—to keep Gloria in check. She was one of those women who had to be reminded of her boundaries.

She'd now crossed one to the point of no return, with someone who was not prepared to put up with whatever she'd been dishing out.

Reece stared at the watercolor above the television, wondering who else had a motive to kill Gloria. He hoped the police solved the case quickly, and that by some miracle Ronald would be proven innocent.

That way, Reece could focus on Sherryn and a return to normality.

Fifty-Three

Justin rested the tubs of ice cream on the floor of the van and buckled his seatbelt. He cleared his throat and Sherryn suspected he was about to come the real point of their ice cream run. He'd insisted on satisfying his craving for the stuff by going out with her to buy it after dinner.

"So, Mommy, everything good with you and Daddy now?" he said, while locking his seatbelt.

"You know very well there's no instant fix. We're still working things out."

"Could you try and work them out this time without one of you leaving? We can't handle that."

She patted the hand resting on his leg. "I know, son."

Justin wasn't finished and waited until she went through the next intersection before speaking. "Something I wanted to find out. You and Daddy been together for so long. How come you all still so tight?"

Sherryn chuckled, thinking for a bit before answering. "We're a good match. Mad about each other, at least until this whole thing blew up. I—"

"The two of you are still mad about each other. You didn't know whether you were coming or going when Daddy wasn't home, and him look as if him was fasting for a month." Gently, he punched her shoulder. "If he was at the hotel one more night, the two of you woulda died and left us orphans."

"That's a bit drastic, but yeah, I did miss Reece." She merged into the roundabout and then glanced at Justin. "I think we've stayed close because we understand each other and want the same things."

"So, if you want the same things, why is it so hard to move on from what happened?"

In their driveway, she switched the engine off and took a deep breath, noticing the temperature had dropped substantially. Night was falling fast.

"One day you'll understand. When you put your trust in someone, you have certain expectations—"

Justin reached for the shopping bag and got out of the van. He closed the door and leaned on it to speak to her through the window. "People make mistakes, Mommy. You always tell us not to hold grudges. That doesn't go for you too?"

Sherryn was stumped. It was true, she'd always told the children ill will festered, which was what her parents taught her, but she hadn't set a good example. Every family member, except Kyle, remained on edge when she and Reece were at odds, because it took her ages to quench her anger.

Regardless of his betrayal, Reece still was and always had been a wonderful father and husband. He never aired their disagreements in front of the children and was always more than willing to make up.

She spun her wedding band to its correct position on her finger, thinking about the many times she'd frozen him out and made him suffer over small incidents. She certainly had some soul-searching to do. When she looked at Justin, framed in the window, his brows lifted and he drummed his fingers on the roof of the vehicle while waiting for a response.

She climbed out to meet him in front of the van and threw an arm around his waist. "I just have one question for you," she said. "When did you get to be so smart?"

Hugging her neck, he said, "I have a smart Mommy, even if she's a crazy bird sometimes."

Sherryn didn't hold back the giggle tickling her throat. She hung on to him, prodding him in the side. "I'll show you what a crazy bird can do."

He squawked, held her off with the plastic bag and ran through the grille, banging it behind him.

She stifled laughter and shook her head. "Is that boy six or sixteen?"

In the kitchen, Justin dished out ice cream under the supervision of Brandon, who told her Reece was in his office. That meant she'd have a bit of private time in their bedroom.

She opened the jewelry cabinet on top of the dresser. The ring Reece had given her lay inside the middle drawer. In the near darkness, she lifted it out to hold it between her thumb and forefinger. The last time she wore it was during the previous week when she cut him with it.

She settled in the rocking chair by the window, which gave her a view of her garden and the roadway. She pictured the well-kept houses and manicured gardens in the community and then wondered about her neighbors. How many of them had the same problems she now faced? How had they worked them out? Was divorce, or a willingness to ignore extra-marital activity, always the answer? How many people bothered to work out their differences?

Wallowing in resentment led down one road. The road to dissolution. Was that what she wanted? Or did she want to get back to the place they were before Gloria Wedderburn came to their doorstep?

Her unhappiness spanned a much shorter period than the years of happiness she'd shared with Reece. Was she willing to throw those years away? And was she prepared to give up a wonderful man because she was unwilling to forgive? Would she continue to punish him while she told herself she wanted their marriage to work?

The baguettes gave her no answer and only winked at her in the darkness relieved by the streetlight slanting into the room. She made a fist, then relaxed her fingers and slipped the ring on her hand.

The door opened, and Reece paused by the door before he entered. "Sherryn?"

"Hmm?"

He flicked the light switch on the lamp closest to the doorway, throwing a soft glow over the room. "You all right?"

She nodded. "Come here, hon."

He came to her in his usual evening wear—sweatpants and tee-shirt. He smelled of musk from the deodorant he wore and was clean-shaven once more.

She tugged his hand, and he stooped before her. With one fingertip, she followed the curve of his lips and the cleft in his chin before making her request. "Tell me what happened with Gloria. Don't leave out anything."

His eye twitched, and his mouth puckered.

She understood that he was trying to gauge her mood.

His breath wafted over her as he exhaled. "I don't—"

"I know you don't want to talk about it, Reece, but I have to know. I want to get past it."

She touched his hand. "Humor me. Please."

"All right," he said, backing up against the bed. He sat, folded his hands together between his legs and talked to her.

Sherryn listened, asking questions when she needed better explanations and swallowing tears when the details grew overwhelming. Reece would never comprehend her need to know everything, but she wanted every scrap of information at her disposal. She didn't understand what drove her to seek out the hurtful details; she simply had to have them.

Each time Reece hesitated, she forced him to continue until she was satisfied she knew all the details of the relationship between him and Gloria.

"That's everything," he said, when he was finished. "And it's a good thing someone saved me the trouble of killing her. Otherwise, I might have eventually done it myself."

"You know I don't like when you talk like that."

A slight movement in the tuft of grass spotlighted under the street lamp across the street caught her attention. A half-grown stray cat was tracking some unlucky prey.

Turning back to Reece, she said, "I hope you're staying away from Ronald. You don't want to be anywhere near him now that the police are looking at him."

His refusal to meet her eyes implied he was still in contact with Ronald. When would he learn that all Waterhouse ever brought him was trouble?

"They've not said I'm free and clear yet," Reece said.

"But if you're innocent, you have no need to worry."

He rubbed his face with both hands. "I know, Sher, but knowing our justice system, I can't help but be concerned."

"I understand, but I also heard another bit of news this afternoon that's connected to this case."

"What?"

"The police are questioning the father of her other children. They picked him up in a speed trap."

Reece tried to recall what the police told him. "But I thought they said he wasn't under suspicion."

"Well, they've detained him, but I didn't hear the entire news item."

He frowned, rubbing his forehead.

"What are you thinking?" Sherry said.

"I know you don't like me going to Waterhouse, but you have to admit they could probably tell me everything."

They or he? Sherryn thought, biting the corner of her lip to hold back a smile.

Reece was dying to call that hoodlum Ronald to see if he had any additional information. She could feel it.

She looked at the wall clock. The children were absorbed with ice cream and television.

If Reece and Sherryn were occupied, Justin would round up the kids when it was bedtime, and later, Reece would go down to secure the house.

His thumbs twirled around each other, and he stole glances at her, no doubt longing to make a phone call.

Hiding another smile, Sherryn got up, turned the lock on the door. She walked back to the bed and sandwiched Reece's face between her palms, kissing her way from his forehead to his lips.

"Reece," she said, "I need you to make love to me. Now."

Fifty-Four

Reece drew an appreciative breath. The aroma of ackee, codfish and fried dumplings surrounded him. It had always amused Sherryn and him that cooking scents traveled upstairs in their house, but were barely discernable on the ground floor. He rose, stretched and reached for the cellular phone on the bedside table. It wasn't there, but someplace downstairs, where he'd left it last night. It needed charging, and he had to find out from Ronald what he'd heard about Gloria's other baby-father.

Getting an update would have to wait for a more convenient time—after he'd given the cell some juice. He wouldn't call from his home phone. Ronald didn't need to have that bit of information.

In the shower, Reece relived the activities of the night just past. He hadn't questioned Sherryn's need to be intimate with him, but had given her the best loving he knew how.

She kept him occupied far into the night, bleeding the energy from him, until he forgot what he needed to do before he went to sleep.

Amusement lifted his lips. A month or so ago, if Sherryn had come on to him as strongly as she did last night, he might have been suspicious. He'd probably have made a stupid accusation, especially in light of her revelation that Judith had taken a lover. Their sex life had dried up under the strain, and like him, she had to be missing their regular lovemaking. He would admit he still didn't know everything about Sherryn, but was certain of one thing. They were well-matched on a sexual level.

The men in Waterhouse never understood how or why he turned down available women, and he had never explained that their trouble stemmed from their refusal to stick with one woman.

Reece had never forgotten the lessons learned from Miss Millicent. In outlining what she saw as women's likes and dislikes, she told him their biggest turn-off was a cheating man.

'If you want to have a peaceful life', she had told him, 'make sure you stick with one woman.'

He had passed on that bit of wisdom to Justin, but hadn't lived up to his own words. Still, he was certain his son understood the principle and strength of his arguments without him having to say he'd had enough casual sex in his teens and twenties to last two lifetimes. Apart from that, Sherryn would kill him if he slept with anybody else.

He valued their relationship too much to run the risk of losing her. His lapse with Gloria had shaken the foundation of his marriage, and he was unsure of his position with Sherryn, who was still sending him mixed signals.

He didn't know why she insisted on knowing all the details of his encounter with Gloria, but supposed it was a woman thing. He sure as heck didn't need a minute-by-minute report if Sherryn slept with someone else.

Shrugging on his shirt, Reece steered his mind away from the uncertainties, and padded downstairs to find the kitchen in chaos.

"Daddy, Daddy," Brandon cried, waving a spoon. "Me and Maurice helped Mommy fix breakfast."

"That's Maurice and I." Sherryn approached Reece, kissed his cheek, and murmured, "Don't say a word."

A hand gripped Reece's shoulder, and Justin spoke from behind him. "Is what happen in here?"

Sherryn rolled her eyes at her eldest. "You're going to hurt their feelings. What's wrong with you?"

Happy to be among them, Reece returned the boys' greetings and sat at the counter eyeing the bowls and spoons discarded amidst a dusting of flour. Two cups of half-drunk Nesquick stood in the middle of the items strewn on the tiles.

Sherryn cleared a space and put his mug down. Reece sniffed the coffee and sipped. Over the rim, he smiled in approval when he looked at Sherryn's sleeveless shirt and shorts.

Her naughty grin caught him off guard. "A little tired, maybe?"

He checked that Justin wasn't listening before responding to her teasing. "I should ask you that, Mrs. Allbright."

"You think you can test—"

Kyle erupted into the room at breakneck speed, his squeal drowning her words.

Celia and Melaine stopped in the doorway, exchanged disbelieving gasps, and backed away.

Reece chuckled when Sherryn caught them. "Come back you two. Help me get breakfast on the table."

Groaning, both girls brushed past Reece on their way to the island where Sherryn had laid out plates and serving dishes. Melaine moved to Sherryn's side and helped shuttle the plates to the table, while Celia glowered at being left to gather the mess of flour and dirty mixing bowls on the opposite counter.

In the dining area, Sherryn called for silence and asked Brandon to pray before they ate.

Reece pursed his lips to prevent laughter from slipping out when he caught Justin and Melaine's eye rolls. One or the other of them would eventually kick Brandon under the table to get him to stop praying so they could eat.

Sherryn always allowed Brandon to continue until he exhausted his lengthy grace. A smile escaped from Reece. The tradition was set to continue, according to Justin who told him that Brandon had Maurice in training.

A fervent 'Amen' went up around the table and when Reece lifted his head, he caught Sherryn studying him. He cocked his eyebrow in a question, and she held nothing back, rewarding him with one of her old smiles.

For the first time since Gloria brought Maurice to his door, Reece felt completely at ease in his home.

Fifty-Five

Sherryn waited until Reece returned from his shopping trip with Brandon and Maurice before she left the house. Both boys were ecstatic. Maurice now owned a PS Vita, and Brandon had more games at his disposal. Reece had not forgotten Kyle, and brought home a radio controlled Jeep, which he was teaching him to use.

Reece's indulgent grin stayed with her, warming her insides while she made her way to see Judith. Barbara pulled into the parking lot behind her and both of them walked into the lobby to wait. The receptionist behind the gleaming wooden counter rang Judith's room.

Sherryn followed Barbara down the passage, around a corner, and up a flight of stairs.

Judith let them in and removed the scarf from her head. "I just wanted to be sure it was you lot."

"Have you spoken to Barry?" Barbara asked, seating herself in one of the matching bamboo chairs around the table.

Judith shook her head. "Not really. He's called several times today already, saying he was sorry, and that I should come home, but I don't trust him. Not after what he did, and the things he said."

"What did the doctor say about your face?" Sherryn asked.

"It'll heal, but I'll look like this for another three or four days."

"Have you heard from Troy at all?" Sherryn asked.

Judith's smile turned into a grimace. "Ooh, I keep forgetting this needs to heal."

She gently touched the split on her lip and nodded. "Yes, I told him what happened."

Barbara kicked off her high-heels, frowning. "What did he say?"

"He wanted to find Barry and let him have it."

"That's just testosterone talking," Sherryn said, angling her head toward Judith. "Seriously though, you know this can't continue if you go back to

Barry. He's called me once already, and I told him off. He sounded apologetic, but I dunno."

"He called me too," Barb added, "and I put him in his place. He can save his tired apologies for someone else. Love has a look, but this right here," she gestured at Judith's face and bruised body, "is not it. If you do take him back, you should wait until he gets counseling first."

Judith sighed. "I'm thinking about not going back at all. Remember I was planning to leave in the first place. That's what got Barry mad."

"It's a good thing Jackie's living on campus, eh?" Sherryn said.

"Not like you and Reece with the kids at home. I suppose that's one thing I don't have to think about. Jackie's old enough to understand a separation."

"I beg to differ," Barbara said, "No pickney is old enough or willing to understand why their father chooses to beat their mother. And they never, ever understand divorce."

Judith gasped. "I wouldn't dream of telling her Barry hit me."

"So how are you going to explain leaving home?" Barbara asked.

"I'll think of something."

"What about Troy?" Sherryn asked. "You gonna tell her about him? That might be a bit tougher for her to deal with."

Judith slouched on the bed. "You know what? I'm tired of living for other people. First, I couldn't leave Barry, because Jackie was too young. Then, I stayed because of what everybody would think." She licked her lips and fiddled with the cord hanging from the waistband of her pants. "After that, I didn't want to leave all that I'd worked for, and have him bring some young gyal into our house and guess what? All this time Barry's been living it up, and I've been vegetating."

She strolled to the window. "Well, no more. I was so caught up in worrying about his threats, I forgot I don't need him. I have money of my own. And if Troy wants to continue our relationship, I won't say no. To hell with Barry."

"You still need to be careful," Barbara said.

"I know. After I leave here, I think I'm going to cool out somewhere on the North Coast for a while. Give myself time to revive."

Barbara smiled. "You know what, Judith? Good for you. I wish I had the courage to do what you're doing, but I guess I'm too set in my ways now to go start over on my own."

Judith turned, and Sherryn was pleased that regardless of the damage to her face, Judith glowed with strength and determination.

"It's never too late," she said. "Matter of fact, I'm going to do what I should have done days ago. I'm going to get a restraining order against Barry."

Barbara and Sherryn gasped.

"Are you sure?" Sherryn asked.

Judith nodded. "It's about time I took charge of my life." She folded her arms. "While I'm at it, I'm going to file for divorce. Things are never going to get any better. I've let him take me for granted way too long. He doesn't respect me any more, no matter what he says. I'm more of a comfort to him than anything else. Kinda like a pair of old bed slippers. It's time to move on with my life."

On hearing Judith's words, a small bud of hope bloomed inside Sherryn. She had no plans to start life on her own, or with anybody else for that matter, because she had a good one. She simply needed to concentrate on pruning the diseased branches inside her that threatened to wither and drain the life from her marriage.

Sherryn pulled into the driveway, honked the horn, and waited for one of the older kids to appear.

A minute later, Justin came out to help unload the van.

Brandon and Maurice followed him outside and then trailed behind Sherryn, raving about their new games. Their focus shifted once they got into Sherryn's office, and she pulled colorful boxes in different sizes from the shopping bags.

"Christmas decorations!" Brandon yelled. "I love Christmas!"

Maurice's joy evaporated, piquing Sherryn's curiosity. "Don't you like Christmas, Maurice?"

He shrugged. "We never have Christmas in my yard. It always feel like any other day to me."

Sherryn rubbed his head, and then chucked him under the chin. "Well, this year it's going to be different. We're decorating the tree tomorrow, and we Allbrights have a great time during Christmas. Don't we, Brandon?"

"Yes!" he yelled, exposing his gap. Both hands stuck out above his head while he did a funny wiggle.

Sherryn slipped a hand over Maurice's shoulder as they giggled. "This Christmas will be a good one for you," she said.

He chewed a fingernail while hope lit his eyes. "You think so?"

"I know so," she said, bumping him up against her side.

He tugged at her shirt. "Me goin' to get a present too?"

While her insides twisted with sadness, she smiled at him. "All our children get presents, so that's a yes."

"Yes!" It was Maurice's turn to make some odd moves while spinning around the room.

It never ceased to amaze Sherryn how little it took to make him happy.

The boys helped her lay the boxes on the side table next to her desk, chattering non-stop.

With her back to the doorway, she sensed Reece's presence and turned to look at him. He held on to the doorjamb, observing them.

A quick flash of regret forced her to look away from him, and a spasm passed through her chest.

Reece stood in the same place, hesitating as if he wasn't sure he was welcome. In the past, he'd have slid his arms around her, snuggled up close, and pressed a kiss to her neck. Instead, he scratched his scalp while biting his lower lip.

Sympathy and love for him made her throat tight. Reece had more than proven his commitment to both her and their family, despite straying.

It was time to move forward.

The boys' conversation faded in the background. She held Reece's gaze as she approached, hiding nothing from him. Slipping her arms around his waist, she hugged him.

He held her close, and when their lips met in a tentative kiss, a chorus rose behind them. "Na-Naaawww!"

Their lips touched again, and the boys went past them making retching sounds.

Reece's lips curved against hers and he kissed her again.

She held the back of his head, and rested her forehead against his. "I've missed you," she said.

He touched his lips to hers, smiling. "I've missed you more."

He intensified their kiss, and slipped his hands under the tail of her shirt.

"We can't," she murmured.

He groaned against her lips. "I know."

Laughing, she slipped away from him. "Patience is a virtue."

"One I don't have, where you're concerned," he said.

But they both knew his words were far from the truth. He would wait forever if that was how long it took to repair their relationship. He'd also bide his time, waiting for her to work through her anger and disappointment with him.

Knowing she was hurting them both with her foolishness, Sherryn closed her head and let go of the need to keep punishing him. She cupped the sides of his face and met his gaze.

"Reece," she said, "I love you."

Tears washed his eyes and he pulled her into a tight hug.

She laid her head against his chest, wondering how it was possible to tell him she loved him when she hadn't forgiven him.

Fifty-Six

From his recliner, Reece absorbed the activities going on around him. The family had returned from church a few hours ago and was now gathered in the living room. Justin hogged the remote, but kept a half-interested eye on what the boys were doing in the corner.

Reece had gotten out the Christmas tree earlier, and Justin opened its synthetic fronds and left Melaine and Celia to string the lights. Sherryn and the younger boys now had the task of putting up the decorations.

With Sherryn occupied hanging ornaments, Reece seized the opportunity to escape. He unplugged the cell phone from the charger and slipped out of the room.

Sherryn eyed him with suspicion in her gaze, but said nothing.

Reece walked into the front yard, dialing as he went. "Ronald, wha' happen, man? Sherryn tell mi she hear something on the news 'bout Gloria baby-father. You hear anyt'ing?"

"Mi all right, but mi not even wa'an talk 'bout dat on di phone. Anyway, di police have him in lock up."

"Really?" Curiosity stirred inside him, but Reece knew better than to press Ronald when he didn't want to talk. "Anything new wid your case?"

"Not a t'ing, but before me go a jail fi Gloria murder, mi prefer run off."

"Dat won't help if yuh not guilty."

"You know how t'ings set up. If dem can't find di real killer, mi don' stand a chance. Dem just goin' to make it look like is me kill her. Yuh know dat too."

Stumped for an answer, Reece grunted and turned to face the house.

Sherryn beckoned to him from the verandah.

He raised a hand to acknowledge her, then spoke into the phone. "Ronald, mi can't talk now. Mi wi' call you later if mi get a chance."

"Reece," Sherryn said over her shoulder, when he reentered the living room, "would you reach the box with the rest of the decorations up on the shelf in the cupboard?"

Justin lounged on the sofa, scrolling through the channels, which raised the question of why she specifically needed him to do what Justin could manage with ease, being almost as tall as he? If he didn't know better, Sherryn was trying to prevent him from doing whatever she thought he wanted to do.

Although he'd gotten Ronald on the phone, he still wasn't satisfied because he needed more information. He put that out of his mind and did what Sherryn asked.

"Here, honey," he said, searching her face when he came back to her side.

She met his steady appraisal, all innocence when he put the carton on the floor beside her. He picked up the newspaper and while browsing the various sections, stayed tuned to the chatter and occasional outbursts of laughter from Sherryn and her small helpers.

She served them lunch afterward, asked him to help Brandon with his homework, and at the end of the day, Reece acknowledged with admiration that he'd been delicately, but firmly sidetracked with domestic duties.

He lay wrapped around her that night, musing on her wily tactics. If she was willing to go to such lengths to keep him by her side, wasn't it best to think about cutting all ties with Ronald, as well as the old neighborhood, when the murder was solved?

On Monday morning, Sherryn's sober warning for Reece to be careful was confirmation that she had launched a campaign of evasive action to keep him separated from Ronald. He waited until he was on the way to the office before making the call to arrange a meeting with Ronald after work.

During lunchtime, Reece ensured he picked up the items Sherryn asked him to get at the cake supply shop, so he wouldn't forget, and at precisely five minutes after five, he left the office and drove over to Waterhouse.

The same dusty roads and depressing zinc fences met him, as well as the ever-searching mongrels, eaten up by mange. They meandered over familiar terrain, sniffing hopefully at the ground.

Ronald emerged from his yard muttering to himself. A brindled dog yelped from the kick Ronald planted on its hip as it dared push past him before the gate swung shut.

"Wha' happen, blood?" Ronald greeted him with an upraised fist, but his eyes roved up and down the street.

"Nothin' much, mi brotha." Reece knocked his fist lightly against Ronald's, observing what he knew was a childish ritual.

Ronald had dragged his clothes on in a hurry. His shirt was rumpled and his pants unbuttoned. He zipped up his jeans before raising reddened eyes to meet Reece's.

.   "So wha' you hear 'bout Gloria baby-father?" Reece asked.

Ronald's words were slow and precise, as if he'd just smoked a heavy spliff. "Boy, you wa'an see, di police arrest him, 'cause di car him was traveling in was carrying ganja."

"Den what happen to him pickney dem?"

Pointing behind him, Ronald explained, "Dem still staying wid dem granny roun' di road."

Ronald sniffed and then folded his arms and leaned in close. "You won' see mi for a while. It not safe round 'ere for you either. Something go down on the weekend, and mi goin' to lie low for a likkle time."

He slid both hands into grubby pockets and shuffled his Reeboks on the cement. "Mi goin' beg you a t'ing to tide mi over."

Light-headed with relief, Reece slipped Ronald the contents of his wallet—four one thousand dollar notes. "All right, take care and walk good."

"You tek care a yuhself too," Ronald said, "and don' come back 'til you get word dat t'ings calm down."

Reece got in the van, watching Ronald's progress down the sidewalk. Whatever he had gotten involved in this time was more than he could handle.

Reece's let his breath whistle through his teeth. Though Ronald's situation was life-threatening, Reece was happy for any excuse to avoid Waterhouse, and at the same time, stay out of trouble with Sherryn.

At the end of the street, Ronald turned the corner, hitching up his pants on his waist. Reece fired up the engine and drove off toward home.

On entering Queensborough, he compared his present life with his past. He'd come a long way. The individually designed houses on spacious lots of land provided a stark contrast to the squalor of Waterhouse. He thanked God again for providing a way out of the aimless life that might have been his had he not escaped the ghetto. Otherwise, he might have been dead already. Half the men Reece knew in childhood had not made it past thirty. In the ghetto, a don was considered a grandfather if he made it to forty.

In view of his activities, Ronald was lucky, living on borrowed time. He had never been able to explain how he dealt with the stress of moving from place to place, staying out of sight for extended periods, and looking over his shoulder when things got hot in the neighborhood. No wonder he looked at life the way he did. Nothing much mattered. Live for today.

Good thing he never had any children, or at least none that Reece knew about.

Reece parked in his driveway, got out, and reached behind his seat. The back of his neck prickled; someone was watching him. He straightened and turned to where Sherryn stood motionless, framed by their bedroom window.

They exchanged a smile, but he felt her anxiety. Wondering what could have gone wrong, he left her order on the kitchen counter, checked on the children, and reached their bedroom in record time.

She hadn't moved from the window, but turned to survey him in a single sweep. She crossed the room and stood before him. Then, she leaned close and breathed in his scent. Shaking her head, she said, "I knew it."

"Knew what?"

She looked away and spoke low in her throat. "You just can't help yourself."

He kissed her temple, grasping her upper arms. "Is everything all right?"

"For the time being," she said, still studying him.

And he understood then that Sherryn somehow knew she had not prevented him from doing what he felt compelled to do—namely, get in touch with Ronald. Didn't she understand that by mentioning the father of Gloria's children to him, she had sent him down that road? Ronald was his main source of information in Waterhouse, making it a given that he would contact him.

He hugged her, rubbing a hand over the smooth skin of her back. "It'll be all right."

She didn't return his embrace and he leaned away to catch her response.

"I don't know, Reece. Not when you won't stay away from that hoodlum." She paced the length of the room before she faced him again. "D'you know he was picked up a short while ago with a whole bunch of other thugs? I heard a news flash on the radio just before you got here."

Reece lowered himself into the rocking chair. A tic danced beside his eye.

What in the world had Ronald done now?

Her voice cut into his thoughts. "You didn't know that, did you? And I'll bet you saw him sometime before that. How do I get you to understand you need to stop going to Waterhouse?"

Her raised hands emphasized her words and her distress, but Reece didn't move or speak, for fear of upsetting her more.

"Doesn't it matter to you that that is how you got that woman pregnant? Because you won't stay away from that blasted place?"

He tried to tell her he had no choice about going there, but she slammed the door and left him alone.

Fingers itching, he pulled out his cell phone and dialed Ronald's number, which rang until the voicemail kicked in. Two more attempts, and he gave up. The police probably had the phone in their possession.

A tremor ran through his body when he realized his mistake. He hoped the cops wouldn't check Ronald's call history.

Pushing against the floor to start the rocker, Reece searched his mind to come up with what he'd heard concerning Waterhouse on the news over the previous weekend. He was certain it had to do with Ronald being picked up by the police today.

He closed his eyes and exhaled, long and slow. It was a miracle he hadn't offered Ronald a drink, as he usually did. If Reece had lingered, the police would have arrested him along with Ronald. He shivered, thinking about what Sherryn would have done if he'd been caught in that dragnet.

She avoided him for the rest of the evening, but to give her credit, the children didn't notice anything amiss, because she made dinner a normal affair. They both exchanged jokes with the kids and few words with each other.

Reece went to his study during the time she and the kids were restoring order to the kitchen and dining room. He had to sort out this latest incident before they went to bed because he wanted nothing standing between them.

He'd bet Sherryn was not only thinking about the danger of associating with Ronald, but with Gloria's drama. She'd feel that if he slipped once, he might be looking at other women. In fact, he wasn't, but Sherryn would have been alarmed if she had a true picture of how available a fair portion of ghetto women were.

A lopsided smile escaped him. Maybe she did know how easy it was to bed them, which formed part of the reason why she worried when he was in

Waterhouse. Not that he thought her concern was unwarranted. If the positions were reversed, he'd be uneasy each time she visited the area, or even glanced at another man.

He rubbed his forehead with his fingertips, still sorting through his thoughts. If only he could go back, he'd do everything differently. But that was not an option, so he reckoned he'd fix what he did have some control over.

When he entered their bedroom, Sherryn sat reading by the lamp on the bedside table. One of her legs rested over the other, and the book hid her face. He closed the door behind him, sat on the bed, and pulled the novel out of her hand, aware she'd stopped reading the moment the door opened.

She stared him in the face, which he read as an attempt to unnerve him.

"I did go to Waterhouse today, but it was only to get some information."

She cocked one brow at him. "You've given up trucking and gone into private investigation?"

"You know I only wanted to find out about Gloria's baby-father."

"I don't know anything." She drew her legs up to hug them and focused somewhere behind him. "Except for the fact that you seem determined to be dragged down by that godforsaken place."

"It's not like that, Sherryn. Today I finally realized what's tying me to Waterhouse, why I keep going back."

She gave him her full attention.

"Ronald is the reason."

A frown contracted her brows and stayed in place.

He strolled over to their dresser, unmindful of the items resting there. "It's taken me a while to figure it out, but I've known him ever since I can remember. We both went to the same schools, well, until he dropped out of high school." Resting both hands on the stained wood, Reece grimaced. "He didn't make anything of himself. He didn't have the drive to succeed I guess, but I've always looked out for him."

Sherryn rolled her eyes toward the ceiling. "Ronald is not a child. He's a loafer, who's been sucking money off you all these years."

Reece dropped on the mattress beside her. "I know, but it's as if I somehow feel responsible for him not making it. I've tried to help him, but he won't keep a job and—"

"It's his life, Reece, and he's entitled to decide what to do with it."

"You think I don't know that?"

"You're not responsible for Ronald, and the sooner you realize that, the better things will be between us."

He sighed. "I hear you. Anyway, I suppose he'll be in lock up, so—"

"Good."

Slightly irritated, he looked closely at her. "You don't understand, do you? He's the only link I have from my childhood that's almost as good as family."

Sherryn straightened her legs and sat forward. "No, Reece. *You* don't understand. Your family is here. Don't forget it! Because the next time you do any foolishness, I won't stand behind you, or forgive you."

She got off the bed and stomped into the bathroom, slamming the door.

He stared at it—that was the second time this evening he'd upset her. Maybe it was time to rethink the way he'd been looking at things.

Fifty-Seven

Reece stepped out of the shower, wrapped a towel around his waist, and padded into the bedroom.

Sherryn, in a pale-yellow sundress, applied lip-gloss before grabbing her handbag off the chest-of-drawers. She turned, bumping into him.

He put out a hand to steady her, before kissing her forehead.

"You should listen to the seven o' clock news," she said, resting a hand against his cheek.

His eye twitched and he sighed. Some unpleasant news was coming.

She left the room, clicking the door shut between them. On the bedside table, the clock read 6:45 a.m. Enough time to put his clothes on, and be ready for breakfast.

Chaos reigned in the kitchen, as usual. The girls buzzed past Justin to the sink to leave their empty dishes. Brandon zipped his lunch bag and picked up Kyle's, muttering that he didn't need to take a fruit to school. Only Maurice was unperturbed, waiting for Sherryn by the door, PS Vita in hand. Reece rubbed his head on the way past him. "You all right?"

He shook his head vigorously, taking Sherryn's hand. She wasted no time. "Come on guys, time to go."

"Bye, Daddy," the kids said while shuffling past their mother.

"Have a good day," Reece said, sitting down over steamed cabbage with codfish and bananas that Sherryn had prepared.

She had gotten the kids out of the house on time, based on the chiming of the hour from the clock over the door.

Reece switched on the radio and listened to the ads playing after the main headline. The news aired for ten minutes, and when the last item was read, the fork in his hand clattered onto the half-cleared plate.

"And on the crime blotters, the police are investigating the murder of Ronald Vincent, of a Waterhouse address. He was killed last night in what police theorize was a reprisal for another man killed in a drive-by shooting this past weekend. Vincent was detained by the

police yesterday and was being questioned in connection with a murder. He was released early last night. His murder brings the total to ... "

Reece moved only when Miss Em dropped her handbag on the counter near him.

"Mornin', Missa Reece. Somethin' happen to you?"

Shaking his head, he got up. "No, I'm fine."

His feet hit the stairs one deliberate tread at a time. In the bathroom, he rinsed his mouth, then changed his mind and brushed his teeth again. He stared at his reflection, feeling as if he was shut up in an empty room. He wasn't grieving. What he felt was regret at the futile existence Ronald had led. Forty-three, with nothing to show for having lived that many years.

Reece didn't know what had become of Ronald's relatives, and wondered how he'd be buried. He supposed he'd have to foot the expense, but he couldn't go to the funeral. Based on Ronald's instruction for him to lie low, Reece had to stay away to avoid being shot as an accomplice. In these days of increasing drive-by shootings, he wouldn't risk his safety. He'd find out which morgue had Ronald's body and make arrangements for his burial.

Reece sat on the edge of the bed, staring at his clasped hands. He'd run countless risks by staying friends with Ronald. What if he'd been with him when he was killed? He'd have been shot dead, and Sherryn left to raise their children alone.

Reece passed the back of his hand over his mouth and got up, surprised to find he was sweating. He had to go to work, but first he had to get his thoughts together. It was weird that only the night before, Sherryn had warned him about Waterhouse. Now he had no ties there, no reason to return. Ronald was all that held him there all those years, and now he was a memory.

Justin's laughing face flashed before him and Reece closed his eyes. Did Justin know where his father spent a good portion of his time and who with? What sort of example had he set for his son, who was almost a man? Keeping company with someone who'd chosen to take a far different path in life than the one Reece trod made no sense, only he hadn't seen it.

Rubbing the back of his neck, Reece walked out of the house and opened the van.

Justin missed little, which made Reece think hard. Fortunately, he'd never taken Justin to Waterhouse, subconsciously fearing that somehow the lassitude and poverty might rub off and contaminate his young life.

But it was foolish to think that way. He'd come from there, and with hard work and a bit of ambition, had made something of himself. With a little determination, Ronald could have done the same, but he'd submitted to peer pressure, and never made it out.

Reece had escaped, but still nursed an inferiority complex that kept him bound to the place where he was born.

Like the gradual appearance of the sun on a hazy morning, he finally understood and accepted that where he came from didn't make him less of a man. In fact, his success against terrible odds made his life remarkable.

"I don't need to be ashamed," he whispered.

Then he smiled and spoke louder. "I don't need to be ashamed."

In his forty-three years, he'd never before accepted that nothing he did would change the fact that he was from Waterhouse. It didn't matter to Sherryn, and she had told him so a thousand times. Nor did it matter to anybody else. The only person hung up on his birthplace was him. Sherryn used it against him only because Waterhouse was still his Achilles heel, despite the number of years that had passed.

He locked the seat belt, cementing the thought that it was past time he got over where his life had started because it had no bearing on his day-to-day existence. He needed to accept the knowledge and move on.

Easing onto the road, he admitted the only thing bothering him now was the lack of a suspect in Gloria's murder. As guilty as it made him feel, Reece hoped the murder accusation had died with Ronald. He didn't see Sherryn standing with him through a murder charge, not after her warning last night.

While he waited for the traffic to move, he pictured Sherryn's face. Finally, she had told him on the weekend what he'd waited to hear over the agonizing months just past. Wrapped up in his relief was the knowledge that she still kept a bit of resentment close to her chest.

Perhaps it was the way she shuttered her eyes when she said she loved him, or maybe it was her soft sigh, hinting at things unresolved and unsaid. He'd grown used to her stonewalling him, but still wanted her complete forgiveness.

Maybe he was overambitious, but he hoped she'd soon reopen the parts of herself she'd closed off from him. He'd have to wait and see.

Fifty-Eight

Sherryn sucked her teeth and flung the magazine into the opposite corner of the sofa. She was restless, without knowing why. Squinting into the dazzling sunlight, she made a note to trim the hedges. They were going too wild. The grass also needed cutting.

Reece hated mowing the lawn, and Justin was too lazy, so she'd have to get their sometime gardener in to do the job.

She hadn't called Reece to find out how he was dealing with the news of Ronald's death.

When he wanted to be, Reece could be described as the strong, silent type, but the news must have had some impact on him.

She regretted that he'd lost a friend—somewhat—but was relieved that the previously unexplained umbilical cord linking him to Waterhouse was severed. She'd always resented the time he spent there. He loved her, she knew that, but she also had a subliminal fear that someday he'd find a woman from Waterhouse who understood him better than she did, based on their shared background.

That had been her biggest worry when Gloria appeared at her door, but her doubts only served to undermine her confidence. She insisted on Reece giving her all the details of his encounter with Gloria because she had to find out whether they had anything together like the relationship she shared with Reece. She'd been relieved to know that what she saw as an ongoing affair was a one-time, unfortunate event—not that it hurt any less—and that she was still the woman he loved and needed.

Her biggest source of comfort was that he hadn't lied to her. His pained account had reduced her to tears, but at the end, she was satisfied that he told her everything.

Meantime, Sherryn struggled not to shoulder blame for his unfaithfulness. Yes, she had refused to have sex with him, but he'd made the choice to cheat.

Reece, being a one-of-a-kind man, went a step further than her when he forgave her for denying him. And when Reece forgave, he did so without reservation.

In hesitating to share her fears about his connections in Waterhouse and how they might hurt his marriage, she'd played her favorite trick on him—withdrawing completely. She sighed, disgusted with herself. How did she expect to work through their combined problems, when she was still playing the old games? Even now, she was holding on to spite by sealing away a part of herself from him.

She sucked her lip into her mouth. For the first time, it occurred to her that whenever Reece failed to get through to her, he frequented Waterhouse—as if the community was a panacea for his problems. Then he'd come home smelling of beer, although he wasn't a habitual drinker.

She moved to the chair behind her desk, hit by a brainwave.

Waterhouse was obviously where he felt most comfortable when she shunned him, and she kept sending him there.

Her mother's advice about talking things out echoed in her ears. Veronica Jones was all for open communication in marriage—she'd always said so.

Sherryn snorted, realizing in a sudden flare of inspiration that she'd adopted her mother's mindset.

It had always puzzled her, the tendency she had to withdraw into herself when displeased. Narrowing her eyes, she remembered sitting at her mother's dining table, where the older woman hadn't done a good job of hiding her prejudice against Maurice. She also recalled her father's murmured words to her that her mother would come around.

Up to now, her mother still hadn't managed to make Maurice feel at ease in her presence. Sherryn smiled again, thinking Maurice had some smarts on him, because he stayed away from Sherryn's mother whenever they were in the same space.

It didn't make sense to Sherryn, but she wondered how it was possible to have grown attached to Maurice in such a short time, yet, she still kept his father at a distance.

As though she willed him to appear, Maurice sailed into the room, flip-flops churning and workbook in hand.

"I'm finished," he announced.

She sat at the desk and beckoned him toward her. "Good boy. Lemme see what you've done."

He leaned in close to her with an expectant air.

A moment passed before she smiled while rubbing his hair. "When you go to school next term, you're gonna do very well, Maurice. I'm so proud of you."

Instead of the grin she expected, Maurice's mouth turned down and he blinked hard to avoid crying.

"What's wrong?" she asked, squeezing his shoulder.

"Nothing. Just that Gloria never tell me anythin' like that."

"Maybe she didn't know better," Sherryn said, hoping to cheer him up.

Standing akimbo, he asked, "Where you think she gone?"

Sherryn ran a hand over the open workbook before attempting to answer. "Well, the Bible says when people die, their souls go back to God, who made them in the first place."

Maurice's rucked-up brows conveyed his doubt. "You mean she gone to heaven?"

"I didn't say that. I said—"

He waved at her. "Yes, that her soul gone back to God. But where God is?"

"God is everywhere, Maurice."

He nodded as if he understood, but she was certain he had more questions. Trying to avoid one of the lengthy debates she usually had with Brandon, she added, "We'll talk more about it another time."

"Just one more question," he said, moving from one foot to the other. "How come you couldn't be my mother?"

A rush of tears forced her to blink—once, twice, and swallow to keep her voice steady. She groped for his hands. "Well, Maurice, when you think about it, I *am* the only mother you have right now."

He gave her a radiant smile, showing an off-kilter tooth ready to fall out. Then, to her surprise, he hugged her neck, kissed her cheek, and whispered, "Love you, Auntie Sherryn."

She swiveled in the chair to hug him close and let her tears fall, murmuring into his neck. "I love you too, Maurice."

Fifty-Nine

Reece longed for closure, but it proved elusive. Ronald's death cut him off from what used to be easily accessible information. Another two weeks slipped by, and he had no idea whether the police still had Gloria's other baby-father in custody, nor was he going to be foolish enough to call them up to ask. So life continued, while he hoped for news that would exonerate him.

Lowering the newspaper he hadn't been able to read earlier in the day, he watched Brandon and Maurice's lively enactment of a car chase. They knelt on the carpet in the center of the room, although Sherryn frequently warned them not to play there. She feared them bouncing against the coffee table and knocking over the bud vase, which always held stalks of anthurium. They never stayed away for long, and continued to shred Sherryn's nerves by bumping the table as they played.

"You're not supposed to kill the driver," Brandon cried.

"Why not? You always get to crash my cars," Maurice said.

"You stupid or what? I'm supposed to overtake you and speed off."

"Is you stupid! Why you must get to pass me all the time?"

Reece chuckled behind the paper, but didn't interfere.

Maurice had come into his own, shedding his hesitance to speak, and getting over an obvious lack of confidence to spar with Brandon. He was intelligent, a quick learner, as Sherryn had confirmed, proudly showing him Maurice's bookwork several times each week.

She walked in, carrying two bowls with ice cream and Jell-o. The boys scrambled into the largest sofa, abandoning the cars in a haphazard crush of colored plastic. Brandon turned on the television before dipping his spoon into the bowl and letting out an appreciative groan. Maurice grinned at him, revealing an open space where his front teeth had fallen out.

Sherryn tapped Reece's knee. "Want some?"

Reece answered with a smile, "Yes, Ma'am."

Going back the way she came, Sherryn rubbed Maurice's head in an affectionate gesture, which made Reece think. Even though she still held something against him, it didn't extend to Maurice. If it were possible, in that smidgen of time, he loved Sherryn more than ever.

She returned, holding a bowl of ice cream out to him. In taking it from her, he let his fingers rest over hers, a question in his eyes.

They needed no words.

Her answer was yes.

Their lovemaking was everything Reece expected it to be, and then some. He relaxed, resting his head below her breast. He strung kisses on Sherryn's belly, happy she'd released more of her animosity.

As the sweat dried from their skin, she ran a hand over his shoulder and cupped the back of his head. Then, she kissed his forehead. "No matter what, you never lose your touch."

Reece chuckled and then pressed his lips to her side, making a vulgar sound. When they stopped laughing, he adjusted his position to cradle her head against his shoulder. "I have to stay in shape, Mrs. Allbright. You think I want some man to run off with you?"

"What man in his right mind is going to run away with a woman who has half dozen children?"

"I don't want to find out, so I plan to stay on top of things." He squeezed her against him. "Look at Judith. Didn't you say she was taking off with some young boy? And she's older than you."

"That's way out of the ordinary. Besides, she hasn't exactly run off with him, yet. She invited him down to stay with her in Ocho Rios, so I doubt they're doing any running right now." She wiggled her brows while her eyes sparkled in the beams of light slanting in from the street.

"I guess not." Reece frowned and ran a hand down her thigh. "D'you think it's gonna last?"

"Even if it doesn't," Sherryn groaned, gripping his busy fingers, "she'll be happy for a time."

"I guess," he said.

They stopped talking and put their energy into what they most enjoyed doing together.

A stinging slap on his bare shoulder roused him.

"Wake up, Reece!"

Groggy from being forced out of sleep before he was ready, Reece moaned and rubbed his eyes while Sherryn shook him.

"I have exciting news," she yelled in his ear.

He peered into her bright eyes. This had to be good.

She was like a playful puppy that refused to be sidetracked from a new game. He rolled his head to read the clock—just past seven. She rivaled the blinding light in the room with her energy.

Sherryn grabbed his shoulder again. "You're not the least bit curious?"

He yawned and rubbed his chest. "When I wake up I will be."

"Come on, Reece. This is the most important thing to happen to you in two months!"

That caught his attention, and he sat up. "What is it?"

She hugged him, pressing his face into the open space where her top button was undone. He caught a whiff of Fendi, which was one of her favourite scents. "You're in the clear, Reece. Free! He confessed! They said so on the news!"

Though he enjoyed the unrestrained hugging, Reece needed to find out exactly what had her so outrageously upbeat. "Who confessed, Sherryn?"

She kissed both his cheeks and came close to ripping his ears off in her exuberance. "Someone named Renford Bayliss."

A hopeful flutter started in his chest. "Gloria's baby-father?"

"Yes! Yes! Yes! He confessed!"

"Why?"

That seemed to dampen her spirit. "She was blackmailing him over his ganja business. They had a fight and he hit her, but truthfully, I don't care. I'm just happy to know you didn't do it."

Reece felt like she'd slapped him. Hard. "Oh, so all this time you believed I killed her?"

The joy on Sherryn's face slipped away. "Reece, after eighteen years with you, there's a side of yourself you never share with me, and the day before she was attacked, you looked at her with such hatred, and I remembered the threat you made against her, and I—"

He brushed her aside and walked to the bathroom, disappointment weighing him down.

"I told you I didn't kill her, and somehow I knew you didn't believe me." He stopped, turning to look at her. "Sherryn, if you, my wife, didn't believe me, who would have?"

Sixty

Sherryn couldn't have felt worse than if she'd hit Reece again, and in a sense, she had. She hadn't meant to say what she did, but in many ways, Reece was a mystery. Some things he never talked about, except to gloss over the surface as though she couldn't deal with anything deeper.

His early history was among the things he kept to himself. His anger was another thing he kept under firm control. Still, she was conscious of him holding on to the rage that sometimes threatened to explode. The last time she witnessed it was when Gloria followed them to the restaurant.

No, she didn't want to think Reece would kill, but she'd be dishonest if she didn't admit thinking he was perfectly capable of it, if he thought he was protecting his family. She'd been proven so wrong. She tapped her fingers on the steering wheel, then sighed before getting out of the van to face the midday heat.

In the building that housed Reece's office, she kept her hand hidden and eased from foot to foot. She greeted Reece's assistant with a bright smile.

"Hello, Sherryn. Good to see you." Maureen pointed to Reece's door. "I saw the van outside, and told him you were here. He said to send you in."

"I appreciate it. Thanks."

He waited for her, positioned sideways behind the desk, staring at the asphalt outside. His solemn air and stern profile combined to make her heart race.

Wiping her clammy hands on her jeans one at a time, Sherryn slid onto Reece's lap. She brushed his cheek and lips with a single yellow rose, before wrapping his fingers around the stalk and laying his hand in her lap.

"D'you know why I'm giving you this rose?"

He shrugged, but didn't look at her.

"I could have given you a red one to remind you of my love, and the passion I feel for you, but this flower ... " She raised his hand to bring the bloom into view. "This flower signifies the joy I feel that you're my husband and friend. I should have taken you at your word, Reece. I'm sorry."

She pressed soft kisses to his unresponsive mouth. "I know you'd do anything to protect us, but please forgive me for even thinking you'd murder someone to do it."

His lips moved under hers. "How d'you plan to make this up to me, Mrs. Allbright?"

"I'm taking you out for lunch."

He wrapped his hands around her waist and murmured, "I'm to be bribed with so-so lunch? Where?"

"You'll see," she said, easing off his lap.

She had dropped Miss Em and Maurice off at the supermarket with a list that would keep them occupied for some time. Driving at breakneck speed, she took Reece home and dragged him into the shower.

In their bedroom, she treated him to everything guaranteed to make him forget his disappointment with her.

Some time later, she hurried out of the shower again to find him buttoning his cuff.

"So tell me again why Renford killed Gloria," he said, "I had several meetings and missed hearing the news."

"Remember how the police stopped him in a speed trap?"

He nodded, while she moved around the room gathering her clothes. "They detained him because of the ganja in the car. The amount was too much for it to be anything but commodity for sale."

She pulled her clothes back on while Reece slipped his shirt into his pants. In front of the mirror, she brushed her hair. "Anyway, they questioned him about the murder again while they had him locked up, and he admitted killing her. Apparently, he didn't mean to do it. The news said she found out about the ganja and threatened to expose him if he didn't pay her to keep quiet."

Reece grimaced behind her. "That sounds like Gloria. Greedy as hell. Maurice said she was always arguing with Renford about money for the other two children."

She hugged him. "I'm so glad this is over. You have no idea."

"Of course I do," he said, returning her embrace. "You weren't the one accused of murder."

She touched his cheek and met his eyes. "What did you ever do to Gloria to make her hate you like that? If he hadn't confessed, you might have gone to jail on her say-so. That's some vendetta."

"She hated me because I wouldn't give up my money as and when she wanted, and she knew I'd do anything to preserve our marriage."

"Thank God things worked out this way," she said, backing away from him. "Come on. We have to leave now."

"I don't understand you," he grumbled on the way downstairs. "You take me home, use my body 'til I'm weak, and then I can't even catch my breath or get somethin' to eat."

When they sat in the vehicle with the engine running, Sherryn gasped at the time. "I better stop at the supermarket first. Miss Em and Maurice will think I forgot them."

Reece squeezed her leg. "Of course she'll know you left them without transportation to go home and, uh, give me some lunch."

He laughed, and the sound delighted Sherryn. "I think she'll forgive me this time, seeing as how she worships the ground you walk on."

"Lucky for you then, but I'm still upset, 'cause you promised me lunch, and mi still don't get any."

"Sorry, babes. We can pick up something on the way back. I'd better get those two lunch as well, to keep them quiet. You mind a BK burger?"

"No, but you said I shouldn't have—"

"Never mind, Reece. A burger once in a while won't hurt."

"I hope you remember that the next time I want one."

She ignored his grumbling and concentrated on navigating through the lunch hour traffic.

Miss Em and Maurice waited curbside in the supermarket parking lot.

Reece loaded the van with the assortment of plastic bags, getting an earful from Miss Em, who clucked at how expensive it was to shop for a big family.

Maurice hung between the seats, frowning into Sherryn's face. "So how come you take so long to come back? The sun did really hot outside and—"

"Was really hot outside," Sherryn said, to distract him.

He repeated her words before going back to his questions. "So where you did—where did you go?" he asked.

"I went to pick up your father, and now we're going for burgers."

"Cool!" He relaxed against the seat, satisfied, and picked up the PS Vita.

A sneaky sideways glance at Reece confirmed that he was holding back laughter.

She pinched his arm. "I just verified something."

"Well?" he said, with his lips pulled into a lazy grin.

"You know how Brandon asks endless questions? I just found out he got that from your side of the family. The budding detective in the back is proof."

He laughed again and faced forward in his seat. "If you say so, Mrs. Allbright."

Sherryn inched through the traffic to buy them lunch, enjoying the extra time with Reece. She dropped him off at his office with a whispered promise to pick up where they left off, if he could cope.

He squeezed her chin before kissing her. "We'll see."

She watched him walk away, unable to imagine what life would be like without him. He was one special man—proud in many ways, and yet so humble in others.

The protests from the backseat about them being burnt to cinders got her moving. She turned the air-conditioning on to appease them, and pulled into the street, chuckling to herself. Though she'd had to work her way back into his good graces, Reece had made it more than worthwhile.

Sixty-One

"Five days left for Christmas shopping, five days left to fill the stocking
… " Brandon and Maurice sang the radio jingle off-key and with gusto. They
marched into her bedroom to sit on both sides of her suitcase. She lifted the
flap, pressed down hard, and pulled the zipper into place. "Do the two of you
remember all the do's and don'ts?"

They nodded, sliding glances at each other.

Sherryn had a remedy for whatever plan they'd cooked up. She wagged a
finger at them. "Remember, anybody who gives Miss Em too much talking
will lose a Christmas gift."

The boys' mouths fell open, forcing Sherryn to hold back a chuckle. They
left when Justin came in and hefted the suitcase off the bed.

"Mommy, what you have in here?" he asked. "You sure you're coming
back on Sunday night?"

She rolled her eyes at him. "I packed for your father and me, if you must
know."

The throb of the van's engine in the front yard reached them at the same
time, which meant Reece had come home.

Justin lugged the suitcase out of the room, stepping aside in time to avoid
being knocked down by Brandon and Maurice, who were racing to get
downstairs.

Sherryn descended the stairs at a slower pace and went in search of Miss
Em, who was in the washroom.

"This is in case of emergency or anything you might need for the kids,"
she said, handing Miss Em a moneybag with cash.

Miss Em engulfed Sherryn in her bosom. "Lawd, Miss Sher, make sure
you and Missa Reece enjoy di mini vacation. Di two of you deserve it after dis
tryin' time dat jus' gone."

She hustled Sherryn toward the living room. "Don' worry yuhself over di
children. Yuh know I will tek good care of dem."

"All right, Miss Em."

Celia curled up in a corner, nose deep in a book. Her older sister and brother lounged together on the sofa in front of the television, snacking on Cheese Krunchies and milk.

"See you on Sunday," Sherryn said.

They answered in chorus and went back to their activities, leaving Sherryn feeling she and Reece wouldn't be missed.

In the passage leading to the front door, Kyle squealed. Reece swung him up to nuzzle his neck.

Next, it was Brandon's turn. Reece stooped to listen to him list all the things he expected them to bring back on Sunday.

Maurice was last. Reece drew him close and whispered in his ear.

With a laugh, Maurice said, "I know dat!"

He cupped his hands around Reece's ear and whispered.

Reece drew back, stared at Maurice for a few seconds, and then nodded. "Yes, I do."

While Maurice hugged his father's neck, Sherryn leaned against the wall, enjoying their exchange. If she didn't know better, she'd think Maurice had said something to bring a sheen to Reece's eyes. Her husband, who never cried, was turning into a softie, which wasn't such a bad thing. Sometimes, he held too much inside.

The drive to Runaway Bay took them two and a half hours at a leisurely pace.

Sherryn insisted that Reece cut his workday short the next time they planned a trip because they were missing all the sights by traveling at twilight. All the same, she enjoyed the smell of the sea and the sound of the waves as the van wound along the coastline.

The décor in the cozy, second-floor apartment featured vivid splashes of reds and yellows, which heightened Sherryn's festive mood. With only a few days left until Christmas, she had already gone shopping for the children and Reece. She planned to relax and revel in their weekend getaway, because when they returned home, they wouldn't have a moment's break from the kids, who were now on holiday.

They had a leisurely shower before driving fifteen minutes to have a seafood dinner in the busy resort town of Ocho Rios. Hand in hand, they strolled along the narrow sidewalks, at ease in the Friday night bustle of locals and tourists.

Reece distracted her on the ride back to the apartment complex by trailing his fingers between her thighs.

She warned him to keep his hands on the wheel, and he behaved himself until they stepped into the cool night, which teemed with the sound of crickets. A heady fragrance wafted from the yellow bell-shaped blooms on the angel's trumpets that filled the garden. She ran ahead of him up the steps giggling, and surrendered to him against the door, where he pressed against her, kissing her skin, but avoiding her lips.

Behind the closed door, they slid their clothes off piece by piece before falling into the plump wicker settee to finish what they'd started in the corridor.

When he was satisfied, Reece groaned against her neck. "Sherryn, my back is going to kill me in the morning. We should move to the bed."

She wriggled against him before grabbing his hand to pull him to his feet. "Does that mean you're getting old?"

"I'll show you old," he said, and smacked her bottom on the way to the bedroom.

On the downy mattress, Sherryn snuggled under his arm. "I have a question," she said. Reece's voice was low and thick with sleep when he asked, "What d'you want to know?"

"What did you say to Maurice before you left home?"

"I told him we'd miss him, and that we'd bring something back for him."

"And what did he whisper to you?"

"He asked me if I loved him like you do."

She exhaled, the sound of it heavy in the room. "It's a pity he had to ask."

"That's how it is when you're basically left to raise yourself. You're never quite sure if you're loved. That was my experience."

She propped her head up to examine Reece's face in the splinters of light piercing the darkness. "Is that why you never talk about your childhood?"

He lay still, and then dragged in a lungful of air. "I guess. Plus, it was a long time ago. I dunno why you find that part of my life interesting. It's more depressing than anything."

"Anything to do with you interests me."

She sat up, drew the sheet over them, and nestled against him, throwing a hand across his waist. "I'm glad you've had a turnaround where Maurice is concerned. Life's a lot more comfortable now that you're back to being yourself. I should tell you, the counselor said that with continued love and care, Maurice won't have any lasting effects from all that's happened."

"That's good," Reece said, caressing her arm. "Sherryn?"

"Hmm?"

"Would you forgive me for everything? I mean for thinking I owned you and for smothering you. I only realized recently that if you didn't love me, nothing I did could make you stay in our marriage—not even the children."

His confession brought tears to her eyes and sadness gripped her at the thought of her stubbornness. "Reece, there's nothing to forgive really. I should be the one asking for forgiveness. I knew you had issues, but continued to play on them by shutting off communication when it suited me. That's so wrong. Not to mention immature."

"I love you the way you are, Sherryn, but it would make me happy if you'd talk to me rather than going into lockdown when you're upset. When you shut me out, I don't know what to do with myself."

Humbled by his acceptance of her faults, Sherryn swallowed the painful mass packed tight in her throat and eased away to look down at him. Tears ran out of her eyes and fell on his chest. She blinked and sniffled, wiping her eyes at the same time.

"Maurice Allbright, what did I ever do to deserve as good and patient a man as you?"

He pulled her close for a long squeeze. "Dunno, but at a guess, I'd say the same thing I did to deserve a woman as wise and generous as you."

A crushing sensation gripped Sherryn's chest at the thought of all she might have lost had their marriage ended in divorce. With a sigh, she acknowledged that life had seasons wherein it ebbed and flowed, bringing good and bad.

In the next moment, a lightness of spirit gripped her, forcing a delighted curl of laughter from her throat. "Reece, you know how you've always wanted six children to complete our family?"

He yawned with a contented groan at the end. "Mmm-hmm."

She floated downward into his arms. "We'll you've achieved that and something extra."

He flashed her a grin and rose above her to crow, "Really? How? Since we haven't been *practicing* in a while."

"That's precisely the reason. I haven't been as careful as I usually am because of everything that's happened." She sighed dramatically and rubbed her tummy.

"Pregnant at nearly forty. What will people think?"

He hovered to brush kisses over her face and neck. "They'll think we still love each other. D'you know how many couples our age are only having sex once per week or not at all?"

"I don't have a clue," she said.

"Plenty," he whispered against her cheek. "This is our covenant baby—she'll be a symbol of our recommitment to each other. You agree?"

"Mmm-hmm. Hoping for a girl, are you?"

"Yeah, to even up the numbers a bit, you know?"

She made small circles on his arm while he continued nuzzling her skin. "You know I love you to bits, right?"

He raised his head, tilting it to the side. "'Course, but I don't mind you telling me so every day as long as we live."

She snorted. "You'd be quite a lucky man."

He laid his head against her chest, laughing. "Believe me, Sher, I'm more than lucky. I'm blessed."

Dear Reader,

If you enjoyed Dissolution and think others would enjoy the story, do share your thoughts in a review and tell your friends about the book.

Be sure to look out for my other titles. For news and updates, you can join my mailing list at http://eepurl.com/n29ZH. A special gift awaits you!

J.L. Campbell

Book Club Discussion Questions

1. In view of Reece's deception, were Sherryn's actions justified?

2. What aspects of Reece and Sherryn's relationship were strengthened by their challenges?

3. How did Reece's outlook on his background and success contribute to his inability to let go of his past?

4. Can you say how the main characters changed as the novel progressed?

5. Can you say how the circumstances surrounding the family affected the way in which

the children viewed their father?

6. What are the main themes in the novel?

7. Which character did you find most sympathetic? Why?

8. What lessons, if any, did Sherryn learn from her children's reaction to the family's

challenges?

9. Did inclusion in the family change Maurice in any way?

10. What lessons did the children learn about acceptance, and appreciation of the differences that exist between people?

Other Books by J.L. Campbell

Savor the taste of tropical living by sampling the Island Adventure Romance series, which currently has five exciting, stand-alone stories that feature feisty women and determined men.

Romantic Suspense (Island Adventure Series)
Anya's Wish (free novella)
Chasing Anya
Contraband
Taming Celeste
Grudge
Hardware

New Adult
Perfection
Fixation

Women's Fiction
A Baker's Dozen-13 Steps to Distraction (novella)
Dissolution
Distraction
Retribution
Absolution

Young Adult
Christine's Odyssey
Saving Sam

Short Story Collections
Don't Get Mad...Get Even (free)
Don't Get Mad...Get Even: Kicked to the Kerb

Contemporary Romance (Sweet Holiday Series)
The Vet's Christmas Pet
The Vet's Valentine Gift
The Vet's Secret wish

Contemporary Romance (Par for the Course)
The Short Game

Meet the Author

J.L. Campbell is an award-winning, Jamaican writer of romantic suspense, women's fiction, new adult and young adult novels. She is the author of 13 novels, four novellas and two short story collections. Her Amazon author page is hosted at www.amazon.com/author/jlcampbell

Visit her on the web at http://www.joylcampbell.com You can also connect with her on Twitter @JL_Campbell or on Facebook at https://www.facebook.com/jlcampbellwrites/.

www.ingramcontent.com/pod-product-compliance
Lightning Source LLC
Chambersburg PA
CBHW031450260626
47154CB00016B/609